BEKA COOPER

BOOK TWO

BLOODHOUND

TAMORA PIERCE

RANDOM HOUSE NEW YORK

Text copyright © 2009 by Tamora Pierce
Cover art copyright © 2009 by Jonathan Barkat

Visit us on the Web! www.randomhouse.com/teens

Educators and librarians, for a variety of teaching tools, visit us at
www.randomhouse.com/teachers

The Library of Congress has catalogued the hardcover edition
of this work as follows:
Pierce, Tamora.
Bloodhound / Tamora Pierce.
p. cm. — (Beka Cooper ; bk. 2)
Summary: Having been promoted from "Puppy" to "Dog," Beka, now
a full-fledged member of the Provost's Guard, and her former partner
head to a neighboring port city to investigate a case of counterfeit coins.
ISBN 978-0-375-81469-3 (trade) — ISBN 978-0-375-91469-0 (lib. bdg.)
— ISBN 978-0-375-83817-0 (pbk.) — ISBN 978-0-375-81475-4
(mass-market pbk.) — ISBN 978-0-375-89252-3 (e-book)
[1. Counterfeits and counterfeiting—Fiction. 2. Police—Fiction.
3. Fantasy.]
I. Title.
PZ7.P61464Bl 2009
[Fic]—dc22
2008025838

Printed in the United States of America
10 9 8 7 6 5 4 3 2 1
First Trade Paperback Edition

Praise for *Bloodhound*

"This compelling first-person narrative, recounted by Beka in the pages of her journal, includes a vivid cast of characters and lots of action. It is fantasy, an excellent police procedural, and an immensely satisfying read."
—*Voice of Youth Advocates*

"Beka is as headstrong and feisty as ever. . . . She truly earns the nickname Bloodhound as she faithfully narrates her story through journal entries."
—*School Library Journal*

"A definite young adult read . . . as usual with Pierce's books, this title is hard to put down!"
—*Children's Literature*

"Beka's detective work will appeal not just to Pierce fans, but to lovers of police procedurals."
—*Kirkus Reviews*

And praise for Beka Cooper Book One: *Terrier*

"Perhaps the book's greatest strength is its raw portrayal of the fine line between law and lawlessness."
—*The Horn Book Magazine*

"Fans of Pierce's previous forays into medieval fantasy will likely savor every page."
—*Publishers Weekly*

Tortall Books
by Tamora Pierce

I want to dedicate this long-delayed second volume
of Beka's adventures to my assistants,
Sara Alan and Cara Coville. I think that without them
I might well have gone just plain nuts.
I would also like to dedicate this book to Joel Sweifach,
my first accountant. Joel, you kept my ship afloat!

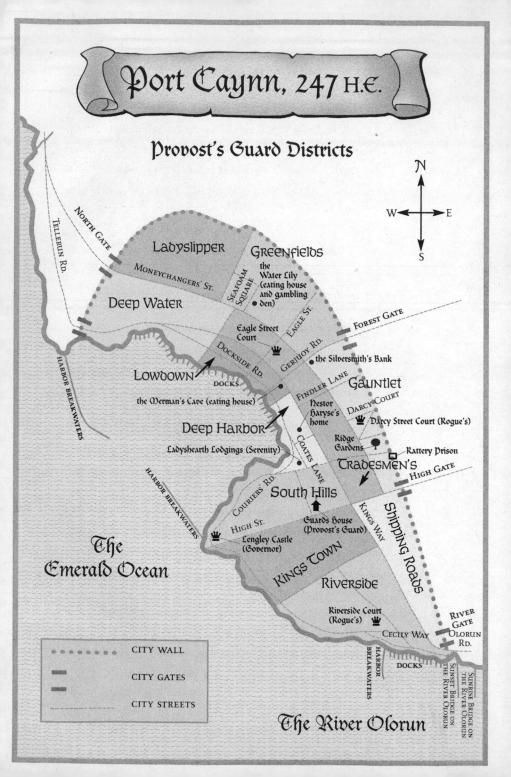

I should have known tonight's watch would kiss the mule's bum when Sergeant Ahuda stopped me after baton training. "A private word, Cooper," she told me, and pulled me into a quiet corner of the yard. Her dark eyes were sharp on my face. We'd gotten on well since I'd finished my Puppy year and in my five months' work as a Dog. I couldn't think what I might have done to vex her.

"Your reports have gotten sloppy." That was Ahuda, never one to soften her words. "You leave out detail, you skip what's said. You used to write the best reports of any Puppy or first-year Dog, but not of late. Have you slacked on the memory exercises?"

I gazed at the ground. Of course I've been slacking. What's the use, with partners like I've had? Ahuda put her brown fist under my chin and thrust my head up so I'd look her in the eye. "Shall I send you back to Puppy training for a refreshing in memory study?"

"Sarge, please don't." The plea left my mouth before I could stop the words. Goddess, not Puppy training again, not even one class! I'd never hear the end of it!

Ahuda took her fist away and propped it on one of her sturdy hips. "Then however you kept your memory quick before, start doing it again. Steel yourself, wench! You're not the only first-year Dog with partners who are less than gold. Work with it!"

She marched back to the kennel. I went to wash and put on my uniform. We had the Happy Bag to collect tonight, me and my partner Silsbee. Our route took us along Fortunetellers' Walk, where I'd be sure to find a shop that sold journal books. I'd thought I wouldn't need to keep one after my Puppy year, but if Ahuda was complaining of my reports, it was time to start again.

I didn't even have Pounce to make me feel better as we mustered for the Evening Watch. The cat had stopped coming with us three days after I'd been partnered with Silsbee. I'd begged him to come. It was Pounce's remarks about folk, and about Silsbee himself, that made it easier for me to walk patrol with the man, but Pounce would have none of it.

He bores me, and he only lets you do boring things, too, my annoying constellation cat said. *I see no reason why both of us should be bored.*

And so I went out to collect our Happy Bag's worth of bribes with Silsbee and no one else, listening to him jabber about the meal his wife had prepared before he came on watch. Those huge meals are one reason that when we reached our patrol route, I visited all the shopkeepers with businesses upstairs. On Fortunetellers' Walk they went up three and four stories, each room with a crystal reader, or a palm reader, or any other kind of reader. Silsbee stood below and blabbered with the ground-floor shopkeepers. They brought him drinks and cakes, stupid loobies. Did they think *he'd* run after the Rat that stole their goods? I did all the climbing in the miserable heat, just as I would run down their Rats when they came.

We gathered the Happy Bag and finished our watch. Ersken invited me to supper with him, his partner Birch, and some of the others, but I was in no mood for it. I just don't feel like I earn that extra bit from the Happy Bag with Silsbee dragging at me all the time. It makes me feel low.

I was walking through the kennel courtyard when I noticed that Silsbee waited by the gate. He crooked a finger at me. "A word with ye, Cooper," he said.

My temples banged. The last thing I wanted was any kind

of speech with that sheep biter when I was off duty, but he was my senior partner. I went to him.

"I'll speak with Sergeant Ahuda, but ye've the right to know first. I'm requestin' a new partner." He dug at his teeth with a wooden pick. "Ye really deserve that name they give ye, Terrier. Y' *are* a Terrier. Ye make me nervous, with yer hands and feet twitchin' and yer teeth grindin', allus wantin' t' chase after every wee noise and squeak. Even in this weather! If I was younger—but I ain't. It's best we say we're not suited before we get fond."

"You're cutting me loose." I said it slow, just to be sure I had it right. It *hurt,* to hear the nickname I was so proud of turned against me.

"Ye give me fidgets." He shrugged and held out his hands as if to say, "What am I to do?"

"You—" I said, trying not to show my fury. "Do you know how many Rats I could have caught and hobbled, had you not held me back?"

"Now, Cooper, don't make me write ye up for sauce." He waved that disgusting toothpick at me. There was a chunk of something on its end.

"You want to hear *sauce*?" Two weeks of working with the louse boiled over and out of my mouth. "You walk a bit, and you stop for a jack of ale. Then you stroll a block or three, till you need 'a wee tidbit,' as would feed a family of five. A cove gets his pocket picked? 'We'll have Day Watch pick that Rat up,' you say. 'There's folk with children to feed on Day Watch as can use the bribes.' Someone cries murder a street over? 'Plenty of folk hereabouts put up a shout because they like to make me run. I ain't a-fallin' for *that* trick again.' Once we get there, any Rats are *gone*—it's enough to make a mot *scream*."

"I'm beginnin' t' see why ye're not well favored when it

3

comes to partners, Cooper," he said. "Ye say nothin' for days, then ye talk sewer muck."

He strolled into the kennel, as smug as a tax man with soldiers at his back. I stood there, shaking, my hands clenched so tight around my new-bought journal that they cramped.

When I came home, Pounce was waiting for me outside Mistress Trout's lodgings. *They'll give you back to Goodwin and Tunstall,* he said, without me even telling him what had happened. *You know you'll be better with them. I will, too. I've been bored.*

"I want my *own* partner," I told him, stomping inside. "Goodwin and Tunstall are a pair. I don't want to be a third forever. I want a *good* partner, like Ersken has in Birch."

Your time will come, Pounce told me.

"When!" I cried. I had no fear of being shushed by my neighbors. My fellow lodgers are Rats, in attendance on the King of Thieves at night. "When! You're the god, aren't you? Tell me!"

I am not a god. I am a constellation. It isn't the same thing. Pounce jumped up on my shoulder and began to purr as I unlocked my door. His side was warm against my cheek.

"Stop that," I said. "It won't do any good." But of course it did. It always does. As he kneaded my shoulder muscles, I sighed and sat upon my bed. Pounce's black fur was like the softest velvet under my fingers. The knots in my temples and jaw loosened. By the time he jumped to my pillow, I was able to change into my nightdress, make myself a soothing tea, eat some bread and cheese, and open this journal. I thought that writing what took place with Silsbee would ease me further, but I have finished, and I am still too angry to sleep. I may as well put down a bit of what has taken place since I finished my last journal, while I was still in training.

I am seventeen years old now, a full member of the Provost's Guard. I have been so for five months. In that time I have had four partners, including Silsbee. My luck in this area has not been good. Between partners I go back to my training Dogs, Goodwin and Tunstall. I remain with the Jane Street kennel of the Lower City watch district, which is yet under the command of Acton of Fenrigh. Kebibi Ahuda is my Watch Sergeant and trainer in baton work.

I live in Mistress Trout's lodgings on Nipcopper Close. My fellow lodgers are Aniki Forfrysning, Koramin Ingensra, and Rosto the Piper, as well as Mistress Trout. Rosto, the Rogue and king of the city's thieves, tried to buy the house and turn it into an inn where his court might gather, but Mistress Trout refused to sell. Instead she persuaded him to buy houses across the street that are also hers. He's had the builders there ever since, turning them into a spacious inn. The work is near enough to done that we've been taking our regular breakfasts on the second floor. Rosto is naming the place after his dead mother. He tells us she was once a beautiful Player called the Dancing Dove.

Rosto still makes it plain he wants me. I yet say no, though nights like this one come when I wonder why I refuse him. Still, a cove as makes a living by violence will live all his life by it, that's my fear. It's no help that Rosto's the Rogue and I'm a Dog.

Curse him for being all tight muscle, with ivory skin and a mouth as soft as rose petals. Curse him for having hair as fair as the sun, and eyes as black as night. Curse him for having the grace of a cat and deft, cool hands.

And now I am having the same argument on paper that I have in my own head, or with Pounce, on too many nights. I know my choice is sensible, but it isn't my common sense I think with, those times Rosto's stolen a kiss from me.

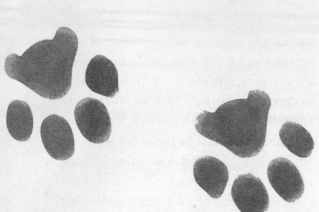

Pounce says I am to stop feeling sorry for myself and get to bed, or he will ruin another good page with his inky paws. I must sleep sometime. But when I do, tomorrow comes, and I deal again with being partnerless.

Curse that cat! I'm off to bed, now that my new journal is started. No thanks to Pounce!

Noon.

I knew I had to tell my friends straight off. Ersken Westover would hear of my dismissal when we went on watch, if our thief friends hadn't already caught wind of it, so Pounce and I went across the street to breakfast at the Dancing Dove, Pounce more eagerly than me. Most of our regular group was there—Rosto, Aniki, Kora, Ersken, and Phelan. All but Tansy, and I chose not to wait for her. With a baby, a husband, and a business, she doesn't always come. I wanted to get the telling over with.

"Silsbee tossed me back last night," I said as Kora passed the turnovers.

For a moment they all did naught but stare.

Then Ersken snorted, pox rot him. Dogs ought to show a united front! Kora put up her hands to cover her mouth. Mages are always discreet. Aniki cackled. Soon they all made merry at my expense, save Rosto.

He didn't laugh. He only raised an eyebrow and said, "That's four partners, then."

I glared at him. I can do that, seeing as how he's got a sweet spot for me. "So?" I asked. "It's not always a good fit, right off. I've said it afore. Even Ersken had two partners."

"I got lucky the second go-round." Finally Ersken remembered whose side he was on. "It was pure chance that Vinehall was transferred and I got Birch. And it wasn't Beka's fault that her first partner didn't work. He died of the red flux. Half the Lower City got it this summer, even you, Rosto. It's not like she *gave* it to him."

"She arrested the second cove herself," Aniki said. "She arrested her own *partner*!"

"He took a bribe to ignore *murder*," I said, still angry. "That's just wrong."

"You told the third one you'd lop his hands off if he put them on you again." Kora could barely say it for giggling. "He thought you'd really do it, too!"

"She would!" Rosto, Aniki, and Ersken said at the same time.

"So what was it with this one?" asked Phelan. He was offering ham to my cat. Pounce, the traitor, tended to that, not to helping me.

"Silsbee." I was tired to death of the subject already and the day scarce begun. "He says I give him the twitches. And he's a lazy, jabbernob, pudding-livered scut." I'd said little to them before. I had been trying to make the best of things, but there was no reason to now. "He eats, he gossips, and he wouldn't chase a Rat if it was a feeble filcher under his own poxy nose!"

They only laughed all the more. I wondered where Tansy was. My oldest friend would surely stand up for me. Why, today of all days, was she not here?

"I'd say you have curst bad luck," Aniki told me, "but the god's truth is, Beka, you want to bag every Rat in the Lower City, and Silsbee is a known slug. The odds were down to fifty to one that it would last another week."

"I'd've stuck it out!" I cried.

"You won plenty of folk some coin when he didn't resign after one night of you," Rosto said idly. "Even more coin when you didn't quit the Dogs by the third day. But no one would wager a copper on it going a whole month."

I had wagered on me making it to a month. That only means I'm a looby. I *tried* not to argue with Silsbee when he'd refused to let me give chase. I hadn't questioned his orders, though my tongue was sore from biting it. I hadn't wanted to lose yet another partner.

"Doubtless he thought you were surly, as shy as you are with them that don't know you." Rosto said it like he was my wise old grandfather. "I'd've thought Goodwin and Tunstall would have made you more sociable with the other Dogs."

"I talked to him," I snapped. "For all the good it did me."

"Goodwin and Tunstall didn't make her *that* sociable," Ersken said. He was trying to feed Kora's cat, Fuzzball, without bleeding for it. Fuzzball could be greedy at times, and his claws were sharp. "Why should they? They're happy when Beka gets kicked back to them, even though my Lord Provost told Ahuda the other day that he wants *two* good pairs, not one great team of three."

I hid my face in my hands. I don't want my lord to be unhappy with me. It's not just that he's my sponsor, or the head of the Provost's Guards. I want to repay him for taking my family out of the Lower City and giving us a decent life. "When did you hear this?" I asked.

"Three days back," Ersken said. I heard wickedness in his voice as he added, "When he noticed that Silsbee rolled his eyes as you came within his view."

Pounce jumped onto my shoulder as I moaned.

Why are you groaning? he asked me. *My lord would see you commit murder before he'd stop liking you.*

My friends looked curious. This time they heard Pounce only speaking in cat, not in human speech as I did, or they would have laughed. Half the time he lets them know what he is saying, and half the time he does not. He likes to tease, does Pounce.

Feet clattered up the stair. Tansy had forgotten to take off the wooden pattens she wore to lift her feet clear of the street muck. She flung the breakfast room door wide. Her rain hat was askew, her gold curls tumbling from their pins. She threw her rain cape on the floor and banged a basket of rolls on the table before us. Her cheeks were red, her eyes sparkling with anger.

"I have never been so humiliated!" she said, panting from her run up from the common room floor.

"You tracked mud in here. The wood's not stained yet," Rosto told her. He is as picky as a cat about this inn he's building.

Tansy glared at him. "Mud scrubs off," she said tartly. "It's not dignified for the Rogue to worrit himself about housekeeping." She was vexed, sure enough. Her Upmarket speech was slipping into the Lower City cant of our childhood. Bending, she slipped off her pattens, setting them outside the room's door.

Aniki poured Tansy a cup of hot tea. "Your day off to a bad start?" she asked as Tansy put on a pair of the slippers kept by the door for us.

"Baker Garnett tested the coin I gave him—and it was false! A silver cole, a thin coating over brass!" Tansy sat next to me and ripped a roll in two. "He had guards in the shop. One of them grabbed me. I gave him the knee in the cod, the scut. *Then* my dozy footman got into it. A flea I put in my cove's ear, not stopping the plaguey bastard before handling a citywoman like me!" She took a gulp of the tea and winced. It was too hot.

"Most citywomen don't jam knees into a cove's cod." Rosto spoke seriously, but his black eyes were laughing.

Tansy shook her head, blushing fiercely. "You don't *understand*," she said. "I've worked so hard to give our business an honest name! Dealing in *coles*—it would be the ruin of me and my whole family, if word got about. No one would buy from us! We'd lose everything!"

"And there's being boiled in oil, if they think you guilty of colesmithing," Kora murmured while she played with Aniki's cat. "Or getting your hand lopped off if they just think you're passing fakes along. Why *aren't* you in the cages?"

"I bribed the baker, of course," Tansy said, and sniffed. I took out one of the handkerchiefs she tucked in her clothes and put it in her hand. "He called off his guard when I wouldn't stop crying. . . . *And* he said he's had two other good customers come in with false coins. Silver, all of them." She blew her nose. "He let me go, but folk were *laughing,* and that rusher who worked for him said *such* a thing to me!"

"I'll send a cove around to have a word," Rosto said. "Don't you worry about that, love."

"Try not to make it a matter for the Dogs," Ersken told him. "Friendly is always best."

Rosto gave Ersken a grin that was all teeth. "I'm the friendliest cove around, Westover," he said. "Ask anyone."

"Living," Aniki murmured.

Rosto glanced at her. "Well, it's Beka you ask if you want to talk to the dead ones, isn't it?" he inquired, all innocent-like.

Fuzzball attacked my fingers. I let him do it, as I was thinking. This baker, Garnett, had seen three customers lately with false silver coins? Respectable folk at that. Tansy's grandfather-in-law had been the Lower City's worst scale and landlord, but since his death Tansy, her husband, and her mother-in-law had gotten rid of the old man's crooked businesses. They'd lost a great deal of money to get straight with the law.

I'd bet a copper of my own that these three false silver cases Tansy mentioned aren't the only ones, not if a *baker* is hiring guards. How many silver coins does a baker see in a day? Most folk buy with coppers, unless they shop for a group, or a big household.

"It's not *you* that's behind this, is it?" Tansy asked Rosto. "Because it would be wrong, very wrong! I don't care if you are the Rogue, I'll speak my mind! You can't meddle with people's livelihood, Rosto! Silver coles hurt us all. If a silver noble won't buy what it's supposed to—"

"Will you *hush*?" Rosto asked, slapping the table. "Mithros's sack, woman!"

Tansy went silent, but she was breathing hard.

"You should learn from Beka," Rosto said. "She says her bit and then waits for a cove to answer. No, I've no hand in these fakes. If you'd a whit of sense, you'd know it. Coles hit the Court of the Rogue even harder than they hit the merchants. You make a bit of coin at first, but if the price of silver goes down, it goes down for all. We'd be cutting our own throats to deal in coles."

Tansy sniffed and blew her nose again. Even as a little girl she would never admit she let her tongue run away with her. "Then you'll keep an eye out?" she asked Rosto. "Afore there's folk begging in the street this winter?"

Ersken and I both sat up. "Hear now!" I said. "Catching colesmiths is Dog business!"

Tansy made a rude noise. "This is *serious*, Beka," she said. "This is *money*. Were it a killer, I'd come to you two, of course I would. But Garnett's hired guards. He's afraid *he'll* be arrested for counterfeit passing, at the least. He's so fearful he's willing to risk offending good customers. That's more than Lower City Dogs can manage, unless maybe it's Goodwin and Tunstall. And you haven't got them, only old flat-footed Silsbee."

"She hasn't got him, either," Aniki said with a smirk.

That distracted Tansy from money, sure enough. She

turned to gawp at me, then rolled her eyes. "Mother's milk, Beka, what happened *this* time? Did you kill him?"

I got up and left, Pounce at my side. So much for hoping Tansy would stand by me. She was more worried about her purse than her oldest friend.

No more can I blame her, despite my stung feelings. She's come a long way from Mutt Piddle Lane, where we both once lived. To be accused of passing false money like a common street mot would have skewered her deeper than any sword. And coles in the marketplace meant her silver that she worked so hard for might not be worth the value stamped on it. She'd be smelling Mutt Piddle Lane just outside her door, if I knew Tansy. Goddess knows I would.

As I climbed the stairs to my garret rooms, I told myself that Goodwin and Tunstall would be glad to take me back. Though I curse when I don't succeed with a new partner, I do like going out with my old ones. We find Rats, and we cage them. Not one- and two-copper Rats, but *big* ones. Each time Ahuda puts me with Tunstall and Goodwin, I can hear the Lower City's Rats groan.

Inside my rooms, I collected my pack, putting bags of cracked corn and bread pieces in it. I made sure it also held my pouches of dirt from all over Corus. I was still thinking about Goodwin and Tunstall as I locked up again. It would be different if one of them took a promotion to Sergeant, like both of them have been offered. Goodwin's a Corporal, Tunstall's a Senior Dog who's turned down promotion to Corporal because he hates the extra writing. I'd happily pair with either of them. But they've been partnered as street Dogs for years. They don't even have to talk, most of the time, they know each other's minds so well. I'd like to have my *own* partner like that.

Have faith that the gods know what they are doing with your life, Pounce said, following me down the stairs.

I don't want the gods meddling with my life, I told him silently as we walked out into the street again. *I want to do it myself. Gods are trouble.*

You don't have a choice, Pounce said.

I don't like the sound of that. I don't like it at all. *I can manage on my own, tell them that!* I said, glaring at him. *And you never mentioned anything like this before!*

I thought it would cheer you up, Pounce said.

I began to trot, not to escape Pounce so much as to get away from what he was hinting at. I've accepted for five year gone that Pounce is magic. Kora was the one who first told me he was a constellation, as close to a god as makes no difference. But he's never spoken of the gods in my life before, and I wish he hadn't. Look at all the folk who have had the gods muck with their lives, folk like Jehane the Warrior, that was burned alive, or Tomore the Righteous, beggared and beheaded, or Badika of the Blazing Axe, who drove off the Carthakis, only to be torn apart in one of their arenas! It never goes well for the god-chosen! Pounce can just tell the gods to leave me be.

Pounce and I got to Glassman Square, where one of my flocks of pigeons was waiting for us, as they do every day. We settled there, me to feed them, Pounce to watch. Slapper was the first to land on me, as ever. I think old Slapper is a high priest among the pigeons, the way he commands the others, here and elsewhere in the city. His blue-black feathers were wet and gleaming today. He must've come straight from a bath in the square's fountain.

I steadied his clubfoot with my hand, not looking him in his staring yellow eyes. He's got tiny, tiny pupils. No one ever thinks of pigeons as mad, but I think Slapper has carried so many ghosts that he's cracked in the nob with it. He'll hit me as soon as look at me, for all I feed him corn and wrap warm cloths around his clubfoot in cold weather. Ungrateful feather duster. Now *there's* one that's god-touched.

I gathered the complaints of the dead from the pigeons while they ate. There were few ghosts complaining of their lot today. None of them said anything I could pass on as good information to my fellow Dogs. Slapper had no ghost at all. He hasn't carried one for more than a week. I wonder if he misses them, or if he is glad not to have some dead human moaning in his ear. I wonder, too, if the Black God ever asks the pigeons if they want to carry ghosts.

On we went to see my dust spinners. For them I brought packets of dust, gravel, and dirt from other parts of town. Stuck in one place like they are, their veils of air spinning tall or small depending on the weather, they savor the taste of other places. In return they give me the bits of talk they've gathered since my last visit.

They're funny creatures, spinners. I don't know how old they are. When I was small, I learned to gather conversations from Hasfush, the one I met first. I think Hasfush is the oldest of the city spinners. My Granny Fern, who taught me how to use this family magic, told me my five-times-great-grandda had listened to Hasfush.

Today we called on Hasfush first. He was spinning short, a whirl of dust, leaves, and tiny stones that rose barely a foot into the air. It was all he could manage with the weather so hot and still. When I entered his circle, I gave him a nice packet of grit from the Daymarket. That cheered him so much that he sped up, growing and rising to my shoulders. He released all the bits of conversations he'd collected over the last week, giving them to my hearing.

As ever, much of it was sheer nonsense, a handful of words or less. There were even pieces in a language that I *think* was Yamani. That was a guess. I've only heard it spoken twice.

Then I heard, "—at this! I won eight silver nobles off the mammerin' scut, an' six of 'em is coles!" It was a cove who spoke, a whiny one.

A mot replied to him. "So find a game and lose 'em to someone else. You want—"

Those two voices were gone.

The next whole bit that I heard sent goose bumps all over me.

"—rot in the rye?" That was a mot, an old one.

"All that rain they've had in the northeast this summer." This was a younger mot, all business. "We'll be lucky if this year's rye harvest is half what last year's was."

"We will sell the rotten stuff. Mix it well with the good. None will notice." The old mot's voice was hard.

"Are you mad? That stuff kills! I'll have no—"

That mot left the old one, from the sound of her voice.

Hasfush was empty of his week's gatherings. I ground my teeth. I would have liked the name of the mot who wished to sell rotten rye, which brings madness and death. It wasn't Hasfush's fault that the two mots had moved on, nor was it a care of his. Spinners take no interest in what comes to them on the breeze.

I thanked him. Then Pounce and I moved on to visit two more Lower City spinners and more pigeons. Neither spinner had anything about coles. One pigeon carried a ghost who nattered about grain crops overall.

I'd give my news to Sergeant Ahuda. The grain inspectors would get the word to check the rye, at least. Hasfush had done the city a favor. I'd add some spices to his next packet. He always likes those. I know by the way his breezes warm as they circle me.

Troubling as the crop news was, my regular meetings with spinners and pigeons did raise my spirits some. We now had advance word on the rye, so I didn't feel so useless. And I'll get another partner. Ahuda wants me to do well. She'd assigned me to Goodwin and Tunstall in the first place. She will keep trying me on whichever Dog is partnerless until the right one turns up. And when it doesn't work out, Goodwin and Tunstall will take me back.

It could be worse. I could have been sent to one of the other districts, which is the *last* thing I want. I belong in the Lower City. The Lower City needs Dogs like me, Dogs that love it for all its bad and good faces.

Once I'd used up all my bird feed and talked to my spinners, I made my way home. I meant to do some cleaning and to write in this journal, but Tansy waited for me on the doorstep of my lodging house.

"I'm sorry," she said before I could open my gob. "I'm sorry I didn't wait for your news. I'm sorry Silsbee is a looby and a lazy one at that." Her eyes were puffy. "Beka, I need a favor." Pounce leaped into her arms and licked her cheek. "Dearest cat, that's sweet, but it scratches. My skin looks dreadful from weeping as it is." To me she said, "Beka, please—come home and help me test my silver."

I stared at her.

Tansy kept her voice very quiet when she said, "Beka, Garnett cut *three* of my coins. I had five silver coins in my purse this morning, and two of them were false. *Two* of *five.* If the rest of my house money is like that . . . My man is too hotheaded—he'll talk. I trust only you to keep it secret."

My tripes turned into a knot. I knew each soul in that

household, from the baby to the kitchen maid. I knew their names, their families, even their birthdays. If Tansy's strongbox was lousy with coles, they might be lucky to live in a hut on Mutt Piddle Lane.

So back to her house we went. We slipped in through a side door and shut ourselves in the little room Tansy uses to work on the account books. With the sounds of the busy household all around us, we took out our belt knives and sharpstones. Tansy opened the lockboxes. Quietly we tested each and every silver coin in them with a cut down the center. We found only three more false ones, in one hundred and twelve coins, which made Tansy cry from relief.

When she calmed down, she hugged me and thanked me. Then she fetched my godsdaughter Joy and had Cook pack up a lunch for me. The noon bells were chiming by the time I got free.

I came home to a pitcher of red gillyflowers in front of my door. Rosto. Once I was in my rooms with the door closed behind me and Pounce, I held them up and buried my face in them. I know why Rosto did it. Whenever aught that was good or bad happened to me, he left me gillyflowers, especially red ones. Goddess knows how he managed it in the wintertime, though I suppose the Rogue could get mage-grown flowers as easy as the King.

It's not like I can give them back, because he won't take them. Still, he knows they won't buy him favors from me.

I'll be that glad when the Dancing Dove's finished and he's moved there. Every time I think of knocking on his door, I remember the things he's done. That just doesn't keep me from thinking that his door is only one flight of stairs down from mine.

I've written enough for the day so far. Time to change to uniform and get my bum to training.

Two of the morning, after watch.

When I got to training this afternoon, Ahuda took me aside. "Silsbee's been transferred," she said in her short way. "He'll be working at the Magistrate's Court from here on. I knew he was a lazy tarse. Now I know *how* lazy. You're back with Goodwin and Tunstall."

I nodded. Given my druthers, I'd druther Silsbee hadn't been lazy.

"He had no partner, and he was next in line," Ahuda said.

I kept my eyes on the ground. If I hadn't known Ahuda better, I could have sworn she was apologizing to me. That didn't seem possible. Ahuda is a bulldog of a woman who's better at tearing pieces out of my hide for letting my guard down.

She thrust me into the center of the yard. "You six." She pointed to half of the Puppies. "Baton work. Form a circle around Cooper here and attack her. Show no mercy. Cooper, try not to break any of them."

So much for apologies.

I broke none of them, nor did I let any of them break me. This year's Pups are spirited, but slow. The work did take my mind off the jokes of the second-, third-, and fourth-year Dogs, who had heard I was partnerless again. It also helped me ignore Ersken and my other friends' arguments with them, and Ahuda's orders for everyone to shut their gobs and train.

As we gathered for muster, the hard Dogs surrounded me—not just Goodwin and Tunstall, but Nyler Jewel, his partner Yoav, Ersken's partner Birch, and their friends. The serious Dogs of the Evening Watch. They said naught about Silsbee. Mostly they patted my back or clapped me on the shoulder. Then they cleared the way for the Day Watch to assemble for dismissal. Goodwin and Tunstall stayed with me. Goodwin propped her fists on her hips, eyeing me, making me feel like she was the tall one, when I know full well she is two inches shorter than me. Her dark eyes looked me over, top to toe. I felt scruffy next to her, though my breeches and tunic were unwrinkled, my boots brushed. Tunstall, his head someplace in the air over mine, scratched his short gray and brown hair, looking more like an owl than ever.

Finally Goodwin said, "We have to do something about this. There must be *someone* in the Lower City who isn't a waste of your time."

Tunstall said, "I hope you have some tattle from your Birdies, Cooper. With half the folk out of the city working the harvest, it's quiet as the grave. I'm bored." He patted a bicep that strained his tunic sleeve. "I'm getting flabby."

I shook my head and told them, "There's naught of use from my Birdies. A gambler got coles in his winnings, but I've no way to track him. I do have this from Tansy." I took out the false coin I had persuaded her to give me and handed it to Tunstall. He looked it over, then passed it to Goodwin. I told them about Tansy's morning at Baker Garnett's.

I'd just finished when the Day Watch cleared the room, and we took our places in the ranks. Once Ahuda sent us out on duty, we went into the courtyard. Instead of moving on into the street, though, Goodwin signed to Jewel and Yoav. Goodwin showed them the coin and had me tell the tale all over again.

Jewel rubbed his chin. "I was startin' to tell Goodwin and Tunstall that Flash kennel brung down a dice game on our court night. Two river dodgers as was gamblin' there had a fistful of false silver. One of 'em got away. One of 'em tripped and fell in his cage and broke his neck."

Tunstall spat in the dust. Goodwin kicked him. "Hill barbarian," she said. "Hasn't Lady Sabine cured you of that?"

Tunstall grinned. "She doesn't try to change me. That's why we're still walking out."

Yoav opened her mouth, doubtless to make a joke about walking not being what they were doing. She caught Tunstall's look and closed her gob again. Folk can say whatever they like about Tunstall. He'll just blink those sleepy brown eyes. Say one word about my lady Sabine, and he'll put a hand of iron around your throat. My lady may not care that folk joke about her bedding a common Dog, but the Dog cares very much.

"Where was this river dodger?" Tunstall asked Jewel. "Kennel cages or Outwalls Prison?"

"Kennel," Yoav said. "Does it make a difference? Cage Dogs turn their backs on their mothers' murder if they're paid enough."

"What about the false coin?" Goodwin asked. "What happened to that?"

"Took to the palace," Jewel said. "No one'd leave *that* in a common kennel, where it might vanish, like."

"I had word of a gambler that won eight silver nobles that turned out to be six of 'em coles," I said. "Near Glassman Square. My Birdie had no names, though."

Goodwin spun her dagger point down on her fingertip. She did that when she was thinking. We all watched her. "We've folk passing coles in the Lower City and Flash District, but no word from any of the other districts," she said at last. "Just down here. This baker, Garnett, took in some coins, there's this gambler Cooper heard of, and its river dodgers in Flash District."

"It might pay to check the Lower City end of the riverfront, to see if other gamblers are passing fakes," Tunstall pointed out.

"The Barrel's Bottom," Goodwin said. She flipped her dagger into the air, caught it by the hilt, and sheathed it. I've yet to manage that trick without cuts. "That's the biggest for gambling, this time of the week. We should start there."

I winced. My luck in the Barrel's Bottom has not improved since I kept my first journal. I've been caught in seven large brawls in that outsized scummer-pot, the first when I was a Pup, the rest since. Last time I got my arm broken.

"If any cole passers know of the two who got caught in Flash District, they'll be shy," Jewel warned Goodwin. "They see you come in the front door, they'll be gone out every rathole in the place. You'll need company." Our team and Jewel's were too senior to have fixed patrols, but it was expected that we didn't work the same streets at the same time.

Tunstall smiled. "I'll talk with Ahuda."

She must have been in a good mood, or Tunstall talked extra well. Not only did Ahuda give us leave to take Jewel and Yoav to the Barrel's Bottom, she let us pull Birch and Ersken off their regular patrol of Rovers Street. Having Birch and Ersken along was an extra blessing. Birch has walked Rovers Street for years. He knows all the Barrel's Bottom exits.

It helped that Friday night was quiet, so we could all be spared. It was hot, too hot to do much. Plenty of folk were out of the city working the harvest. Walking down Jane Street, me and Ersken listened as the Senior Dogs wagered on when the streets and drinking houses would fill up with returning harvesters. Autumn is the Dogs' busiest season. Along with the harvesters and those that come to buy their winter's supplies come the thieves and gamblers to clip them. It's best we get this business of coles done with now. It will make a pretty mess once the crowds come.

Around the corner from the Barrel's Bottom, the Senior Dogs halted to give us our assignments.

"Ersken goes through the front door," said Birch. "Walk about slow-like, lad. Look over the games, and now and then give a pile of silver a wee poke with your baton, but not so much as to disturb the coins. Let them know you're there, eyein' the money. If you're payin' a bit too much attention to the coin, they'll sweat. They won't know why you're lookin', but they'll know it ain't good. Like it says in *The Book of Law*, the guilty run first. We'll be waiting for them."

"Don't interrupt the games," Goodwin cautioned. "They hate that."

All of us nodded.

"The regulars know Ersken," Birch told us. "They'll know I'm hard by."

"And them with aught on their consciences will scatter for the bolt holes," Jewel said.

"Which I'll be showing you," Birch replied. "Wait till I return, Ersken."

As he led us away, I looked back at Ersken, worried. He's put on weight and muscle since our Puppy year, and he's better with his baton and those brass knuckles that Kora gave him. Birch wouldn't have kept him if he thought Ersken wasn't tough enough for Rovers Street. All the same, there's a difference between working the street with a tough Dog and walking into the Bottom alone.

He has his whistle, I told myself. We're all close enough to hear.

Then I saw Pounce sit down by Ersken's feet and felt better. Pounce is as good as another Dog.

Birch put me at a side door that opened on a tiny alley. A

pair of torches over the door gave me light as I waited there, my baton in hand, my sap in easy reach. In my free hand I kept a piece of spelled mirror that Kora had given me for Midwinter. It would show me anyone who might try to sneak past under the cover of magic. I never asked her how much it cost, but to me it's worth my weight in gold. I've bagged five mage-spelled Rats using that mirror. With it and my weapons, I might be outside the rowdiest den on Rovers Street, but I was ready to bag me some Rats. And if there was a brawl, I would do my part.

But there was no brawl. Folk were too hot, seemingly. Instead, they ran. The first three that scuttled out my door were known to me. They were part of Aniki's band of rushers: Bold Brian, Reed Katie, and Fiddlelad. They grinned when they saw me and held up their empty fambles.

"Back with Goodwin and Tunstall?" Reed Katie asked me with a wink, a laugh in her sweet voice. Word moves fast in the Lower City.

"What do *you* think?" I asked her. "And why are you three sliding out the back way? Put your hands down."

They lowered their arms. "You don't fool us," said Bold Brian. "Westover's in there, lookin' as innocent as a babe. If he's about, Birch isn't far behind."

"An' if the two of them's huntin' in the Bottom, we're off," Fiddlelad told me, running his fingers over his fiddle. "We thought Rovers Street would be restful once Birch got him a first-year Dog for partner, but Westover's sharp. 'Tis best to tread a measure when they're about."

" 'Specially when Westover wears that baby face of his," Reed Katie added. "He comes in looking all innocent, you *know* sommat's in the wind."

Mayhap I've been worrying over Ersken for naught. Seemingly he's building some repute for himself. I prodded Reed

Katie's purse. "So what were you up to in there, you three? Gaming? Winning silver?"

They laughed and showed me four silver coins between them. "We don't gamble, not in the Bottom," Fiddlelad said. "Play's too rough here."

"We was havin' but a cup of ale, whilst Fiddlelad earned coin playin'," Bold Brian told me.

All of their coins were cut to show they were silver clean through. The three of them were earning better since Rosto became Rogue, but most of their purse coin was still copper.

"Since when do you cut your silver?" I asked them. "Or were you given these already marked?"

"Checked 'em ourselves." Bold Brian had given me two silver nobles. "Aniki warned us about coles this afternoon."

"Just mind who you tell that to," I said, worried. "We need no panics."

"Aniki said the same," Fiddlelad told me. "Brian only mentioned it now a'cos we're talkin' with you, Cooper."

Bold Brian said, "You don't mind, Cooper, we'll clear out. Time we let you be about your business."

In case I run into trouble, I thought, but I waved them on. Five more mots and coves came through the door, but only one of them carried silver, and that was true coin. I was starting to get bored when I saw a reflection in my charmed mirror—a fat Yamani fellow inside a curtain of magic. I turned as if to look inside. When he eased by me, I checked the mirror a second time to make sure I knew his height and where his head would be. Then I snapped my baton around his neck from behind. Whilst he choked, I threw him against the side of the building and groped for his hands so I could tie them. With that done, I felt for the magic charms at his neck and cut the cords they hung on. He started cursing me then.

Once I saw him clear, I hobbled his ankles with a second thong, then searched him for weapons. He carried only a pair of daggers and a dice box. Seemingly he relied on magic to keep him out of trouble. Though his skin and features were Yamani, he wore his hair like any cove of the Eastern Lands, cut along the sides of his head instead of in a topknot. His clothes were the tunic and leggings most local coves prefer.

As I went through his pockets, he complained, "How might such a pretty lass be so cruel?" His accent was that of Port Caynn.

"Compliments do you not one whit of good," I said as I took the purse from his belt. I inspected its contents in the torchlight. It held a few coppers and at least ten silver nobles. A search of the rest of him gave me another purse, hidden inside his tunic. It was stuffed with silver coins. "And I *hate* colemongers."

"I know naught of coles!" he protested.

I took out a silver coin from the hidden purse and cut its face with my dagger. Brass gleamed at the bottom of the cut. I dropped that coin on the ground and fished out another, cutting it as I had the first. It, too, was a cole.

He was sweating. "I won them in play on the boat from Port Caynn."

"From who?"

"Some fellows. Decent enough, but—they'd not like my giving their names to the law in Corus, I'm certain."

I grabbed his hair and banged his head against the wall. "You'll not like what will happen to you if you *don't* tell me who you won those coles from."

"I cannot tell, Guardswoman! I must have played five people on that boat!"

"Then we'll round all of them up," I said. He shook his

head and kept shaking it, though he wrenched his own hair in my hand as he did it. "Very well, then. Who are you?" I asked.

He refused to speak.

"Tell me or tell the cage Dogs, it makes no difference. They will get the truth out of you sooner or later," I warned him. Sometimes just the threat of the cage Dogs will make a Rat spill. Not this one, though. He was still holding his tongue when the other Dogs came for me. They'd caught another cole-monger, a mot built like a barge. She looked like a fighter of some kind, dressed as she was in a metal-studded leather jerkin, leather breeches, and boots, with metal-studded gloves folded over her belt. She wore empty sword and dagger sheaths on the belt. Jewel had her weapons.

My cove lit up when he saw her. "Tell them! Tell them we won the coles on the boat! This stone-hearted doxie won't be-lieve me, but maybe these fine Guardspeople will!"

"He's a gabblemonger, but he's tellin' the truth," the mot told us as we walked them down the street. "And it's a gold noble for each of yez if you'll send for the advocate to the Gem-cutter's Guild. She'll bring a mage with truth spells. We'd as soon avoid any rack or Drink or thumbscrews your cage Dogs got waitin'."

"It's true," my Yamani said. "The guild will pay our fees and yours. All our wrong lay in gaming with the wrong folk."

"The Gemcutter's Guild," Nyler Jewel repeated, just to be certain.

"We carry packages for the guild, to and from Port Caynn," said the Yamani.

Jewel groaned. He looked like he'd bit into a pickle with a rotten tooth. Tunstall spat on the street. Yoav swore. Some of the city guilds could walk their people away from plenty of things. If we couldn't prove these two guilty of cole passing, the Gemcutter's Guild would have them out of the cages before dawn.

"Gambling's a pleasant way to pass the time. She's my guard until the packages are delivered." The Yamani nodded toward the mot. "We spend a night in the city, and in the morning we take goods back to the port."

"Be reasonable," the mot said. "You know cage Dogs get lies as often as not with their tortures. A mage is a certain thing. Just send to the guild—they'll get someone to come for us. And the advocate will pay them gold nobles over to yez, nice as honey in the comb."

I could nearabout hear the Senior Dogs' teeth grinding. I asked, "If you're so clean and you're to be bought free of cages and charges, you may as well give up the names of your gamester friends and that boat you came on."

"And your own names as well," Goodwin said.

The mot gave us a hard grin. "We will, once our release papers are signed. If yer cage Dogs haven't been gnawing on us. Then we'll be happy to say what you want to know."

I looked down so no one could see me smile. She had sack, this mot, giving back hard answers when she'd been nabbed by hard Dogs for passing coles. I hope she is honest.

Birch and Ersken came out of the Barrel's Bottom. "It's clear, and the staff inside cursing us," said Birch. "Are these two all we have to show?"

"It gets better," Tunstall growled. "They work for the Gemcutter's Guild." He ruffled his hair. "One of us will have to go to the Guild's Advocate. And why should the advocate believe we have two of their Rats?"

"Hey!" cried the Yamani, insulted. "We're no Rats!"

The mot acted like she hadn't heard. "Where's the magic charms he wore about his neck? That's your proof. And I'd give a rosy copper to know how he got caught with them on, unless he was so rattled he forgot to work the spell." She gave the Yamani a scornful look.

"I worked them!" he said. "But the young Dog there caught me all the same, the mot with the ghostly eyes."

Jewel and Birch looked at me. Ersken and my partners knew about Kora's Gift. "My friend Kora gave me a mirror that shows what's behind an illusion," I explained. I pulled the Yamani's charms from my pocket. I'd hoped Kora would tell me how I might use them, but that was out now. I wouldn't be allowed to keep them. They'd go to the Senior Dogs, or maybe even the Watch Commander.

The mot selected one made of the costly blue stone called lapis lazuli. She handed it to me. On it was carved the sign of the Great Eye, for eyesight, but there was something wrong about it. I turned the charm about and realized the Eye was carved upside down on one side and closed on the other. "Show it to the Gemcutter's Advocate," the mot said.

I left Pounce with my partners. I knew where the advocate lived from my days as a message runner from the different kennels. She was well enough, for someone who was paid to get Rats out of their rightful sentences. Still, there were times when we nabbed someone wrongfully, and then the advocates have their uses.

It was a fair way from the Barrel's Bottom, and I took it at the trot. The servants didn't keep me waiting at the gate very long. Scarce ten minutes after I'd handed that strange eye charm to the manservant on duty there, he returned with the advocate, who was pulling on her robe as she walked.

"Fetch my horse and two grooms suitably armed and prepared to ride," she ordered the servant. To me she said, "How many of our people do you have, Guardswoman, and where are they held?" She is always that way, straight to the point and no mucking about.

"Two of them, Mistress Advocate, and they'll be at the Jane Street kennel," I replied.

"Very well. You may go about your duties," she told me.

And that was that. She did not ask me the prisoners' names or the charges. They never do, these busy, important folk. She and I both knew she could buy them out of the cages, given the guild's heavy purses.

I returned to my partners as quickly as I had left them. Our captives were gone, tucked into a cage cart for transport to Jane Street and their advocate. We six Dogs and Pounce returned to Rovers Street.

We spent the rest of the night in every drinking den and gamblers' hall on the side that lay within our district. We brought in seven others with more than two of the silver coles, but we'd no good feeling from them. The Yamani and his guard were our best bet for a scent of the colesmiths responsible for this run of false coin.

"So who told the colemongers there was good coin to be made here?" Ersken asked after we'd mustered out. We were yawning over our reports, wanting to get them wrote up before we went home. I kept having to shove Pounce over to write mine. He likes to nap on my papers. "One of those colemongers that Flash District had?" Ersken suggested.

I shook my head. "I'm thinking mayhap it's whoever made the coles, or who's in charge of passing them on. Gambling's a good way to do it, right? Folk will gamble for silver when they won't buy things with it. Silver makes folk like them that live in the Lower City crackbrained. They gamble and win, they gamble and lose. If you've a fistful of coles and you know how to gamble, you can trade your coles for coppers and your coppers back for good silver at the games. Your gamblers go out and play with other folk, sending your coles further along. No one asks your name, they hardly look at your face."

"And they can't describe you for the Dogs," Goodwin said over my shoulder. She took my finished report from me and read it over. "Good, Cooper. Tidy, as ever." She gave Ersken and me a sheet of parchment each. "Flash District sent these over and Ahuda had them copied. We'll show them around. It's the cole passers they had, and lost."

We looked at the drawings. They could have been anyone.

"I know," Goodwin said. "Come on, you two. Let's have a late supper at the Mantel and Pullet. Lady Sabine is buying."

As much as I wished to see my lady, and as much as it pained me to turn down a free meal, I was near asleep on my feet. I begged off. Walking home woke me enough to write in my journal. I've been thinking hard to see if there's aught I've forgotten, turning the fire opal stone I got as a Puppy over in my fingers. The bits of bright color my candle strikes from it spark my thinking.

So is there a colesmithing ring in Port Caynn? Or just a lone colemonger like the Yamani or his river dodger mot?

Time for bed.

Saturday, September 8, 247

Noon.

Poxy, plaguey, sheep-biting Tunstall.

The morning came on even hotter and more miserable than yesterday. The pigeons were pecking at my shutters. I was rolling over for another hour of sleep when someone hammered on my door, shaking dust loose from the cracks.

"Murrain take you, I'm a Dog and I'm dragging you clean to Outwalls!" I cried at last. Clad only in my nightdress, I grabbed my baton and undid my bolts, ready to break someone's nob. "If y' think this be a joke, ye'll chuckle through gaps—" I yanked the door open. There stood Tunstall, looking fresh and cheerful, wearing a cityman's clothes instead of uniform.

"Cooper," he said, shaking his head in a woeful sort of way. "Talking cant like a Lower City gixie. And you such a careful-bred thing. I take no pity on you. I left my beautiful lady all sweet in bed so we could go and roust Mistress Tansy's baker."

I scowled at him. I wished I could do more than scowl, but I like him too much. "When was this decided?"

"Last night, over supper. Goodwin tossed me for it, and I lost." He shrugged, a true eastern hillman. The gods had decided on the toss of a coin, and that was that.

"But I'll miss breakfast with my friends," I complained.

"So you will," he said. "I am missing breakfast with my lady. Is Pounce around?"

Pounce trotted through the door between my feet, meowing a greeting.

"We'll wait downstairs," Tunstall said.

Pounce led him away while I closed the door. I dressed in cityfolk clothes, long blue tunic over undyed breeches, half mot, half cove. The garments stuck to my skin before I even put my boots on. I did my hair in my long braid but left out the spiked strap so I might pin it up in a maidenly coil. And I fetched my basket. Tunstall didn't think to bring one. He was a bachelor. He took his meals at eating houses and seldom shopped for food. He wouldn't know folk no more went to the baker without a basket or bag than they went naked. There was no use telling the world we had Dog business there.

Tansy's baker, Garnett, had his shop on Stuvek Street. Pounce curled up outside the door while we went inside and looked around. It was a prosperous-looking shop. Apprentices worked his counters, whilst Garnett supervised the money box. There were the guards on each side of him, just as Tansy had said. They were a pair of rushers who had seen more shining days, but doubtless they were good enough for a baker.

The moment he saw us, Garnett was on his feet. Mayhap we still looked like Dogs, in or out of uniform. "What may I do for you?" he asked, polite enough. Then he got a good look at Tunstall and knew him.

Tunstall smiled. "We'd like a word, Garnett. No trouble, just a word, mayhap three."

The baker looked at me and sighed. "Your hair's too long and it ain't black, so you ain't Goodwin. You must be Cooper. Bad luck either way."

I kept silent. I'm not chatty with strangers when I'm not dressed as a Dog.

Garnett called for one of the counter folk to take the cash box and ordered the guards to stay with it. Then he led us into the back room. It was small and godless hot, a place for light bookkeeping only. A feeble breeze came through the slats in the shutter. Garnett took the comfortable chair behind the desk. Tunstall had a chair. I had to lean against the wall.

Garnett looked up at me, then at Tunstall. "What brings two Evening Watch Dogs to my place so early of their day? I doubt it's for the baking, for all you carry a basket."

"A Birdie told us you've hired guards because folk are slipping you coles," Tunstall said agreeably. "Now we've seen the guards for our own eyes, right, Cooper? And we're curious. Jane Street has had no report from you. When did you find you were receiving coles?"

Garnett drooped in his chair. "Me and my wife check the coin. We do it every week, afore we sort out taxes and pay and expenses and the like. Three weeks runnin' we found a few coles in the week's takings. We used to check one in ten. That first bad week it were fifteen coles in all, so we decided to check three in ten. The next week we found twenty-seven. Then we checked all our coin, startin' two weeks back. Last week it were fifty-five, more'n half the week's gain. That's when I hired the guards, to keep folk from causin' violence when I caught them in the shop."

"What did you do with the coles you had?" Tunstall wanted to know. "You didn't report them."

Garnett turned white and looked at the floor.

I tapped my foot on the tiles.

"Cooper," Tunstall said.

It would be in here, somewhere. He'd need it close so he could put the dry coins back in the money box. I went around and yanked open the drawers of the desk. Garnett started to grab me, until he saw Tunstall clean his nails with his dagger. Then Garnett just covered his face with his hands.

I found the jar of silver paint and the brush in his bottom drawer. I put them on top of the desk.

"You painted silver over the bronze cut in the coles. Then you paid out the false coins to someone else as good ones," Tunstall said. "You've committed colemongering yourself, Garnett.

34

What you say from now on decides whether you visit Magistrate's Court or not. Who has tried to pass coles to you that you can name?"

"Mistress Tansy Lofts had two. A journeyman carpenter buyin' for one of the weekly guild suppers had five. That came from the guild's own fund, so they'll do the reportin' of it to the kennel." He sighed again. "I s'pose you're wantin' to speak with the others? I only have the names of six." He looked at Tunstall, who gave him a pleasant smile. Garnett took a scrap of parchment from a pile of them, uncapped the ink bottle, and picked up a quill. He made his letters carefully. I guessed he'd not been writing so long as to be comfortable at it.

Tunstall watched him for a moment, then looked at me and raised his brows. I got the hint and asked, "Have you recorded the extra coppers you made them pay as a penalty? For your Crown tax?"

Garnett's hand jumped. He left a streak from the parchment straight onto his leather blotter.

"Cooper, you startled him," Tunstall said with mock reproach.

Tansy hadn't mentioned Garnett making her pay a fine. She must have been too ashamed of having coles to say he'd charged extra so she might leave without him calling the Dogs. But it was a reasonable guess. He had to get money for his guards *somehow*. From the way he'd jumped, he'd not set any of it aside for the King's taxes or for the Dogs' Happy Bag. Naughty baker.

Garnett blotted the line of ink. He was sweating beyond what the heat called for. "Of course I kept the record," he muttered. "Why shouldn't I charge a fee, when I've been given false coin? I have to make up all the money I'm out, after takin' in so many coles before!"

"He lies," I said. "He no more kept a record of it than he reported the coles he got."

Garnett wiped his face on his sleeve.

"Tell the truth, now, Master Baker. It will do you good," Tunstall prodded.

"I didn't record it," the baker said.

"There—that's better. How much is your fee?" Tunstall asked.

Garnett sighed. "Five coppers." He didn't have the air of a liar this time.

"Half a silver! You've a granite set," Tunstall said.

Garnett hung his head. "Better half a silver noble to me than several silver to the cage Dogs, and the court Dogs, and maybe a bath in boilin' oil despite all they pay," he said. "I *know* my neighbors ain't colesmiths, but Dogs is hard, suspicious sorts. They haul you in, and things get expensive and painful fast."

Tunstall picked up the list. "Six names. That's not so bad." He gave the paper to me and stood. Then he leaned on Garnett's little desk so that he towered over the shrinking baker. "Not a word to anyone, Garnett. Or me and Cooper and Goodwin will visit you again. Start recording that fee you charge, for the tax and the Happy Bag. And send what coles you have left to Jane Street. We know it's hard to find you're getting paid in bronze for hard work. But you don't want us chewing at your ass."

Tunstall never raised his voice. He hardly even growled. Garnett would no more warn the folk who'd paid him in coles than he would eat his own hand. Having six-odd feet of sleepy-eyed barbarian looming over them did influence people to do as they were bid.

Outside, we found Pounce waiting. He followed us into

the shade of a nearby tree. Tunstall gave him an ear scratching while I looked at Garnett's list.

"We already know about Mistress Tansy, so we needn't worry her," Tunstall said when I gave the paper back to him.

"My cousin Philben is on that list," I said. "And this Urtiz fellow doesn't live so far from my lodgings."

"Seek out at least one before watch today and talk to him like a neighbor," Tunstall said. "I'll see who I can find out of the other three names. Don't tire yourself out." He looked at the sun, shading his eyes with his hand. "It's going to be cursed hot again. You'll need your strength for duty tonight, and I'm sure you have errands and such."

"It's no bother," I told him. "I don't have anything special to do."

Maybe, and maybe not, Pounce said at my feet. *Maybe I have plans for you.*

This was one of those times when Tunstall understood him. "Do they involve me, *hestaka*?" Tunstall asked. Ever since Pounce saved his life at Midwinter, Tunstall has called him *hestaka*. It means "wise one" in Hurdik. That's what Tunstall calls the hillman speech. Whenever Tunstall says *hestaka,* Pounce fluffs up his chest and looks smug.

No. My plans include only Beka, Pounce replied.

"Then I will leave you to your day. Cooper, don't let your guard down with that cousin. Even family goes wrong."

"I know that," I said as Tunstall turned to leave. "Tunstall?" He looked back. "I know we promised, but . . . will you *really* let Garnett off? By my rough count he's sent at least one hundred and four bad silver coins back into the city's money. There's probably more that he didn't mention. Men have gone to Execution Hill for less."

Tunstall patted my shoulder. "Don't worry, Cooper. I just didn't want him scaring our six into running before we talk to them. I will give Day Watch the word to pick up Master Baker Garnett this afternoon. He'll be spared the worst. We'll speak for him. But he'll tell the cage Dogs everyone he passed those coles to, if he wants to walk or use his hands easily again."

I nodded, feeling better. Garnett knew as well as any that the more bad coins got into a city's money, the shakier *all* our money got, yet he'd looked after himself first. He would have to pay for that.

"Off you go, Cooper. I'll see you at four." Tunstall ambled down the street, hands in his pockets. He looked every inch the country cove enjoying the city, if you didn't notice his body was set so that if someone hit him from the side, he wouldn't be knocked over. I would have bet a week's pay his eyes were roving, taking in everything around him. Dogs don't survive in the Lower City, on duty or off, without paying attention. Of course, as long as Tunstall's been a Dog, he's never really off duty.

I still had Pounce to manage. "What's this you're telling me about plans?" A passing gaggle of lads stared at the girl who talked to her cat. I glared at them. They laughed and raced on by me.

We set off down the street, Pounce trotting at my side. *You think too much, that's your problem. Have I led you astray before?*

I could think of dozens of times that his advice had gotten me into trouble. "Yes." I wiped my forehead on my sleeve.

You're being petty. You always come out all right.

"I had the highest healer's bill of any Puppy in Corus," I reminded him. "How many broken bones and slashes have I gotten because you yowled, 'This way'?"

*Yet you preen like a pigeon when they call you Terrier. You
don't mind the bruises and cuts then.*

"Why do I argue with a cat?" I always ask myself that,
when I know there's only one answer: I don't learn. I can't even
say it's because he's a *talking* cat. He's a cat, and cats just aren't
reasonable. "Cousin Phil's likely to be hiring out at the Daymarket, this time of year." We turned onto Jane Street. "Best catch
him there. If Delene hears of him gambling, she's liable to lay
him out with a pot."

'Twas then I heard a four-legged dog yelp. I looked about
us. Across the street I saw the scent hound Achoo with her
newest handler, Ercole Hempstead. Hempstead yanked at the
hound's leash, dragging her when she clearly did not wish to go.
My tripes twisted in pity for her. Achoo had been her happiest
last year, when she'd been handled by my friend Phelan Rapp.
Then Phelan had quit the Dogs to join Rosto's side of the law.
Achoo had gone from one handler to another, each of them less
patient with her than the last, though veteran Dogs always said
that when she was put on a scent, she never failed to track down
what she was asked to find. I'd heard that she hated hound kennel life after living with Phelan in his rooms, but all of her other
handlers insisted that hounds be kenneled. And it seemed that
they didn't have the right character to match with hers. Given
my own record with partners, I felt plenty of sympathy for her.

Watching her now, I thought that Achoo looked like she
just wanted to sniff around where she stood. Who could blame
her? She was a scent hound. But Hempstead was having none
of it. He raised the free end of the leash and struck her with it.
She yelped, cowering. He was a big, burly man, and she was a
skinny creature who stood no higher than his knee. That blow
must have *hurt*.

I ground my teeth. "Festering slavemonger's byblow . . . ," I whispered. I'd like to give him the end of that rawhide!

Will you do something? Pounce demanded.

I looked at Pounce. "He's a ranking Senior Dog, and a handler. He'll order me about my business."

Another yelp from Achoo hit me between my shoulder blades.

If you don't stop him, you are not the girl I believe you to be.

"*You* do sommat, you're so clever," I muttered, but Achoo's whimpers called me across the street. I dug my hands in my pockets as I approached them. "Excuse me, Senior Guardsman Hempstead," I said. "I know this hound. She does better with gentleness."

He glared at me. He was going to write me up, I could see it on his face. "Mithros's shield, you *dare*—ah. Goodwin's pet. Tunstall's girly. Think you're as good as a Senior Dog and experienced handler, do you?"

I ducked my head. "No, sir. Only, I was told you got this hound but a week ago, and I've known her in times past." Achoo slunk past Hempstead to nudge my hand. I took it from my pocket to pet her ears. A glance told me she was hard-used and half starved. Her curly white fur was matted. She used to weigh more than thirty pounds, but she looked like she might weigh only twenty now. I felt cold all over. I cannot abide anyone who mistreats animals. "Sir, she likes to stop and smell things, when she's not on the job. For fun, like, or practice."

"She's got no discipline. She's useless! Won't obey a command in plain Common instead of some foreign jabber! No sense of who's master!" He leaned in. I could smell the drink on him. He was swilled, and the hour not even noon. "Just like you. *Terrier.*" He laughed.

"She's a good worker. She's one of the city's best scent hounds." I hate tosspots. 'Twas a drunkard got one of my friends killed when we was Puppies. "She deserves better even if she is silly off watch. Plenty of us are silly off watch, Senior Guardsman." I stepped on thin ice, but Achoo licked my hand like I was her only friend. Her ribs showed through her coat.

"Then I'll just tell Sergeant Ahuda you've the handling of her, eh?" He grabbed my hand and shoved Achoo's leash into it. "You, all untrained in scent hounds, you can work this miserable scut. They should sell her for bear meat anyway. *You* work her, then come tell me my trade. We'll see how clever you are!"

He walked off, laughing.

I'm glad he's gone, Pounce said. *A man like him should fall into a midden and break both legs.* His tail switched to and fro. *Maybe I'll take a little trouble and arrange it.*

I stared at Pounce, wondering if I ought to say he should not joke about such things. I thought the better of it and raised the leash in my hand to look it over. Achoo shrank back. She feared her own leash. To Achoo it wasn't just a tool of her trade anymore. It was a tool for punishment.

I saw her cower and decided to wait until later for a word with Pounce. Right now this poor hound had been passed to yet another strange new handler.

I crouched so our eyes were on a level. "No, it's all right, Achoo." I ran my hands over her as gently as I could. She had welts on her poor body. There would be no combing her fur. Those mats had to be cut off. As she stuck her nose in my ear, I glared at Pounce. "This is *your* doing." I said it quiet, so as not to frighten the creature under my hands.

But at least I'll help. Pounce came over and sat at my side. Achoo lowered her nose until it touched his. She took a sniff and sneezed three times.

You're going to be all right now, as long as you listen to Beka and to me, Pounce told her. *Beka growls, but she feeds her animals first. And she'll let you smell whatever you like.*

Achoo looked at me, then nudged Pounce with her nose. He stumbled backward.

None of that, Pounce warned. *Treat me with respect. I'm not an ordinary cat.*

"You're cat *meat* if you foist any more creatures on me, scent hounds or no," I told him. "I'm not a trained handler. Doubtless they'll just take her from me again." I was trying to decide how I might bathe Achoo without hurting her. And there was still my cousin Philben to find. How do my days get so busy?

We went home, to begin by getting a meal into the poor starved beast. I was feeding Achoo meat pasties I'd crumbled into a bowl of fresh goat's milk when I heard feet on my stairs.

Kora looked in. "We missed you at breakfast. What's this—another creature?" she asked, with a nod for the pigeons that fed on corn at my windowsill, as well as at the cat and hound. Then she noted Achoo's condition. "Beka, what happened to this poor animal?"

Once I told her Achoo's story, Kora ordered me to leave the hound to her. I was glad to do it. Kora has a way with creatures and, unlike her preparations for humans, her animal medicines work. Since Pounce had given Kora Fuzzball, she had collected a second cat, a pup, and a pair of lovebirds. Ersken said he couldn't wait until they moved into the Dancing Dove. There was scarce room in Kora's bed for him. She was a fine one to talk about my creatures! At least the pigeons don't live with me and Pounce.

"You won't know her when you see her again," Kora told

me as I left her with Achoo. "Hempstead, you said her handler's name was?"

"Kora, don't you go magicking any Guardsmen," I warned her. "No matter how much they might deserve it. It's not the kind of thing I can turn a blind eye to."

Kora gave me a sidelong look as she rubbed Achoo's ears. "Beka, I would *never* test you that way."

I snorted. Then I looked at Pounce. "Are you coming?"

I will stay with Achoo, he said. *Until she knows Kora better. I can translate. You won't need me to talk to your cousin.*

"She has a cousin?" I heard Kora ask as I went out the door.

Several, Pounce replied. *Most of her family on her father's side did not like it that she lived at Provost's House, or that she became a Dog. They prefer that she stay away.*

"Tell *all* my secrets, why don't you?" I called as I rattled down the stairs. I felt uneasy in my tripes, though not about Pounce speaking to Kora of my family. It was Kora being clever about Hempstead that worried me. I know full well that Kora might do something devious to the handler, if Pounce does not.

On the other hand, he deserves to be punished somehow. What I don't know won't hurt me.

I shook those worries off and headed for the Daymarket, listening to the pigeons on the ground and the window ledges as I walked. The ghosts they carried were still quiet. If folk were getting killed, they knew why and accepted it. I loved these calm weeks before the harvesters returned to Corus. They were restful not just for me as a Dog, but for the Beka who heard the pigeons' ghosts. Once folk with big hauls and then money in their pockets reached the city, it would be another matter. Killings would pick up then.

I located Phil easily. He was at the Daymarket fountain with his fellow carters, as I expected. They were hunkered down in a circle, their eyes on the ground. As I walked up to them, I heard the clatter of a dice cup.

I grabbed Phil by his ear. He came up with a yelp, scrabbling at my wrist. His friends started to laugh.

"That your woman, Phil? Looks a bit skinny for your usual taste!" one of them japed.

"Stuff yer gob!" someone said. "Don't you know who she is, you crackbrain?"

Phil twisted around to look at me. "Mithros's staff, Beka, wha'd you want with me? You ain't in uniform! You got no call to haul me about like some Rat!"

"I don't?" I asked. I leaned in so his friends wouldn't hear me whisper, "Coles to Baker Garnett, Phil." I looked at the coins in front of the gamblers. All were coppers. "Any of those yours? Do you have a bet down?"

His mouth opened and closed like a fish's. Then he shook his head.

I let go of his ear and tucked my hand in the crook of his arm. "We'll talk, all nice and cousinly." Gentle-like I towed him out of earshot of his friends.

"If you was nice and cousinly, we wouldn't have this talk at all," he groused.

"I didn't hit you, did I? It's just a few questions, and I'll be on my way. Oh, and maybe a look in your purse." I've never had to deal with family as a Dog before. I can't say I care for it.

We perched on the driver's seat of his cart. I looked at Phil as he wiped his brow with a ragged handkerchief. When I was eight, before fortune smiled on us and my Lord Provost brought Ma and our family to live in his house, Phil was my handsome older cousin. He helped Mama carry baskets of laundry and brought us bundles of food from my Granny Fern. Now he was a husband and father to four little ones of his own. There were crow's-feet at the corners of his blue eyes, and he didn't laugh so much anymore. Providing for a family did that to Lower City coves. I hoped I wouldn't have to deal hard with him.

"Your purse," I said, and nudged him with my foot.

He glared at me. "I'd think you'd trust family." He edged away and upended his purse on the bare spot of bench he'd left between us. I took the worn leather bag from his hands and made sure he'd kept no coins back from me. "You're a cruel, suspicious mot, Beka Cooper. You always were. Doggin's the right work for you."

His coins were all coppers. "You gave your only silver to Garnett?"

"No. I had two other coins. Once I knew they was tainted, I went to a friend with a forge—no, Beka, I'll not give up her name! She melted the coins down and separated silver from bronze. She bought the raw metal, so I saw a bit of money back. Not what my day was worth for curst certain, the sarden belly robbers."

I'd no interest in anyone who melted down the coles only for the metal. "You *saw* them melted?"

"Mithros strike me if I lie. Goddess tears, Beka! Mayhap I weren't raised in Provost's House, but I know what harm coles do."

I patted Phil's arm and picked up his coppers, sliding them back into his purse. "So where'd you get the coles? Gambling? You know Delene will have your hide if she catches you dicing." I jerked my head toward his friends and their game.

"Ah." Phil shrugged. "This here? It's a stupid little two-and three-copper game. I'm out if I lose that much. I'll not play with my little ones' bellies, no, nor Delene's, either. If I lose, I go without. And I *never* gamble for silver. That's beggin' to get bit. I made that coin on the straight, Beka. That's what turns to glass in my gullet. One of the boats from Port Caynn brung in bales of Copper Isles silks. The coves as was bringin' it in hired me to cart it up to Starshine Warehouses. Durward, him as hired me was called, and the other fellow was Talbot."

"Had they last names?" I asked him.

The look he gave me could have peeled whitewash from stone. "Like they'd give their lineage to the likes of *me*," Phil said. "They showed me coin and goods and asked if I could do the work. We haggled over price and I did the job. Pus suckers was probably laughin' at me all along. *They* was the gamblers. Durin' the ride up Palace Way they was talkin' about how they cogged some slick port coves out of a purse of silver." Suddenly Phil grinned. "Mayhap they're the ones that got bit, if the coles came from that purse."

"What boat did they come on?" I asked. "Did they say where they were going once they'd sold their goods?"

"The boat?" Phil squinted at the sky. He flinched. "Beka, there's a demon bird a-glarin' at me. He's—" He flung up his arms as a pigeon came flying down at us.

I ducked, but Slapper caught me on the head anyway, two good, sound buffets with his wings. "Stop it, you ungrateful louse!" I yelled. I grabbed for the dreadful beast. He fastened his beak on my hand and wrenched. I yowled, scrabbling in the small bag of feed I carried in my tunic until I had a handful of corn. I shoved Slapper onto the seat between Phil and me and dumped the corn before him. The moment the crazed pigeon saw there was food nearby, he yanked his beak from my flesh and stood on the bench. He stumbled, his clubbed foot skidding on the wood. I balanced him and got pecked for my pains. "Curse you, I'll yank a wing feather if you do that again!"

He was too busy eating to listen.

"Goddess save me and mine," whispered Phil. He now sat all the way at the edge of the seat, eyeing the bird. "You're sure he's no demon?"

"He's just cracked, is all. This is Slapper." I didn't blame Phil for being flinchy of the bird. He looks like any moment he'll start to spout prophecy.

I set down more corn. Slapper stabbed at me with his beak, but I yanked my hand clear in time. "Missed me," I told him. He smacked me with a wing. "A love tap," I said, and looked at Phil. "I need the name of that boat and where else they might have been going."

"You do talk to 'em," Phil whispered, staring at the bird. "I heard you done, but I thought it was just gabble."

"Did you hear they don't listen? My life is wearing on, cousin, and so is yours. Give me all you know and I'll take myself and this cracknob feather duster out of your way." Slapper hit me again. I swear, the pigeons that know me best have gotten saucy.

Phil wiped his forehead again. The sweat rolled from his face in beads. "The boat . . . 'Twas the *Merry Molly*. She comes upriver twice a week. And she only returns to Port Caynn."

Slapper had finished his corn. I scooped him up carefully, gripping both wings one-handed. He couldn't even get his head around to bite, which pleased me to no end. "Very well, then, Phil. We're done, unless I find you've lied to me. And then it won't be me you explain yourself to. It'll be Goodwin, or Tunstall."

He winced. "I didn't lie, Beka. There's no point to it. I'm already out five coppers to Garnett that I didn't have, thanks to those two merchants. Though I'll say this, I'd prefer dealin' with any other Dogs than get this kind of treatment from family."

It hurt like a pinch in the peach, I won't deny it. But what could I have done? "If you think other Dogs would treat you better, you've been buying dreams from hedgewitches. Be on about your game, then, if you're fool enough to play."

I jumped down from the wagon, Slapper tucked under my arm. When I found a quiet corner, I put down another handful of corn and let him go. I jumped back, so he missed smacking me yet again before he settled to his meal. "You're getting slow, bird," I told him.

Otho Urtiz lives on Lambert Street, on my way to Nipcopper Close. I knew I would find him there, it not even being eleven. He is a minstrel who works steady and late at Naxen's Fancy and some of the city's other fine eating houses. He'd be abed yet, or just waking up.

His landlady interrupted her washday work just long enough to tell me where his rooms were. When I knocked on his door, a slave answered. For a cove of Urtiz's reputation I expected someone prettier, and smaller, too. This mot topped my five feet and eight inches by six inches more. Her hair and brows were brown and straight, her eyes brown, her nose lumpy, her teeth bad. She had a scar across her forehead. Her shoulders and waist were broad as a man's, her scarred hands like stone. In a tan wool dress she looked a joke on the very idea of a woman. Her apron was a parting giggle. She would have done better dressed in a tunic and breeches.

"Who wants to see Master Urtiz?" she asked. Her voice was as dull as her clothes.

"Say that I've come regarding his recent visit to the baker Garnett," I told her. "I doubt he'll be wanting me singing more of it than that out here in his hallway."

"Ashmari, it's well enough." Otho Urtiz even spoke musically. He stood in the doorway to his bedchamber, wearing plain breeches and a tunic and carrying a lap harp. I'd interrupted his morning practice. Interesting to think that a Player so accomplished still did that. He was as I'd seen him before, scarce five feet and five inches in height. He is fifty-three by all accounts, with long black hair he wore loose today, and a short-cropped black beard. His eyes are green-hazel. "So Garnett has noised the truth of those coins about, Mistress—?" He looked me over with eyes as sharp as a veteran Dog's. His brows went up and he set his harp aside. "He swore to keep it to himself, but perhaps you were more persuasive than most."

"It depends on what you have to say. For now, I only need information. How did you come by the coles you paid to the baker?"

Urtiz sighed. "It was gambling. You know there are horse races on the Common?"

I nodded.

"I've an eye for horseflesh, so I like to go there and wager against the sheeplings who *believe* they know horses. There were crews up from the riverboats. I found myself a likely coney, fresh from Port Caynn, and won twelve silver nobles from him. I bought some bread on my way home. That was when I learned he'd paid me in coles. Lucky for me I had enough copper to pay off Master Garnett. Word hasn't gotten around the city about false coin. I went to the slave market and bought Ashmari." He grinned, showing teeth. "Money changed hands so fast the slave peddlers barely had time to count it. No one was bidding on her. They meant to sell her to the mines. They were glad to take eight silver nobles for her, what with the King's tax and the market fees. The other coins I threw in the river."

"You paid for a slave with coin you knew was false. That's a crime, Master Urtiz." I wanted to laugh at the trick played on the life peddlers. I hated them. One of Mama's men had a buyer for my sister Diona and was waiting for him to get the papers when Mama and I caught them and told the buyer her man had no right to sell her. We almost lost her that day.

Distracted by memory, I forgot to watch the woman Ashmari. She rushed me from behind, her hands gripped together over her head in one giant fist. Only my instincts got me out of the way, or my head would have been crushed. The blow glanced off my left elbow, numbing it. I spun and tried to trip her. It was like trying to trip a tree.

She grabbed me by the waist and lifted me over her head. All the while she cursed me: "Sarden puttock—gutter piece— hedgecreeping scummer . . ."

I seized her hair and swung my legs up, then down, kicking her in the chest. She grunted and dropped me. For all her size, she'd had no training in fighting. I kept my hold on her hair and dragged her head down until I could slam my knee in her forehead. It was as square a hit as ever I'd made. She went loose, falling to her knees. I darted around and got my arm about her throat. Only when she was purple did I yank off her apron and use it to hobble her arms at her back. There were rawhide ties in my purse. I never go out without some. Those I used to bind her ankles.

"You've got my trade all wrong, you looby," I told her once she was properly done up. "I'm a Dog, not a whore."

"You whore for the law," she mumbled.

I looked at Urtiz. He was dead white, frozen in place by the hearth. "She tries my patience," I warned him. "You know the law about masters who keep vicious slaves." Except I couldn't send this ugly creature back to be sold for working meat. No more could I send the man who'd saved her from the mines to the cages.

"Let me kill her," Ashmari begged, struggling against my bonds. "I'll not slave in mine or quarry! You saved me, let me save you!" She fought the apron binding her arms. "Master, I'm beggin'! You know the colemongers' fate!"

"I'll give you five gold nobles. Let me free her, let her escape, before you hobble me," Urtiz said, with sweat on his brow. "Guardswoman, I swear, the coin is right here. Only let me free her, and I'll go with you quietly. She was trying to protect me! Not just five nobles—I have jewels. Let me buy Ashmari's freedom and you can have the rest. It's enough for you to retire on."

I stared at them both. Goddess save me. Urtiz was one of those who liked to free slaves. That's why he'd bought Ashmari. And now he'd pay a fortune to bribe me so he could do that. Not get me to turn a blind eye while *he* escaped, but wait until he'd freed *her*. Why? Was it a vow to a god, or his ancestors, or something? Whatever it was, *I didn't care.* I only wanted to know how Urtiz had gotten his coles.

Look at this mess I've written. Maybe this is what Ahuda means about my reports.

The truth is, I must think of a way to write this up for Ahuda so she, Tunstall, and Goodwin don't suspect about Urtiz's bribe. They'll never forgive me for turning it down.

"Listen to me good, you crackbrain pair of scuts." I kept my voice soft, in case the landlady was listening. "I came here for answers about the baker's coles. *That's all.*" I was shaking, I was so angered. "Has neither of you the sense to grow herbs in dirt? Getting me involved in fooling with the slave laws! Leave me out of that!"

I knelt and untied Ashmari's feet, pocketing my rawhide thongs when I was done. As I worked, I warned her, "Kick me and I'll break your toes, understand? I'm that vexed with the pair of you." I undid her apron to release her arms. Then I looked at Urtiz. "You'd best free her now, before she gets the two of you in real trouble. Not every Dog's a looby like me."

Ashmari rubbed her hands and then her feet, staring at me. "You're one strange cur," she said.

"That's no way to talk to the Guardswoman," Urtiz told her.

"You're both featherbrained. Why do the likes of you two care what happens to the likes of me?" Ashmari clambered to her feet. "Everything made sense before I ran into you." She went to a corner of the room and pulled a standing screen around it so we couldn't see her.

Urtiz shrugged. "I make apologies for both of us, Guardswoman—?"

"Never mind my name. Who lost those coins to you? Tell me that and you can forget I ever came by." I just wanted to get my information and go, before they acted out any more tragedy for me.

"Hanse. His first name was Hanse," Urtiz said.

I tapped my toe, letting him know my patience was running out. "Hanse is a common name, minstrel. I've two Hanses in my watch. No one will know I've gotten the name from you, so cough it up."

Urtiz sighed. "Hanse Remy. I don't know what boat he came on, I swear."

"Describe him for me."

Now, at last, he stopped toying with me. "He dressed well. Like a merchant, though he wore his hair cut only a quarter of an inch thick, like the professional soldiers do. He was near six feet tall. Blue eyes. Brown hair and eyebrows. A mole on his left cheek. Scarred hands. In his late twenties. His accent was from the valley of the River Tellerun. There were worn places on his belt where he would normally keep a sword and a fighter's dagger."

I nodded. His memory was good, but I expected that. Minstrels, the best ones, are trained to use their memories the same as Dogs. "Is there aught else you can tell me?"

"Only that when you hobble Master Remy, give him my regards." There was a flinty look in Master Urtiz's eyes. "I like being cheated no more than the next man."

I took my leave, before Ashmari decided she ought to try to kill me again. The day was wearing on. At least I have a full budget of news for Tunstall and Goodwin for tonight.

On coming home, I stopped at Kora's open door. She sat on the floor making written charm designs as Pounce and Achoo looked on. Cleaned up, Achoo was skinny, with greenish ointment that glistened in a couple of open sores and welts. There weren't as many sores as I remembered, so Kora had used her magic ointments. Achoo's fur was cropped ragged and short, none of it more than an inch long. It looked more amber-colored than it did when it was long. She was clean from nose to tail.

"She was mostly white when I left here," I told Kora while Achoo sniffed me.

"Sometimes it happens, when you cut their fur short." Kora blew on her charm to dry the ink. "It'll grow out white again, you'll see. I charmed off the fleas and ticks, and gave her something for worms." Kora wrinkled her nose. "Be glad you weren't here for that."

I *was* glad. There was only one way for a creature to rid itself of most kinds of worm. "What do I owe you?" I asked. "I don't know what the mages for animals charge—"

Kora waved it off. "Don't be a fool, Beka." Her eyes glinted wickedly at me. "Or let me go at that Hempstead."

Pox. She remembered his name. "He's not worth it," I said.

Kora rubbed Achoo's ears. "Being friends with such an upright Dog is very bad for my spirits," she told the hound. "Mind she doesn't make you feel low. Not that you'd notice, being trained to the work and all." Kora gave me Achoo's leash.

I took the hound on up to my rooms. Pounce talked to Achoo softly as we climbed, in animal sounds I did not understand. Only when we were inside did I inspect Achoo's leash and collar. Kora had cleaned and oiled both, but that did little to improve them. Both were made of worn, twisted, dirty leather, not at all up to Dog standards.

There is naught I can do now. I can only hope that Hempstead left none of his hairs tangled in the leather. Mages can do a fearful lot with a cove's hair.

It is stifling in here, even with every shutter open. There is no breeze at all. While writing in this journal, I have sweated through my clothes.

Tonight's watch will be nasty, if the heat does not break.

Long after watch, near dawn.

Pox rot this cursed watch. I am so weary I can scarce hold my pen, yet what must I do the moment I unlock my door? Achoo greeted me, whining and dancing. She trotted to the edge of the stair and back, her tail between her legs.

She couldn't have been plainer if she'd spoken in Common. She also was plain about expecting me to hit her because she had to go on an errand that came from sitting indoors all through my watch. I closed and locked my door and went downstairs with her. My head was spinning, I was so weary.

Achoo raced down the steps and out the door. She must have been full to bursting. I found her in the street, not even the courtyard, doing her business over the gutter. I had to admire the person who'd trained her to go through doors and gateways to find a gutter. Even my lord Gershom's or my lady Teodorie's hunting hounds, trained though they are, forget themselves indoors sometimes.

"Good Achoo," I said, reaching to scratch her ears. She cringed away from me. I turned my hands over and crouched slowly. It was hard to do it and not fall over. I let her come to me. She sniffed my hands. I scratched her chin a little, then gently did her ears. I never let her suspect that I was in a killing rage at her last handlers.

When she leaned her head back, showing just the tips of her teeth in a hound's grin, I lurched to my feet. She stepped back from me. "Time to go inside," I told her, keeping my voice gentle. "Elsewise I'll fall asleep right here."

She followed me back up to the room, her feet thumping on the steps.

I've managed to write this much, but the letters are dancing on the ~~pg~~ page. I told the easy ~~parte~~ part about coming ~~hom here~~ home here. I will write more of this ~~nyt~~ night after I sleep. I ache in my every bo⟍

Sunday, September 9, 247

Ten of the clock on Sunday morning.
being yet a record of the events of the Evening Watch of Saturday, September 8th

It is too hot to sleep more this morning, and no matter which way I turned, something hurt. I woke to Achoo panting in my face, making me hotter still. "I am surprised you held your water so long," I grumbled as I pulled on my breeches. All my body ached.

Achoo went out with Kora at breakfast time, Pounce told me. *She has a charm that slides the bolts on the door.*

I was too weary to be angry. Instead, as Achoo took care of her necessities, I drew a bucket from my landlady's well and dumped it over my head. Lifting it hurt my arms dreadfully, but it was worth it to feel cool all over. I led Achoo back upstairs. She was in fine fettle this morning, her tail waving like a banner. I gave her and Pounce cold meat pasties for their breakfast and settled down to finish my accounting of yesterday's watch, the Evening Watch of Saturday, September 8.

First I had to check with Mistress Trout that I would be allowed to leave Achoo tied in the backyard this evening. Five coppers bought her agreement. I left Pounce to bear Achoo company. I set them both up in the kitchen garden behind our lodging with a bowl of water and their supper. Achoo I tied to a long rope attached to a post, in case she got the urge to wander. Then I reported to training.

When I got there, Ahuda was waiting for me. Her arms were crossed over her chest.

"I'm informed you consider yourself a scent-hound handler now," she told me.

I winced as I handed her the notes on what I had gathered from the pigeons and the spinners. I should have figured Hempstead would rush to bleat his tale in Ahuda's ear. "Sergeant, I never tried to take Achoo from him. He was the one who thrust her on me."

"Never mind, Cooper. I'd have taken the poor thing myself, except I'm no street Dog. We don't have any more handlers." She rubbed her nose. "It's not what I would have chosen, but it may serve. It won't hurt you to have a handler's skills. Stop by my desk after your watch musters off duty, and I'll give you the allowance for the hound's food and care. You still see Phelan, don't you?"

Phelan had been Achoo's handler before he'd left the Dogs. "Yes, Sergeant, I do."

"Have him teach you the commands until I can get you regular training. It's just as well you're between partners, wouldn't you say? Now get in that yard and warm up."

Word raced ahead of me, as always. By the time we walked into muster from training, Goodwin greeted me with, "You're turning us into a menagerie, Cooper, is that it? First a cat, now a hound—what's next, winged horses?"

"Always wanted to see those," Tunstall remarked with a sigh. There was a light in his eyes as he added, "Always wanted to ride one."

"Didn't that barbarian nursemaid tell you winged horsies are stories, man?" Yoav teased. "You go ridin' stories, you're due for a long fall!"

"Hempstead *made* me take Achoo," I told Goodwin. "Besides, you should see her. Skin and bones and open sores."

Tunstall went to spit on the floor. He stopped, seeing Ahuda's eye on him. "It's a tiny soul that'll beat an animal, even one as silly as that Achoo," he said, his voice a soft growl.

"Muster up!" Ahuda bellowed. We took our places in the ranks. Ahuda gave us our orders for the night and called up the Senior Dogs for anything special.

When Ahuda dismissed us to duty, we walked out into the courtyard, where the heat smothered us. It clung wetly, filling our noses and lungs. We all grumbled, each in our own fashion. Saturday is a big market day. Plenty of folk come out when their jobs are done. On a night like this, with the heat so bad, tempers would be short.

The free-roaming Senior Dogs and Corporals bunched up near the gate to choose their routes. Goodwin picked the Market of Sorrows for the three of us. The lordlings and rich merchants who came to look over the slave merchandise after dark would be short with the beggars and street folk. Things would go smoother if we were there to stop trouble before it began.

"Any word?" Jewel asked me. "Ahuda said you had sommat troublin' on the rye crop."

I told him what I'd learned while the others listened, frowning.

"That's bad," Yoav said. "If it gets out, it could start a panic."

"I gave it to Ahuda," I told them. "She's always careful with the delicate things."

Tunstall growled. "I'd like to get my hands on the kind of snake that would sell folk rotten grain."

We all growled our answer. Everyone would be looking at any seller of rye now, alert for anything that didn't look or smell as it should. The Senior Dogs and us lucky enough to be partnered with them lingered a little while longer, talking about the harvest in general. None of us were eager to rush out into the heat and the business of the watch. Despite the shadows granted to us by the city walls and the coast hills, the air felt just as hot and sticky as it had during full daylight. At last our knot of Dogs undid itself, Jewel and Yoav going one way, Goodwin, Tunstall, and me another.

We'd just ambled a couple of blocks down Jane Street when Tunstall halted and put a hand to his ear. I'd heard something, too. We all waited, listening. Then we heard it clear. Somewhere from the direction of the Nightmarket, Dogs were blowing the General Alarm signal on their whistles.

We turned down Sophy Street at the trot, bound for the Nightmarket's eastern edge at Feasting Street. We knew this was bad. Five regular pairs and two roving ones had the Nightmarket on Saturday. If the ones who sounded the whistle continued to do so, it meant that fourteen Dogs were in trouble there.

Goodwin halted us a block short of the Nightmarket. The whistles had continued to blow. "Weapons check," she said. "Mother, watch over us."

"So mote it be," Tunstall and I whispered. The Great Mother Goddess was not who either of us prayed to first, but we would take all the help we could get. I checked my knives swiftly, though I'd done so before leaving the kennel, and made certain my arm guards were tightly laced. I mourned the absence of my armor, which lay snug at home, because I'd decided it was too hot to carry. Then I drew my baton and gave Goodwin the nod. She and Tunstall had gone through the same checks that I had, though perhaps they had not hated themselves for leaving their armor at home. They were wearing their gorgets, which made me kick myself again. *They* had thought it was worth at least wearing their neckpieces. Mine wouldn't have made me sweat *that* much more.

"Keep breathing, keep learning," Ahuda says.

Goodwin held up her whistle, which hung on a thong

from her gorget. Tunstall produced his, hanging around his neck. I showed her mine. "Very good, Cooper," Goodwin said. "Let's go."

We emerged onto Feasting, the eastern edge of the market, batons in hand. Our view was blocked by the rows of stalls in front of us. The trouble was doubtless in the heart of the market, where there was more open ground. We swung down to the Rovers Street border of the market and trotted along until we found the edges of the crowd. The open heart of the market was filling up with the kind of cracknob who always came to see what the fuss was about.

Using our batons and elbows gently, ordering these loobies to go about their business or go home, we muscled our way to King Gareth's Fountain. It stood at the heart of the central square, four shallow bowls of lesser and lesser size along the length of a carved stone pillar thirty feet in height. It gave a determined climber a good view of the square between Stuvek Street and Rovers Street. A handful of lads and gixies had already climbed it to take in the events at the south side of the market.

"Up you go, Cooper," Goodwin said. "You're the lightest."

"Not to mention the most junior of the team," Tunstall added.

I undid my weapons belt, and gave it and my baton into Goodwin's care. They would only hinder me as I went up.

I clambered up the sides and over the three lowest bowls, shifting the lads and gixies who didn't want to make way. Lucky for us all they let me pass once they saw my uniform. Standing in the last bowl, hanging on to the crown-tipped point, I could see where the problem was.

The crowd had turned into a boiling mass of hornets at the front, all its attention centered on a line of Dogs—eight at the center with one a step back on each side, whistles to their lips. That was all but two of the pairs assigned to the market. The line of Dogs stood at guard, their batons horizontal in their grips, before the Two for One bakery. In front of Two for One hung its famous slate sign, *Day-old loaves, 2 for 1 copper.* Only someone had crossed out the *2* and chalked the number *1* in its place.

"Bread!" them in the crowd were shouting. "We need bread!" Mostly those in the lead were women armed with naught but market baskets. Behind them were others, coves and mots alike, better prepared for a brawl with bottles, stones, sticks, and jars.

It was unthinkable. Two for One had sold day-old loaves of bread two loaves for one copper ever since I could remember. They bought up much of the city's fresh bread at the end of the day and sold it here the next day at that rate. In the Lower City, even one copper made a difference.

"Move on!" shouted the burliest of the Dogs. It was Greengage, one of our Corporals. "Be about your business. I'll have no trouble tonight!"

"Easy for you to say!" I heard a mot cry. "You're paid a decent wage! One copper, two, it's no skin from your cheek!"

The two Dogs at the ends of the line of guarding Dogs took a deep breath and blew the summons to all Dogs in the area. They were right. Ten Dogs, or even fourteen when the two other pairs arrived, weren't enough for this crowd, and the folk in it weren't calming down.

"Bread," folk in the rear of the crowd began to call. "Bread, bread, bread."

"Eat this, cur!" I heard someone yell. "Here's fare ordinary folk can buy!"

I looked back at Two for One in time to see a rotted cabbage head hit Greengage straight in the chest. It splatted brown-gray sludge over him and the Dogs on both his sides.

Down the fountain I went, ordering the others who climbed it, "Get home afore you get your bones broke!" On the ground again, I told Goodwin and Tunstall what I'd seen. Goodwin returned my belt to me and watched as I buckled it on, making certain everything was settled where I could reach it. Then she handed me my baton.

We all gave each other a last swift going-over by eye to see that all buckles were done up and all laces were tied. Then Goodwin nodded to the left. That would be our direction around the fountain, toward Two for One. She and Tunstall moved first into the crowd, then I stepped in behind them, as we had done at other crowd fights, so I could guard their backs.

Folk around us surged forward, punching their neighbors and shrieking, "Bread!" as sweat poured down their faces. The heat alone might drop a third of them soon enough. Our job was simple. We ordered the brawlers home. If they disobeyed, they got a taste of the baton. Rushers with clubs or blades in their hands got the baton to the head, hard enough to drop them. We didn't need anyone up and about who'd come with a mind to draw blood. Our job was to clear these folk out. And we had to get them that weren't fighting out of the way. It was hard, fast work and left me no time to think about how frightened I was. I'd never been at the heart of a riot, only its edges. I felt beat at by the noise alone.

Goodwin was tangling with a tattooed cove and Tunstall with two drunken Rats when a mot grabbed my braid and yelped in pain. She had found the spiked strap woven in it. I gave her the baton to the belly and let her stumble away, gasping for breath. A cove to my right was keeping a fainting mot on her feet. At the same time he reached for a child who screamed in the grip of a grinning rusher, a child stealer like as not. I lunged for the little gixie, slamming the child stealer's elbow with my baton. He squealed and took one hand off the girl. I wrapped an arm around her waist, then rammed the cove's cod with my baton. He went down under the feet of the mob, wailing. Quick as I could, I thrust the girl into the man's free hand. "Papa!" she cried, reaching for him.

I grabbed the fainting mot and got her arm over my shoulders. "There!" I ordered the cove, pointing to a stall where other cityfolk huddled, wanting no part of the violence. I shoved the three of them under the scant protection of the stall's awning and looked about me for my partners. I could see naught of them in that lump of heaving flesh.

Again I threw myself into it. My ears rang with screams and the never-ending chant of, "Bread! Bread!" More than once the crowd's force picked me off my feet and bore me along, held up by the bodies of them that were packed in around me. That was the worst, when I had no control over where I went. I was in the power of this beast of sweaty arms and faces and dozens of screaming heads. When it let my feet touch the ground, I fought to keep them there.

Over and over I banged the unlawful on knees and shoulders, then dragged folk clear of the mob—women, mostly, and little ones. I had to switch baton hands twice as my arms began to ache. Part of me knew I would hate the next day, when I woke up to feel all those places where the brawlers landed their own blows on me. I didn't feel them now, that was all that mattered. That and the knowing that other Dogs were here, same as me, bringing order to this mess. I could hear their whistles high over the beast's roar, letting me know they were nearby.

It wasn't all clean-cut battle. I was running out of places to get the helpless who couldn't run out of harm's way. Folk that might have ducked a common market brawl came to this one to tell the shopkeepers what would happen if any more prices went up. Word of a bad harvest on top of so many hot days made the Lower City folk lose what sense they had.

The stall that had sheltered the first people I got out of the fight didn't exist anymore. The mob had torn it to pieces for clubs. I went looking for those who'd hidden there. They were in the next row of stalls, tucked inside one. I dragged two of the women, who clutched as many little ones as each could manage, down the row, trusting that the others would follow. I *wanted* to get them clear of the market. I hoped that the sight of a street with no mob on it would give rise to some sheep-like instinct to run home, or to Jane Street kennel.

Then the mob crashed into the row ahead of us, smashing through the walls of two stalls on either side. Both places sold drink. I saw mots and coves handing around jacks, tankards, and bottles. I turned my people back, toward the main square.

"Here." A light-haired cove, slender and muscled like an acrobat, appeared in front of us like something from a dream. "This way." He gathered up two children and set off, sure we would follow. When a river dodger rose in his path, ready to club him down, he leaned to the side and kicked high, catching him in the breastbone. I shoved the mot I'd been towing after the fair-haired cove and turned to make sure the others followed. Then I wiped my sweating forehead on my arm and moved alongside our little group, bashing any that threatened us.

The cove led us to the Jack and Pasty, the oldest of the square's places for food and drink. Mother's mercy, it was built of stone and roofed in slate. The windows were shut and barred. Only a door in the front was open. It was guarded by a big, slope-shouldered cove armed with a staff as thick as my wrist.

"Not dead?" he asked our leader with good cheer, his voice loud enough to cut through the roar. "Curse it, Dale, I had a bet on that you wouldn't make it." He passed each of us a flask of barley water. I drained mine and thanked him.

The light-haired cove—Dale—grinned at the big one as he ushered our group into the shelter of the Jack. "You always lose when you bet against me, Hanse, admit it." He looked at me. "If you find more, Guardswoman, we've started a collection in here." And he winked.

I nodded and headed back along the edges of the crowd. I needed to find Goodwin and Tunstall, so I got out my whistle and blew our private signal. I'd not gone far when I heard an answer nearby. I swallowed my fear of getting back into the thick of it and plunged in. Now that I wasn't spending all my wits on getting those cityfolk to safety, I listened harder to the whistle calls. I heard seven different sets, not counting my own partners'. That meant every pair assigned to the Nightmarket was engaged and calling for help. Ahuda must have the word by now. She would be sending every pair that could be spared from their own duty here in the Lower City. We dared not use everyone. The Rats would take advantage of our absence and go after those we'd left unprotected.

Finally I saw Tunstall's head over the dense wall of blind, furious bodies. I brained a huge cove who wouldn't drop when I struck his knee, then dashed sweat from my eyes. I didn't know if the salty drops came from the heat or my own fear anymore. Every second I stumbled, shoved by half-mad folk. I was scared I wouldn't live to reach Tunstall.

Suddenly paving stones flew into the air. Columns of

brown river water followed them, blasting holes through the mob. Mots, coves, children all went flying if their luck was ill enough to put them in those powerful blasts. Folk screamed. There were mages nearby, mages with the codes to free the spells on the riot founts. Those pipes of river-fed water were made for just these times, to soak a mob. I clambered up the back of the cove whose skull I'd been trying to break. Maddened with fury and who knew what else, he barely felt me. He was struggling with a pair of tough rushers near as big as he was. I knelt on his shoulders, clinging to his hair. Five more riot founts blew water into the sky, showering folk around them.

It wasn't enough. If anything, them as hadn't been blasted were glad for the cool of the spray. The only good the riot founts did for us Dogs was that the water's hard push upward knocked out any who stumbled into the columns.

There was Tunstall, three yards ahead. I marked his place in my mind. A last thought made me glance at Two for One before I dismounted. The old bread shop was burning.

Then I heard a roar like a bull who'd been cut with a rusty axe. I knew that roar. Tunstall! I don't know when I drew my long boot knife, but I used it, smacking sidelong as I would use a baton.

Folk are much quicker to notice a blade than they are a stick.

Goodwin was holding off the mob with a torch in one hand and her baton in the other. She stood over Tunstall, who was propped up against the base of King Gareth's Fountain. Both of Tunstall's legs were stretched out before him, and not properly. They bent in directions straight legs are not supposed to.

"The sarden tarses stepped on his legs when he went down," Goodwin yelled. "They were the size of oxen!"

"That's no good," a cove said behind me. I turned, my blade up. It was the big man, Hanse, who'd been at the Jack and Pasty. "Doubtless they're both broke, the way they look." He hunkered down beside Tunstall. "It'll hurt to move you, barbarian."

Tunstall rolled his eyes at Hanse. "Call me barbarian twice and I'll hurt *you*," Tunstall said, but there was no vigor in it. His dark face was ashen, his lips blue. He had what the healers called shock. We needed to get him out of danger fast.

"Right, then." Hanse bent, gathered Tunstall's arms under one of his, hoisted Tunstall over his shoulders, and stood.

Tunstall started to roar but never finished it. His eyes rolled up in his head as he fainted.

"Just as well," Hanse shouted to Goodwin.

"You got a place to go?" Goodwin yelled.

"We've a snug little fort we're holdin'," Hanse called. "Ask your friend, here."

"Then take him there," Goodwin snapped. She smacked a cove with her baton and kicked him away from Hanse. "Cooper, go with them—"

I shook my head. I could hear new whistles shrilling over the low snarl of the mob. "They're calling us in!" I cried. "Come on. It'll take both of us to get Hanse and Tunstall to the Jack and Pasty."

Goodwin took Hanse's left side, I his right. We grabbed others who looked like they wanted only to escape and towed them along, dealing harshly with any that got in our way as we ducked the riot founts. I truly cannot remember how we made it across sixty-odd yards of packed square. I will say as much in my formal report, and let Ahuda take me to the laundry for it if she likes. I thank the gods for the mage-made balm that Kora found this summer. Without it to rub into my arms and shoulders, I doubt I could write this down while it is fresh in my mind.

Make it to the Jack and Pasty we did. A stocky fellow with a cord-thin beard, or maybe it was a long mustache, guarded the front door and window. He opened the place for us. I stayed outside with him, in case any had followed us. Truth to tell, I hated to see old Tunstall all ashy and broken like that. It made the world seem cracked, like it might fall to pieces any moment.

The stocky cove introduced himself to me as Steen. He explained he was one of Hanse's crew of caravan guards and that others guarded the shuttered windows around the sides and back. They'd been looking for trinkets for their lovers at home when the fighting started. I soon learned why he'd been left on his own to protect the door. He was very comfortable with the club he carried. Any of the rioters who thought we looked worth a try soon joined the growing pile of unconscious busybodies in front of the shop.

I don't know when the air boomed, nearabout scaring the sweat out of me, if I'd had any left. Steen hawked and spat. "Mages," he called. "They finally noticed the riot founts weren't doin' the job. That sounds like the start of a freezin' spell—good idea, now they have the square all wet."

I looked at him and raised my brows. "You've done this afore, is that what you're tellin' me?" I was that tired, to be speaking street cant.

Steen winked. "A time or two. Not in Corus. They do things this way in Galla and Tusaine. I heard they were plannin' to try it here." A breath of heavy air touched us. "Here we go."

I raised my hand through a breeze that had the weight of thick honey. The brawlers a couple of yards away moved slower and slower. Steen dragged me inside before we were entirely caught in the spell.

Once Steen and I were within stone walls I felt normal. "They's layin' a freeze spell outside," Steen yelled to the folk inside the Jack and Pasty. "Yez may as well set. 'Twill be a while afore they break this mob up, doin' it thataway, and ye'll freeze if yez go outside."

While the others gasped and wondered when they might go home, I looked about for Tunstall. They'd put him on one of the long tables near the hearth. Someone had a small fire burning there. I hobbled over to Goodwin, who was wiping down Tunstall's face with a cloth.

"How does he go?" I asked.

"Left leg's broke in three places, the right in two, according to Master Lakeland," Goodwin said, pointing to a short, fat cove. He directed four men as they placed another long table near Tunstall's. There was a pregnant mot on that. Lakeland is a healer who works over on Messinger Lane. He isn't the best, but he would do until we could get Tunstall to a kennel healer. Goodwin asked, "What's going on outside?"

"Freeze spells," I told her. "Why didn't they use that on the mob last year?" I thought of all the buildings and lives lost back then.

"You think that kind of magic is there for just any hedge-witch to use, young Terrier?" Master Lakeland asked as he rolled up a shirt and slid it under the pregnant woman's head. "It takes a fearful lot of power."

"Wasn't that riot spread all over the Lower City?" Dale, the fair-haired cove, came over as I took a seat next to Tunstall. "I heard somewhere that the bigger the crowd, the harder it is to magic the whole thing."

"It's true," Lakeland said, checking the pots in the hearth. "Boiling already?"

"They was still hot when we found 'em in the kitchen," replied a gixie who was watching the pots there.

"Clever girl," Lakeland told her. He looked at the rest of us. "This square's circled about and the riot is largely only here. The mages can hold it with freezing spells. The Dead Men's Riots went from the Commons almost down to here. No one could freeze all of that."

"And the mages would charge more than the Crown is willing to pay, I'd wager," Dale remarked cheerfully.

Tunstall stirred and moaned. Lakeland put a hand on him. I saw yellow fire trickle over Tunstall's face and sink in. My partner went quiet again.

"Keeping him quiet is the best I can do till you get him to your healers," Lakeland told Goodwin. "This mot beside me is starting labor. She'll need me soon. I'm not so good with broken bones. Your friend has two broken legs, and he's been healed often. I'd have to work like a slave to get a simple healing to stick, let alone a complex one. Too many healings and the patient gets resistant, see?"

"I know," Goodwin said, and sighed.

"You look worn out." Dale offered me a cup of something. I think it was ale. I shook my head. "You've had a busy night," he said.

"I'm fine," I said. "You're not from here, Dale—?"

"Dale Rowan, of Port Caynn," he said with a grin. He looked all right: straight nose, large eyes, brownish-blond hair and small beard, and that slender, lean-muscled body. "I'm a courier for the Goldsmith's Bank. That's how Hanse and I came to be here—I often travel with the caravans he guards. No one bothers a skinny lad like me with Hanse and his rushers about."

Hanse yelled something to Dale. I leaned my head on the table where Tunstall rested, just to shut my eyes. I must have gone to sleep. Goodwin roused me around three by the chimes of the city's clocks, when the King's soldiers opened the door to let us out. I looked about for Dale, but he, Steen, and Hanse were already gone.

They carried Tunstall to the Mother of Healers' temple. Goodwin and I reported at last to Jane Street. Ahuda was still there, waiting for all of us from Evening Watch to report in. She ordered us home.

I came home to free Achoo from her rope tie in the garden. She slobbered and jumped up, pawing at my weapons belt, all because she was glad to see me. Pounce, though, was different. He stood on Mistress Trout's chicken coop, staring at the sky. I spoke to him three times before he so much as looked at me.

"Are you all right?" I asked. "Are you missing the other constellations?"

Pounce jumped down and walked inside ahead of me. *I do not miss them,* he told me. *They are troublesome, and some of the young ones misbehave. You look like you have been fighting.*

I frowned. Pounce *always* knows what I have done, even if he is not with me. Finally I told him, "It was nothing. Just a small riot," as I unlocked our door. "Tunstall got both legs broken."

That got his attention. I told him what had happened as I fed him and Achoo dried meat I'd left to soak before I went out. Then I tried to write up the night's events, but I was too weary to finish. I dragged myself to my bed to sleep.

I remember trying to turn over, to find myself up against a warm body. My face was buried in coarse fur that smelled of roses. Kora's soap is rose-scented. I shoved Achoo. My arms gave me warning twinges of pain. "I don't recall saying you're allowed to sleep on this bed," I told her. I could as well have talked to a sack of flour. "There's scarce room for me and Pounce." I pushed at the hound again. Achoo moaned. I pushed harder and she yelped, fighting to sit up. She planted a paw in my eye in the doing. I brought away a hand covered in greasy ointment. I'd hit one of her sores by accident.

"I'm sorry, I'm sorry," I told the hound, scratching her ears and gentling her, talking in my softest voice. "I never meant to hurt you. Easy, now."

Achoo washed the goo off my hand. Then she washed my face.

"Pounce, tell her there's only room for the two of us. She'll do fine on the floor. None of my lord's hounds sleep on a bed," I reminded the cat.

This bed was comfortable enough for three while you were asleep, Pounce told me. *Let the poor creature be. You ought to be happy she still likes humans after the way she's been treated.*

"I *am* happy Achoo still likes humans," I said. "I just wish she didn't like sleeping with them. It's too hot!"

I was about to give Achoo the order to get down when I saw that she slept once again. I pushed, taking care not to touch her sores, but it was no good and it made my arms hurt. In the end, I put my back against hers and went back to sleep despite the heat. I must track Phelan down and learn the proper words to command a hound.

I had the burning man dream again. It's like it was four months ago. I see that cove run into the curst Cesspool building with his torch. I hear the bang as he slams the door and the clack as he bars it. I'm blowing my Dog whistle as hard as ever I can, but no sound's coming out. And I'm trying to run to the building, trying so hard my legs ache, but I'm too gods-curst slow, no matter how hard I push.

Then all of a sudden the whole thing is on fire. Flames stream out of all of the windows. Even though I couldn't see the faces of them that were jumping out of the building the night it happened for real, in the dream I always see them. They're burning just like the real dead burned that night, and in the dream they wear faces I know. Today it was my sisters and my brothers. They were burning alive. I was running hard to save them, but my feet hit the mud so slow, one at a time, and the burning building was moving away from me. My brother Willes was getting ready to jump. I reached out to him, my mouth open to scream.

That's when I woke. Pounce was kneading my shoulder hard. Achoo pawed my ribs, whining. I'd sweat clean through my nightdress. I always do when I have the burning dream.

"Did I shout?" I mumbled.

You never do, Pounce said.

"Good." I stumbled to my washbasin and splashed water on my face. I'm glad I don't scream. I don't want anyone to know I have such babyish nightmares.

Achoo trotted over to the door and sat beside it, looking at me. I stared at her for a moment before I understood what she wanted. "Can't you just magic yourself out, like Pounce?" I asked. There was no answer, not from the hound. I pulled on breeches and a shirt and took Achoo outside. Then we returned and went back to sleep.

I woke around ten. Filling out the rest of last night's events had to wait until I'd taken Achoo outside, fed her and Pounce, then dragged my aching body to the bathhouse. Only when I'd returned, slathered on that special balm for my sore muscles, and eaten a cold pasty could I fix my mind on writing.

And here are Kora, Aniki, and Rosto with food. It is just after noon and they are eager to give me the news they gathered while I was getting bruised from head to toe. I will write my proper Sunday journal tonight.

One of the morning, after watch.

Rosto, Kora, and Aniki had all kinds of news, not to mention a basket with a proper lunch. It is strange—Achoo was glad to see Kora, who had cared for her wounds, and gladder still to see food, but she kept trotting back to me to sniff my hair, my neck, and my hands. It was as if she wished to reassure herself that I was well and present. At last I had her lay down half in my lap as we all sat on the floor between Rosto's and Kora's rooms to eat. All the windows and doors there were open to catch the tiniest breezes. The others had already told me the sun was far too bright for us to sit outside, and the open windows did create a wind of sorts through the house.

While my friends shared out hot pasties, crocks of soup, buns, new-made jellies, and fresh apples, they told me the latest news of the Bread Riot. It was hard to eat around Achoo, with her head sticking up between my arms, but she was polite and only sniffed my food. Her main concern seemed to be my health. She ought to weigh ten or fifteen more pounds than she does, all of it to cushion her elbows and ribs so they don't jab my poor bruises so much. As soon as my own belly stopped growling I fed her and Pounce. The others mostly talked.

The Nightmarket was cleared and closed until notice was given by the Crown, they told me. Soldiers stood on guard to make sure of that. Night Watch, with Day Watch assisting, was still on duty, hobbling those who'd been up to murder and theft when the freezing spells were put on them. For them as weren't assigned to clean up after the riot, there was extra work, too. The city's Rats always tried to take advantage of the Dogs being distracted.

"I went to see Tunstall at Mother of Healers," Rosto told me as he peeled an apple with his dagger. "I knew you'd want word. There's a basic healing in place on his legs, and magicked splints, but the healers won't let him go. No bouncing on home right away this time, like he's used to doing."

"Pox," I muttered. "Any word on how long?"

"Now, they wouldn't tell the likes of me that kind of news. Hard mots, those goddess healers." Rosto offered me a chunk of apple.

"There's army all over the riverfront, standing guard on the grain warehouses," Aniki told me, rubbing Achoo's side. "Word's gone all over the city about the price change at Two for One. A lot of bakers didn't open this morning."

"The harvest isn't that bad!" I protested, though I remembered the problem with the rye crop. "The bakers are panicking over naught! There was no need to raise the price."

"Perhaps, perhaps no," Kora said, looking at me sidelong. I sometimes think mages practice some kind of mysterious look. That was Kora's, a slide of the eyes to her left or right, shielded by brown lashes over brown eyes. "Everyone knows the Crown went into the storage granaries to serve bread for the Prince's celebrations this summer. I hear the northeastern rye crop has the poison mold. The King *says* there will be plenty for all over the winter, but he'll be sure to feed his nobles first, won't he?"

"That's why we've been picking up grain loads from the Copper Isles and the Yamanis, love," Rosto told her calmly. "Kings look after their own people, be they crowned or Rogue."

I looked at him sharp. "You've been laying up foreign grain." I said it to be sure of what I heard.

Rosto smiled just a little. "It's my second year as Rogue. My newness is wearing off. Folk are remembering I'm a stranger to Corus, to Tortall. This is a bad time for me to forget it's a Rogue's duty to feed his people in hard times."

Aniki kissed Rosto noisily on one razor-sharp cheekbone. "There's my clever lad!"

"You can't trust kings and nobles," Rosto said, looking at me. "Only them that know how real folk live."

"You're one to talk of trust," I said. "If you knew aught of the colemongering, would you even tell me?"

"Some of my people have been bit, but it's at gambling. Especially that new card game from Port Caynn, Gambler's Chance," Rosto said. "And we were able to get some of the money back." He and Aniki both gave me hard smiles. "I'll tell you this for nothing. The coles are coming on the boats from Port Caynn."

"I'd've done better if you'd given me *living* gamblers," I snapped. "We need to question them, find out where they got the coin!"

"We *did* question 'em, while you were dancing with mad-brained cityfolk last night," Rosto told me. "*We* weren't tearing up our own shops."

"They told us they got it gambling—dice, horse or dog racing, dogfights, cockfights, cards." Aniki fed Achoo some pasty. With what I'd given her, Achoo had a round bulge in her belly. "And you'll know who they are as soon as you find them."

Rosto got to his feet and stretched. "Had them branded, we did," he said lazily, as if it were a courtesy he'd done the colemongers. "A coin with an X through it, on their right hands. So every time they shake a dice box or pick up a card, folk will know. And here you thought we'd killed them, Cooper. Not very trusting, are you?"

He sauntered out of my rooms, clearly pleased with himself. I struggled not to throw something at his head.

"He did it for you." Aniki gave Achoo a second pasty. "I was worried folk would think him weak if he let them live, but he wanted to leave you a trail to follow. It's too bad they all ran for Port Caynn on the first morning boats."

I rubbed my head. It ached, along with the rest of me. "I'll let them know, when the search goes to Port Caynn," I said, feeling tired all over again. "The Dogs there can look for gamblers with brands on their fambles. We'll be busy enough nabbing them that lose their coles here in the city."

Aniki and Kora began to clean up. "It's not so bad if it's just gambling, surely," Aniki said. "Rosto bears down on the dens, folk grumble—"

"Or they'll find a reason to get rid of him," Kora interrupted, lifting Pounce to her shoulders. "Gambling's one of those things folk *have* to do. They're always saying they'll win enough to buy a snug house, or a new mule, or training and a proper job for one of their children. Work is for every day, but they gamble for the future."

"And they *lose,*" Aniki said bitterly.

"However it may be, folk won't stand for it if Rosto interferes," Kora told her. "If the danger's in silver coles, they'll gamble in coppers."

"It's not poor folk gambling that sweats me," I told them as I checked my supplies of pigeon food. I knew I ought to write up my official report to keep Ahuda from nattering at me, but I'd yet to feed the birds that day. "Poor folk don't win that much silver. But if it gets into the hands of the nobles—if *they* start gambling coles like they gamble silver—"

"We're cooked," Aniki said. "The treasuries will be rotten with the stuff."

"We'll stop them," Kora said firmly, like there was no question of the outcome. "The Rogue and the Dogs, you'll see. Stop fussing, Beka. What do you have to do before muster?"

I smiled at her. Member of the Court of the Rogue or no, Koramin Ingensra is a good friend. "I want to get Ahuda's report writ up so she won't be pestering me for it all night."

"All right. Me and Aniki will walk Achoo and bring her back after I've seen to her sores. You get to writing, and whatever else you must do." Kora finished packing up the leftovers and leashed Achoo.

I will go with Kora and Aniki, Pounce said. They understood, because they nodded. *You are not fit to be around when you must write long reports.*

At least I had the details of the night before in my mind from writing it up in my journal, and reports for Ahuda were much more direct. I spread out my paper and ink and went to work. I left spaces where I would need to add those things done by Goodwin and Tunstall that I had not seen. I'd collect that information later.

I was nearabout done when Kora brought Achoo and Pounce back. Achoo danced over and gave my hand a small lick. I rubbed her ears gently, touched by her greeting. "The army's everywhere," Kora told me. "You should have a quiet night. Everyone's scared to budge." She nibbled her lip for a moment, then said, "With the army here to keep the peace, all the Lower City bakeries have raised prices. By the time the army goes, folk will be used to the change."

It was no more than I'd expected. "By how much?"

"The same as Two for One, mostly. Day-old bread at a copper before now costs two. Fresh bread is three coppers, not two. But worry about that later," she added, striving for cheer. "Look who I found." She opened the door wider to show me Phelan.

Achoo barked at him and wagged her tail, but she did not go to him.

He smiled. "I heard you'd been promoted to scent-hound handler."

Since Achoo was then trying to climb into my lap, I glared at him. "I'm not sure it's a promotion." I looked at the hound. "Since when are you so fond of me?"

"Tell her *dukduk*," Phelan said. Achoo went stiff and looked at him.

It sounded like *dook-dook*. "What in the Mother's name is that?" I asked. "You frightened her." Achoo looked up at me and whined a little.

Phelan leaned against the frame of my door. "I didn't frighten her. I just gave one of the commands she's been trained to, but I'm not her handler anymore, so she's confused. Right now, she's decided that person is you, but it's not firm. When we're done teaching you the commands, she'll *know* you're her handler, though I warn you, she will test you, now and then."

I looked into Achoo's face. Her hind legs were sliding off my lap. "How splendid for us both." There was something in the way she looked at me, some manner of trust, that made me want never to disappoint her. There is such a clean soul behind this hound's eyes. "Doubtless you'll come to regret it."

"*Dukduk*," Kora said thoughtfully. "It sounds foreign— almost like Kyprish." Achoo glanced at her, then whined at me. Seemingly she didn't approve of others using the words that I was supposed to say.

"It's supposed to be foreign," Phelan told us. "Our trainer, the one who taught Achoo and me when Achoo was a pup, said it's best if we use commands in another language, so the hounds won't hear them all the time. It's better still if we don't say them right. That way even a native speaker won't give the commands the way the hound knows them. You see how she twitches just hearing us say it." Phelan grinned. "My old nursemaid was a *raka* from the Copper Isles. She said I had no ear for her language at all. If I ever needed to use it, I should just write what I needed to say. Achoo's commands are all in my manner of Kyprish."

Dukduk. I set it in my memory, then told Achoo, "*Dukduk.*"

She slid from my lap and sat on the floor, her eyes on me the whole time. It was like magic.

"*Turun—tooroon*—is for 'down,' as in, lay down flat," Phelan told me. Achoo looked at him. "You see?" Phelan asked. "She hears me, but she won't obey. She will never obey me again. She's all yours, Beka."

I rubbed my head. It seems like so much responsibility. Don't I have enough, with my pigeons and my dust spinners? But there sat Achoo, gazing at me with those curst brown eyes. When she saw I looked at her, she wagged her tail, just a little.

"*Turun,*" I told her. Instantly she lay flat, her paws neatly before her.

"Shall we go downstairs and work with her a little?" Phelan asked. He pulled a folded square of paper from his pocket and brought it over to me. "I wrote the words and how they're pronounced here. But it would go better if we could go through them once. We'll need things for her to smell. Dirty clothes are best."

Kora went through my laundry basket as I looked the paper over. "Achoo, *kulit,*" I said, reading the word for "leash" as Phelan had spelled the pronunciation. Achoo trotted to the door and stood on her hind feet to take the lead down from the peg where Kora had hung it. She brought it to me, tail a-wag.

"She remembers what she's been taught," Phelan said. "She likes to chase butterflies and leaves blowing in the streets, but that doesn't mean she hasn't always known her work." He came over to us and knelt to pet Achoo. "I didn't do well when I left you, did I, girl?" he asked her softly. "But you belonged to the Provost's Guard, not to me."

Achoo licked Phelan's hands.

"Right," Phelan said, getting to his feet. "Let's go outside."

Down the stairs we trooped, our steps loud enough that Rosto shouted for quiet from inside his rooms. Achoo barked at him in reply. I checked my paper for the right command.

"Diamlah!" I said. That was "quiet."

"Dee*ahm*lah," Phelan corrected me.

I glared at him and said it as he'd told me to. Then I added, "Do I need to say 'good girl' in Kyprish?"

"If you do, someone will think you're gargling bones," Kora murmured. When we looked at her, she gave us her sweetest smile. "I speak Kyprish."

"Whatever for?" Phelan asked.

"I just like it," Kora said, and shrugged.

Mages are strange.

We walked around the house to the kitchen garden. "I *told* you I was bad at it," Phelan told Kora. "Too bad for a mot with such nice taste that mine is the dialect Achoo knows."

"Dukduk," I told Achoo, and she sat. I tried to remember if *anyone* had ever done what I told them to do right off. I couldn't think of who it had been if they had.

"Fix the leash to her collar," Phelan told me. He, Kora, and Pounce sat on my landlady's bench as I did so. Once I'd secured leash to collar around Achoo's throat, Phelan told me, "When the two of you are on duty, most of the time you will need her to walk on the side that doesn't wield the baton. Wrap the rest of the leash around that hand until you have just enough for her to be comfortable walking right behind your elbow on that side—your left, is it?"

I did as Phelan said and ended with a considerable length of leash about my hand.

"As you walk forward, give Achoo the command *tumit,*" Phelan told me. "That's 'heel.' She's to walk just behind you, off your leg. She would walk there with a leash or without it if you give that command, but you're both new to this, so you should keep her on the leash to start."

"Tumit," I said, and walked toward the entry to the garden. Achoo stayed with me as we went out onto the street and returned. We stopped in front of Phelan, Pounce, and Kora. *"Dukduk,"* I said, feeling like a fool who uttered nonsense. But Achoo sat, nonsense words or no.

We tried "greet" and "friend" on Kora, then "stay" and "wait." Next came "smell," using one of my soiled shirts. I took it out of the yard and hid it in the front hall of the lodging house. Achoo looked at me anxiously when I returned. Seemingly she did not like me leaving her.

Kora passed me another of my soiled shirts. I held it under Achoo's nose and spoke the order to smell it: *"Bau."* She gave it a thorough going-over as I gathered her leash in my hand. Then she sneezed. That was how she'd gotten her name—she sneezed when she had a scent. "Achoo, *mencari,*" I told her. "Seek."

"Put that shirt in your belt," Phelan ordered. "If she loses the scent on the trail, you'll need to use it to give her the scent again." I did as he'd bid me.

Achoo raised her nose in the air, her nostrils flaring. She looked back and forth, testing each breeze. She came to me and sniffed me from toe to waist.

"Tell her no," Phelan said. "You want her to find that scent, but not on you."

"Tak," I told Achoo, fumbling with the page of written commands. *"Mencari,* Achoo."

She turned, then trotted toward the gate to the street, yanking me after her.

"You want 'slow'—*pelan,"* called Phelan, laughter in his voice.

I tugged on the leash. *"Pelan,* Achoo, all right? *Pelan!"*

She stopped on the doorstep of our lodging house. From the look in her eye, she plainly wondered why I couldn't keep up when I only had two legs to manage, not four. In we went. She found my shirt almost instantly. Dragging it from its hiding place, she gave it a terrier's shake, one eye on me as if to see what I would do if she kept shaking it.

I can't spare any shirts for Achoo toys. I had to make her let go, but I couldn't take it from her. She was trained not to give it up without the right command. I squinted at the paper and cursed the dark hallway. Achoo shook my shirt again and pawed at it.

"Stop that!" I ordered. "Pox, he doesn't have 'stop' on here. Give! Achoo, *memberi!"* I held out my hand. *"Memberi."*

Achoo hesitated, eyeing me. She shook it again.

"I said, *memberi,"* I told her. "Don't diddle me, wench."

She thought it over a moment more, then trotted forward and dropped the shirt at my feet, her tail wagging.

I looked around. No one was there to see me. I knelt and scratched behind both of her ears, mindful of her sores. "Good girl," I told her softly. "Good hound. Just, no mauling my clothes about, all right?"

Achoo licked my face.

"Silly thing," I whispered, touched. Pounce isn't much for animal affection. "Don't do that. Folk will say we aren't tough."

She licked my face again.

Back to Phelan, Kora, and Pounce we went. Phelan apologized for forgetting to put the word "stop" on his list. It was *berhenti*. I had a chance to use it almost immediately when the flock of pigeons descended on us from above. Achoo thought they had come for her. She raced at them, jumping and biting, yanking her leash from my hand. I'd been stupid enough to let my hold on it go loose. That's a bad idea with a hound who likes to chase things.

"Achoo! *Berhenti!*" I cried, lunging after her. "*Tak*, Mithros take you! *Berhenti!* They're friends—*kawan*, curse it all, *kawan*!"

She halted in mid-leap to stare at me. I suppose in her world no one had ever claimed pigeons as friends before.

I turned to Pounce. "Will you explain it to her, please?"

He jumped down from Kora's lap and stretched. *Very well. I doubt she will understand about the pigeons if I don't.*

"I'll get the bird food." Kora jumped up and ran into the house.

"Achoo will be quicker to obey as she gets used to you," Phelan told me. "I see some of her handlers let her get bad habits. She's never had a female to work her, either, that may have sommat to do with it. She has to get accustomed to your voice."

"I've seen handlers give their hounds treats when they do

tricks or work well," I mentioned, watching Pounce talk to Achoo. I couldn't hear anything, so he must have spoken to her in her mind.

"Ah—thank you for the reminder!" Phelan said. He took a packet from his tunic and opened it for me. It was full of strips of dried meat, each about two inches long. I sniffed them. Unless I was mistaken, they were goat and mutton. "You want to keep plenty of these with you," Phelan told me. "Hounds love to be praised, and they love to be petted and scratched, but a hound loves you best of all if you look after her belly. Reward her with jerked meat—not too much, but then, you're a sensible mot, Beka—and she'll love her work with you. Oh, aye, you know I've brought the treats out, don't you, girl?"

For a moment I thought he meant me. Then I saw that he spoke to Achoo, who was watching us, her tail wagging. She had seen, or smelled, the meat.

"Kemari," I said. When she came, I gave her one of the strips. "Good girl," I told her as she gobbled it.

"Don't give her meat for everything," Phelan warned me. "It's good to start with, but you want to keep it for harder or unusual work."

I looked at him and sighed. "I'm not a dolt, Phelan Rapp."

We spent a couple of hours in the garden with Kora, Achoo, and Pounce. Kora had thought to bring my journal with the bird food, so she tended Achoo's sores while I fed pigeons, taking notes from the ghosts who rode them. Then, when we ran out of bread crumbs and corn, Phelan, Achoo, and I went back to work. Phelan explained how the usual hunt went as Achoo and I practiced commands and Kora hid things at greater distances for us to find. Pounce took a seat atop Mistress Trout's chicken coop and napped.

Phelan also taught me hand signals to show Achoo for

when it was too dangerous for us to talk. They were the same as the ones Dogs used for those times, but I had to hold my hand where Achoo could see it to make the open palm for "stop," two flicks of the hand for "guard," and so on. We practiced those several times until I knew them well.

We halted when it was time for me to get ready to go on duty. I thanked Phelan and even kissed his cheek. "Just remember, she will test you by refusing orders sometimes," he told me before he left. "Don't get angry and shout. Repeat the order in a firm tone. Make certain that she knows you are the head hound in her pack. They have to test their handlers now and then, just to make certain that you are in charge." He rubbed her ears, saluted Kora and me, and ambled off with his hands in his pockets.

"He misses her, doesn't he?" I asked Kora as we went inside. "Being a handler, and having Achoo."

"He's got some curs at his rooms, mongrels that he's taken in," Kora said. "But the handlers get attached to their hounds, it's said. The good ones do. They prefer the hounds to any human partner."

"Well, I doubt I can be as good as Phelan," I told Achoo once we were inside my rooms with Pounce. "But doubtless I'll be better than Hempstead."

When we were about to set out for watch, Pounce refused to climb down from my bed. *I must watch the skies tonight,* he said. *Try to manage without me.*

I put my hands on my hips. "Are you sulking because I have Achoo? I didn't *ask* for her, you know. And she's hardly the same as a constellation cat."

I am not *sulking because Achoo has joined us,* Pounce said. There was enough amusement in his voice that I had to believe him. *I do have other concerns that do not revolve around you, Beka. Now, will you argue with me and be late for training?*

I winced. Sergeant Ahuda does *not* like it when we miss the physical training before our watches begin. "Achoo, *tumit,*" I said. Off we went on our first night as a hound-and-handler pair.

It did not begin well. I couldn't move as fast as I'd like, with all my bruises and twisted muscles. Worse yet, Achoo decided she was in love with a seller of cooked meat. She nearly dragged me onto his grill. Underweight she might be, but she was strong. The cove laughed himself to tears at the sight of me tangled in her leash. Then he'd added insult to injury by feeding the hound scraps until I untangled myself and got her under control again.

"I'm the one holding the leash," I told her as I dragged her off. "Not you. We'd best get that straight right now. *Tumit!*" With no more fuss Achoo trotted beside me as if she hadn't nearly tugged me onto the brazier among the sausages. My arms were one big ache.

Ahuda sniffed as we entered the training yard. "We'll be lucky if you can walk patrol tonight without falling over," she said, taking in the riot bruises on my face and my all-around stiffness. "So this is the hound, is it?"

"Achoo, *dukduk,*" I ordered. Achoo sat. *"Turun."* Achoo lay down in the dust as if she had taken my orders all her life.

"Hmf." Ahuda stripped off a glove, turned, and threw it across the training ring. Puppies and Dogs scattered to get out of the way. They must have thought that the glove alone might carry some of Ahuda's power to hit.

Then she removed her other glove and held it before Achoo's nose. "Seek," she ordered.

Achoo looked at Ahuda as if she had no more understanding of the command than a flea.

"Seek," Ahuda told her again.

Achoo sneezed. She had the scent, all right. She just wasn't going to follow it.

I reached down and undid the lead from Achoo's collar. *"Mencari,"* I said.

Achoo stood and cast about, her nose in the air. Then she raced across the training yard. She returned almost instantly to drop the glove at my feet. I bent, dusted it off, and returned it to Ahuda.

"Sit," Ahuda told Achoo.

Achoo yawned.

"You've been in the Guards longer than Cooper," Ahuda said. Her voice was dry, but I saw a tiny curl of a smile at the corner of her mouth. "You ought to know to obey a sergeant." To me she said, "You might actually be good for poor Achoo. And since neither one of you's fit to train out here today, you may as well go in and wait for muster."

I wasn't the only Dog she excused from training. Ersken was inside, and five more of us that had been caught up in the Bread Riot. We all looked as if we'd been stuck in a barrel with a lot of rocks and rolled down Palace Way to the river. At least I escaped black eyes. Ersken had a beauty.

Goodwin was one of the first of the rest of the watch to arrive. She looked worse than I did, and I knew she spent well on healers' creams and potions. I went to her, wanting her details for the report of last night's watch. I wrote them down as she told them to me.

"My report can stand for Tunstall's," Goodwin said when she'd finished.

"Have you seen him yet?" I asked her. "I didn't wake till nearabout noon, and then I was writing, and training Achoo."

"I visited a bit. We'll take his supper to him later," Goodwin promised me. "The Daughters of the Goddess were keeping him asleep most of the day. Even with the healing, his legs hurt him enough he'd just annoy us if he was awake." She tugged my braid. "Thanks to that big cove Hanse, he's alive to grouse."

"Meeting him and his friend Dale was the gods' own luck," I said. " 'Twas a pleasure to watch them fight."

"A pity we didn't talk to them more about Port Caynn," Goodwin said. "I heard them say they'd come from there on the riverboat."

I cursed under my breath. Here I'd gone to sleep when I could have questioned them or Steen.

Goodwin nudged me with her arm, like she sometimes did, then winced. So did I. I guess neither of us smeared enough healing balm on those arms. "Don't gnaw on yourself, Cooper. I was too worn out myself to think of it. If we were on duty every second, we'd be dead husks like some of the older ones, not fit for human company. I'll stay human, thanks all the same."

I still hated missing the chance to get information out of the Port Caynn travelers.

Day Watch was filling up their muster ranks. They were worn out from being called in early to help clean up the rest of the riot. Our lot greeted them with more friendliness than usual. They'd worked for their pay this time. They returned the respect. A quarter of us were missing, laid up either at home or at the temple hospital like Tunstall.

Ersken tugged my braid, carefully, on account of the spikes in it. "I never thought I'd say it, but I'm glad the army's in the streets. We need the help. Not that I'll be telling them."

Jewel, who heard, snorted. "Catch the army around the

Court of the Rogue, or workin' the Cesspool. It'll be normal duty for us there, certain enough. And the Cesspool folk will be worked up, what with bread prices goin' higher."

I nodded. I'd brought my gorget, saps, arm guards, and new stiffened leather breastplate, heat or no. I also meant to draw one of the broad-brimmed leather and metal hats before we left the kennel. It would protect my head from any rain of muck that might come from above when we reached the worst parts of the Lower City. I know the Cesspool folk. I was born there, after all. Their children cried from hunger already. Knowing bread prices have doubled will make their parents crazy enough to chew off their own arms.

"Day Watch, you served well," Ahuda told them. I saw the Dogs of the Day Watch bow their heads, startled. Ahuda rarely praised anyone, let alone an entire watch. Our Evening Dogs decide to add their bit. Nyler Jewel started it, stamping his foot, hard and regular. Yoav and Goodwin picked it up, then those of us closest to them. As the Evening Watch stamped their approval, the Day Watch Dogs stared at us.

"It's good for them," Birch muttered to Ersken and me. "Keeps them off balance."

"Dismissed!" roared Ahuda. We ended our stamping. Day Watch filed out, thanking us with a hand to the shoulder here, a wrist clasp there. That was enough. We didn't want them thinking that a show of respect for a day well worked meant we liked them or wanted to marry their brothers.

"Form ranks!" Ahuda cried.

I took my place near the back, with the first years, Achoo plopping herself comfortably at my right side.

"Those of you assigned to duty in the Nightmarket and on Stuvek Street last night, step forward," Ahuda said. "All of you, line up in front of me."

We stared at her as the pairs she'd summoned limped up. Why did she want the Stuvek Street pairs? I wondered. They would have been the closest, the ones best able to respond to market whistle calls.

Ahuda leaned over the top of her tall desk to look down at the line. "What is wrong with what I see?" she asked. Frost formed on her words. "Turn and face the watch."

The line reversed so we could all look at their faces. Corporal Greengage wasn't there, nor was his partner. I'd heard someone say they were both in beds next to Tunstall's. Every mot and cove of that line sported bruises and bandages, save two. One was a ten-year Dog named Tillyard, the other a seven-year veteran named Marks. They were as unmarked as when they went on duty last night. Someone in the ranks started to growl. Others took it up.

Achoo was shivering. I rubbed. "It's all right," I whispered to her. "Easy, sweetheart. You're not the one that's in trouble." She leaned against me, her head tucked into my knee.

"Tillyard and Marks. You had Stuvek Street near the Nightmarket. Yet here you are, looking like you spent your watch very agreeably," Ahuda told them. "If last night was any sign, we're in for a bad winter. We don't need curs that won't carry the load. Drop your gear where you stand." She looked around. "Senior Corporal Nyler Jewel, cut away their insignia."

Jewel stepped forward, his dagger at the ready, and got to work. I felt for my own Dog badges, carefully sewn on my tunic. I check them every laundry day to make sure no stitch had come unraveled. I couldn't watch as Jewel cut Marks's and Tillyard's badges off and passed them up to Ahuda. Then he stripped away their leather thongs that carried the pendant with the Provost's arms. Mine is leather. Marks's was brass, Tillyard's silver, practically new.

I couldn't see their faces. They both stared at the floor. Tillyard's hands were behind his back. Marks kept his clasped white-knuckled on his belt. They had to be afraid to speak. Even their friends wouldn't protect them in that room of growling Dogs. How could they have done that? How could they have turned away from other Dogs in trouble? I was scared green, but not so green that I'd ignore my partners, or the city-folk who needed help.

"Don't think of collecting pay for the week," Ahuda told Marks and Tillyard when Jewel was done and back in the ranks. "Get out. Don't let any Dogs see you for a while. And don't think we'll give you scuts a reference for guard work."

They walked out fast. I glimpsed their faces then. Tillyard was crimson with rage, or shame, while his partner was ashen. Both men's faces ran with sweat. It was amazing they didn't skid out of the room, so many people spat at them.

Ahuda waited for the door to close before she looked at us again. "Any of you think you're not up to more like last night, now's your time to go, or don't report for duty next week," she said. "We can't handle cityfolk in a bad winter *and* worry if we can count on our fellows. If bad times are coming, all we have is each other. If you're not up to that, go now, and we'll understand." She looked us over slow. "It's been, what, eight year since the last hungry winter?"

I shivered. My family was in my Lord Provost's house by then, fed and warm. The Lower City was cold and hungry. My lord gave us permission to take extra food and fuel to Granny Fern and some of our other Lower City kinfolk. We had to do it in a cart, with a couple of strong menservants to guard us. Folk still tried to jump in and steal what we carried.

"Those tarses at Two for One got an early start to jumping the prices, curse them for leeches, but the other bakers are following their lead," Ahuda went on. "They won't pass up the chance to make extra coin. The real shortages will come, and then we'll have our work set. Keep your tempers. Remember that we live here. And prepare. Now, as for tonight. The army's in the streets. Nightmarket is closed. The pairs assigned to Nightmarket tonight, see me for re-assignment. The rest of you have your patrols. Take extra care in the Cesspool. They gave Day Watch some trouble. Gods bless you all."

"So mote it be," we replied quietly.

"Dismissed for watch!" Ahuda ordered.

"Tumit," I told Achoo, and stepped out to meet Goodwin. We walked out into the steamy, sickly hot courtyard. It was empty of people come to the kennel with their complaints. Thunder boomed overhead, low and sullen. Goodwin looked up. "We're going to hate all this extra gear in just a little while," she said.

By the time we reached the end of the silent Nightmarket, the rain was pouring down so warm and heavy we could scarce see. Our leather was turning into a soaked burden on our aching shoulders and backs. Our hats were good for keeping the rain off our faces, at least.

Achoo actually enjoyed being drenched. She trotted along, tail in the air, smelling every doorway. She'd even grin at us now and then as if to say, "Isn't this *fun?*"

I hope there was little crime done, because the rain continued so hard we couldn't have seen or heard it. In that way we were wrong about the Cesspool and the Lower City. Only we Dogs, the army, and a few running folk were out and about in that. For the whole night, save for supper in a Charry Street eating house, we saw mayhap sixty people. Ten of them were in the eating house.

Thus passed our watch. Now here I sit, all of me wrinkled

like my granny from the wet. I own no piece of leather gear that is not soaked through. I have soaked three cloths in trying to dry Achoo, and she has soaked half my room, shaking off. I shiver despite the fire in the brazier next to me, the blanket wrapped about my shoulders, and even the small cup of mead I am allowing myself to warm the chill. Achoo, now well dry, and Pounce are in bed, plainly wondering why I am still up. I am going to join them.

For the first night in weeks, it is cool in my attic room.

Monday, September 10, 247

Pounce was not home Sunday night when Achoo and I came back from watch. Achoo sniffed for him, whining, but he was nowhere in my rooms nor in my lodging house. I think she is so new to life with us that she takes any change ill.

I wrote up the watch fast, in cipher, and went to the half of a bed that Achoo allows me. Monday was Court Day. I had to be awake at dawn.

So I was. Pounce had yet to return. Once I'd cleaned up and dressed myself for court, I fed Achoo, telling her we would be outside very soon. I left food for Pounce and for the pigeons on my windowsill. Then I put Achoo's leash in my tunic and told her, *"Tumit."* I would wait until we were at court to leash her. She is doing far better at staying beside me without one.

Down the stairs we went. There is no light in the stairwell, but I know the way by heart.

I do not remember what happened after that. Goodwin says that I must have gone through the front door. From the footprints in the mud, two coves of good size were waiting for me on each side of it.

My hero was Achoo. Her screaming barks as she attacked the coves were loud enough to wake Kora. Ersken was not there to help. Kora always makes him sleep at his parents' house on Monday so he won't disturb her as he prepares for Magistrate's Court. She roused to Achoo's odd, loud barking and came at the run. Seeing her with the light of her magical Gift blazing in her hands while they were fighting off Achoo, the coves fled. Achoo did not give chase, Kora says, but stayed by me as Kora got Aniki and Rosto.

I wish she had not woken Rosto.

Aniki went for a kennel healer, and then to court, to tell

Goodwin why I had not come. Rosto would have taken me to his room, but Kora would not let him move me until the healer said it was safe.

I know none of this. I did not even come fully to my senses until near midnight on Monday. I woke to Goodwin dozing in a chair beside my bed. Achoo slept at her feet. Pounce sat beside my hip, staring.

How does it feel to be a fool? he asked me.

I tried to sit up. Lightning went through my head, making my tripes leap. Somehow I turned to the side of the bed opposite Goodwin to vomit, though very little came up. Puking, though, made my head bang more, so that my gut heaved and heaved. My head hurt, my neck hurt, my shoulders hurt. My ribs were shot through with pain. I thought I was dying.

A hand lit by Gifted fire in deep blue pressed against my forehead. Coolness like cold water spread through my poor skull, making the throbbing go away. Down through my body that wonderful chill went, settling my sore muscles, my painful bones, and my miserable belly all together. When the person who owned the hand pulled me back, I obeyed, stretching out flat on the bed once more. Now I noticed my ribs under my nightdress were wrapped, I had a splint on one arm, and there was a bandage on my head.

There was also Achoo, who had jumped onto the foot of the bed. She was scrabbling at the blanket over my feet, whining frantically, staring at me with eyes that looked like they might weep at any moment.

"Achoo," I croaked. "I'm all right. Easy—umm—" For a moment I searched my brain and found every memory sliding away from me. What had happened? I rubbed my head.

"Achoo, be still or I will tie you up in the courtyard again."

Goodwin said it in that way she has, the one that is very convincing. Achoo gave Goodwin a guilty look and only pawed me twice, silently.

I saw the paper on which Achoo's commands were written in my mind's eye. I felt better instantly. "Achoo, *mudah*," I said. "*Mudah,* girl, *mudah.*"

"And what does that mean?" asked the stranger with the blue Gift.

I looked up into the healer's face. "I'm telling her to be easy, Master Healer. As you have made me easier."

He smiled at me. "It's a joy to work with someone so young. Your bones heal up right away, without the resistance of the older Dogs. That knock on the head would have been serious for someone like your partner, here."

I put my hand on my head and felt the bandage. "Did you cut my hair?"

"No, Guardswoman Cooper. But you had a bloody wound to bandage once we'd put ointments on it." He smiled at me, the smile crinkling his whole face.

"Cooper, this is Master Sholto," Goodwin said. "Sir Tullus sent him to tend you. We're in the infirmary at Jane Street."

"Sir Tullus's healer!" I grabbed Goodwin's arm and pulled her close. At least, I tried to. She leaned toward me, because I didn't really have the strength to tug on her. "Goodwin, I can't afford a healer who tends knights!" I whispered, very soft. My heart was beating fast in panic, and I knew I blushed with shame.

Master Sholto rested a hand on my shoulder. Calm settled over me like a veil. "Sir Tullus pays my fee in these cases, young Cooper," he told me.

"He does it whenever something happens to a Dog on

their way to his court," Goodwin said. "That's why nobody ever dares claim they got sick and couldn't attend. They'd best really *be* sick when Master Sholto arrives."

I looked around. I'd been tucked into the corner of the infirmary, but I knew enough from my visits to recognize the place. "How did I come here?" I asked. "Why don't I remember?"

"You had a very nasty blow to the head, Cooper," Master Sholto said kindly. "You may come to remember what happened, or you may not. Blows to the head have that effect."

"And I say you took sick with stupidity," Goodwin snapped.

"Guardswoman, a little kindness is in order," Master Sholto told her.

"With respect, sir, not in this instance," Goodwin replied.

Master Sholto threw up his hands and went to the far side of the room, where a handful of other patients waited for him.

Goodwin looked at me. "Cooper, how many exits does your lodging house have?"

I rubbed my eyes, that itched me some. "Three. Four, if I go through Aniki's rooms and onto the neighbors' roof."

"And what is a Dog supposed to do when she leaves her home?" Goodwin demanded.

I was beginning to have a bad feeling I knew what had happened. If I was right, then so was Pounce, and I *am* a fool. "Choose different ways to come and go. Listen first and go carefully, in case enemies lay in wait," I muttered.

"And why do Dogs act so?" Goodwin asked.

"Dogs make enemies," I said, quiet-like.

"Which is why two coves were waiting for you when you danced out your door yesterday morning." Goodwin said it cold. I could nearabout see clouds form around her words, though the air was not *that* chill. "Did you even stop to peek out through those spy holes Rosto had put in?"

"I don't remember." Now I was grateful for my loss of memory.

Achoo says she did not, Pounce told us. *Achoo apologizes. She says the wind was against her. That is why she didn't smell them.*

"Achoo's excuse, at least, is a good one," Goodwin said, rubbing Achoo's ears. "Cooper has nothing to excuse her. She made a habit out of leaving her lodgings every day through her front door. Plainly these men, just as any Dog's enemies, learned it, and they nearly killed her yesterday."

Master Sholto had returned. He frowned at Goodwin. "You've scolded enough, Guardswoman. You're upsetting my patient. She must be calm, or my spells will not take."

"She needs to remember her Dog work," Goodwin told him while looking at me. "I lost one partner for a time, two nights ago. Yesterday morning I almost lost the other for good. I would like her not to be such a looby again!"

She got to her feet and left, her back stiff with anger. Master Sholto watched her go, shaking his head.

"I am sorry, Cooper," he said.

I wanted him to go away because I was going to cry and I didn't want him to see it. "She is right. They teach us, don't develop habits, because they'll get you killed. I thought I was safe because I have powerful friends." I meant Rosto and Pounce, but I wasn't going to say so. I was too tired to explain. "I was wrong and I got a cracked head for it."

Master Sholto nodded and walked away. I covered my eyes with my arm, though it made my ribs ache, so I could be private with my tears. I hated myself for crying over a scolding I deserved.

I was done when Master Sholto returned with some herbal drink. I downed all of that.

"You will be able to return home in the morning," he said as he helped me to lay back on the pillows. "And you will feel very much better. I would give the Trickster, the Goddess, and great Mithros some offerings, if I were you."

I nodded. "Thank you, Master Sholto," I whispered as he tucked my blankets around me. This time, when he left, he took the lamp. There was yet enough light that I could see Achoo inch her way up along my side so she might stretch out. I didn't think she was allowed, but I was too weary to stop her. And it was nice to have her there, all warm at my side.

Pounce still sat by my feet. His purple eyes were fixed on me. *You have gotten too dependent on me,* he said. *You must never believe that I protect you. Always look after yourself, just as if I were an ordinary cat. My own tasks have taken me elsewhere of late, and they may take me again. Will you be so careless again?*

"No, Pounce," I whispered.

What does Ahuda say you must rely on?

"Dog eyes. Dog ears. Dog instinct." I think I spoke it out loud. My eyelids were shut. I tried to say it again—Dog eyes. Dog ears. Dog instinct. I don't know if I did.

I woke in the middle of the night. My pack was at my bedside, with my journal in it. I wrote the above until I felt sleepy, then slept until I was roused by the muster of Day Watch in the main room of the kennel nearby. Looking at my journal, I am shocked at the awkwardness of my writing during the night. I remember shaping the letters poorly, but I didn't know until now how clumsy I truly was. It is a little better today, around noon.

This morning Kora, Tansy, Ersken, and Tansy's husband,

Herun, brought me home in a wagon that Herun and Tansy use for their business. I told them that I could walk, but nobody listened to me. They too were scolding me about my folly in becoming predictable. They were so busy nattering that it wasn't until we came to Mistress Trout's lodgings that I could ask if there was any word of them that jumped me.

Herun just shook his head and drove off for home. It was Kora, Ersken, and Tansy that traded looks as they helped me into my rooms, trying not to stumble over Achoo. My bed was all made up fresh, with clean sheets and a light blanket for the cooler air that came through my open window. There were gillyflowers, red and white, in pitchers and bowls all around the room, a new table with wooden chairs, and two new, brightly colored rugs on my floor. Aniki sat at the table, where a solid meal was laid out. I knew that if I questioned my friends or asked who had paid for anything like furniture, blankets, rugs, or food, they would pretend not to hear.

I let them ease me onto one of my new wooden chairs and demanded, "Who jumped me? It's plain you know. Is he in the cages?"

Ersken sighed and grabbed a hot onion tartlet. As he juggled it, waiting for it to cool, he said, "It's a 'they,' and we've yet to catch them. Jewel and Yoav had a Birdie who told them Madon and Geraint Pell were in their cups and bragging how they taught an upstart bitch the price of hobbling their brother Kevan."

I swore. I'd hobbled Kevan Pell two weeks ago for a buffer. A week ago Monday he'd been sentenced to the northern road crews. It was hard for him to cry innocent when he'd been leading a string of five cows to the city gates when I hobbled him. He'd told me I'd weep for doing it, but I ignored him. Every Rat says the same.

"If the brothers are as fog-brained as Kevan, they'll be found quick enough," I said.

We were near done eating when Rosto arrived. He looked like the cat who'd been at the cream. If he felt tender over my bumps and bruises, he hid it well. "Are you well enough to walk to the bathhouse today, or shall I help?" he asked, his eyes twinkling very wickedly. "I'm told I'm a fair hand at washing hair. And backs. And—"

"I'm not one of your doxies, Rosto," I said crossly. I hate it when he flirts with me like he does with any other mot. "I'm well able to bathe myself. Will you join us, or will you strut?"

Rosto winced. "Ouch!" he said. "Nothing wrong with your bite, I see. Actually, I came to take Master Pounce to task, for letting you walk into a trap."

"I told you, I can *look after myself*," I said just as Pounce replied, *I am not her nursemaid, Rosto the Piper.*

The others began to clear the table as Rosto and Pounce glared at each other. Achoo only shrank close to my ankles and stayed quiet.

Finally Rosto said, "I've killed men who were that good at looking after themselves." He took a pear from the table.

"Have you seen the Pells yet, Rosto?" Ersken asked. Aniki froze where she stood. Kora gave him a little shake of the head. Ersken ignored her, watching Rosto with his calm blue eyes. "Any tips on where they might be found?" He is so good about Kora's allegiances that sometimes they forget he is a Dog, and he will ask the questions they do not want him to ask.

Rosto, halfway into his bite of pear, stopped and took it from his mouth. "The Pells live on Spindle Lane, I know that much," he said, his voice chilly. "I imagine they're playing the ghost game now that they've muddled with a Dog. You might try the Sheepmire drinking dens."

I looked at him. He was being too helpful. The red gillyflowers all about my room were starting to look like splashes of blood. I got to my feet, slowly. "I'm off to the bathhouse," I said.

Of course Aniki and Kora wouldn't let me go alone. They went for their things, and Ersken went with Kora. That left me with Rosto.

He put his finger on my lips. "Before either of us says anything foolish, think of a king's position, love," he whispered, his eyes holding mine. "Say our little prince was beaten half to death outside his nursery door by a band of rushers. The King *has* to do something, doesn't he? His borders have been breached, his area of safety. The rushers came to his house and attacked one of his people. What would we say of a king who doesn't deal with that? Of course, this is His Majesty, King Roger, we're talking about."

"Of course," I said.

"It doesn't have anything to do with who was beaten so bad. It could have been Her Majesty, the Lord High Magistrate, any member of the King's household," Rosto said. "The important thing is, an example has to be made."

He kissed me so very gently on the forehead. He knows I might have punched him in the gut if he'd tried to kiss me on the mouth, him with blood on his hands. Even the blood of two men who'd done their best to spread my brains on the street.

After the bathhouse, I talked Kora and Aniki into letting me stay in my rooms with Achoo, Pounce, and the pigeons for company for a while. The first thing I did was take up my journal. My handwriting is not of the best, so I print slow and plain and larger than usual as the shakes work their way out of my arms and my fingers come to feel less like sausages. But it helps my mind, too, writing these things down.

And I can feel the magic working through me, mending all the soft parts that Master Sholto said would take longer to get strong. The bones he could knit right off, but they won't be quite as hardy as the unbroken ones for another day or so. But each time I wake from dozing, I am better. I do owe the Trickster something. After all, I will be back on duty soon. With the kennel healers, I might have been out of work for a month, and that would bite into my savings. I can't afford that, not with a hungry winter coming and another mouth to feed.

And this mouth! She eats ten times what Pounce does! Even with the allowance I am paid for her food, it is not enough.

I hope that once Achoo makes up for lost meals, she will slow down.

Despite the bath, I feel dirty because deep in the heart of me, I am glad that Rosto will kill the Pell brothers, if he hasn't done so already. I would nab Rosto fast if I got evidence that he did it, though it might mean my life and the lives of all I love to nab a Rogue. They're too important to the city, though no one says as much. They keep the slums and the Rats from overwhelming the cityfolk and the Provost's Guards. Rogues *have* been taken in the past, but never for sommat as small as the murder of a commoner. And Rosto is far too clever to do it so he might be caught. He knows that even though we are friends, if I caught him in wrongdoing, I would hobble him.

I hope I would.

Midnight.

Goodwin came by after watch. She was out colemonger hunting with Birch and Ersken and didn't stay long. She only came to pass one piece of news to me, along with Tunstall's greetings from his sickbed, and his promise of a lecture about carelessness.

Her news made my gut sink. "Jewel and Yoav found the Pell brothers in King Gareth's Fountain," Goodwin said. "We had bets on where they would end up, but no one wagered on that. No one expected someone to have the sack to put them at the center of the Nightmarket, not with the army crawling all over the place."

I ran my hand over the cover of my journal. "How was it done?" I forced my voice to be calm. I needed to know. Rosto is a knife cove.

"It wasn't blades. They were got the way they got you, but it was made a killing matter for them," Goodwin replied. Half a smile curled the side of her mouth. "No one would be looby enough to try to pin it on Rosto, even if they'd been diced like an onion, Cooper. We're going to need the Rogue, come winter." She hoisted a small cloth bag onto my lap. "Lady Sabine wants you to have these. They're Vivianos."

I stared at the beautiful apples. "My lady must have paid high to get Vivianos so early in the season!" They are my favorite kind of apple, and the most costly.

"No, she didn't. Her family has orchards." Goodwin put her hand on my shoulder. "As far as we're concerned, Cooper, the matter of the Pell brothers is settled. We can't prove Rosto had a hand in it. I'll wager he made certain plenty of folk will say he was with them all the time the Pells were getting beat to death. So you work on healing. I'll stop by tomorrow night after watch, let you know what's going on."

I nodded and walked her to my door to see her out. Once I'd bolted my door, Pounce cocked his head. *I must go, too.*

"Where?" I asked, maddened by so many sudden absences.

But he vanished.

Feeling lonely, I took Achoo outside through the cellar door that opened onto the alley. When she finished, we climbed back to my rooms and I wrote up this day.

I wish I'd thought to ask Goodwin what they had learned about the colemongers.

Three in the afternoon.

I wish that Achoo was a constellation like Pounce, so she could appear and disappear in the street to do the necessary early in the morning and late at night. She is so gentle about rousing me, though, that I cannot be vexed with her. She paws me lightly, and there is a look of true regret in her brown eyes. How can I be cross? So I pull my breeches on over my nightdress and take her down, as I did this morning, using the kitchen door instead of the front. I neglected to write in last night's entry that I carry my baton with me as well. Also, I use Rosto's spy holes, which have a light spell sunk into them that makes it possible to see what is beyond the door as if it were brightest noon.

It wasn't until I was at the top of the steps on our return this morning that I noticed the pain was not so bad as even last night. My ribs hurt only a little, my gut not at all. My head aches much less.

"I hope Sir Tullus pays Master Sholto a good wage," I told Achoo as I went back to bed. "He is worth it." I will make offerings in thanks to the Goddess for Master Sholto, and to Great Mithros for Sir Tullus.

The city clocks were chiming ten when I woke next. I cleaned up and dressed for the day in breeches and a tunic. Mayhap I could not visit all of my pigeons and dust spinners, but a few wouldn't tire me too much.

"Achoo, *tumit,*" I said. She followed me down the stair and out through the kitchen cheerfully, head and tail high. It was plain to me, as we stepped outside, that this was Achoo's kind of day, cool and sunny, a few clouds in the sky, a light breeze that carried off any bad smells. It bore instead the scent of woodsmoke and cut hay from the cast, harvest scents.

We walked east ourselves, down Nipcopper Close, then left on Westberk. The Nightmarket rose before us, all shabby and tattered in the bright September light. The soldiers posted at intervals along Stuvek Street were allowing folk to pass through, rather than forcing them to walk around the closed market to go where they wished. At twilight, doubtless, they'd be turning folk away, unless they were bribed proper. I doubt that the rushers who fetched the Pells' corpses here were all that clever about sneaking them in.

I passed the soldier that was guarding the join of Stuvek Street and Peachfuzz Lane, looking around me. Every shop and stall that stood yet was locked and barred. All showed damage. Many had lost awnings, shutters, even entire walls. Two for One was a blackened ruin on my left. I stopped and waited, stretching my back out, while Achoo gave Two for One a good sniffing.

When my spine bones stopped popping, I called, "Achoo, *kemari,*" and she trotted over as if she'd been doing it to my command all her days. "Good girl," I told her, and gave her a bit of dried meat I'd warmed in my hand on our way from our lodgings. She bolted it and whuffed softly, a polite way of asking for more.

"No," I said. "Oh, pox, what's the word? *Tak.* I shouldn't spoil you." Achoo sighed and looked down. My heart went all soft and I gave her the other piece I'd been holding. "But that's *it,*" I told her, trying to sound masterful. "Now we're going to do some work."

I'd been saving the little stir of air beside King Gareth's Fountain for a day when I was alone and had a bit of time. Not only was this such a day, but now I had a need of it. We stepped up to the north side of the fountain. Folk were avoiding the area, having heard already of the dead men left here yesterday and not wanting the Pell brothers' ghosts to follow them home. I have no reason to fear ghosts, knowing they will come to me or no. I also knew that, unless they were hungry, they would not visit me here.

My interest was in the small whirling round of dust at the fountain's base. It spun right before the spot where the word *Gareth* was carved into the stone. The swirl was the tiniest of dust spinners, no more than three inches high and six inches wide. It had been there since midsummer, born on the breezes that had blown while the city was sick with the red flux. Unless a windstorm came to feed it stronger currents of air, or unless I did something, it would die in the winter cold. I hated it when they died so young, before they'd had a chance to really taste life in the open air.

I pulled a bag of dust from my pocket. I'd made it up a while back, when first I noticed other such young spinners. Sometimes I am able to make them stronger, sometimes not. In bags like this I put samples of street grit from every part of Corus I visited, in the hope that the new spinner could draw on the strength of the city to live, not just on that of the place where it whirled.

I do confess, I work all this out as I go. Having never met anyone like me, and knowing that my lord never found a mage who had heard of any like me, I craft what I may and pray that it works.

"Achoo, *dukduk,*" I said after she finished slurping from the lowest dish in the fountain. I still feel silly when I give her that word to get her to sit. *"Diamlah."* She sat, cocking her head as she watched me. I barely noticed that Pounce had appeared beside her.

I opened the bag. Closing my eyes, I prayed to the Black God. It seems to me that he is the one I should speak to in these matters. If he claims the pigeons, and the ghosts, mayhap he governs the things of the air, like dust spinners. No one has ever told me he does not, in any event. This is the first time I asked him about it, though.

"Great One, if you wish it, allow this spinner to grow high and strong like its brothers and sisters in the city," I whispered. "Allow it to feed on and carry the air that blows here. And—whatever else seems fitting to you. Forgive me. I've never tried to talk like a priestess before. So mote it be."

Mayhap this is why priestesses and priests train for years, to talk so elegantly.

I stepped into the heart of the spinner. It spread to fit around both of my feet, losing most of its height. Holding my bag at a slight angle, I narrowed my eyes against blowing dust and began to pour a thin stream of dust straight down into the spinner's edge. I continued to pour until my bag was empty. All of the dust in it had gone into the spinner. None lay on the ground. Now I closed my eyes and, like a looby, lowered my hands to my hips and raised them slowly above my head.

"Come up," I whispered, hoping that no one could see me. I lowered and raised my hands twice more, because everyone knows these things work best in the Goddess's threes. Twice more I whispered, "Come up," hoping the spinner understood either my words or my thoughts.

I waited. Then I heard the scratch of grit blowing over cloth. Slowly the hems of my tunic began to flutter and flap. I felt windblown dust on my hands. It moved no higher. At last I opened my eyes. The spinner had grown and widened. It spun now as high as my ribs, and it had picked up bits of twigs, cloth, and leaves from the riot. It was wider, too, wide enough to leave an inch of air around me.

I closed my eyes once more and invited it to release whatever talk might have become trapped in its breezes. A roar exploded in my ears. I shrank, covering them, but the roar was in my head in truth. No amount of ear covering could stop it. The noise came from the riot. It sounded like a screaming monster made of human voices. I wondered if a spinner could go mad, but this one spun on, not even burdened by the roar.

"—here. Right . . . here." It was a mot's voice, breathy, as if she carried sommat heavy. She was much closer than the roaring mob, and she was familiar.

"Easy, Clary. Gods curse those two—what were they, oxen? Ahh!" It was Tunstall! It was Goodwin and Tunstall, when Tunstall got hurt.

"I'm sorry, I'm sorry," Goodwin whispered. "Get your back against the fountain. Now easy. Easy—"

And then silence. He must have sat on the spinner. I pulled my nails from my palms, where I was digging them, and wiped my eyes on my sleeve. I asked my little spinner if there was aught else she had for me. There was more roaring from the riot, and scraps after that.

I was about to step from Raaashell's hold—she had named herself while I took the word scraps from her—when I heard something new. I nearabout missed it, the voices were so soft.

"—got to be *here*? What purpose does it serve—" It was a cove. I heard strain in his voice, like he bore a load.

"Cork it! No names, are you *cracked*? She might catch them with her magic and then it's the cages for us! You think you'd last against the Drink, or the hot irons? The rack?" This cove too sounded strained, and frightened.

Neither of them said anything more. Raaashell had a few more scraps for me, but they were not like the last bit for importance. Either word was getting out among the Lower City Rats that someone had ears where they did not expect them, or someone who knew what I could do had given these Rats their orders. It was impossible to tell by what little I'd heard.

I thanked Raaashell and stepped clear of her. Free of the burden of human words, she grew until she spun as high as my chest.

Very fine work, Pounce said. *You've thought about this a bit.*

"Some," I told him, brushing myself off. "Achoo, *bangkit.*" She came over to me, frisking and wagging her tail. I looked at Pounce. "Any chance you'll say where you've been?"

Pounce met my eyes with his purple ones. *It is the business of stars, Beka. Even if I spoke of it, you would not understand a word in five.*

We walked on out of the Nightmarket. I felt weak all over again, the result of helping a spinner to grow. We returned to our rooms for yet another poxy nap.

I finished my nap, and did all of the offerings to the gods that I promised in return for their help in the last few days. That brought me to Holderman Square and a good-sized flock of pigeons.

It was the rust-colored pigeon, the one that liked to sit between my feet and peck at corn, that carried the whining ghost.

"How did I come here? Stupid mumpers, clingin' to their coin. Time was, you beat a Dog well, folk bought your drink all sarden night. So I went out to take a piss, an' it went dark, an' . . . an' they hit me. They kicked me, they beat me."

Another pigeon in black and gray fluttered down beside

me. "Shut up," its rider said. "Shut yer whinin'. Always 'Poor me,' always runnin' t' Ma."

I gently put more corn before me. "You were Geraint and Madon Pell in your life," I said, keeping my voice down.

"In my life?" cried the whiner. "In my *life*?"

"You thought you were riding pigeon-back for a wager?" the surly one asked. "You thought this mot here were a giantess?"

They both looked up at me, their birds' eyes sharp and not quite pigeonly.

"Do you know me?" I asked them, curious.

"There's a shinin' about you," the surly one told me. "Yer hands and face, they shine."

"Ah," I said, and wondered if I should tell them who I was. It didn't seem like it would do much good, and they still had information I wanted. "Who killed you?"

"And how would we know that?" the surly one asked. "We was comin' out of the alehouse, and I saw two coves I didn't know pop a cloth over Geraint's head. I'd not had even time t' squeak afore someone put a pigsticker to my throat and told me t' stand quiet whilst they did the same t' me. The beatin' started once the cloth was tied around my head."

"I saw no more after they wrapped my head in cloth," Geraint complained. "Did they beat *me* to death? We are poor folk! Who will get revenge for us?"

"Well, the Dogs might," I said. "Oh, wait! You half killed a Dog, didn't you?"

"Would've killed her all the way but for that curst hound of hers," Madon Pell grumbled. "Rippin' and tearin', and makin' enough noise to rouse the neighborhood. I shoulda hit Cooper harder, and *then* took care of that hound."

"You can do it now," I told him sweetly. "Achoo, *kemari*."

Achoo had been playing with some of the laundress's

children over by the fountain in the square. At my command she came galloping over, scattering the pigeons.

"That's the hound!" cried Geraint. "Gods save us, it's going to kill us!"

The brothers and the pigeons who carried them fled. I hugged Achoo about the neck and whispered to her, "You are so fierce. Yes, you are. You're fierce enough to be a hunter."

We came home to rest again as I wrote in this journal. I felt guilty about the Pell brothers, but not guilty enough. I should want to tear up the earth to find their killers. I have done so for others, time and time again. It is very wrong of me that I have no wish to do so for them that bashed me about.

I will work on that. I've another day before I return to duty, after all. Mayhap by then I can get more good information from the pigeons and other dust spinners.

Strange. A messenger just came for me. I am to report to Sergeant Ahuda at six of the clock this very evening, after I see the healers for a last examination. I wonder what stirs?

I must clean my uniform if I am to look presentable. I thank the gods that someone, Kora, I suspect, washed it after my mishap, or got me a new one.

Midnight.
Well.

I hardly know what to think, my head is spinning so. It is not from injury or medicine. The chief of our kennel healers has pronounced me fit for duty, though she says I may yet have a headache or two. I had supper on the way home, so it is not for lack of a meal, either. Mayhap it is from too much thinking?

I dither.

*　*　*

I wasn't certain that I should bring Achoo to the meeting with Ahuda after my examination, but I am an official handler of a scent hound now. Pounce too insisted on coming with me. I knew better than to say no. He would just magic himself in otherwise.

The walk to the kennel was a good one. Autumn is my favorite season. The cool breezes blow the collected summer stinks from the streets and alleys. The sky is the brightest color of blue, and the harvest is coming in, such as it is. We can gather it, cook it up, store it, and pray that it will be enough. And we can sleep our nights through, not waking because it is too hot to sleep. I am sure summer has yet a little more misery to send to us, so I enjoy this taste of autumn while it's offered.

The Daymarket clock was striking six of the evening exactly when I finished with the healers and took Achoo and Pounce into the kennel's muster room. Goodwin was there, lounging on the side of Ahuda's desk, deep in talk with her. I'd expected Goodwin to be out on patrol with another pair. She held a sheaf of papers in her hand.

Ahuda saw me first. "Good, you're here, and on time. We can't keep them waiting."

Goodwin inspected me. "Better and better," she told me with approval. "Achoo looks well, too. Master Pounce, you are always elegant."

"Did you expect anything different?" Ahuda asked, poking Goodwin's head. She turned to look behind her. "Karel, take the desk for me."

Corporal Karel normally roamed to make sure all the patrols and cage wagons were in their rightful places. Tonight he was still there to take over after Sergeant Ahuda climbed down from her tall seat. I tried not to stare. I knew there had to be times she left her place once the watch began. She is human, after all. I am nearly certain of it. But the desk looked funny, with Karel up there and Ahuda standing beside Goodwin.

"Let's go, Cooper," Ahuda ordered. She took some papers from a shelf under the desk. "Is Achoo trained? If you tell her to sit and be quiet, she will do just that?"

"Yes, Sergeant," I replied. "She's trained me well."

"Good. You haven't been to a meeting like this. No slipups, understand? The cat stays outside. Bringing your pet will reflect on Goodwin and me." She did not lead us into the Watch Commander's office, as I expected. Instead we went up the narrow stairway at the back of the muster room, next to the hall that led to the cages. I'd never been up those steps, had never cared to climb them. All that was up here was more cages, storerooms, and a large meeting room.

Ahuda took us to that door.

I will not wait outside, Pounce declared. *It is not what I expect, nor what my dignity deserves, Kebibi Ahuda.*

Ahuda *jumped.* I was startled to realize that Pounce has never spoken to her before. She'd have heard he can talk, though. Ahuda hears about everything.

She recovered quickly. "I will no more tolerate disrespect from you than I will one of my own Dogs, Master Saucebox," she warned. "If you come in, you are to be quiet and well behaved."

I am a cat, he replied. *It stands to reason I will be quiet and well behaved.*

Goodwin put her hand on the door latch. "And here we go," she said. She opened the door.

The room within was big and plain, with a big, plain table

and chairs at its center. Windows set in the walls would admit daylight when open, but with twilight setting in, branches of candles were lit and set on the table.

My lord Gershom of Haryse, the Lord Provost, sat at the head of the table. He was very much the great man tonight, his tunic gray silk brocade, his cloak ruby silk trimmed in gold braid. A gold and silver brooch held the cloak at his shoulder. His long silver hair was pinned back with a matching gold and silver clasp. He even wore a round cap, crimson silk within and along the upturned rim, and gold-stamped leather above. For him to be dressed so splendid, he had to be attending some engagement of the nobility, something for which Lady Teodorie had dressed him special. She would be furious if he got Lower City muck on his grand clothes.

Sir Vannic haMinch, the District Commander for the Lower City and Watch Commander for Day Watch, was there. He was a redheaded cove with blue eyes and peppery ways. He wore his tunics like someone else picked them out and he wanted to wear them down so he might choose the replacements himself. He'd been a great fighter in his younger days, I'm told, but if he'd been so good, why give him the Lower City and the Dogs for his older years?

Sir Acton of Fenrigh, Commander of the Evening Watch and my own Commander, was present. He is a plain man of middling build who dresses plainly for work. Tonight he wore a brown wool tunic with an embroidered neck band, and a second band of embroideries down the front, over his right side. I saw the signs for peace and calm among the vines that were embroidered on his clothes, but they were well worked in. I understood why he might hope for those things on his watch, so soon after the Bread Riot. He nodded to us.

I knew the fourth cove, too, though I was shocked to see him here. I forgot myself and outright grinned at Sergeant Nestor Haryse of Port Caynn. Nestor is a cousin of Lord Gershom's on the wrong side of the blanket, his mother being a peasant mot my lord's father had kept for a mistress on their home estates. My lord is patron and friend to Nestor despite the ten-odd years' difference between them, for good reasons. Nestor is the only one of Lord Gershom's family who has any liking for the Dog's trade.

I knew Nestor from my lord's house. He often took the half-day's journey from Port Caynn to visit his noble cousin in Corus. When I was fourteen, I had wanted so badly to marry Nestor one day. I had plenty of company among the maids. Nestor is but an inch taller than me, built on a stocky and muscled frame, with hands that are big enough to crush melons. His curly brown hair has a gold shine to it and his short beard is a little darker. He's got a long nose that's only a bit bent in two places, which is good for a Dog who's served twelve year. He's got dark, blue-gray eyes that carry his sense of humor readily. What I like best about him is his voice. To me it's like dark, warm smoke, very easy to listen to.

Sadly for my wedding plans, I learned that Nestor is a bardash. I envy the men who have enjoyed his favors. He has always treated me with friendship, which I value now more than my old romantic feelings, and he gave me every encouragement to become a Dog. Now he winked at me.

Jewel and Yoav were present. They held the same sheaf of papers that Goodwin and Ahuda did. So too did Nestor and the nobles. There were wineglasses set before every place, including the three empty seats. Bottles stood at the head and foot of the table. Platters of cheese, bread, egg pastries, and almond fritters were set on the table as well. What kind of meeting was this?

"Now that we're all present, I would like to get this meeting under way," my lord Gershom said. "Sergeant Ahuda, Corporal Goodwin, Cooper, please take a seat. Cooper, are you able to take notes?"

I had seen the paper, pens, and ink bottle at one of the empty places. "I am, my Lord Provost."

"Then if you will perform that service for us?" my lord asked. "How *are* you, Cooper?"

I glanced up at him and smiled. "Very well, my lord. I am cleared for duty," I said, and looked down at the paper and pens. I hoped he didn't ask me anything else in front of all of these people. I looked at Achoo. *"Turun,"* I whispered. She lay down behind my chair. Pounce walked over to Goodwin and curled up in her lap. Goodwin stared at him for a moment. I think she actually blushed with pleasure.

Lord Gershom reached down and brought out his battered leather pouch. I knew it well. When I was small, it was one of my tasks to keep it clean and polished. I remember working dirt out of the stitching with a little pick, then buffing the leather to a fine, warm glow with all the strength in my arms. My heart pinched me as I wondered, Who cleans it for him now? Whoever it might be, he or she didn't have my way with the buffing cloth.

My lord opened the pouch and removed several thick bundles of paper. Two he passed to Sir Vannic and Sir Acton. Two more he gave to Nestor. "Senior Corporal Guardsman Jewel brought this document to me yesterday. I had it copied for the eyes of all of the Watch Commanders of the city," he told them. "Sergeant Haryse, one is for you, and the other is for

Deputy Provost Sir Lionel of Trebond in Port Caynn." Lord Gershom watched Sir Vannic, Sir Acton, and Nestor as they glanced through the pages, his eyes sharp under their shaggy gray brows. "The work was done by a number of Evening Watch Dog teams in the Lower City District and Flash District. Jewel compiled their reports and brought the results to me. It's a hunt they pursued on watch and on their own time over the last week, following rumors and reports they picked up. Ahuda approved the work, Acton. Jewel, Yoav, Goodwin, and Cooper were among those who took part in the collection of this information."

For a long time the room was silent as the two Watch Commanders and Nestor read. Quietly Yoav poured cups of wine for Ahuda, Goodwin, and me. Jewel filled plates with some of the food from the table and set it before us, just as quietly. I touched none of it. My mouth was stuck together, it was so dry with nervousness. I wanted to hide under the table. This was far worse than being in Sir Tullus's court.

Achoo took a nap. Pounce kneaded Goodwin's thighs while she scratched his ears. Reaching into my pocket, I turned my fire opal over in my hand to calm down. I can feel its bright fires against my fingers, even when I can't see them.

Sir Acton finished reading first. He began to leaf through his copy of the report again. Nestor put his copy down next. He got up and went to stand under a window. Finally Sir Vannic finished as well. By the time he set the report down, his mouth was tight.

"I'd heard only the usual," he said. "There are always a few counterfeiters with a small forge, turning out a hundred coins here and there. Rarely in the Lower City—it takes money to buy the metals involved."

"This is no small operation, if all the facts in this report be true," Sir Acton replied.

"They are true, Sir Knight," said Nyler Jewel. "As true as those of us who collected them could tell." Yoav, Goodwin, and I nodded. Thinking of folk like the Yamani cove and his river dodger guard, my cousin Phil, and Ortho Urtiz, I was as positive as I could be that they'd all told me the truth as they saw it.

"These colemongers are clever, to let their work trickle in through the gambling dens," my lord said.

"Their copy of the silver noble stamp is very good," Nestor added. He came back to the table and set three silver coles before the Watch Commanders and Lord Gershom. All had been cut across one face to show the brass underneath. The nobles picked the coles up to examine them. "We seem to have a similar problem in Port Caynn," Nestor explained as he took his seat.

"Why hasn't word of this gotten out?" Sir Vannic asked. "The Council of Lords has heard nothing, have they, Lord Gershom?"

My lord shook his head. "I've had no word from my bank. The people would be in a panic. Prices would be soaring. . . ." His eyebrows shot up. "The Bread Riot."

"That was more about the harvest talk," Jewel said. The nobles and Nestor looked at him. "You haven't heard? They're saying there's a blight in the northeastern rye fields. And that the rye sellers mean to blend the rotten stuff with the good rather than go poor."

"These are serious accusations," Sir Vannic told him. "What kind of proof have you?"

Nyler pointed his thumb at me. I looked at my notes and said, "One of my Birdies—beg pardon, Sir Knight, one of my informants, one of the most trusted—heard two rye merchants from that part of the realm speak of it."

"I'll send the right people to look into that," Lord Gershom told us. "It's certainly true that the harvest this year is going to be a thin one. We can't stop word getting out, not when people are coming in from the fields."

"And we won't be able to stop word from spreading about false silver. We've had to make arrests," Ahuda said. "Those who shopped at Garnett's bakery know he was testing silver. If folk weren't so worried about the harvest, they'd be more panicked over this, for certain. The reason you haven't heard more rumors and more panic, my lords, is because the Dogs who have been on this hunt know how to keep things quiet. You've them to thank." She met Sir Vannic's eyes. He was the one to look away first.

My lord Gershom broke the silence. "Unfortunately, we can see from this report, the rate at which these false coins are entering our moneystream is picking up. We must expand the investigation, but *quietly*. The Watch Commanders of the other districts must be placed on alert, as well as the other two commanders for the Lower City. What else is needed?"

I was grateful that I was assigned to take notes. Otherwise I never would have been admitted to a meeting like this one, and despite being nervous, I was glad to be in attendance. I do love knowing secrets.

The talk went on for over an hour as these experienced folk spoke of what had to be done to halt the spread of coles. I will not write out here every word of what I put down then. They made plans to alert the treasury, and both the Gold- and Silversmith's banks. Next they worked out a plan for the districts, whereby each commander would choose a squad of Dogs who had proved themselves absolutely trustworthy, able to keep their gobs shut. That squad would be in charge of investigating the gambling dens and rumors of false coin in their districts, bringing the Rats they hobbled to a central lockup created by my lord's personal Dogs.

The main thing everyone at the table returned to was the need for silence and secrecy.

"Now we can get to my request," Nestor said at the end of it all, while I was rubbing the cramps from my hand. "I would like someone to come to Port Caynn and look around. I have the sense, and I think most of you do as well, that the coles are coming upriver from Port Caynn. Outsiders might see the problem with sharper eyes. I'm up to my eyeballs in work these days, as are my people. I would appreciate the help." He looked away at the window again, and I frowned. "Sir Lionel doesn't agree that the problem could be a serious one, but he was good enough to let me come to learn what Lord Gershom made of it."

"Very well," my lord said as I rushed to write. "We need to choose someone to follow the scent to Port Caynn and stay on it. That Dog, or those Dogs, must know enough about the problem here to discuss it with the Deputy Provost, Sir Lionel of Trebond. I'll want them to stay on the chase in Port Caynn and beyond, and to call for help in numbers if it's needed."

"That choice seems clear to me," Ahuda said. "Sir Acton can't spare Jewel and Yoav." She gave a nod of courtesy to Sir Acton, who returned it. I kept my head down so none of them would see me smile. Everyone knew Ahuda ran Evening Watch, and Sir Acton agreed to her choices. "After Jewel and Yoav, Goodwin, Tunstall, and Cooper are the Dogs who know the most about all of this. Tunstall's off the streets for a while now.

Why not send Goodwin and Cooper? Goodwin's one of our best, and she's worked in Port Caynn before. Cooper can use the experience in a strange town and with investigation. She's already shown a talent for that."

I wasn't smiling anymore. Leave Corus? I'd been to Port Caynn twice in my life, when my lord was kind enough to take me, for half days only. I no more knew its streets than I knew the palace. I'd never dealt with its Dogs. I don't know their names or their families.

Goodwin was the next to speak. "I—" she began to say. Then she stopped and ran her hands over the table's edge. When she looked up, she nodded. "No, that's true. Cooper and I are the best ones to send. We've talked to plenty of folk about this already. I have ties in Port Caynn to a silversmithing family that may be useful, and I have ties to the Goddess temples, as my lord Gershom knows. Cooper's Birdies will be in Port Caynn as well as here. Ahuda's right, she's got a knack at investigation, and she'll have no partner at all if I'm away."

"And you can put it about that you're shepherding Lord Gershom's pet," Nestor said.

I glared at him. I *never* play upon my lord being my patron, never so much as speak his name when I'm with the Dogs!

Nestor smiled at me. "Don't glare so, Cooper. It's to your advantage. If I say that Goodwin's stuck with taking my lord's ewe lamb about Port Caynn, like you're playing at studying how Dog work is being done there, no one will think you are there for any manner of serious work. They'll expect you to visit the markets and the taverns, not to report to anyone for duty. You'll be able to go where you like."

Even if I could have brought myself to speak before them all, I would not have done so. All of them were nodding, even

Goodwin. Nestor had given Goodwin and me a fine tale to hide behind, and it would be my duty to swallow and live it.

Goodwin made it worse when she announced, "That's all well enough, but I'll say it right out—we'll need fat purses. We'll need to spend, and maybe gamble ourselves."

I almost said, "Oh, not me. I'm a dreadful gambler." But I couldn't. Everyone there was senior to me, except mayhap Achoo. I bit my cheek and kept silent.

"You must lose more than you win," Sir Acton said. "You want the gamblers to welcome you."

"I will see to the purses," my lord said. "Check your city-folk clothes. If you have no dresses for the more elegant gambling houses, you will need to purchase them. How long will you both need to wind up your affairs in the city?"

Goodwin took a deep breath. She is very fond of her husband, for all she complains of Tomlan's snoring and the way he leaves his clothes on the floor. "Friday morning, my lord. Right, Cooper?"

She nudged my calf with her boot, in case I thought to argue. I looked up long enough to say, "Of course, my lord."

"I'll go ahead of you and set up an appointment with the Deputy Provost," said Nestor. "If you take a ten of the clock boat for Port Caynn, I'll have someone meet you at the river docks when you get in. He'll bring you straight to Guards House. That way I can make sure you're assigned to report to me again." He winked at me. "We'll have it all arranged, smooth as a cat's whisker."

Mind what you say, Pounce said from Goodwin's lap. Seeing only Nestor grin, I could tell Pounce had made certain Nestor and I alone heard his remark. Nestor did not so much as twitch. He was used to Pounce's ways.

"Then both of you, Goodwin and Cooper, report to me at Provost's House tomorrow night at six of the clock," my lord said. "I'll have your papers and your funds at that time. Dismissed."

I stood when Goodwin did, bowed, and left with her, Pounce, and Achoo.

Goodwin did not believe in dawdling. "We need to see Tunstall," she said over her shoulder as she rattled down the stairs. "He'll have a tantrum to throw. It's best he do it where no one important will hear."

I followed her out of the kennel at the trot. "Because we're going away?" I asked.

"And he's not, even though he'd have to do it in a sedan chair," Goodwin replied, her voice hard as we strode up Minch Way. "Between us, Cooper, I'd as soon it was the two of you jauntering off to the port. I get stupid and mopey away from home, and I've a feeling things are going to get worse here. We'll be needed. Instead we'll be off in Port Caynn, gaming away good money and acting like we're up to our teats in muck. How in all the gods' creations we'll get *you* to play a curst loose Dog I have no idea."

"Can *you* do it?" I asked.

To my shock, she laughed. I *think* it was a laugh.

"I *was* loose once, Cooper."

I was so flummoxed I stopped dead in the street, staring at her back like a country looby seeing the palace for the first time. She'd turned onto Honor Lane before she realized I wasn't at her elbow.

"Don't stand there, Cooper, come on!" she called. When I ran to catch up, she said, "You never heard?"

I shook my head.

"Ah, well. I gave it up." She said it as carelessly as if she had given up wine or mead. Again she caught me gawping at her. She shrugged. "I was given a silver kiss to stand watch as coin and a shipment changed hands. I never asked what the shipment was. I was paid to guard, not to question. That time things went skewed. I ended in the gutter, buried under two corpses and not sure I wouldn't be the third by dawn. I promised the Goddess I would change my ways if I lived." We'd reached Tunstall's lodgings. She began to climb the outer stair to his door. "You can guess the rest for yourself."

So that is how Goodwin came to the service of the Goddess. But *Goodwin,* loose. My head hurt just to consider it. She can't have been much older than me, because I've been hearing stories of her hardness with the law for years.

I followed her up and waited while she banged on Tunstall's door. His place has changed much since Lady Sabine began to spend her time there. He'd always had plants on the railings and in the boxes around his windows. Tunstall is the best gardener I know in the Lower City, for a man with only window and porch boxes. He grows tiny, beautiful flowers, breeding them like some breed horses and chickens, until he has roses no bigger than my thumbnail.

The new changes were fresh paint on the doors and shutters, and fresh boards on the stairs and railings. Tunstall owns the building. He'd redone it when he and my lady had been seeing each other nearly a month. He'd tired, he said, of renting rooms in dreadful places, so he wanted to bring her back to a decent one. There were shops on the ground floor, closed at night, and the folk on the third and fourth stories knew better than to pry into the landlord's business. They liked the new paint and stairs, too.

Lady Sabine opened the door. For a moment we only stared at her. Over her shirt and breeches she wore a long, sleeved garment like a loose coat. It was made of rich blue silk and reached to her calves. Heavy bands of silver braid encircled the edges from collar to hem, even the cuffs. A pair of blue silk roses looped around with a thin silver braid held it lightly closed across her chest. It looked like the most comfortable thing in creation. I want one. I wonder if my sister Lorine might sew me one, though not in silk.

My lady stared at us, too, but not for the excellence of our dress. "Clary? What's wrong? Why aren't you on duty? And *Beka*? Are you supposed to be out of the infirmary? Come in— oh, there's a hound? And Pounce?"

"Cooper handles a scent hound now, my lady," Goodwin said as she went inside. "Achoo knows how to behave."

My lady offered her hand. "*Pengantar,* Achoo," I said. Achoo sniffed my lady's hand. *"Kawan,"* I told her. "Remember *kawan.*" Achoo, allowed to be herself now, wagged her tail and gave Lady Sabine's fingers a lick. My lady crouched to give Achoo's ears a good scratch. She spared a hand for Pounce as well.

The rooms smelled of juniper, rosemary, and cinnamon. There was a fire on the hearth, and a brazier burned near Tunstall's bed to ward off the chill.

"Why aren't you on patrol, Clary?" Tunstall growled. "Cooper, get your bum over here."

"He's foul-tempered with pain and inaction," Lady Sabine murmured.

I didn't blame him in the least.

They'd put up a bed in his sitting room, with mounds of pillows so he could prop himself up. Both his legs were stretched out and covered with a blanket, but I could see the shapes of the splints on them. He was dressed in a wool tunic of his favorite pale yellow. He was clean-shaven. It was plain my lady would not allow him to let himself go.

"So you let two Rats get the jump on you at your own *door*?" Tunstall growled at me. "Over here." He pointed to a spot right next to the side of his bed.

I went. I'm here to testify that whatever was the matter with his legs, his arms were fine. He smacked me a buffet on the shoulder so fast I didn't see it coming.

"Was that necessary?" Lady Sabine demanded of him, her hands on her hips. "She's probably shamed to death already, if I'm any judge. She is *also* just healed!"

"I didn't hit her that hard," growled Tunstall. "Just hard enough she'll remember to act like there are Rats *everywhere,* so she'd best be on watch *everywhere.*"

My shoulder ached fiercely, more fiercely than my new-healed skull. I know he's right. Hadn't I been kicking myself already?

"Cooper is safe from those two tarses, at least," Goodwin said. "They ended up mysteriously dead last night." She sat in Tunstall's favorite chair and put her feet up.

"Dead?" asked Lady Sabine, raising her eyebrows.

"Mysteriously," Goodwin repeated, twiddling her thumbs. "No one saw aught, heard aught, knows aught."

I squirmed, feeling *very* uncomfortable. "It wasn't because I asked him to do it." I spoke without thinking, because I couldn't keep it in. "I can defend myself!"

Lady Sabine took one of my hands in both of hers. I felt her sword calluses against my fingers. "My dear, no one who knows you believes you had anything to do with this," she said, her deep voice kind. "Rosto did it because it was necessary."

"He told me something of the kind," I said. "About the

king having to go after any that attacked a member of his household in his own house."

"He's cleverer than most Rats, I'll give him that," Goodwin said. "Rumor is that Rosto's family was nobility in Scanra."

Tunstall snorted. "Merchant, mayhap. The nobility wouldn't let one of their own sink so low."

Lady Sabine only pursed her mouth and said naught.

"The Pell brothers are old business—" Goodwin said.

Tunstall looked at me. "Kevan Pell's brothers?"

I nodded.

"*Now* will you remember you make enemies with every hobbling?" he demanded.

"Yes, sir," I said, and rubbed my forehead. "I'm not likely to forget."

"Tunstall, enough," Goodwin told him, to my startlement. As if she hadn't chewed my head when I first came to after my beating! "If you'd seen her laid up, you'd know her lesson will stick," Goodwin went on. "And we've come with better meat for our stew. Cooper, sit down. That is, if my lady permits?"

Lady Sabine had eased into her chair, next to Tunstall's bed. "Cooper, go on, sit," she urged me. "You look pale."

Not as pale as she was yesterday, Pounce commented. He waited until I was seated, then jumped into my lap. Achoo settled over my feet.

"Have an apple," Lady Sabine told us, pointing to a bowl on a low table next to Goodwin.

"My lady, thanks for the apples you sent," I told her. "Vivianos are my favorite." I looked at the one I'd plucked from the bowl after Goodwin chose her apple. This too was a Viviano.

"My father has a turn for raising apples, and the Vivianos

132

are his pride," Lady Sabine told me. "I will be sure to tell him that they eased a good Dog's sick leave."

Such a compliment from my lady made me sweat. I took a bite from my apple so I wouldn't have to say anything in reply.

"Zia," my lady called. She looked at Goodwin and me. "We have fresh-made cider, barley water—Clary, are you on duty, or will you have something stronger? Beka?"

Tunstall stirred as a small girl of twelve or thirteen came out of the rooms in back. "Zia, I will have the bitter brown—" he began.

"You will have the tea the healer prescribed," my lady said firmly. "And nothing stronger. It interferes with the spells. Doesn't my big strong Dog want to be on his feet breaking heads sooner before later?"

"Tyrant," he said. He relaxed against his pillows with a scowl.

Lady Sabine kissed his forehead. "Sheer self-interest, my love. The longer you are in bed, the more tempted I will be to kill you. I am much too fond of you to enjoy a world without you." She looked at us and raised her brows.

"I am off duty, and I will have ale," Goodwin said, grinning.

I'd finished my bite of apple. "Cider, please," I said quietly. The sight of a serving girl in Tunstall's rooms was interesting. She must be in Lady Sabine's employ, which made sense. I know my lady does not cook, and she does not keep slaves.

The girl Zia curtsied. "Tea for the master, ale and cider for the mistresses," she said. "My lady wishes . . . ?"

"I will have the rose hip tea, Zia, and thank you." Lady Sabine watched her vanish into the back rooms again. "I couldn't manage my barbarian without her," she said when she looked at Goodwin and me again. "She has all those delightful, feminine skills I lack."

Tunstall took her hand in his. "But she can't whack a Rat with a longsword like you," he said, and kissed my lady's fingertips.

It's delightful and lonely to watch them together. They are so different, but they fit so well. I've known married folk who've been together twenty year and had ten children who don't fit as they do.

"So what's the news, and why aren't you on duty?" Tunstall asked Goodwin. "It must be good to bring you roaring at my door."

"It is, trust me," Goodwin said, her mouth full of apple. "It will fill you with joy. My lord Gershom presented our collected report to Sir Vannic and Sir Acton." She told them all of it, checking the details with me. She left the surprise for the end. "Cooper and I are off to Port Caynn the day after tomorrow to sniff about there for a while. Nestor Haryse is going in advance to prepare the way."

"Scummer, pox, and wound rot!" roared Tunstall, slamming his fist down on the bed. "Gods curse the pig-tarsed mammering craven currish beef-witted bum-licking gut-griping louts that did this to me! May every flea, leech, and hookworm in all creation find and feast on them!" And then he spun off into a round of curses in Hurdik that made Lady Sabine laugh. Finally he ran out of breath and glared at us, his brown eyes bulging in his head. "You know what this means?" he asked us. "*Do you know?* Ahuda's been hinting she wants to shake up the cage Dogs, put a *real* Dog among them to smarten them up! Once I'm on my feet, with you and Cooper gone, that Dog will be *me*! Rank and mewling paperwork instead of the street, and those lily-fingered *grubs* babbling in my ear all the cursed day! I won't have it! And Cooper's too young for a hunt!"

"She's done better Dog work than most third years, and she'll be with me," Goodwin told him. "You know she's got a knack for investigation. Stop whining, you great jabbernob."

"Take one of your maps," Tunstall advised me. "Remember what you did with the Shadow Snake? Mark where you find coles. Mayhap the places where they turn up will ring about the forge, if it's in Port Caynn."

"Do you think it will be that simple?" Lady Sabine asked us.

Goodwin shrugged. "We *may* get lucky. I don't believe in luck, myself—"

"Nor I," Tunstall admitted.

"Me neither," I said.

"But the one time we don't look for luck might be the time we get some," Goodwin said.

"I'll remember the map," I told them, fixing it in my memory.

"Go armed even when you sleep," Tunstall said. "You're taking Pounce and Achoo?" He yawned.

"We can't leave them," Goodwin said. "Pounce would follow, and the hound is glued to Beka. Tunstall, you're worn out."

"I'd see you out, but they tell me my shins will break like cheap pottery," Tunstall said wearily.

"Two weeks and you'll be back to your work," my lady told him. She walked us outside. "He's glad to see you up and about, Beka. We both are." She went inside and closed the door behind her. I'm glad she didn't wait for me to answer. I was too confused and awkward to know what to say.

Goodwin insisted on walking me to my lodgings, though it was opposite her way home. "I know Pounce and Achoo are as good as a pair of Dogs, but I don't trust the Pell brothers' kin not to make a try for you if they find you away from Rosto's doorstep," she said. "Isn't my lady something? I feel better, leaving Tunstall in her hands. She'll keep him from acting stupid."

"That she will," I agreed.

"I wonder if she'd watch my Tomlan. If I'm not there to do the shopping, he lets himself be cheated by every vendor with a sad tale," Goodwin told me. "*And* he gives away every copper in his pocket to urchins who could easily find work." She took a deep breath. "But they're right—it has to be you and me. We can be spared. This is an excellent chance for you, Cooper. If we can get a scent of the counterfeiters, it could bring you to the Lord Chancellor's notice. It's always good for your career to have friends in high places."

"I like my career on the streets," I muttered. "Same as Tunstall."

Goodwin snorted. "Even Tunstall needs the right friends sometimes. You're both lucky you have *me* to watch out for that side of things."

"You don't think I'll fall on my bum, then?" I asked. I was glad for the chilly dark that hid my face. "Even if I did let the Pells get the jump on me this once?"

Goodwin tweaked my ear gently. "Cooper, if I'd thought that, I would have suggested Jewel trade partners with me for this hunt. Now listen, and practice our tale. After the Pell brothers cracked your poor head, Lord Gershom decided to send you away until the rest of the family rushers are taken and questioned. If you're to move up in ranks, you'll need to see the way other towns handle their Dogs, so you've been sent to Port Caynn, with me, your partner, for nursemaid."

I almost took hold of her arm, but lost the courage for it. "Goodwin, I never do that. No more does my lord! He don't favor me, and I don't ask for favors! If *that* were so, why am I in the Lower City, instead of Upmarket, or Unicorn District?"

Goodwin took out her baton and set it twirling, like she does when she is thinking. "True. Ah—I have it. You're in the Lower City because of my lady, who dislikes you. And it's my lord who put you with Tunstall and me, seeing that we're the best Dogs to keep you from getting killed." She glanced at me. "No one you care about believes any of it, Cooper, and that's all that matters. If you haven't learned it by now, folk will listen to the silliest muck, so they'll gobble this tale up. My lord gives us plenty of coin to look busy and stay out of the way, I play the loose Dog, and you play the pretty pet."

"I hate it," I grumbled.

"I know you do, so give it *plenty* of practice," Goodwin ordered. "That pout you're doing is very good, for example. You'll want to use it." I growled and spat, which only made Goodwin cackle.

We parted at my lodgings, Goodwin saying she'd see me at my lord's tomorrow night. Achoo, Pounce, and I climbed to our rooms. I'd just put down food dishes for both hound and cat when Pounce said, *I will not go with you.*

I stared at him. He looked at me from where he sat on my bed, his eyes steady. "Tell me I just heard you wrong," I whispered.

I will do no such thing. You heard me correctly. My problem with my group of stars has proved more complicated than I can manage from here. This hunt of yours could not have come at a better time.

"But I *need* you," I said. "Going off on my own with

Achoo and Goodwin, in a strange city, I need you to talk to, and help me out!" I was begging him, and I hated myself a little for it. Did the Pell brothers hurt me in a place the healers couldn't reach for me to act so—so *weak*?

I mentioned this to you before, remember, Pounce said. *Come over here and sit.* I obeyed, quivering all over. Pounce has been with me for five years. He was there when Mama died, when I went through training, and my Puppy year. He never had to go away for more than a day or two before. Pounce settled on my lap and I buried my fingers in his fur. *You have become too dependent on me. You will have Achoo and Goodwin. You will do well,* he said firmly. *My first duty is to these stars, Beka. I have known them for thousands of years longer than I have known you.*

"Duty is duty," I whispered.

You freed yourself of Mutt Piddle Lane without me, Pounce said.

"That was luck," I retorted. "I never thought Lord Gershom would take us into his house just because I helped him nab a gang."

You made that luck. You were terrified of those Rats, yet you tracked them to their lair despite your fear. The Dogs frightened you when they would not take the information of an eight-year-old child, yet you were brave enough to stop a nobleman on his horse to give that information to him. You do not need me, Beka. You only think you do.

He stood and rammed his head into my face several times, purring as he did so. Then he was gone. Only his parting words were left in my mind. *I will see you when your hunt is done. Seek and find, Terrier.*

I couldn't help it. I cried like a silly gixie whose kitten was lost. I finally stopped when Achoo jumped onto the bed and licked my face all over, but I started again as I wrote all this.

I'll take Achoo outside. Pounce is gone, and I have to sleep, so I will continue to heal.

He did say he will return.

Thursday, September 13, 247

Three of the morning.

What is the point of going to bed if you will just lie awake? Not only did I have to think of all that must be done, dreading the days to come, but now I could not forget that I would do it without Pounce. I am so undone by the thought that I could not sleep. Achoo did her best to console me, but in the end I left her in bed alone. I set about packing instead, uniforms, breeches and tunics, and my few dresses. I made certain to put the special Dog tools and devices, like my mage-proof gloves and my lock-stuffing clay, into my pack in case I need them. We are only supposed to gather information, but as I have learned over and over in this work, everything goes awry, given time.

Then there was breakfast to face, and my friends. Ersken was plain jealous. He didn't believe me at first when I said I'd as soon it was him going to Port Caynn. Kora and Aniki took it in stride. Kora promised me some charms to take along. She and Aniki offered to feed my pigeons and dust spinners. I was glad to take them up on the offer.

Tansy was cold and distant to me, chewing over some tough bit of vexation. She finally spoke out over the egg pie. "You and that barbarian partner of yours had Garnett *hobbled,*" she hissed at me as Kora served out the pie.

I was trying to remember if I'd packed dress shoes. No, I owned no dress shoes since my last pair wore out. I would need the curst things for gambling and eating houses. "What?" I asked Tansy.

"My baker, Garnett—he was taken away." Tansy kept her voice down as the others chattered and passed bread and drink. "Yesterday, folk said, for passing false coin, him and his guards. And they told me you and Tunstall was there in the morning. So you gave Garnett up, and everyone knows I'm friends with you. They'll think it was me turned him over to his death!"

"Be grateful it was the Dogs that got him." Tansy should have known that Rosto would hear. "They'll keep their gobs shut about whatever Garnett says under questioning. My folk wouldn't. Then all the town would know he was passing coles on even before I had him strung up somewhere noticeable."

I looked at Rosto. He was getting fair cocksure, first hiring the murder of the Pells, and now talking this way in front of me. "He's getting tried under King's Law, proper," I told Rosto. "And that's the end of it." To Tansy I said, "Be grateful he's not sending other coles out into the moneystream, to enter your coffers through someone else's hands. Either you're a good city-woman or you're not, Tansy. Make up your mind to it!"

She put her face in her hands, then looked up at the others. "I'd never sing on anyone here. Never!"

Rosto slung an arm around her neck and kissed her cheek. "Never thought you would, love. And we're real careful to talk civilized around Beka and Ersken. On account of we don't want to ruin beautiful friendships." He winked at us.

"Oh, good," said Ersken, feeding a bite of pasty to Kora. "I'm attached to my friendships."

Rosto leaned forward to eye me. "So you're off to Port Caynn. How long?"

I shrugged. "As long as it takes."

Rosto's smile was as thin as a knife. "Mind those saucy sailor coves, Beka. Their hands are nimble, and they mean no good to a pretty mot like you."

Phelan laughed. "Our Beka's ironclad against the wiles of common seamen, aren't you, lass?"

I got to my feet. Achoo stood with me. "If you mean to talk nonsense, I have errands," I told them. "And I smile all the time. I just don't do it for nonsense from coves who only mean to get under my skirts."

That made them laugh, as I meant it to. I left them that way, thinking well of me. None of them had noticed Pounce's absence, so I did not have to tell them that he'd left me on my own.

I bought a pair of the thin useless slippers that look good with a dress. Hairpins, too, I needed, and a leather belt to wear under a dress, the kind that would carry weapons. I bought a jar of soft soap, a cloth pouch of sticks for cleaning my teeth, and willow bark tea to ease my monthlies, which were due. I also purchased seed and corn for the pigeons and bread enough for a few days. I reminded myself to leave coin for Kora to pay for more. All these things I left at home.

Next I took myself to Granny Fern's. I had to let her know I would not be visiting for a while, and that she must call on Aniki or Kora if she needed anything.

Granny knew I'd nearly gotten killed by a Rat's kin. "You need to watch all around you, lass," she said as I did a few of her chores, the ones that were none so easy for her anymore. "Here I thought you knew better."

"Everyone slips, Gran," I said, hanging her fresh-washed curtains.

"You can't afford to, not when you're a Dog. At least you're alive to talk about it." She cocked her head at me. "And now you're off to Port Caynn. Watch them sailor lads. They'll have your skirts up and a babe in your belly afore you know what you're about."

"Everyone keeps warning me about sailors," I complained. "Why can't someone tell the sailors to stay clear of me?"

Granny snorted. "Oh, you're the fierce one now! Just take care no one else catches you unawares and knocks you on the nob! Master Pounce, why didn't you—" She looked around. "He's not with you. He's always at your side, that cat."

I wrung my handful of sheets out extra hard. "He's got duties in the Divine Realms, Gran. He told me he'd be away for a time."

She stared at me, drumming her fingers on her forearm for a few moments. At last she said, "Then you truly need to be on the watch, don't you? You won't have your magic cat looking out for you."

"I have Achoo," I reminded her. Achoo lay on her back, wriggling in the bit of grass that was growing in my gran's yard.

Granny looked at Achoo and raised an eyebrow. "Fills me with trust, that one."

I fixed all that needed fixing and did Gran's shopping for that day. Before I left, I brought up something that had troubled me. I knew I shouldn't, but she is my gran. My cousins help her out at times with coin and work, but they have their own worries.

"Gran, I'll be needing silver in the port. I'll trade you coppers for whatever silver coin you have, equal up," I told her.

She had three silver nobles. I gave her three silver half-nobles and the rest in coppers, while I tried to think of the best way to tell her the rest. "I think the silver mining hasn't been good of late," I said at last. "I was you, I'd get my coin in copper for a time."

Granny squinted at me. "Warnin' me off silver, are you? I heard a bit of gossip."

"I know of no gossip, Granny. Don't hearken to it," I answered quickly. "No more should you spread any and say it's come from me!"

"Lucky your cousins mostly get paid in copper and goods, eh?" Granny patted my arm. "Did you think Philben would keep *his* gob shut about coles? You aren't the only one as can think, girl. Are the Dogs going to do sommat? Seems to me the Rogue is the better cove to put a stop to it, if the colemongering isn't his to start with."

"Gran, for the gods' love, it's talk like yours that starts riots!" I said, keeping my voice down. "*No,* the Rogue has naught to do with coles! Will you just put a stopper in it?"

She looked at me and sighed. "Girl, do you ever take a breath and wonder if folk don't put out bait for you? To see if you'll bite? You'll never get a man if you don't relax."

My dear old gran. It's a wonder her children aren't every one of them mad as priests, if she mangles their wits as she mangles mine.

"Granny," I told her, "this is dead serious. I can't relax, no more than any Dog. I'm not shopping for a man. That's the *last thing* I need."

"A good swiving would freshen you right up," she said. "I've heard folk say the Goddess never meant for mots to be brawling like soldiers and Dogs, elsewise why put wombs in them? You'd best think on that, Beka, afore someone cuts yours clean out, and you never have children of your own."

There's no denying it, Gran has good days and bad. I kissed her and took off. I'll keep my womb to myself. The first looby who tells me I'm not fit to do a Dog's proper work because of it gets a kiss from my baton.

Back home, and then I did the rounds of my pigeons and dust spinners, including Raaashell. I told them I'd be going, I didn't know for how long, and that Aniki and Kora would look after them. I can't say if they understood, particularly Raaashell, since she was so new. It's not like our conversations were so promising. The spinners took my gifts of dust and continued to spin. The pigeons stuffed themselves. They had plenty to say, or their few ghostly riders did. I just couldn't make head nor tail of most of it. It was my own fault. I was just plain rattled. How would I manage without Pounce?

When I realized what I was thinking, I was more upset. I *do* depend on him a great deal, more than I should depend on anyone but myself.

Home I went again, to clean myself up. I changed into my uniform and went to Provost's House. I got there an hour early, so no one might complain that I hadn't left time to say goodbye to my brothers and sisters. I tied Achoo in the kitchen yard, my foster aunt Mya being particular about animals in the kitchen. She was the head cook at Provost's House.

Although the kitchen was as mad as ever, Mya found me right away. "Beka!" Her little wren's face lit up. She came to embrace me, then stopped. "Oh, I've flour on me. I'll smutch your uniform. You haven't come in so long!" She beckoned to one of the message runners. "Tell my lady that Rebakah Cooper is here."

I must have fidgeted or done something to let Mya know I didn't like that. She smiled up at me.

"Beka, you know my lady will be unhappy if she does not see you. It's polite. She requires it," Mya said, her dark eyes warning me.

"I know," I replied. "I'd just hoped she would be out, or something." My lady Teodorie does not approve of me. My lord never had any children who liked the low and dirty life of the Dogs as he did. The young folk of his household who took up Dog work did so because it seemed like a decent living, nothing more. In me he had found someone like his cousin Nestor, who loved it as he did. I would talk to him about the ins and outs of the cases at the end of the day. Having me at Provost's House renewed Lord Gershom's love of being

Provost at a time when my lady had arranged a position for him that she thought was better fitted to his bloodline, and to hers. Since she did love her husband, she decided to hate me instead.

It helped not at all that my brothers and sisters wanted to better themselves in ways that Lady Teodorie valued. The girls were good, obedient maids. Diona was skilled at handling clothes and dressing hair. Lorine was a fine seamstress, bidding fair to be a much-favored designer of clothes. My brothers Willes and Nilo were good with horses. Will was a trusted messenger already, while Nilo was learning how to train horses for different tasks.

I answered Aunt Mya's questions about my recent days, even telling her about Silsbee and the riot, but my ear was cocked for that messenger. I wanted this meeting over with so I could return to the kitchen and warm up. I'd done Rat watches on freezing slate roofs in January that were more comfortable than a few minutes in my lady's solar.

The messenger returned, but not at the trot Lady Teodorie required. He walked. His eyes were huge in his face. He looked at me and said, "My lady says she don't wish to see Guardswoman Cooper. She says she don't wish her servants talkin' with someone that has no better sense than to stay with the Provost's Guard when bein' in it almost got her head bashed in twice in one week. She says Guardswoman Cooper is to wait for my lord in his library."

She'd heard about the Pell brothers as well as the Bread Riot. Only my lady Teodorie would make both of those my fault. Her disapproval meant that it would do me no good to try to see my brothers and sisters. They took their directions these days from the look on my lady's face.

Well, a murrain on her! I did proper work during the riot, and the Pell brothers taught me a lesson I needed to learn. If my lady expected me to come begging for a better position, I hope she had food and drink to keep her while she waited. She has *no right* to judge what I do.

I'm sure I didn't hear Aunt Mya mutter the word I thought I heard her say. "Go on to the library, dear," she told me. "I'll send you in a bite to eat while you wait."

I nodded and kissed her cheek. "I've got a hunt in Port Caynn," I whispered in Aunt Mya's ear. "Tell my brothers and sisters I said goodbye, and gods all bless."

She clung to my hand. "No bad thoughts, now," she said, gently scolding. "Don't tempt any bad spirits. Gods all bless, Beka."

I do regret not being allowed to say farewell to my brothers and sisters. There's no knowing what will happen to me on a hunt.

I fetched Achoo and took her back inside with me. The servants gawped as I passed them on the way to the library. Word goes around quick. I was relieved to shut the heavy door behind us. At least in the library I felt comfortable. It smelled of leather, cinnamon, juniper, and bay, my lord's own scent. Reports from the different watch districts, each with its own color of seal, were scattered on his desk. His leather case lay atop them, open to show the colemonger report and notes. Letters were strewn everywhere, some writ by elegant scribes, others scrawled notes from Dogs. The servants knew better than to straighten my lord's desk.

"Achoo, *turun*," I said, pointing to a place on the floor. "And *tinggal*. You're in a nobleman's house, remember."

Achoo gave her very soft whuff, as if to say she knew very well what was expected of her. She curled up on the space I had pointed out, watching me as I turned my attention to the walls.

Here Lord Gershom displayed his maps. Everywhere there were no shelves of books, my lord had maps that could be drawn down to full view of the eye. There were tables on which maps could be laid and studied as well. The precious documents were stored underneath. My lord required a good knowledge of Tortall's many cities and towns, and of the great distances between, to understand the reports that came to his desk.

One wall map drew me. My lord would have been studying it with a keen eye since he'd had our information on the colemongers. It was the map of Port Caynn. Port Caynn is two cities divided by a ridge, half on the southeastern shore of the sea harbor, half on the northeastern shore of the Olorun River. The northern half is the better half, where the monied folk live and the harbor is deeper. The big cargo ships and naval vessels dock there in the shelter of a breakwater built near sixty year ago, by King Roger's grandfather. The southern shipping is the river traffic—cargo barges, small boats, fishing smacks, and the like.

Two bridges spanned the river where it emptied into the sea. They marked the end of the river dodgers' run to the port, and posed a barrier for any as tried to raid inland by sailing up-river. They were low and solid, raised in the deep riverbed by magecraft in times long past. No seafaring vessel could sail through their low arches, but folk could travel back and forth between north and south Tortall with ease.

The place was built on rising ground. My calves and bum always ached from clambering about after my visits there. I'll have to get used to that.

The door opened. I turned. It was my lord, followed by a servant with a tray of food and drink. My lord pointed the lad to a table kept clean for the purpose, and thanked him when the boy had put everything down there. Once he was gone, my lord looked at me.

"Stop bowing, please, Beka. I feel like I should bow to *you*." He made a face and shoved his long hair away from his eyes. He had not tied it back today. "I just had an interview with my lady. I understand she was informed you were in the house, and was not pleased."

I looked at the floor. What could I say? I never talk to a man about his wife. That goes ten times for ever saying a bad word to my lord about my lady.

"Time will mend this." My lord filled two cups and offered me one. "She will come to see that it is improper of her to interfere with your family, as it would be improper for you to interfere with hers."

Well, he could think that, I suppose. The thought of me interfering with House Haryse would have been funny if I hadn't been so angered with my lady. I checked the cup I'd taken from his hand. It was filled with peach nectar, cold from the cellars. I sipped it. Didn't it serve me right, to be forbidden my family, after I'd worked to keep my time with them as scant as possible? Now I had none at all.

"Is this Achoo, then?" Lord Gershom asked. "She won't come to me, will she?"

"Not unless I bid her to, my lord. They're only supposed to answer their handlers. Achoo, *kemari. Kawan.*"

Achoo came dancing over to smell my lord's hands and leggings, wagging her tail. She circled him, showing that she was pleased to meet him.

"This is a great honor," my lord said. "I've been hearing of your exploits, Achoo. But you're not looking as well as I expect for the finest scent hound in the Lower City." He looked up at me with a frown.

"Her last handler was a brute," I said.

My lord went to the door and looked outside. "A bowl of chopped meat and another of water for a scent hound," he ordered the messenger who always stood there when he was inside. My lord looked back at me. "Does she have any favorite meat?"

I had to smile. My lord was famous for spoiling his hounds. "She will eat anything, my lord."

"See to it," he ordered the messenger outside. He closed the door and took a chair across the small table from mine, then snatched a pear from the plate. I took up one of Aunt Mya's spice cakes. I can't resist them, not even if it means eating in front of my lord.

"Tell me, how did poor old Tunstall get his legs broken?" he wanted to know. "I sent my own healer to him yesterday, and she says she can't do better than what's being done. I've been so busy reading the information on this colemongering that I haven't finished the Bread Riot reports."

I heaved a sigh of relief. My lord's healer was *very* good, as good as Master Sholto. If anything more could be done for him, she would have taken care of it, and not counted the expense.

We were yet talking about the Bread Riot when a footman brought Goodwin and the messenger came with Achoo's bowls of meat and water. Lord Gershom stood when Goodwin arrived. Achoo whuffed and wagged her tail, but did not get up. I was impressed. She clearly wanted to go to Goodwin, but she waited for me to give her permission.

"Pengantar," I said. Achoo happily bounded over to Goodwin, to lick her hand and dance around her.

"Hello, Achoo, hello." Goodwin bent to scratch Achoo's ears. She was actually pale, something I'd never seen, not even when her jaw was broken or the healer was stitching up a six-inch gash in her side. "My lord, is there no one else to send?" she asked. "Already my Tomlan speaks of the gatherings he will hold when I am gone from the house. He is threatening to have the plaster newly painted indoors before winter sets in. No, Achoo, I don't need kisses."

"Achoo, *kemari*," I said. She returned to me, looking a bit sad. The sight of the bowl of meat and the bowl of water set by my chair cheered her up. Oddly, she did not fall on it, as she would have done at home. She stood there, looking at me. She waited for something, but what?

"She wants the command to eat, Cooper," my lord said.

I knew it, but why did she want it now? "She's never needed it before, my lord."

"Have you fed her away from home before?" he asked. "The scent hounds are trained so that no one can poison them."

Just the *thought* of someone trying to poison a sweet creature like Achoo makes me angry. I stroked her head and told her, "*Makan*, Achoo." She began to eat as if she was starved.

My lord poured Goodwin a cup of the peach nectar. "As for your problem, Clary, no, I want *you* on this hunt. You know Port Caynn better than the other Dogs who did the original investigation into the matter of coles. You're the most senior Dog involved except for Nyler Jewel. You and Tunstall have more experience in hunts outside Corus than any other Dogs from that investigation, and Tunstall is laid up. I don't want to bring in anyone outside your original group, to keep word that we are concerned from spreading."

Goodwin scowled at her cup. "With all due respect, my lord, I hate it when you make sense."

Though Lord Gershom's face was sober, his eyes sparkled with a laugh. "If you are so worried that you will be distracted, I can have Master Goodwin locked up."

"No, I thank you," Goodwin said, waving the offer aside. She took the chair my lord indicated. "He will only amuse the Rats with his wild tales, and hire them to work in his carpentry shop when he gets out. Too friendly by far, my Tomlan." She sighed. "Isn't Sergeant Haryse here?"

My lord shook his head. "He's gone back to Port Caynn to set things up—a place for you to stay, a meeting with Sir Lionel, and so on. The bill for your lodgings will come straight to me, by the way. You won't have to worry about paying for it out of the hunt funds."

Goodwin smiled. "Thank you, my lord. The less time I spend keeping the books, the better." She looked around, frowning. "Cooper, where's Pounce?"

My lord raised his brows. "Yes—where is he? I haven't seen you without him nearby in years."

So I had to tell them. I won't write it out here. I didn't cry then, but I would if I wrote it out, and I am tired of crying.

My lord was shaking his head by the time I was done. "Whoever knew that stars need Pounce to make them behave," he remarked. "I'd have thought they just did so, regardless. Well. We have arrangements to settle." He took a pouch from the desk and came to stand before us. We got to our feet. The pouch was all red silk and embroidered with magical signs in gold. He opened the mouth and offered it to Goodwin. "I had a pair of Dog tags made up for the two of you," he said. "Take them and hold them in your hands."

Goodwin reached into the pouch and brought out something small enough that I could not see what she held. She put both hands together and closed her eyes.

"You'll have heard of Dog tags, Cooper," my lord said.

"Only that they are a magical device that is used by

partners on a far-reaching hunt," I replied. Now I was curious, *very* curious.

"When there's a chance partners may have to split up and the hunt's a high-stakes one, they're issued these," my lord said.

Goodwin opened her hands and offered me two round pieces of glossy black stone, each on a silver clasp. "Take them both," she said. "Hold them like I did, and concentrate on me, whatever you think of me when we work."

I put my hands together flat and closed my eyes like Goodwin did. What *do* I think of her when we work? She is tough. She cuts to the bone of a problem with a few words. When all is going to Chaos, she is right there beside me, planted as solid as stone.

"That will do," my lord said. I opened my hands and eyes.

Goodwin plucked one of the stone circles from my hands. "Look at the other side of the circle, Cooper," she told me. I did. There was a basic compass cross dug into the gleaming stone and painted white. "Now think of me and watch it." I did as I was told. A bright green dot appeared in the stone and moved around the heart of the compass cross as Goodwin walked a full circle around me. "It's simple, but it's very useful if you get separated from your partner in a strange city," she told me. "Keep it with you always, understand? And don't lose yours. They cost at least five years' pay for the likes of us."

"The gods willing, you won't need to use it," Lord Gershom said as he took his seat behind the desk. "But I prefer that you have them and not need them to needing them and not having them."

Goodwin and I took our seats again. I turned the tag over in my hand before I tucked it into my belt pouch. The green dot had vanished as soon as I'd turned my attention to my lord's talk. Now the tag was simply black stone, a bit cold in my hand. I suppose mages do have their uses.

From a bottom drawer in his desk my lord took two leather cases, both with the kind of buckles that opened only with a magical password. "The word on these is *Terrier*," he said with a wink at me. "And the charm is on the whole case, so that only a high-level mage can open it. None of this cheap spelled-the-buckle-so-cut-the-leather nonsense." He put them beside each other on his desk. Next he put a box on his desk and opened it with a touch to the charmed lock.

"A special courier took copies of the counterfeiter report on to Sir Lionel, the Deputy Provost, so he will be prepared for your visit," my lord told us. "Here is my letter to the Deputy Provost, in Goodwin's pouch." He took a sealed document and placed it on one of the leather cases. "Two copies each of your orders, that you are there to observe Port Caynn Dog work and write it up for me. You will show those to any Watch Commanders who may request them." A sheaf of papers went on top of each leather case. "A copy for each of you of the Port Caynn map." Two folded packets went onto the stacks. I had to stop myself from lunging for my copy of the precious map. "The books of accounts you'll keep for the journey, and your tickets of passage on the riverboat *Green Mist* to Port Caynn." He placed small, leather-bound volumes and two strips of thin wood on top of the papers. "And this." He held up one folded and sealed paper. His face was grim. "Should you need to question any Rats more deeply than you can manage on the street, this document orders any Watch Commander to give you immediate and full use of his question chamber and the services of those cage Dogs versed in torture. I want you to use it, Goodwin, if you find someone you feel won't give up the goods."

"What about truth spells, my lord?" Goodwin asked.

"Torture isn't dependable if you want the truth. Too often the Dogs who use it are clumsy. I'd feel better for letters that will get me the use of mages and truth spells."

My lord shook his head. "The Watch Commander, Deputy Provost, *and* the Governor must sign off on the use of truth spells and a mage to wield them, Goodwin. I don't trust that many people in Port Caynn, nor should you."

Goodwin frowned. "I never had to deal with three nobles to approve, my lord. When did this happen?"

"They passed the law two years ago in the Privy Council, that's why you didn't hear." My lord glanced at me. I knew what this was. He had enemies in the Privy Council who were always trying to limit his power. Denying us the use of mages and forcing us to use the mauling of torture was one way to do it. Truth spells are a powerful weapon, and I cursed every lord and lady on the council for taking it from our hands.

"Make certain you get the pouch with the warrant for questioning, Goodwin," Lord Gershom said. "Cooper's too junior to use it. Remember, employ that order at need," my lord instructed. "We are not having a festival dance. Now, most important, you will require funds." He placed two leather pouches that clinked on top of the cases and set his box on the floor. "This for immediate costs." He opened the lighter-colored bag and poured some of the contents into his hand. Out tumbled a mix of silver and copper coins. "The silver is good," my lord added dryly.

I could see the deep cuts across the surfaces of the coins from where I sat.

"Don't want us taken up for passing coles, my lord?" Goodwin asked.

"It would be inconvenient," he replied. "This is for the long term." He opened the darker pouch and showed us its contents—gold coins. It was as plump as the other purse. I gasped. "We don't know how long you'll need to be there or what costs you'll meet," my lord explained. "I expect you to place this with the Goldsmith's Bank in the port and draw on it to meet your needs. If you need more—" He held up another folded and sealed document. "A letter of credit, to be given to the bank when you place the coins there. Cooper, let Goodwin handle the monies, but learn how she keeps the accounts. Every copper must be marked down, even the coin you win and lose at gambling, understood?"

We nodded. I would have done so anyway, just because I keep track of every copper I spend or give in alms. I have to, if I am to be certain all my bills are paid on my salary. My lady insisted we learned to keep accounts as well as learned to read and write, and I am tolerably good at it.

Lord Gershom still rested his hand on the cases, not ready yet to turn them over to us. There was a small frown on his face. "Sir Lionel," he said at last. "His wife is Prince Baird's oldest daughter. This may or may not make a difference to your hunt. In my opinion, which is not to be repeated, Prince Baird isn't interested in anything that doesn't involve a horse, a hound, or falconry. But still, watch where you step, in case his highness remembers he's a father."

"You don't trust Sir Lionel?" Goodwin asked.

"I don't *know* Sir Lionel," Lord Gershom replied. "He's had that post for five years, and I know no more about him than I did when His Majesty ordered me to place him in Port Caynn. I do know that his reports for the last few years have detailed remarkably peaceful times for a seafaring town, but they give me no good reason to conduct an inspection. I don't like to hang over my deputies unless I must. It creates ill will."

"He may be keeping the peace very well," Goodwin suggested.

My lord smoothed his mustache. "Which is a thing that *can't* be done in our other port cities," he said. "So why is it so easy in the largest of them? Never mind. My questions aren't yours. Let's send you two on your way."

Goodwin had fetched her pack with her. She and my lord put the papers in the cases. Then she loaded cases and purses into her pack. "We will not betray your faith in us, Lord Gershom," she said, her face grim.

I stood beside her. "You know we will not." Without my command, Achoo came to stand at attention beside me.

"I never thought for a moment that you would," Lord Gershom told Goodwin and me. "Once a week I'd like one of you to hand-carry a written report back to me personally, also by riverboat. I know it's a full day to go there and back, but I want to be absolutely sure that I'm getting all the news that you gather, and you may as well keep an eye on the river gambling as you come and go. Other Dogs will be hunting the river and gambling connection, but you may catch something they'll miss, going only once a week." He got to his feet. "Hunt well, my Dogs. Bring the enemies of the kingdom back to me in hobbles."

We bowed and left him. Goodwin, Achoo, and I were on our way out through the side gate when I heard a whisper from the nearby shadows. "Beka!"

My youngest brother Nilo rammed into me and nearly got himself thrown into a dung pile. I *would* have tossed him there if my sister Lorine hadn't warned me with her call. She and my brother Will came forward at a more dignified pace, watching over their shoulders in case any of the other servants had seen them. I dragged Nilo into the shadows so we weren't easily spotted.

"You shouldn't be here," I told them, giving Nilo a hug in return. Lorine and Will had more years and more dignity. They kissed me on the cheek. "My lady wouldn't like it." I looked around, but Diona wasn't with them. It stood to reason, her being closest to Lady Teodorie.

"What my lady doesn't know won't hurt her," Will said, but he kept his voice down. "Mya said you're going away."

"To study the Dog work in Port Caynn. Here. Try to look like you're well brought up," I ordered them. "Senior Corporal Guardswoman Goodwin, this is my sister Lorine, my brother Willes, and my brother Nilo. You three, this is my partner, Guardswoman Clara Goodwin."

Lorine gave a very proper curtsy, and the lads neat bows. Goodwin nodded to them. "Well done, to say goodbye to your sister," she said, approval in her voice.

"And you don't want to get in trouble, so back inside with you. I'll write," I told them. I gave them each a kiss on the cheek and watched them go. I waited until my eyes dried before I turned to Goodwin. "They're more respectable than I am," I explained.

"They do you credit," she said as we walked through the gate. "Why the secret farewells?"

As we ambled onto Palace Way and downhill, I explained about my lady not liking me. Goodwin shook her head. "After twenty-three years of marriage she still thinks she'll make some prancing courtier out of Lord Gershom. She can't, or won't, see that he loves this. Some wives are like that. Some husbands are like that. They drive off the Dogs they marry, not seeing the Dogs love the work, and that any who want to live with them must make room for the work, too. I got lucky with Tomlan. He doesn't understand it, but he took it when he took me. Pray the Goddess you get one of those, Cooper. It's that or take a Rat, like Ersken has, and hope you never have to choose between the Rat and the work."

We parted at Jane Street. Goodwin insisted no one would attack her, since they didn't know what was in her pack. "Just be careful," she warned me. "Meet me at Seven Dock at ten in the morning. We'll catch the *Green Mist* from there."

I was watchful, but no one lay in wait for me, wanting to settle a score. Instead Kora and Aniki were home. They dragged Achoo and me off to the Unicorn Tavern, to enjoy my last night in town. We had to begin our enjoyment all over when Ersken, Birch, Jewel, Yoav, Ahuda, and my other friends on the Evening Watch arrived. We danced, we sang, we went out and serenaded Tunstall and Lady Sabine, and we ate. Then we danced some more. Achoo did tricks, Rosto came and played his pipes, and Kora did a few bits of magic. Phelan brought one of his curs, who also did some tricks. After that, Phelan had me show everyone how nicely Achoo did the things I told her to do.

Then I came home to write all this down. I will catch a few hours' sleep before I need to take myself, my luggage, and Achoo to the docks. No one need know how much I miss Pounce, or uneasy I am over going on a boat, which I have never done, and trying to do Dog work in a city I do not know. In the time since I helped to capture the Shadow Snake and stop the Opal Murders, I have mostly forgotten my greatest failing, except in Sir Tullus's court. I am so curst shy I can barely speak when it comes on me.

Friday, September 14, 247

Two of the afternoon.

The remainder of this journal I will write in Dog cipher, to ensure the privacy of my notes and also so I may shorten how much writing I need to do. Being in a new city, on a hunt, with a scent hound, there will be so much more detail to note down against my final report to my Lord Provost. I will need all the help I may get to keep my writing hand from falling off.

I hope I will be able to read this later. The boat rises and falls sommat as I write, so that my reed's point is less than steady on the page. I'm told it's worse on the sea, so I shouldn't complain. Rather, I pray that I will never go to sea. Then I brace myself, and continue to write of my day so far.

I was able to hire a cove to carry my trunk to the river. I walked along beside him, dressed like a citymot in a blue dress and veil, with Achoo on her leash at my side. Most citymots didn't wear a leather pack on their shoulders, but I wasn't about to let that pack go into my trunk. It held all that was important, but for my fire opal. That was in my free hand, its edges digging into my palm.

As ever, the docks were crowded and noisy. My trunk bearer followed Achoo and me around carts, mules, and men loaded down with anything money might buy. We dodged swinging cranes and overseers with whips until we came to Seven Dock, where the *Green Mist* was waiting. I saw Tomlan Goodwin right away, standing beside a pile of bundles and a big trunk. He waved cheerfully when he saw me.

I had my cove drop my trunk beside Goodwin's things and paid him off. Then I turned to Master Tomlan. He was down on one knee, rubbing Achoo's belly while my hound wriggled on her back. That's Master Tomlan Goodwin for you. Even I relax around him. He's got a broad countryman's face, with brown hair edged with white around the ears. His eyes are a bright, bright blue, filled with humor, and there is always a smile on his mouth. He's solid built, due to being a master carpenter, but the years have put a small paunch on him. This morning he wore a fine blue wool tunic with yellow and red embroideries, red leggings, and sturdy leather shoes.

"All ready to travel, then, Beka?" he asked me. "My Clary's off giving the captain your passage tickets. I packed yez both a basket, so you'll not starve on the way. These cargo boats take their own time."

I smiled at him. You have to smile at Master Tomlan, he's that friendly. Mayhap that's why he and Goodwin have been together these many years. It would take an easygoing man to bear her and her tongue. I near worship Goodwin, but she's not easy to share time with.

"She tells me you're nicely healed after those lice jumped you," Master Tomlan went on. "I've no pity for them getting their heads knocked in, none at all!"

I looked at him, startled. "But it was murder, Master Tomlan."

"Some folk need murdering," he said coolly.

"Tom, that's enough. Cooper's a good servant of the law." Goodwin had returned. For a moment I could do little but gape. She was handsome in a dark cherry dress with long, close sleeves. The dress was cut to her ankles and girded about her waist. She wore a round cape for river travel. It was made of dark brown wool matched both to her dress and to the strong breeze down on the water, and held at her shoulder with a brass clasp made like a chain. Even in cityfolk dress she couldn't get away from being a Dog.

Her short black hair was tucked under a white veil and round red cap. The cap was stitched over with yellow and black embroideries in the shapes of eclipse moons, warning folk she was a magistrate in the Goddess's courts.

"Cooper, you'll freeze in just a dress," she greeted me. "Haven't you got one of these curst bothersome capes?"

"In my trunk," I said. "I'm not cold."

"I hope you can carry that trunk if we can't find a carter when we get there," Goodwin said.

"Love, there'll be plenty of stout lads willing to carry your things," Tomlan said, wrapping an arm like a leg of beef around her shoulders and kissing her cheek. "She's always cross on the road," he told me.

To my startlement Goodwin threw her arms around his waist. "What will I do without you, Tom?" she asked, her voice gone all funny.

I turned away. I didn't want to see her like this, or him, for that matter. I understood it in Tunstall and Lady Sabine. They'd met little more than a year ago and still had some kick in their gallops. But surely Goodwin and Master Tomlan were well past this sort of thing by now.

Three river dodgers of a more respectable sort than I was used to came striding down the docks toward us. "Are these your goods, then, mistress?" the one in the lead asked. "Pick what you'll need on board and we'll stow the rest. We need to shove off soon."

Since they'd come from the *Green Mist,* I stepped forward. I didn't want them seeing Goodwin acting, well, odd. "I'm with her," I said, taking the basket from the pile. I also kept her leather pack. The weight told me our coin was in it. "The rest can go, with my trunk, too."

The talker looked at Achoo. "Tell me the hound is stayin' on land where she belongs."

"She goes with us." *That* sounded like the Clary Goodwin I knew. "She'll stick to our skirts, too. You never mind about the hound. Beka, what have you got? My pack—good. And that basket."

"Don't waste my cooking, woman," Master Tomlan said. He kissed me on the cheek. "Keep an eye on my lass, will you, Beka? Keep her from harm."

I actually heard myself giggle, which is what happens to a person when she wears skirts, I swear. The idea of me saving Clara Goodwin was too rich to stop me from *some* kind of laughter. "We'll do fine, Master Tomlan," I told him.

"Travel safe and travel well, both of yez," he said, one hand on Goodwin's shoulder, one hand on mine. "Mithros shield you, Goddess heal you." He squeezed my shoulder and hers and left us.

The river dodgers had carried our things aboard the *Green Mist* during our goodbyes. Goodwin and I hoisted our packs on our shoulders, while I carried the basket and Achoo's leash.

Like any child of the Lower City, I'd spent plenty of my days down here, listening to the river dodgers talk about their work. I knew this ship, and others of its construction, was a shallow-bottomed craft, with sails angled to catch any bit of breeze. I know the prevailing winds come out of the west here, so the voyage to the port is slow. Those who can afford to do so ride or go by cart over land. Them with time to spare don't mind taking the boats, and them with large cargoes prefer it. From the talk of the crew I learned *Mist* was well loaded with crates, sacks, and bales in the hull, and more on the deck.

Already some of our fellow passengers had got up a dice game and a card game, using bales of tanned hides for table and seats. Goodwin and I chose a place upwind of the hides, on some crates destined for a bookseller's shop in Blue Harbor.

Barely had I gotten myself situated on my crate when a bird came hurtling down from the sky. It attacked, slapping my head, my face, my hands when I put them up to defend myself! Finally the crackbrained beast plopped onto my lap and relieved itself of a walnut-sized dollop of dung.

Goodwin laughed so hard that she wept.

Slapper stood on my knee, bracing his clubbed foot. He glared up at me with crazed yellow eyes.

"You fen-sucked, puny claybrain, what in the gods' names are you *doing*?" I cried, seizing the bird and lifting him. "I ought to kill you!"

He got a wing free and hit me across the bridge of my nose so hard my eyes watered. I shook him.

"That's no way to treat the god's messenger," Goodwin said between gasps.

Achoo, wagging her tail, barked. It sounded like she was agreeing with my partner.

"God's messenger be blowed," I muttered. "I'll message him clean back to the Peaceful Realms!"

Goodwin scooped the dollop of pigeon dung from my knee with a handkerchief. Then she poured cold water from her flask over the spot. I squeaked.

"You don't want the stain to set," she told me with a straight face. "I think he's upset that you were going to leave him behind." She began to chuckle again.

"You go *nowhere* if I wring your stinking neck," I told Slapper. "I haven't a bite of food for you. I'll have to buy it in Port Caynn!" I threw the curst annoying bird into the air.

Goodwin picked up the cloth tucked over the top of the basket, revealing fresh-baked rolls. She handed me one. "I'd start tearing it up, if I were you, Cooper."

Once Slapper's belly was full, Goodwin looked around. We were on the far side of the river, having passed crossways over most of its two hundred yards' width. Now the crew spread more sail. We were in the deeper channel on the north side, near the western edge of the city. Here flowed the large boats headed for the coast. The ones bound inland had the center deep channel, while smaller boats ran on either side.

Ahead on both sides of the river lay the forested edges of the hills. Nobles hunted up there, and kept fancy lodges. The kingdom's great roads passed among those trees. I could see the one that ran along the northern edge of the Olorun, heavy with traffic at this time of day. Within a mile it disappeared into the forest. The southern road lay in the open for ten miles or so, passing through a good-sized village before it wound up through the trees and the hills. That was the way I had traveled with my lord on my two earlier trips to the port.

The folk here painted their sails bright colors, so I felt surrounded by butterflies. Some of the small boats were actually floating shops, carrying fruit, vegetables, cooked meat, cloth, trinkets, even magic charms and potions. They slowed to offer food and goods for sale to them on other craft. A few were fishing boats, going for what catches they could bring to the city's tables. Others were couriers flying merchant, bank, or royal flags. The larger ships had their own banners, from distant lands or Tortall itself. Though they had them, the slave ships needed no banners. Their stink made all of us draw back, our hands over our noses.

Goodwin soon tired of the parade of vessels. "Watch our things," she ordered. She wandered over to the dice game like any bored citywoman. The boat's slight rocking was enough to make my gut uneasy, so I was happy to stay where I was. Achoo sprawled beside Goodwin's pack, her feet twitching in a dream. Her sores were almost entirely healed. Slapper had taken himself up the arm on a mast and was grooming himself.

One of the river dodgers came over and hunkered on the deck beside me. "That was a sight, when yon bird came after you," he told me, pointing up at Slapper. "What was that about?" He was a short, stocky cove, two inches less than my height, of maybe twenty or twenty-one year, with nice eyes.

I looked down, glad the veil slid forward to hide my face a little. "He's a pet," I said, cursing my uneasiness at talking to strangers when I am out of uniform. "I've no idea how he found me."

"Oh, they're clever birds, pigeons," he said in a friendly way. "My father bred 'em for messenger birds. Feed 'em from your hand twice or thrice, and they'll look to you ever after, 'less you're cruel to 'em. They can be trained t' remember places two hundred mile apart." He looked up at Slapper, who hacked at a dodger who needed to crawl out on the same cross-mast where he sat. "I don't suppose you can call 'im away? My mate'll knock 'im bum over beak off that yardarm."

"Is that what it's called?" I asked, curious. "Yardarm?" I raised my voice. "Slapper! I'll wring your scrawny neck if you don't get off there!"

Slapper always preferred the enemy he knew. He took off and dove at me. I raised my hands to protect my face. Achoo looked at Slapper and barked. The crazed bird threw up his wings, stooped, and landed on a crate beside Achoo. There he strutted, limping on his bad foot and cooing angrily until he settled and returned to his grooming.

My new friend grinned. "Slapper, is it? Good name." He chuckled softly.

"Marco! Marco, there's work to be done, and not the kind you do with pretty mots!" roared the captain.

Marco, it seems, was my companion. He winked at me and trotted off to see what the captain needed, while I tried to sink into the crate and everyone around us laughed. I hate it when folk say I'm pretty. Pretty means no one takes a mot Dog serious.

We moved into what the river dodgers call the Little Lake, a broad open basin between Corus and Port Caynn. Hills covered with trees ringed it. There were still plenty of boats, but now they had more room to move. Ours slid to the right, keeping close to the side channels. The dice game went on. Others had gotten out backgammon boards and cards. They drew folk who wagered on their games. I would have liked to play backgammon, having learned from my lord, but it was more important to watch our things. It would be a poor start to our hunt if a riverboat foist got his fambles on our papers and our coin.

Instead I called Achoo to me and gave her a proper grooming, head to toe. Her sores were now only pink, tender flesh, as were her welts. I worked around them carefully, not wanting to hurt the new-healed injuries. Achoo loved the brush and comb. She lay splayed on her back when I asked her to turn over, all four paws in the air, pointing different ways, her tongue lolling from her mouth. I'd never seen a creature so happy as she was.

"It takes so little to please you, silly thing," I said, brushing her belly. She'd had at least one litter of pups, mayhap two, but the sign of the closed womb was etched deep into her collar. Some previous handler had not wanted Achoo to have more.

"We'll talk about pups down the road," I whispered as I fluffed her chest fur with my fingers. "When I swap leather insignia for bronze and can afford bigger lodgings, mayhap."

Up by Goodwin's dice game, one of the players stood and stretched, then fumbled in his belt purse. "You've the better of me, mistress," he told Goodwin, handing her some coins. "A poor farm lad like me had best watch himself!"

Someone came up behind me on the deck. I could sense him there, though he'd made no sound. Now the cove leaned against the crate just behind my shoulder. Achoo stirred. I put my hand on her to keep her calm.

"Your companion had best watch out," a boyish voice said close to my ear. "That noisy fellow is no farm lad."

I looked around, shielding my eyes from the sun, to no avail. The new cove's face was in shadow. He wore a gold hoop earring and he had good shoulders, though they weren't heavy.

"Sorry," he told me, and jumped to the deck so he could face me proper. Now I could see him clear. It was Dale Rowan, the light-haired cove who'd helped us in the Bread Riot. I noticed now that his eyes were gray and large, with a deal of humor in them. He had brown hair streaked with blond, a small brown beard in the shape of a crescent, and brown lashes longer than mine. His clothes were good, yet simple enough for a river voyage on a crude boat—a tunic of autumn brown with hem embroideries of pears and grapevines, yellow leggings, and leather shoes that laced up over his ankles.

He frowned. "Don't I know you, Mistress—?"

"Depends on what you mean by 'know,' " I said. "Where's your friend Hanse? Or Steen, for that matter?"

He looked harder at me. "They went back to Port Caynn yesterday, and how would a nice young maid like you know— Goddess tears and Crooked God's teeth, you're Cooper, the

Dog." He put out his hand, grinning at me. "If it hadn't been for those ghost eyes of yours, I might still be guessing. Hello, hello! I was going to call on you at Jane Street when I came back the next time! I see you're none the worse for wear. How's Guardsman Tunstall?"

"Laid up," I said. "Off duty for at least another couple of weeks, and grumpy with it."

Dale was nodding. "That's the problem with old Dogs— the good ones, anyway. You can only get so many healings before it's just not as complete as the first. What about Guards-woman Goodwin?"

I smiled at him. "You were looking at her."

His brows shot into sharp peaks over his eyes. "Wait— that's *Goodwin*?"

"She looks different in cityfolk garb, doesn't she?" I asked slyly.

Dale turned back to me. "So do you. Pretty, but different."

I waved the compliment off. "What makes you say that cove she's gaming with is no poor farm lad?"

"Him? He gambles all up and down the river and rooks all the sheeplings that drop into his fambles." Dale shook his head, contempt on his face.

"What?" I asked. I knew *rook* was "cheat," but I didn't spend much time in the gambling dens. I usually track tougher game.

"Cheating all the cityfolk and countryfolk who drop into his hands," Dale said, looking at the gamblers. He smiled at me. "What are you and Goodwin doing on the river?" He found a seat beside Achoo. "And who is this?"

"Achoo is a scent hound. I'm her handler." Slapper, doz-ing in the sun atop my trunk, stirred and fluffed his wings. "And that over there is Slapper." The cross-grained creature went back to sleep. I think if I hadn't claimed him, he would have flown at me again. "Me and Goodwin are assigned to Port Caynn for a while, to study their Dogs' methods, since Tunstall's laid up." I wondered if I should say my lord wanted to get me out of the way of enemies, and decided that was the sort of thing he ought to hear from others.

Dale grinned. "Are you, then? There's a bit of luck! Where do you mean to stay?"

I shrugged.

"We've no word yet. They'll let us know. It's good to see you, Master—?" Goodwin had returned, her belt purse bulging.

"Dale Rowan," he said, offering her his hand. "It's good to see you again, Goodwin. I was asking Guardswoman Cooper how your partner Tunstall was doing."

"Master Rowan," Goodwin said. "Will you take lunch with us? My man packed enough for an army. Cooper, open up that basket."

"Call me Dale, Guardswoman," he suggested, smiling at her.

As I spread the cloth that protected the basket, Goodwin nudged Achoo aside and folded herself into a tailor's seat on a crate. "Then you'd best call her Beka and me Clary, off duty, at least. It'll be good for Cooper to know someone in Port Caynn. I've friends in town, but she's only been there twice. I doubt she'll get on with the older folk I know."

"I'd be happy to take Beka around, if she doesn't object," Dale said. "I confess, I had hopes in that direction."

I stopped in the midst of setting out pasties, about to protest, then remembered I would have to go about the town to obey my orders. The fact that Dale was glad to take me about made me ashamed, because I couldn't go with him honestly. I'd be there looking for colesmiths and those passing coles, of which he might even be one. I would have been glad to see him again for his own sake, with no secrets between us.

I glanced up. He was smiling at me with those lovely gray eyes all alight. I gulped and opened some wrapped sausages with fingers that trembled a little.

"I'm shocked you walked away from Arval with a full purse," Dale told Goodwin when the silence went too long. "He doesn't usually let folk leave the game before they've lost all they've won back to him."

Goodwin smiled cruelly. "I pleaded an errand of nature and gave him the slip. Mayhap he's used to countryfolk who don't recognize those dicer's calluses on his fingers."

Dale held up his hands for her to inspect. He has very nice hands with long, elegant fingers. I do like a cove with fine hands. "I have a gaming cove's calluses, too, Clary."

She looked him in the eye. "Do you cheat, then?" she asked bluntly.

Dale laughed. He *laughed,* at Goodwin when she was being her toughest! "I don't have to," he said. "The odds are in my favor if I play the games right. The bones fall so many ways every so often. If they're honest, and I keep my wits about me, I've a good idea what my odds are."

He talked dice games with Goodwin as we made a good meal on what Tomlan had packed. Then the boat's captain took Dale away for a backgammon game.

Goodwin watched me as I packed up. "He's got a lot of charm. He might also be one of the Rats we seek."

I looked at her. "Do you believe I'm a fool, Goodwin?" I asked her. I confess, I was hurt she might think it.

She sighed. "No. Your life might be easier if you were. A

fool for love is happier than a Dog with a heart that's all leather."
She stretched. "Take a walk around the deck, Cooper."

I did as ordered, Achoo bearing me company off of her
leash. When I found a nook along the rail between two stacks
of barrels, I stopped for a moment to look at the river and the
trees. To think that people live all their lives out here, far from
the people and business of Corus! I think I could go mad, staying more than a short walk from the markets, without the Common to dance on, or the temples and the festivals to ease my
eyes when I tire of the everyday sights.

A hound's yip and a mot's angry screech brought me back
to the moment. I'd thought she was used to me enough to stay
close. I had thought wrong.

Away from my nook between the barrels, near the bow,
Achoo had spotted a dragonfly. Just as I spotted her, she leaped
for it, rising a good four feet in the air. I was impressed. The
mot nearby was not. She shrank against the rail as Achoo
flopped onto the stack of hides in front of her.

"Whose animal is this?" she cried. "It's going to attack!
Save me!"

"Achoo!" I cried, running toward my hound. "Achoo,
kemari!"

Achoo scrambled to her feet on the stacked leather and
gave me a sheepish look. The woman inched further down the
rail toward a well-muscled fellow passenger. "Save me!" she cried.

"Don' be a fool, woman!" he advised. "Her tail's waggin',
or it was until this mot came." The other passengers who
looked on laughed.

I wanted to kiss him, but I had to deal with Achoo. I
pointed to the deck before me. "*Kemari,* right sarden now,"
I ordered.

Achoo snapped at the dragonfly that buzzed by her face. It

was a halfhearted snap, meant more to show me that she was her own mistress than an attempt to grab the dragonfly.

"Achoo, either you sarden *kemari* or it's oatmeal for you for a week," I promised her.

I don't know if she understood my words or my tone, but she jumped from the stack of hides and slunk over to me, head down, tail between her legs. She knew she had been bad. I put the leash on her. She wagged her tail the tiniest bit, but I shook my head. "You know that you are supposed to come at my first order, never mind that you weren't supposed to leave me in the first place. Don't even try to cozen me."

"That creature is savage!" cried the mot. "I will report you to the captain for letting it loose on the boat!"

"Report us, then," I said. "But I doubt he'll be impressed by her viciousness in hunting dragonflies." I gave the leash a small tug. "Achoo, *tumit.*" We left the woman, who was scolding the onlookers while they laughed at what I'd said. I doubted she would say aught to the captain, not when there seemed to be no one nearby who would support her.

When I went back to our things, I was shocked to find Goodwin busy over needlework. Of all the things I could imagine her doing to keep her hands busy, it had never occurred to me to think of her with needle in hand. Even more startling, she was at fine embroidery, the kind of elegant stitchery that was sewn onto sleeve and tunic hems and collars. I stood for a moment, watching her needle dart as she stitched a pattern of blood-red silk keys between two gold borders. This was expert work, not the kind of craft a woman might do for her own family.

I leaned in closer. Goodwin wore thin white silk gloves as she stitched. Of course she did. Her work-rough hands would catch at the fine threads if she left them uncovered.

"Cooper, if you're going to stand and stare, the least you could do is get in the way of the sun and provide me some shade," she told me without looking up. "Otherwise, sit down."

"I'd no notion," I said without thinking.

"It's not something I talk of, overmuch. It kept my mother happy, all right?" She said nothing more as I took my seat. Finally, as Achoo stretched out on the deck, Goodwin muttered, "As long as I could do this kind of work, Ma thought I might give over the nonsense of being a Dog and be a proper wife, selling needlework to make a bit of meat money on the side, as she did. After she passed on, I kept it up. It wasn't the coin so much, by then. More like the remembrance of her, and pride in the craft."

I watched Goodwin's needle dart fish-like, making the red keys rise from the black cloth of the strip she worked. "My sisters do fancy work," I said after a time. "Mostly for my lady Teodorie, though Lorine wants to make elegant clothes for the nobles."

"My lord mentioned once your sisters are fine seamstresses. And I've seen your clothes are always well turned out," Goodwin added, eyeing a line of stitches. "You do your own sewing?"

I nodded. "I do mending for all of us at Mistress Trout's," I said. "Kora does the laundering—well, she has gixies help with it, these days. Aniki sees that the cutlery and blades are sharp for her, Kora, Ersken, Rosto, and me. And she makes sure we've wood for our fires. It evens out."

"A good arrangement. Will you keep it up when they move into the Dancing Dove?" Goodwin snipped a thread and chose another for her needle. "Or will you move there with them?" She gave me a sharp look.

Achoo leaned against my side. "Oh, you're a good girl

now?" I asked, and scratched her ears. To Goodwin I said, quiet-like, "I don't know, but I don't believe so. That inn's to be the new Court of the Rogue. It wouldn't be right, me living there. I'll stick to Mistress Trout's." I sighed. " 'Twill be lonely, though."

Goodwin set her stitch. "Maybe some more Dogs will move in there. It's not like living across from the old Court of the Rogue, in the middle of the Cesspool. The Dancing Dove is part of the Lower City. You might have better company than you think."

I shrugged. I would worry about it when my friends moved.

We'd been silent for a time when she said, "You've been practicing the tale we will tell?" I nodded. I'd thought about it often when I couldn't sleep. "Good," Goodwin replied. "Keep doing that. I've been thinking about our work. There's another thing we should sniff for." I waited as she tied off a knot. Goodwin snipped off her thread, then set the needle down and flexed her hands before she went on. "Where do they get their silver? The brass is easy enough to come by. It's cheap. They can buy a few baskets of brassware in the markets, the stuff that's so battered none will use it, and they have what they need. But silver's another matter."

"It's only sold by the Silversmith's Bank," I said, remembering our lessons in colesmithing. "The melted silver is molded into ingots. Those are stamped by the Crown. It's illegal to have block silver without the stamp. Anyone who buys more than three ingots has to give their information to the bank."

Goodwin nodded. "It's the silversmiths the crown's Ferrets will be on first."

I nodded. The silver- and goldsmiths were always at the

top of the list of suspects when the hunt was on for counterfeiters. One time in four a colesmith *was* a silver- or goldsmith, sad to say. "It may be a silversmith this time," I said.

"Oh, of a certainty." Goodwin was threading a fresh needle. "That's the quickest question answered. We'll know that within a week. But if it's not—where do the colesmiths get their silver? The mines are all controlled by the Crown. Keep your eyes and nose open, Cooper. If we find that source, we're close to breaking the whole ring. It's good odds we're after a ring, not a lone colesmith."

I agreed. "No one cove or mot could turn out this many coles alone."

"Exactly. We're looking for a gang. Don't worry, though, Cooper. The entire hunt doesn't rest on us, remember that. I've heard naught but good of Nestor Haryse. He'll have solid Dogs to help in Port Caynn, and we know who will be working on this thing in Corus. Once my lord convinces the Crown, we'll have the Ferrets on it, too." She looked at me and I nodded. I didn't say I wanted *us* to be the ones that brought down the game for our hunt. I'm sure she thought so just as much as me. She always says it's a wonder two such eager Dogs get on so well in one partnership.

"I think I know what the answer will be, but I will ask. Cooper, have you any notion of how to play this new card game, Gambler's Chance?" Goodwin asked, changing the colored threads in her needle.

I shook my head. "I've heard of it, but I haven't seen it played."

"Pox," Goodwin muttered. "I would have liked to learn it *before* I got to Port Caynn." She smiled crookedly at me. "I suppose I'll have to learn it on the fly." We continued to talk over small details of our hunt to come. The sun moved enough to provide us with shade as we made a list of the places we would go in Port Caynn.

The boat slowed on the lake. We had encountered the clog that began where the lake narrowed and the boats downriver approached the jam at the bridges. I took out my journal and began to write of the first half of this day, to have this much done before we report to the Deputy Provost.

Goodwin has noticed what I'm doing, but she says nothing. Her fingers dart over her work while her eyes go to dicing games on other boats nearby. Slapper flies now and then for amusement, returning for more food. Achoo sleeps.

I must finish. I see Dale coming back. At least the next two hours won't be boring, with him to talk to.

Ladyshearth Lodgings, Coates Lane
Midnight.
We did not reach Guards House, headquarters for the Deputy Lord Provost in Port Caynn, until well past four of the afternoon. We'd come in view of the Sunrise Bridge by one, but it had taken us two more hours to glide under that, then the Sunset Bridge, to tie up to the river docks, and see our things unloaded.

Before we parted from Dale, he'd left me with a list of five places where he might be found.

"And you'll remember them, right?" Goodwin asked as we watched him angle off through the crowds on the dock. "He's a gambler and he wants to further his acquaintance with you." She glanced at me. "We've begun already, Cooper."

"I'm not that fond of lying to folk," I told her. "Not telling someone I like why I'm really here is the same as lying."

"We're on a hunt, Cooper," she said. "When you're on a hunt, you do whatever it takes. Think back to the Opal Murders, and the Shadow Snake. This is the same. Folk will die of hunger if we don't nab these colemongers." Some cove shoved into her, not looking where he went. Goodwin shoved back. "Mind your step, cityman!" she ordered.

The cove turned on her, hand raised. Achoo was between them in an instant, her lips curled back from her teeth, her ears flat, her hackles up. I moved in next to her as me and Goodwin quickly checked our purses, in case he'd been a foist. Our coin was safe.

The cove spat on the dock and retreated.

"Beggin' yer pardon, mistress." A thick-built cove had come up to us. He touched his broad-brimmed hat. "Master Dale Rowan said yeh needed a carter t' carry yer things wherever ye're wishful t' go. He give me a siller noble for th' work, mistress." He grinned, showing blackened teeth. "Though ye're welcome t' give me a bit of extry consideration, like."

Goodwin eyed the cove. "Dale Rowan sent you. And how do you know him?"

The carter looked surprised. "Ev'ryone on the docks knows Master Dale, mistress. He's on an' off th' river once or twice a week some weeks, mayhap more. He's an open hand with th' coin, is Master Dale. Tips on the races, too."

"Free with coin and a gambler," Goodwin said, hands on hips. To look at her, you'd think she commanded a household and children for her day's work, and never missed a speck of dust. "His wife must be one discontented woman."

Our bluff cove laughed at that. "Master Dale's not married, so his coin's his own, and his nights too," he told us. "It'd take a curious kind o' mot t' keep *his* interest for more'n a week! Now, mistress, will yeh be havin' that help? I'd hate to give his siller back."

He gave us a funny look when Goodwin directed him to Guards House, but shrugged and said it was all the same to him.

Our carter negotiated several narrow streets behind the docks. At last we made the turn onto Kings Way, the broad, open way that was what the Olorun Road became when it entered Port Caynn. Three carts could pass down the street without hindrance, which was a fine thing, because it was thick with horsemen, sedan chairs, herdsmen taking their flocks home, vendors, and all kinds of folk on foot. There were far more people here from foreign places than in Corus. The sight of all those Yamani, Scanran, Copper Isle, and Carthaki faces and costumes took me back at first. There were also more Bazhir in the port city, come with horses, goats, and sheep to sell or looking for animals to buy. I'm sure there were Gallans, Tusainis, Barzunnis, and Marenites, too, but they tend to look more like us than the others.

Quick enough I spotted some filches and cutpurses, then a clump of doxies and spintries on a corner by their bordel. I began to feel more at home. The mumpers had their posts on the ground. The best way to see them was on the bridges. I had forgotten how many bridges there are in Port Caynn. If the bridge is big enough, as they are on Kings Way, folk set up businesses there, like the mumpers.

I picked out servants and Rats trying to pass as servants for purposes of burglary. Best of all, I saw Dogs, strolling along with batons swinging, eyes on everyone and everything.

"A sharp-looking crew for Day Watch," I told Goodwin quietly.

"They get the best up on Kings Way," she said. "They put on their good face for the visitors."

On the cart climbed. We were coming to the only part of town I really knew, since I'd visited it on both my trips here with Lord Gershom. The ridge that divides Port Caynn in two is crowned by High Street. Lengley Castle, where the district governor lives, stands at the south end, overlooking the sea. Guards House is north of the governor's palace. It has a good view of both sides of the ridge, the part where the river docks are, and the part that makes up the deep harbors. Both times I was here, while my lord met with his Deputy Provost in Guards House, I would run up the stairs to the observation deck and look out at both sides of Port Caynn. I'd pretend I was the Rogue or a Deputy Provost.

As we turned onto High Street, I saw the cold gray stone block of Guards House to our right. I wondered at the strange way they did things here, so different from what I was used to. All of this city's court hearings are done in Guards House. Prisoners stay in each kennel's cages only a short time before they are taken to Rattery Prison, which stands at the north end of High Street. Were I Provost or Lord High Magistrate, I would have arranged things so my Dogs didn't have to travel so far from their kennels and homes to go to court, but every city has its own way of doing things.

Our carter drew up before the gates of Guards House. A pair of Dogs came forward as Goodwin slid down from her seat. She showed them the gold insignia she wore around her neck. "We've orders to present ourselves to my Lord Deputy Provost," she told them. "Sergeant Nestor Haryse was to set an appointment for us—Goodwin and Cooper."

The Dogs unloaded our gear while I saw to Achoo and Slapper. Goodwin slipped our carter some extra coins, which won us a big grin.

"Bless you, mistress, and you, girl! Stands to reason a

friend o' Dale's would be as openhanded as him!" He gave us a cheerful wave and turned the cart, heading back toward the river docks.

One of the guard Dogs led us inside, to a desk sergeant. He took charge of us and our gear, sending word of our arrival to Sir Lionel. He also gave the fish eye to Slapper and Achoo. I ignored the fish eye. If Dogs have to report here as soon as they arrive in town, the sergeant must see they come with all kinds of gear and family.

We didn't wait long before the runner came back, saying we were to follow him to Sir Lionel's office. That was when I turned to my animals. "You're to wait," I said, quietly, so Master Fish Eye didn't hear. "Understand? *Tunggu.* I *mean* it. Folk don't cut me extra yardage here. *Tunggu. Turun,* while I'm thinking of it." Achoo lay down with a patient sigh. Slapper relieved himself on my trunk.

I followed Goodwin, looking back as I left the room. Mother's mercy, both of them stayed where I'd put them. Pounce *never* would have done that, just because he was a cat.

The runner showed us into Sir Lionel's office. The walls and ceiling were made of fine, polished wood, the moldings well carved. The only other decorations were maps of the city, one for each Guard District. There were maps, too, of the outlying districts. Unlike Corus, which is a command of itself, the Deputy Provosts are in charge of countryside as well as the cities and towns where they are situated. Sir Lionel's reach covers the same area as the district governor's, north along the River Tellerun to opposite the city of Arenaver, east to the Great Road North, then south to the outskirts of Corus.

For all he is a Deputy Provost and a noble, his office is plainer than my Watch Commander's. There are no carpets on the stones of the floor. There are no hangings on the bare spaces of the walls. The windows have horn panes, not glass. For now they stood open, letting in courtyard noises. One bookcase has some volumes of law. The candlesticks are brass. So too are the inkwell and quill stand.

Two men came in. Nestor was one, dressed in full uniform. He gave Goodwin and me the tiniest of nods. The other was Sir Lionel of Trebond, the Deputy Provost for Port Caynn District. Goodwin and I bowed. He was two inches taller than me, with deep-set brown eyes, a long nose, and a thin mouth. He was lean, and his cheeks were red and weathered. His ginger-colored hair was combed straight back from his high forehead and hung in a slight curl below his ears, as if that curl was all it was allowed. I had a notion he was a hunter, better with hawks than with a boar spear. He dressed well in a calf-length tunic of gray wool. The embroideries at his hems and cuffs were modest, black and white sea lions on strips of blue. The needlework looked like something a daughter might make for him.

Goodwin stepped up to Sir Lionel's desk and held out our orders. He took them, holding them a moment while he looked her over, like a man about to buy a horse. Then he did the same to me. I tucked my hand in my skirt, where I could feel the lump of my fire opal through the cloth. I squeezed it. I'd not had to impress anyone for a long time now.

"Corporal Goodwin I know, though hardly out of uniform," Sir Lionel said. He had a thin, tough voice. I would not want to be guilty of breaking his rules. "You would be Rebakah Cooper, then," he said, and raised his eyebrows. "You are too young for such a mission."

I could feel myself blushing. I knew that, but Lord Gershom had disagreed. Wasn't that good enough for his Deputy Provost?

"Permission to speak," Goodwin said.

Sir Lionel nodded.

"Cooper is a good Dog, and she's my partner," Goodwin explained. "She's been partners with Senior Guardsman Tunstall and me in the bad cases we've hunted down this last year. She would surprise you."

"We'll see." Sir Lionel broke the seal on our orders and read them. I tried not to fidget. I wasn't used to being left standing like this, any more than Goodwin was. Either Sir Lionel had a stick up his bum, or other districts go to pains to say you might be good in your home district but *we* do things different.

I risked a peek at Nestor. He stood with his legs planted apart, his hands clasped loosely in front of him. He looked as if he could stand like that all day and never cramp up. I eased my feet apart some to balance my weight better.

Sir Lionel set down our orders. He finally said, "You may sit, all three of you." We settled in the uncomfortable guest chairs.

"We've had some trouble with counterfeits, largely in the better class of houses of pleasure and some of the jewelers' shops," Sir Lionel told us.

Houses of pleasure? Good Goddess, the man meant bordels. Why didn't he just say so?

"If, as the report sent to me claims, the coins are spread by gambling, I have heard nothing of it. Still, successful gamblers like to spend their winnings. Those are the first places they go. We've heard no warnings from the Silversmith's Bank." Sir Lionel's eyes went to Nestor. "You have a thought, Sergeant?"

"Only that it's hardly to the banks' advantage to report an increase of coles, Sir Lionel," Nestor said. "They'd be the first ones under investigation. Their stock of coin would be locked up until it could be examined for fakes."

"True enough," Sir Lionel replied. To Goodwin and me he

said, "I will meet with those of my Watch Commanders that I trust with this news tonight. We'll create a plan to hunt the counterfeiters here. Lord Gershom has made it plain that he wishes the two of you to have a more roving hunt, letting your instincts take you across Guard Districts if need be. To that end, I am turning you over to Sergeant Haryse's guidance. He can give out the tale that you are assigned to his watch district, though you will not be assigned to a particular watch. He is also familiar with the less . . . law-abiding parts of the city, and is respected there. Sometimes I think he is *too* fond of those areas, which is why he will not accept promotion away from the streets."

"I feel as if I do more good in the street, Sir Lionel," replied Nestor. "All of my friends are there."

"Impudent Dog," muttered Sir Lionel. To us he said, "Sergeant Haryse will handle your communications with my office and with my lord Gershom. It would look ill for two loose Dogs, as you must appear to be, to deal regularly with Guards House. I believe Sergeant Haryse has found you lodgings. He will also advise you in all other matters, including assistance, should you need it."

"Discreetly," Nestor murmured.

"Above all, discreetly," Sir Lionel agreed. "We do not wish to start a panic. You must take care not to start false rumors and panics, Guardswomen. We have a peaceful city here, and I will not tolerate the creation of agitation among my citizens by you outsiders."

"Permission to speak," Goodwin said a second time.

"Granted," replied Sir Lionel.

"With respect, Sir Knight, you are uncomfortable with our presence," Goodwin went on, as formal as I'd ever heard her. "Given the long history of cooperation between Corus and Port

Caynn, I'm not sure why. Only good has ever come from our districts working together."

Sir Lionel shook his head. "I have no problems in working with Corus, Corporal Goodwin. My problem lies in first, the fact that we have a peace here, and I fear that you will break it, and second, in the fact that both of you are women. I would be far happier if my lord Gershom had sent men. I feel, along with others, that women's souls are more tender, more vulnerable." He stopped and looked at Goodwin and me. "Neither of you has the least notion of what I mean. Life on the street has coarsened this young girl as it has coarsened you, Corporal. I can only pray the Gentle Mother that you two do not create so much trouble that my people are put at risk getting you out. Take care in your investigations. At the first sign of difficulty, call on us for help."

He nodded, cool as snow after such an astounding speech. Nestor and Goodwin rose. Goodwin had to poke me with her foot to make me realize I had to get up, so dazed was I. We were dismissed.

Nestor led us back to the desk sergeant. "We'll take your gear to your lodgings," he said over his shoulder. "Then I thought you might want a decent supper before you turn in for the night. Is that well with you?"

"It depends on those two," Goodwin said, jerking her thumb at Achoo and Slapper. "They came with us."

Rubbing the top of his head, Nestor looked at the animals.

"Watch the pigeon," the desk sergeant warned. "One of the lads tried to shoo 'im off and got pecked in the nose for his trouble."

"He's a watch pigeon," Goodwin said, straight-faced. "Mean as a snake, but easier to feed."

The desk sergeant laughed.

"Actually, I am acquainted with Slapper," Nestor said. "The last time I tried to feed him, he bit me. Twice. Now, I didn't get to meet the hound properly in Corus."

"Achoo, *bangkit*," I ordered. *"Berdiri."* Achoo sat up at attention, her chin high, her eyes straight ahead. "She's a scent hound, about two years old."

"Pleased to meet you," Nestor told Achoo.

"Achoo?" asked the desk sergeant, coming down from his tall chair. "*The* Achoo?"

"There's only one Achoo amongst the Corus scent hounds, sir," I replied.

The sergeant crouched before her. "We borrowed her a year back, Nestor. She sniffed out them dreamrose smugglers for us. This is a fine hound, and someone's been treatin' her like scummer." He glared at me with ice-blue eyes. His gray mustache seemed to bristle at me. My tongue froze in my mouth.

"Sergeant Axman here was a handler of scent hounds before they nailed him to this desk," Nestor explained. "He breeds them now for us."

"What's the likes of Achoo Curlypaws doin' with a junior Dog?" the sergeant demanded. "No offense, youngster, but with her record, this hound ought to have a senior handler."

Achoo made the smallest of grumbling noises deep in her throat. It could have been a growl, it could have been a low whine. She has very good manners.

I looked at the hound. Achoo *Curlypaws*? I had no notion she even had a last name! When I get home, I need to go to the scent hounds' kennels and read all the paper they have about her. *NOTE—MUST DO SOON!*

Goodwin told the sergeant, "Her last senior handler treated Achoo like scummer. Then he dumped her on Cooper

186

when Cooper objected. It's only been in the last few days that Achoo's wounds have healed under Beka's care."

"May I say hello?" Nestor asked. "Aside from Master Pounce, I've never petted a legend before."

"*Kawan,* Achoo," I said, pointing to Nestor. She wagged her tail. I pointed to the sergeant. "*Kawan.* You can say hello," I told them. I could tell Sergeant Axman wanted to look her over, but he was too polite to ask. Now he could do so.

Once Nestor was friends with Achoo, he and Goodwin went to get a cart from the stable yard. Sergeant Axman was still petting Achoo, crooning to her in some soft language that Achoo seemed to like very much. I dug the remains of a roll from my pocket and fed them to Slapper. For once, he didn't try to pummel me with his wings or peck at me while he ate.

I was thinking about Sir Lionel's peculiar notions about women. I've never heard such puke, not from anyone. Who was this Gentle Mother? Another face of the Great Goddess?

I wished so badly that Pounce had been there to explain. Instead I whispered to Slapper, "He said me'n Goodwin are coarsened. And he said women's souls are more vulnerable and tender! Has he never seen a mot bowl over some cove that's bothering her?"

"It's this cult of the Gentle Mother teachin' that women are delicate souls." Axman swiveled so he could look up at me. "You're supposed to be too pure to dirty yourselves with combat." He barked a laugh. "Tell 'at to *my* old woman. She's been in His Majesty's navy since she was old enough to tie knots. Some of these lady knights'll cut you from crown to cod, you even look at 'em disrespec'ful."

He couldn't be too bad if Achoo liked him. I nodded. "I know one who does that if you get between her and her end-of-day ale."

"Exac'ly so. There's a sergeant in Corus, Ahuda—" he said.

I grinned. "She's my Watch Sergeant."

He grinned back, showing three missing teeth. "She's a caution, that 'un. If we had five like her here, there'd be no Rats in all the city."

Goodwin and Nestor returned. "Then we'd die of boredom, Sarge," Nestor said. We gathered up our things and hauled them out to the cart. Just to show Goodwin I could, I carried my trunk myself.

"Cooper, you were actually conversing," Goodwin said as we climbed into the cart. Nestor took the reins and glanced back at me.

"He heard me telling Slapper about that Gentle Mother stuff. He was explaining it to me, but it's still moonsongs, far as I can tell." I settled Achoo in the cart. Slapper waited until we were sitting still, then landed in a corner, muttering to himself.

Nestor said, "Why are you talking to pigeons, Beka? Where's Pounce?"

And here I'd thought I wouldn't have to explain it anymore. Wearily I told Nestor why Pounce wasn't traveling with me. He whistled when I was done. "We'll just have to see to it that you have so much to do, you'll hardly miss him," he told me. He waved to the Dogs on guard as we rattled through the gate. "Serenity, that runs Ladyshearth Lodgings, has an understanding with the Provost's Guards regarding payment. That's where you'll stay. It's on Coates Lane, about five blocks from my house, on the edge of Deep Harbor District. The walk to the kennel and the heart of things is easy. The area's a safe one, though, and the house itself is very safe. Several of our woman Dogs stay there."

He turned off High Street, bound downhill, into the southwestern part of the city on that side of the ridge. Below lay the deep harbor, its blue water sparkling. The big oceangoing ships were scattered over the harbor waters and tied up at the docks, preparing for the night. Some were sailing out between the great breakwaters, taking the evening tide out to sea. I'd loved watching the big ships on my last two visits. They look beautiful, like low-skimming gulls.

I'd already memorized the map Lord Gershom had given us, using the tricks we learned in training. Going by that, we now entered the South Hills District. Tradesfolk lived hereabouts, from the looks of the shops and the dwellings, much like where Goodwin and her man live back in Corus. Very tidy, very respectable. I felt like a flea on the bum of a nobleman's dog.

Ladyshearth Lodgings was near the northern edge of South Hills District, on Coates Lane. I could tell just by looking that this place was too costly for me to afford on my own. It was set off the street, behind a waist-high stone fence. As we approached and passed through the open gate, I noticed that some of the stones had magical runes cut into their faces as protection from thieves and the like. The house itself was stone on the ground floor, wood painted with moon designs for the two upper stories, and a roof that was tiled, not thatched. Even the shutters had been painted with the three moons, crescent, full, and dark. An herb garden was planted around the front of the house.

A short, plump woman in a flour-smutched wool dress came out of the open front door. The mot wore a linen head cloth that covered her hair, but from her brows the color was dark and going to gray.

"Tinggal," I ordered Achoo while Goodwin and Nestor climbed down from the cart. I shouldered my own pack and gathered a couple of Goodwin's.

"Welcome," the woman said. "I'm Serenity. Don't bother with 'Daughter' talk. I'm not a priestess at home. I hope you like the rooms I set aside for you. Nestor says you'll be with us for an indefinite time, so I tried to give you something comfortable." Chattering to Goodwin, she led us inside and up to the second story. "Just press your thumbs to the lock hole to the right of the door. Then the locks will only ever open to you or to me. The spell is one of my best and has never failed me. I will let the maid in to clean, unless you wish to do that yourself. Set your chamber pots and laundry outside the door of a morning, and the maids will tend to them. You may also take your meals here, if you like. Breakfast is from dawn until nine of the clock." She steered Goodwin through one door and me through the next. Nestor followed me with my trunk and set it on the floor.

I stared after her as she bustled off, Nestor following her downstairs. Magicked locks? The room itself was more than I was used to. There were fresh rushes on the floor. The bed was made up with a good blanket and better coverlet, and clean linens were stacked on shelves over the bed. Two chairs with fat cushions sat on either side of a hearth—a hearth! Only wealthy folk have hearths in their bedchambers! There was a stand with a washbasin, a spotless chamber pot, and a large table and chair I could use for meals or writing. Embroidered hangings brightened the walls. I opened the shutters and found myself looking over a vegetable garden, a bit of grazing, a shed for animals, and a chicken coop. The birds scratched on a bare patch of dirt. Along a corner of the yard flowed one of the city's many streams, crossed by a small bridge.

I closed and bolted the shutters and went into Goodwin's rooms. I sank onto her bed. "Gods be thanked the Provost's Guard pays for this, Goodwin! I could never afford it," I told her. "My room probably costs for a week what I pay for two months at Mistress Trout's! What if I break something?"

She shook her head. "Cooper, you worry too much. We've been given an open hunt. That means we use our own judgment about the money, and we have lodgings where we can feel *safe*. My lord must truly believe you won't spend foolishly. Normally only ten-year Dogs or older are put on open hunts. If your dress is torn, they pay for a new one. If you need to feed old Slapper, they will pay—he's your Birdie, after all!" She punched me lightly on the shoulder. "Let's help Nestor bring up the rest of our things. He says his lodger prepared supper tonight, to welcome us. Enjoy this while it lasts. You'll hate going back to your old ways."

But I *like* my old ways, I thought, trudging down stairs that were doubtless scrubbed every day. I'm *used* to them.

Nestor met me in the door. He had Slapper in both hands as the bird twisted, trying to get his beak in Nestor's flesh. "What's the matter?" he asked, his eyes twinkling at me. "Is this place fancier than you're used to?" I nodded. "Cheer up, Beka. I'll wager you'll get plenty of hunts when you're in muck and ice to your eyebrows. Enjoy this while you can."

I watched him return to the cart to help Goodwin. "I hope you're right about the hunts, though I'd prefer no muck and ice," I muttered. On outside I went. Achoo was sitting in the cart where I left her, looking miserable. Serenity was trying to get my hound to sniff her hand.

"Achoo, *bau*," I told her. Achoo cheered up immediately. She hated to seem unfriendly. She gave Serenity's hand a good sniff as Serenity looked at me. "She's a scent hound," I explained. "She belongs to the Provost's Guard. And—well, I have a bird, too." I held up Slapper.

"I saw it, the poor thing," she replied. "Did you rescue it when you found it so crippled?"

Slapper began to struggle. I gripped him one-handed and took Goodwin's last pack from the bed of the wagon. I hoisted the pack onto my shoulder. "No, mistress. He just came to me as he is, and I can't seem to get rid of him."

Serenity smiled. "You've a good heart under that gruffness, Rebakah Cooper, or you wouldn't come with two animals looking to you! I have cracked corn for the chickens. I'll bring a bowl of it up to your room for your poor friend—what is his name? I know your hound is Achoo."

"He is Slapper, and I thank you for the corn," I said, trying to sound as grateful as I felt. "But be careful of him, I beg you. He is a cranky thing, and he hits with those wings of his. And pecks."

"I imagine the foot gives him pain," she said wisely. "I'll get that corn."

Nestor laughed and climbed to the seat of his wagon. "I'll wait here until you're ready to leave."

By the time Goodwin and I had all our things stowed, Serenity had not only brought me cracked corn for Slapper, but a water bowl each for him and for Achoo. I thanked her and offered her a couple of coppers, but she waved them off. " 'Tis my pleasure to help with your creatures. Now go along. Nestor is waiting to carry you and Mistress Goodwin off to supper at his home!"

Life is so different if you or your master has deep pockets to pay for it.

We got into the cart again, Goodwin on the seat beside

Nestor, me in the bed, and rolled on downhill. Nestor's house was tucked between two others just like it, wooden buildings of two stories with attics above. The painted designs on Nestor's walls were brighter and prettier than his neighbors', showing dancing goats, smiling fish, and tiny flying horses circling bright green vines.

"Why is everything all painted?" I asked Nestor. "Not all the houses, but enough of them."

He looked back at me. "Gershom never told you, the times you were here?" I shook my head. I'd feared my lord would think it a silly question. "Plenty of us worship at Oinomi Wavewalker's shrine, for the obvious reasons. She likes pretty things. Besides, the paint helps keep the wood from weathering."

He drew up before the house and Nestor whistled. A mussed serving girl threw the door open. "Have Haden take the cart to the stable round the corner," Nestor ordered her. The gixie turned and screeched into the house, "Haden, master wants ye!"

A lad the age of my brother Nilo trotted out as Goodwin and I got down. He took over the reins and had the cart rattling down the street before we'd even reached the door.

"Don't wreck it!" Nestor bellowed after him. As we followed him in, he told the gixie, "If he wrecks it, I'm selling your brother to the Copper Isles."

"Where they'll curse yer name forever, sir," she said, not a whit afraid of him.

"Impudence. I am surrounded by it. I am *starving!*" Nestor bellowed as the gixie skipped up the stair and through an open door. As Nestor led us inside, he explained, "The ground floor belongs to my lodger, Okha Soyan. My rooms are on the upper story."

We followed him up the stairs and into his home to enter a main room clearly meant for sitting, work, and eating. Two doors opened off of it. I guessed that they led to a kitchen and a bedroom.

"I bespoke supper early. I hope you don't mind," Nestor told Goodwin. "I'm not fit company till I've had my evening meal."

"An early supper is fine," Goodwin said. "We'll want to settle in tonight, when we'd normally be out and about, right, Cooper?"

I nodded. I was more interested in watching the person who came in from the room that must be the kitchen, from the good smells that came from it. I knew from his visits to Provost's House that Nestor's lodger was in truth his lover, and I confess I was curious to see the man who had dashed my fourteen-year-old marriage hopes. Nestor had never said Okha was a Carthaki, back when he'd mentioned him to me, yet Carthaki Okha clearly was. Okha's skin was light brown. His black hair was shoulder length and made glossy by some kind of hair oil. He looked to be the same age as Nestor, thirty-one. His eyes were large and dark, his nose short, his mouth thin. He is two inches taller than me, which makes him five feet and ten inches. He is slender in build and graceful, far more graceful than me.

Okha's tunic was autumn orange. I didn't recognize the style of the embroideries. Very dramatic, they were, in black, white, and green zigzags on his hems and collar. He wore slippers stamped with black designs. Large bracelets with odd beaded designs were on his arms, amber drops hung from his ears, and amber beads circled his neck. He wore kohl around his eyes, red paint on his lips. His nails were colored orange, like the Bazhir and the Carthakis do.

Looking at what I've written, I can see that I've described Okha as I would for a Dog report. I do that all of the time, with near everyone I meet when I have their names. But I also want to write of Okha in such a way to sort out how I feel about him. I was so in love with Nestor back then, and I was cracked jealous of a cove I'd never met. I half expected to hate Okha on sight, but I don't. I like him, a bit, and I don't trust that. I don't trust liking someone on sight. If Pounce was here, I could ask him, but he's not. I can trust his instincts more than mine. But he's gone, and I'm left floundering. I couldn't even see how Achoo is with him because she was at Serenity's. ~~Is that a Dog thing to want other opinions~~ Never mind, Beka! Leave the muddling for scholars!

"We were just waiting for you to get here," Okha told Nestor, letting Nestor kiss his hand. Okha's voice was musical and light for a cove's. He smiled at Goodwin. "I'm Okha Soyan. I dance and sing in some of the taverns and gambling houses."

I watched Goodwin, worried how she might handle meeting Okha. You can never tell how folk will greet a bardash or a honeylove. Many don't care, but most screech of unnatural minglings if they so much as see two grown mots or two coves touch hands. It's not what I would like for myself, but I won't speak for what others do. I have enough trouble keeping my own life untangled.

"Clara Goodwin," she replied to Okha's greeting without the tiniest of frowns. "Clary, to most. This is Rebakah Cooper."

Okha turned that bright smile on me. "I'm delighted to meet the famous Beka," he told me. "Nestor has kept me up to date on your accomplishments. He's as proud of you as if you were one of his own trainees." He looked at Goodwin again. "I hope you like our supper. Truda and I did a little cooking."

Goodwin raised her brows. "An entertainer who cooks?"

Okha chuckled. "Often, Mistress Clary, the two are the same. Please, take a seat." He'd steered Goodwin over to a table already set with tankards, spoons, and linen. "Will you have wine or ale?"

Nestor had gone into the kitchen. I sat beside Goodwin while Okha went to bring the ale to the table. "Very graceful," she murmured. "He makes me feel like a clod." She raised her brows at the look on my face. "Stop fretting, Cooper. I'm not going to start screaming. How they live is their own affair."

Nestor and Okha halted as they slid past each other in the narrow kitchen door. Okha bent and kissed Nestor's mouth, then went inside the other room. I looked down. Why in the Goddess's name are so many older people kissing in public of late?

"I'm going to change," Nestor told us. He vanished into another small room at the back of the main one.

I glanced at Goodwin. She was tapping her cheek with her finger. "Okha might help us to meet folk at the richer gambling dens," she said quietly. "It's worth asking."

Okha returned with an ale pitcher and filled cups for Goodwin, Nestor, and himself. The gixie Truda came a moment later with raspberry twilsey for me. It was wonderfully chilled, and cut the dust of all that racketing about in carts.

Okha and Truda had not brought together a meal as much as a feast. I've never been welcomed with such open hands. We had little leaves and fennel for a salad, cuttlefish in black sauce, Carthaki chicken with ginger, cloves, and fruits, fried mushrooms with spices, and cheese fritters. There was even a beet soup that I liked, despite not caring for beets.

I listened to the others talk about news from the palace and news from the port. They discussed ship trade, the harvest and the rye blight, the Bread Riot, and omens. Folk were saying that a sword had appeared in the harbor foam and had broken up, a sword like the one on Tortall's flag. Okha scoffed at that one, since foam is always breaking up. The bad harvest itself was supposed to be an omen that King Roger's crown was in trouble.

Once Truda had cleared the plates and left us with our drink and bowls of cardamom and anise seed to chew, the conversation turned to why we are in Port Caynn. Nestor had sworn Okha to secrecy yesterday about the reason for our presence. We had to trust Nestor's judgment, and Okha had news for us.

"I've taken about ten coles in fees for the last three weeks," he told us gravely. "The other entertainers are whispering about it, too. They're no fools. In the bordels they've stopped taking silver. It's copper nobles or gold pieces. The customers don't like it, but they pay. And I am certain the customers have begun to wonder." When Goodwin looked at him, Okha shrugged in an elegant way. "It's impossible to keep false coin a secret for long. It raises a stink, like bad eggs."

"But you say you don't know who's passing the coin to you," growled Nestor.

"I would have no clients left if I tattled," Okha replied. His face was calm. He didn't seem to mind that Nestor was vexed. "You have known that from the beginning, my dear. I can be useful in some ways, but a Birdie I am not."

"Perfectly sensible," Goodwin said. "Folk already know you live in Nestor's house. Chances are you're the first person they'd eyeball if he came sniffing around."

"Exactly," Okha said with a pleased smile.

"I know," Nestor said. "I *do* know. It just makes things curst complicated."

"Well, maybe Cooper and I will uncomplicate them for you," Goodwin said. "That's why we're here."

The evening ended soon thereafter. Both coves walked us back to our lodging—not to protect us, they insisted, but because it was too nice an autumn night to waste.

Goodwin and I set a time to meet in the morning and went to our rooms. First I took Achoo out by the brisk stream that flows through the rear yard of the lodging house. When we came back upstairs, I fed her and set about writing the rest of this long day's events in my journal. The worst of it is done now. I can sit here with the shutters open, Achoo curled beside me. From this seat I have a fine view of the city lights. The sound of the creek is peaceful.

I am not sleepy, though. I want to be out there, finding the gambling dens. I want to get a whiff of the smithy that turns the coles out, and the network that carries them inland. I wonder if this is how Achoo feels, all quivery and wishing to be taken off the leash.

Saturday, September 15, 247

One of the afternoon.

Though our bodies knew Evening Watch hours best, Goodwin and I were up around dawn, not being used to such an early bedtime. First things came first. I took Achoo outside, then brought her back in and fed her and Slapper. While I cleaned up and dressed in uniform for the day, Slapper flew out to in-. spect our new territory.

Goodwin rapped on my door. "Cooper. Breakfast."

There was a room just for dining on the ground floor. Three mots were seated there in Dog uniform also, eating with their heads down. They nodded or grunted when Goodwin and I came in, but seemingly none were in a mood for talk. We took our seats and let a maid serve us pease porridge and fresh-baked rolls. The tea was a strong mix of herbs, a true eye-opener loaded with mints and some ginger. By the time we were ready to leave, I was eager to face the strange city.

Goodwin and I set off down Coates Lane, Achoo beside me. The city was stirring. Folk were opening their shops. Coates Lane was too narrow for all but the smallest carts, so we had only horses and mules to avoid, in addition to folk with loads on their shoulders.

Overhead on our left shutters swung open and a mot leaned out. " 'Ware scummer!" she cried, and emptied a chamber pot into the street. We dodged it and two more before Coates Lane emptied into Dockside Road.

Happily there were no houses on Dockside, and thus no chamber pots. Here the risks came from wagons, carts, horses, mules, and ships' cranes. The waterfront was wide awake, ships having come in on the tide to offload cargoes. Goodwin soon decided it was a little too busy for us and took an alley away from the bay. She had to tug me, since I was gawping, but I went quick enough when a sailor asked my name and when I came off duty. Up to Kings Way we went. Goodwin knew her way along the cross streets. I followed our path on the map I'd memorized, making certain that my information was true. We were bound for the Goldsmith's Bank at the southeast corner of Gerjuoy Road and Moneychangers' Street.

Once we'd reached the bank, Goodwin handed me a fat purse. "The moneychangers' booths are on the Gerjuoy side," she told me. "Get those changed for copper and for gold bits."

I bowed my head. "Um—Goodwin," I whispered.

I could see one of her fists go to her hip, over the grip of her baton. Her weight shifted so she rested on that hip. She was thinking.

"I shall guess. You've never been inside a guild bank before," she said quietly.

I nodded.

"Well, Cooper, it's easy enough that I taught Tunstall how to do it, and him barely able to speak Common Eastern," she informed me.

I swallowed a chuckle.

She went on. "There are tables with flags over them and clerks that sit behind them. The flags show where they change that realm's money. Whose money do you want to change?"

"Ours," I replied. "So I go to the tables with our flag over them."

Goodwin nodded. "And you ask the clerk behind the table—?"

"To change our coin for coppers and gold bits," I answered. "And I get a receipt."

"I knew I forgot to tell you something," Goodwin said.

"Exactly. Get a receipt. Trust me, the greatest danger is dying of boredom in the line. I'll be in the offices on the far side of the building. I'll take care of the rest of our coin and the letter of credit. You meet me in the waiting room there when you're done."

With that she strode off to the far side of the bank. For a moment I wanted to beg her to let me stay with her. I'll say it here, though nowhere else. I was terrified. These folk jostled me as if I was nobody. I could hear at least five different languages being spoke, when at home it's Common Eastern, with maybe some Bazhir and some Hurdik unless you're down by the docks. The clothes were just as mixed, and there were more brown- and yellow-skinned people than I am used to.

I looked at Achoo. She stood beside me, her paws set firm in the road, her nose up, scenting the air. I suddenly noticed that the bowed shoulders and the drooping tail of the hound I'd first met were gone. Achoo was happy. She was healthy, well fed, and ready to do her work in this place that held all kinds of information for her to find.

"You're right," I told her softly. "This is what we are made to do. We *should* take pleasure in it."

I stood up straight and took a deep breath. I am a Dog on my first hunt, with the best partner and the best hound in Tortall. I will not disappoint them.

I entered my assigned door and found myself in a great hall well lit by tall windows. Banners hung overhead showing the gold scale insignia of the guild. There were stalls at intervals along the far walls, some with the flags of foreign lands so folk would know those coins were changed there. A member of the guild, wearing the guild's badge, sat at a desk in each stall, ready to do service. A well-armed guard in leather armor, also sporting the guild insignia, stood before the stall, to guard the privacy of those that entered, and to take care of any Rats who thought to help themselves to the coin.

I took my place in a line before one of the stalls that changed Tortallan coin and tried to wait with patience. At last I stepped up to the moneychanger's desk. I took gold nobles from my purse and stacked them before the mot, twenty coins in all. When she began to remove silver nobles from one of the boxes at her side, I shook my head.

"Half copper nobles, half gold bits, if you please, mistress," I said, keeping my voice down. "No silver."

The moneychanger's hand jerked. She stared at me with shock and a little fright. "No silver?" she asked quietly, and coughed.

"None, mistress," I replied. Her reaction was interesting. She knew. She knew the silver coins weren't to be trusted, and she was afraid.

"But—but—that's a fearful lot of coin for you to be carrying, Guardswoman . . . ?" She let it dangle.

"How I carry is my affair. I'll take no silver. You know why, don't you?" Now I was no longer a stranger in a new town, but a Dog on a scent. I took a closer look at that box of silver coin beside her. She closed it, but not before I saw that every coin in it had a greasy shine. They looked as if a mage had touched them with some oil that would show if they were coles. It was more costly than the stroke of a knife, but it didn't give the test away to most folk.

"The guild knows?" I asked her. "They know there's a problem with silver?"

The moneychanger didn't even look up at my question. She just hurried to count out ten gold nobles' worth of gold bits. Then she pulled leather pouches, each holding one hundred copper nobles, from a large box at her feet. She put them on the table and shoved them all at me. As I stowed all that coin in my pack and tunic, she wrote out a receipt.

"You've not answered my question," I reminded her. Her hands were shaking.

"It's forbidden to discuss guild policy, Guardswoman," she said. Her voice and her mouth were tight now. She did not look at me. "You may be assured this *has* been reported to your superiors, and they are taking care of the matter. This is hardly a concern for street Dogs." She thrust the receipt at me. "Good day to you."

She had given me a gold bit more than she should have done. "Is this a mistake?" I asked. "Did you forget the guild's fee for changing my gold?"

She did not look at me. "I forgot nothing. Surely even a young Dog knows what that coin is for."

I pocketed the gold bit separate from my other coins. The gold equal of two silver and ten copper nobles was a heavy bribe. I scooped up my receipt and left the hall, thinking hard. If the moneychanger had thought our talk was worth a gold bit, then I'd wager the Goldsmith's Bank had *not* reported the coles they had received to the Deputy Provost. Surely Sir Lionel would have told us if they had, instead of bragging about his peaceful city. Moreover, the bankers must have known for at least a few days, to pull together the mages and potions they'd needed to test their silver coin.

I could point to all manner of reasons the bank would not want word to get out that they suspected the silver. A panic was the most obvious. The Silversmith's Guild would lose, but so too would the gold- and coppersmiths as folk scrambled to get other coin and prices went mad. I don't know exactly what will happen, but riots and high prices in other years have taught me what I will have to face. I don't want a panic. But the bank is breaking the law, not to notify the Provost's office. And if things are unsteady here, Sir Lionel must be told.

I was out in the street, off to meet Goodwin, when movement at the corner of my eye grabbed my attention. A merchantish-looking cove was talking with a friend, two arms' lengths away from me. A young pickpocket brushed his side.

"Achoo, *tinggal*," I ordered. I lunged for the gixie. She swerved away from me, deeper into the crowd in the street. I lunged again and seized her by the sleeve.

"Hand it over," I ordered. "And come along with me." Then I realized, what would I do—take her to the Tradesmen's District kennel? I'm not sure if I'm allowed to nab anyone here. At home I'd not even bother to nab her. She was too small a Rat to worry about. Do the Port Caynn Dogs care about mice? I needed to think.

She was crying already. They all cried the minute a Dog had them in hand, the little ones, to make us pity them. "Please, Guardswoman, we was hungered at home," she told me. She fumbled in the side slit of her tunic where she'd stuffed her prize.

Behind me I could hear the witless coney had finally noticed his coin had been lifted. He started to shout, "Thief! Thief!"

The gixie handed me a fat red purse. I took it in my free hand, not loosening my grip on her. Now would be the time she'd try to kick me or hit me to make me let go. I was surprised she'd not done so before now.

Instead she wiped her eyes. "I give it back," she said. "Why don't ya let me go? I'm no golden filch, baggin' twenny purses a day."

Achoo barked a warning, but I never saw whoever rammed me from behind, knocking me facedown in the muck of the street. Achoo snarled. There was a thump, and she yelped.

"Achoo!" I cried. I jumped to my feet and went to my hound, who'd been knocked flying, no doubt by the same mammering canker blossom that had bowled me over. I looked around quickly, but the gixie and her rescuer were gone. Then I went over Achoo with my hands to make certain naught was broken, while Achoo whimpered and licked my face. "Don't go grabbin' folk like that, you silly creature," I whispered to her, hugging her for a moment. "You're a scent hound, not a pit bull nor a man hunter. You might've gotten your fool nob cracked." Achoo wagged her whole self and made a kind of happy groaning noise, as if I wasn't insulting her.

Sure that Achoo wasn't hurt, I took stock. All I had for my trouble was a bad scare for my hound, the coney's red purse, and a lot of laughing cityfolk who enjoyed a Dog's humiliation.

"See if I save your purses for *you*," I grumbled. I wiped my face on my sleeve. "Achoo, *tumit*." She fell in step at my heel as if that tarse had never hit her. We went back to the coney, who was still hollowing.

I thrust the purse in his face. "Here," I told him. "Keep your hand on it from now on."

"But that's not my—" he said as he took it and looked inside. He closed his mouth, then opened it. "My—my thanks, Guardswoman." He bit his lip, then gave me a silver noble. "My thanks to the gods that you were here!"

I took the coin. It was a generous bribe, but now I was suspicious about that purse. "You were saying this isn't yours," I told him.

"No, no, I was wrong. The excitement, and . . . I thought I took the brown purse today, but I just remembered it was the

205

red-stained, to go with my tunic." He waved a hand at his tunic, which *was* red.

I looked at the coney-cove again. "You lie," I told him. "The gods will punish you if you've claimed coin to which you have no right."

" 'Tis his purse, you impudent Dog!" said the coney's friend, who'd been silent until now. "He paid for our morning meal with it!"

I could do nothing when they both swore to it. They turned and walked off in a huff, the picture of two righteous coves whose honor had been insulted.

I drew my dagger and scraped it across the front of the silver noble the coney had given me, before we'd got so un-friendly. The metal curled away. At the bottom of the cut was the gleam of brass.

Achoo and I made for the banker's door. My mind was busy with what I'd just witnessed. What if that whole purse was full of coles? Had I gotten in the middle of a trickster's game? The gixie nudged the coney a-purpose while she lifted his purse, for all he didn't notice right off. She *wanted* him to cry, "Thief!" She'd let someone catch her so she could hand over a purse bulging with silver coles. The rusher that knocked me down was in the crowd in case she couldn't escape anyone who caught her. Then either the coney got the false purse in return and said not a word, thinking himself richer, or the one who caught her kept the purse. So would more coles get into the moneystream. The gixie would keep the good money, having exchanged it for false.

What was the purpose of that? Who gained?

Something made me glance back. A small body, sized about the height of a ten- or twelve-year-old, shifted from my sight behind larger folk.

"Did you see that, Achoo?" I asked her softly. "Our spy got careless. I don't suppose you could fetch him."

Achoo looked up at me and gave her soft whuff.

"No, I suppose you can't." Without her able to answer as Pounce did, I had to make up her replies. For a moment I missed Pounce so fiercely that my heart felt squeezed. "You'd need sommat of his to sniff, same as if you were seeking him. That's *my* part of the job, and I haven't done it."

I looked forward at the bank, sifting my memory of the morning. Had that been the watcher in drab brown clothes, on the way to the docks, or to Moneychangers' Street earlier? My memory caught on glimpses, but they could have been glimpses of anyone of that size, dressed so plainly. Wasn't that the whole point of a tracker?

If we had one on our trail, we'd seen him again soon, or her. I was reaching for the door to the bank's offices when Goodwin opened it. "Cooper, you're a mess. Did a wagon roll over you? No, explain later. Come inside and give me my half of the coin. It'll be safer."

I followed her. There was a waiting room for the bank officers with a clerk to take names and a guard to keep order. Several coves and mots in merchants' dress sat on the benches, giving us the fish eye. Goodwin moved so none of them could see what we did.

As I handed over her half of the gold bits and copper nobles, I told her what I had seen in the moneychanger's stall. Then I waited to see if she would say I was full of chicken dung.

"Hunh," she said as she stowed her coin in her pockets and tunic. She gave me a round brass token with a hole punched through the top. It had the Goldsmith's Guild scales on one side and a number on the other. "Keep that close," she ordered. "If you need funds or the letter of credit, show that to these people and they'll provide. I have one of my own. Now, let's see about the silver."

Back we went to the moneychanger's side of the building. Achoo and I stayed outside, so as not to give the moneychanger a whiff that sommat was off. Goodwin went in, a gold coin in her fist.

I kept watch for the pickpocket gixie, in case she returned. This was a good place to try her trick again. The crowds were thick enough, and plenty of folk had purses at hand, coming and going from the banks at opposite corners of the crossing. I did not spot her, though I did see a pair of Dogs take up position across the street from me. They eyed me, memorizing me, and I gave them the Dogs' two-fingered salute in greeting. I figured Nestor would have told the Day Watch throughout the harbor area what me and Goodwin looked like. I looked around anew for our tracker lad, but saw naught. He'd vanished again.

"Dale told me, and here's the proof," I heard a man say. I turned and faced Hanse, the big, slope-shouldered cove who had carried Tunstall out of the riot. He gave me a huge, well-pleased grin. By the light of day I could see his hair, cropped very close, was brown, his eyes bright blue in his tan face. He looked just as cheerful, and as ready for trouble, as he'd done the night of the riot. His brown wool tunic had a simple green braid trim at hems and collar. He wore green leggings and shoes that laced up his calves, sturdy for trudging through the street muck. A short sword and a dagger hung from his belt, both well used and well kept.

"I run into him last night, and he told me you and Goodwin were in town. I thought he was pullin' my leg, but here you are," Hanse said. He reached out his hand. We clasped fore-arms, like soldiers might do. I wouldn't be surprised if he'd been in the army once. "Me and the crew just got in two days ago. We had a short jog upriver and back, guarding some goods. What brings you so far off your turf, Cooper? And how's Tunstall?"

"Grumpy," I replied. "Healing, but grumpy. He's down for the month. They sent Goodwin and me to study Port Caynn Dog work. Tunstall gets paperwork when he's out of the splints."

"Oh, that's hard," Hanse said, making a face. "I had paper-work once. Got myself thrown in jail to get out of it. Had to punch an officer to do it, too. It was worth a flogging to get clear of the pens and the ink. Now who's this?" He crouched and offered his hand to Achoo.

She looked up at me.

"Achoo, *pengantar*," I told her.

Hanse chuckled. "What's that foreign gobble? Can't the poor thing speak like a proper Tortall hound?"

"It's the way she was trained," I told him as Achoo wagged her tail and sniffed Hanse's fingers. I felt more comfortable talking with Hanse than most chance-met strangers. After all, we'd been in a riot together.

He gave my hound's ears a scratch and glanced at me. "Achoo?" he asked.

"When she's got the scent, she's been known to sneeze," I explained.

Hanse straightened. "And here's the lovely Goodwin," he said. "Would you be rememberin' me, Guardswoman? Hanse Remy."

Goodwin came to us, tucking sommat into her pocket. She

offered her hand to Hanse and returned his clasp. "From the Nightmarket. It's good to see you—Master Remy, is it?"

"Only Hanse," he said. "Caravan guards aren't masters of much, for certain."

They talked about Tunstall and our visit here, but I wasn't listening. Hearing both of his names together, I realized they were familiar as a pair. "Hanse" is a common enough name, but where had I heard "Hanse Remy"? Had Dale said it?

"Cooper, are you daydreaming?" Goodwin asked. "Hanse would like to take us to supper tonight at the Merman's Cave. Steen will be there, and maybe Dale."

I blushed and mumbled my thanks. I'd have to wait till later to pry that name from my memory. Goodwin and Hanse settled it, and Hanse was on his way.

"That's a lucky break," Goodwin said when we could no longer see him. "The Merman's Cave isn't a place two mots ought to go alone, but if there is anyplace that will have gambling and loose talk, that will be it. Let's walk this way." We turned up Moneychangers' Street. We put two silent blocks between us and the Goldsmith's Bank before Goodwin took a silver noble from her pocket and handed it to me. "I changed a gold noble in there for silver," she told me. "I wanted to check your findings, and you're right."

I glanced back for our tracker. This time I caught a glimpse as he turned to look in a window. I smiled to myself. He'd be cursing for letting me get that much of a look at him. Facing forward, I inspected the coin as Goodwin and I walked on. The metal had been well wiped, but there were traces of oil in the lines of the stamp.

"They're either very dirty in the bank vaults, or they're testing these coins," Goodwin told me. "We need to alert Sir Lionel. 'Peaceful,' he says. Peaceful doesn't mean good, not at this guild bank. It's rotten with coles, if your visit and mine are proper measures. Otherwise, why would they test all of their silver? This gives me the crawls, I don't mind telling you."

"There's more," I told her. "Mayhap not so big a thing, but neither is it good." As Goodwin steered us northeast, away from the bay and toward Guards House, I explained my encounter with the gixie pickpocket and her return of the false purse.

"What a curst odd game," said Goodwin, frowning. "Return false coin for good, and let your coney spread them about the town. Who benefits? We heard no report of such a thing in Corus. Could they be moving the coles this way? The colesmith sends them out with filchers, who trade with coneys, only the coneys are carriers. The carriers take the coles somewhere else . . . ? Or spend or gamble them away?"

"It seems too complicated to work," I said. "It leaves too many folk to turn into Birdies the minute the cage Dogs heat up the irons or show them the rack."

Goodwin sighed. "It does. Two games, then, but surely only one colemonger gang. There are still far too many good coles, good copies, for it to be even a whole fistful of small colemongers. Ratpox, I wish we knew more!"

"Coneys wouldn't be willing to tell us anything no matter what," I said. "Either they've got a windfall, or they know they've got a purse full of coles and they're liable to be nabbed. They'd spend the coles or get rid of them any way they can." I looked around us. We were on Mouse Lane, a street for small shops and homes. "Where do we go now?"

"Remember I'd mentioned silversmith friends?" Goodwin asked. "Isanz Finer, the old man, isn't in the business anymore, but at one time he could make silver talk as clear as Pounce."

"But what can he say that we need to know?" I asked,

confused. And why would someone want to flood the money-stream with silver coles? I wondered. Wasn't the whole idea of making false coin the fact that you spent them like real ones? You don't give them away.

"Isanz can find out where the silver comes from, Cooper," Goodwin said. "He could tell you if he worked Copper Isles silver, Yamani silver, hill silver, Barzunni silver. I'll bet a week's wages he can point us to where this stuff began."

"Surely my lord has royal mages tracking the silver by now. They'll tell us where it's coming from," I said.

"Everyone knows mages can track royal coin. That's because they've spelled Crown silver," Goodwin told me. "I'll wager you buttons for badgers these colemongers are getting silver from someplace else. Silver that's *not* carrying a Crown spell."

That shocked me. "But the mages could work out where the silver's coming from. Can't they?"

Goodwin was shaking her head. "Cooper, I've been on cole hunts before. Mages like you to think they can do near everything, but that's not always so. Throw dirt from someplace far away into a melt, and even though it sinks to the bottom, it sets a mage to chasing his tail. And you needn't even do that with silver. You know how they use silver charms to purify wounds and curses and bad thoughts?"

"It never purified *my* bad thoughts," I told her without thinking, like she was Kora or Aniki.

Goodwin thumped my head lightly, but she was smiling. "Silver purifies, is the thing. That's its power by nature. And once it's been melted down, there isn't a mage who can tell where it came from. It throws off all the magic that was in it, even the magic of the place where it was born. That's where my friend Isanz comes in." She pointed. "Turn here. I was working

Port Caynn once for a few months, when Tom and I were in difficulties. Isanz's son took me dancing. I learned a great deal from the old man." She halted. "Here we are."

We'd come up before a small cluster of silver businesses. There were three forges, two on one side of the street and one on the other, and a good-sized shop next to the lone forge. A big house stood beside the shop.

"All these belong to Finers," Goodwin told me. She pointed to the forge beside the shop. "Isanz's oldest son's." She pointed to one of the shops across the street. "His oldest daughter's. And his youngest son-in-law's. Two of his other sons and one of his other daughters work in the forge, and one of his sons and one daughter-in-law run the shop. The grandchildren and great-grandchildren are apprenticed out to silversmiths all over the city."

"Then why does he live up here?" I asked. "Shouldn't he live with the other master smiths, in one of the better parts of town?"

Goodwin shrugged. "He likes being close to Tradesmen's District."

Turning to look about as we did had given me another chance to check for our watcher. He was nowhere in view, but there were plenty of doors and alleys he could have popped into. What I wouldn't give for a scrap of his clothes to give to Achoo! *She'd* find him for me in the flirt of a goat's tail!

"Cooper, this is no time to daydream!" Goodwin stood beside the path that led around the side of the big house. Achoo and I trotted to catch up as she led the way back to the kitchen. There she knocked on the open door.

"I think you'd best stay," I told Achoo. Seeing her eye the geese and chickens in the yard, I pointed to a spot by the fence around the vegetable garden and ordered, "I mean it. *Tinggal.*"

Achoo sniffed the air and leaned toward the fowl.

"Achoo," I said, glaring at her. "Shall I get the leash?"

Achoo leaped at a butterfly passing overhead.

I unslung my pack. "I'm getting the leash."

Achoo flattened her ears and went to the spot by the fence. She stood there, looking back at me.

"Tinggal," I ordered. "And no more mucking about!"

With a sigh and a look that told me I was a brute to happy-natured hounds, she lay down.

"Cooper!" Goodwin bellowed. I ran into the house.

The kitchen was large and well lit, more than enough to serve a house of this size. It should have been easy to move about, but the women of the house had to work around a tiny old man at a table next to the largest hearth fire. Here he shaped silver wire as fine as thread, winding and curling the wire on tiny pegs. The finished creations were designs like lace, made all of silver wire. I couldn't help but stare. The old cove's knuckles were knobby with age, but his fingers were as precise as a fly's feet in handling his tools.

"Cooper, you gawp like a countrywoman who just saw the King," I heard Goodwin say. She stood next to a mot of her own age who just plain grinned at me. "For your information, that is Master Isanz Finer. This is his daughter, Wenna."

"Daughter and busybody!" snapped Master Finer without looking up. "Pestilence and scold!"

"And how would this house run, Da, if I were none of those things?" Wenna asked, seemingly unbothered by his insults. She turned to talk with Goodwin. I stepped out of the way of a manservant carrying a joint of mutton, which brought me closer to the snapping turtle by the hearth.

"Never seen a *real* craftsman work in that city of yours, eh, wench?" he asked, still not looking up from his work. He never fumbled or hesitated. Delicate twists and curls formed under his fingers. "A crew of layabouts, charging too much for shoddy work, those Corus smiths! Forget true craft! Make it glitter with some mage potion. They don't care that the work looks drab when the magic wears off. Then they undersell honest craftsmen!"

I hardly knew what to say. I didn't dare try to defend Corus silversmiths to him. He might bite my nose off.

"Luckily, Isanz, we aren't here to invite you to Corus," Goodwin said over my shoulder. "Just as well. You'd put our smiths out of business. My partner Cooper and I are on more serious business. May we speak privately?"

Now he looked at us with eyes that were an amazing shade of green. "Craft is deadly serious to me, you fribbety female! Look at you, back again after you toyed with my poor lad's heart—"

"Your poor lad is married these ten years and has five children to show for it," Goodwin told him coolly. "He hasn't stopped thanking the Goddess I chose to stay with my husband and keep bashing folk for fun."

"Da just misses you. None of us argue with him the way you did," Wenna told us. "I've had cakes and drink sent to the little sitting room. Da, I even set out a tankard of Goldenlake ale."

Isanz put his tools aside and got to his feet. "Why didn't you say so?" He grabbed a knotted walking stick and led the way. Goodwin and I followed him down a short hall to a small room set up with cushioned chairs. There was a table laid with tankards and plates of cakes, and a small brazier to keep the chill off. Isanz and Goodwin had ale, while there was barley water for me. Goodwin must have told Wenna my preference.

Once the door was closed and Goodwin had taken the

first sip from her tankard, Isanz put his down. "You're too senior to have a temporary place here," he told Goodwin, his eyes sharp. "They know of the coles in the capital, don't they? Did the report come from here?"

Goodwin looked into the tankard as if her answer was a casual one. "The other way around. The Lower City Dogs brought word to the Deputy Provost from Corus. What do *you* know of coles, Isanz?"

He cursed. "I sent two of my boys and two of my students to talk to the Watch Commander here in Tradesmen's District. They went representing the lesser silversmiths of Tradesmen's. About a month ago we reported a sharp rise in the coles coming over our counters, and the Watch Commander said he'd take care of it. Then we reported it to the Silversmith's Guild. We've not heard a word from Dogs nor guild since."

"Which watch?" Goodwin asked.

"Day, of course. Evening Watch is as crooked as the coastline." Isanz took a swallow of his ale.

"How long ago?" Goodwin put her tankard down.

"Ten days. Ten days, and we've taken in more coles. Kept 'em, too, waiting for guild orders to hand them over." Isanz looked at Goodwin, then at me. "If you didn't come about *our* report, why are you here?"

Goodwin nodded to me. I placed the cole Goodwin had taken in change from the bank on the table between us and Isanz. "Isanz," Goodwin said, "you know more about the whys and the wherefores of silver than any cove I've ever met. We need to know where the colemongers get their silver."

The old man's eyes brightened. He picked up the cole.

"I think it's coming from somewhere that isn't under Crown supervision," Goodwin said. "But where? Are foreigners behind this, destroying our coin to soften us up for invasion?

Normal colemongers would keep stores of coin and dole out their coles little by little. They want to get rich, not flood us with false silver and drive the value down. Or do they get silver from inside the country somehow? Either way, we must plug up that end of the operation. You're the cove that can tell us where to look."

Isanz leaned back in his chair. "Well," he remarked, his voice quiet. He looked from Goodwin to me. "The two of you are on the hunt."

"We're one part of it," Goodwin said. "But few know Cooper and I are involved, and we want to keep it that way. I doubt they'd think to come to you. But I know you. I think you'll get farther, using your powders and glasses on whatever silver you can melt off this coin, and the ones you've kept, than all the King's mages."

"Mages! Fah!" Isanz spat on the floor. His daughter would not be happy about that. "You leave it to me. Mages look for influences, and stirrings in power. I look for what is always there."

"Alone?" I wanted to keep the word to myself, but decided to speak it anyway. This venture was too risky for me to keep quiet. "Will you do this alone, Master Finer?"

He hesitated. I think he wanted to lie, mayhap from vanity. At last he shook his head. "No. I have a granddaughter and a great-granddaughter I have been training in just this work."

Now Goodwin looked troubled. "Isanz, I doubt that it's a good idea to bring in more folk than we must. There are too many lives at stake already."

The old cove sighed. "My eyes are not what they were, Clary." How he could say that, doing the fine silver work I had seen in the kitchen, I do not know. "I am not as sharp with the colors and the fine distinctions."

"The what?" I asked.

He glared at me. "Never you mind, mistress! This is my family's secret, mine! I will not be surrendering my craft to one who is not my own blood!"

Oh, forgive me, Master Snapping Turtle, I thought angrily. I did glare back, even if I was polite and held my tongue.

"I'll swear my girls to silence, Clary, a *second* time, since I already swore them to keep my secrets. We will be careful," Isanz told Goodwin after a final glare in my direction. "You ought to get *her* teaching in curses." He pointed his bony finger at me. "She's got the eyes for it. Now, begone. If I'm to do this, there's preparations I need to make."

"How long?" Goodwin asked, not moving from her chair. "How long will the work take?"

"Some days, I think. It's not magic, to be done with a whisk of hands and a poof of smoke!" Now he stood, and we did, too. "I'll send for you—where?"

Goodwin gave him our direction and kissed his cheek. Then we said our goodbyes to the lady of the house and went into the rear yard to retrieve Achoo. She was actually where I'd left her. I gave her a strip of dried meat for a reward. "Good girl," I whispered to her as she wagged up a small breeze. "*Very* good girl!"

Wenna followed us out. "You've done him some good, Clary, I have to say! He's got color in his cheeks, and he's stepping along as if he was sixty again," she told Goodwin as she walked us to the gate. "You'll come back?"

"Of course," Goodwin said. "But thank Cooper for his improved spirits. Once he'd insulted her a few times, he was in the pink."

Wenna laughed heartily at this and waved goodbye to us as

we passed down the path to the street. Only I could see the worried look on Goodwin's face.

"Do you think he can keep it quiet?" I asked her softly.

"I believe so. He used to be as silent as the Black God. The secrets of what he does have come down in his family through generations." She shook her head. "I flinch at gnats, Cooper, that's all. He's surrounded by family, and they are watchful." She rubbed the back of her neck. "To tell the truth, I don't like what I'm seeing here. This town seems like there's rotten money in its veins. I can tell you're thinking the same. How could Sir Lionel keep telling Lord Gershom all is well here?"

"My lord says Nestor's true to the bone," I told her. "Whatever's going on, it's not under Nestor's nose."

Goodwin nodded. We were headed toward Deep Water, down the long strip of Tradesmen's District. "So Nestor keeps an eye on South Hills and much of the docks, possibly. But a sergeant's reach only goes so far."

"Where do we go now?" I asked.

"The main gaming district. It's called Flowerbed. We might as well get to know it, particularly the alleyways. It's off toward the Deep Harbor District." Goodwin pointed to the part of town opposite, that climbed up toward the city wall at the base of Queen's Heights.

I figured now was the time to tell her. "Goodwin, we've had company."

She nodded. "He picked us up near our lodgings. I haven't gotten a good look at his face yet, have you?"

I shook my head. "A lad, twelve or so, dark brown hair, quick on his feet."

Goodwin shrugged. "Whoever he watches us for, what can he say? We visited the bank, met with old friends, and now we're walking through the parts of town with shops. In a bit we'll take our noon meal and go back to our lodgings on a different path. I hope he gets blisters."

"*I'd* like to know who paid him to watch us," I muttered, stopping to look at a shopkeeper's tray of brooches. A glance to the side showed me no watcher.

"Whoever it is will be dead bored by the time his day's report is done. Sometimes you *want* to be followed, Cooper," Goodwin told me. At the next stall she picked up a length of bright yellow cloth and held it up to her cheek. "What do you think?"

I winced and kept walking.

We were four blocks past Gerjuoy again when two coves and a mot stepped out in front of us. They wore leather jerkins and were armed with long knives and a trove of hidden daggers. I knew the blades were there by the print the hilts showed against their clothes. Stupid tarses. I sew stones in the hems of my tunics so they hang away from my hidden weapons, and I use flat hilts.

Goodwin and I both stopped, hands on our batons.

"Here's a sight to make me eyes go all watery. Two Dogs, as fair as the May, out o' their patch and bein' all careless-like." The talker was the shorter cove, a rusher built like a barrel. "Like they was thinkin' we'd let 'em go any old place."

"But they're *Dogs*." The mot had a voice as rough as a corbie's and the black eyes to match. She wore her black hair cropped so short it showed the scars on her head. She might be a former soldier, since many wore their hair cut so. I hope she was ashamed, going from the King's service to being a Rat. "They allus go wherever they want." She sneered as she said it.

"Stow yer wind, you two," ordered the third of them, a bony cove like a skeleton. He had cold, dead gray eyes that gave me the shudders. If my eyes are like that, no wonder folk don't like them. "You Dogs. Come along wiv us."

Goodwin eased her feet apart, balancing herself. Behind me I heard the low rumble of Achoo's growl. I was already balanced, my baton gripped in both hands. If these Rats were here to harm us, doing it in Tradesmen's District as the day drew on to noon seemed like idiot work.

"I don't like the tone of your invitation," Goodwin replied. "And my old mother told me never to go along with strangers."

Achoo turned. Her growl got louder. I risked a look around. Three more rushers, all coves, came up from behind. I swung to face them, setting my back to Goodwin's. Achoo stood just off my left hand, head down and hackles up. For a dog of middling size, she looked dangerous.

"Guardswomen, please, let's not have this fuss and bother." A doxie past her prime came forward. Her face was painted white. Her eyes were lined with black paint and shaded with blue. Her dress was a shrieking shade of green, her hair a dyed red that nearabout blazed. "I beg pardon for my rough friends. I got a rock in my shoe and they came ahead of me. They never thought I might be wanting to use my silken gloves, and not the leather ones." She patted the arm of the rusher who stood in front of me. "Never you mind their rudeness. The truth is, I come from Her Majesty Pearl Skinner." She looked at us and cocked her head to one side in a way that was mayhap winning, ten or twenty years ago. "Pearl Skinner? The Rogue of Port Caynn?"

Goodwin shifted slightly so she might keep an eye on the mot's face. "And why should this make us any more eager to go along with you?" she asked.

The doxie smiled. "Because you want to know what our

Rogue might have to say to a pair of visiting Dogs. She gives you her word, in the name of the Great Mother Goddess, that you will be safe."

Goodwin looked at me. I looked at her. We shrugged at the same time and put our batons away. We could have fought. Sooner or later the local Dogs would have come and put a stop to it. These rushers might have gone to the cages for a short while before the Rogue got them out again. We'd go about our business, until we got trapped in an alley or picked off one by one, to get beaten or killed quietly someplace with no witnesses.

"Achoo, *tumit,*" I said.

"Lovely creature," the doxie said. She meant it not at all. "Follow me."

I glanced back as they led us down an alley off the main street. I saw the flick of a brown tunic as our watcher twitched out of sight. He was still on our track, then, and he didn't belong to the Rogue of Port Caynn.

We turned down a smaller street, then into another alley. Halfway along, once the rushers made sure no one was close enough to see, we took a set of steps down into the cellar of what looked like an abandoned house. Achoo whimpered.

"Hush," I told her. Achoo looked at me with sorrow, as if to say, "You *like* entering strange, dark places?"

"Here's the tricky part for you, but you've still got Her Majesty's word," the doxie told Goodwin and me. Two of the rushers were taking torches from a pile inside the cellar door. "You have to take the blindfold."

I clenched my fists.

"Do it. How often do you get to meet the Rogue of Port Caynn?" Goodwin asked. She let them slip a dark scarf over her eyes. "Don't touch the hound, you lot. She'll have your throat out."

"Achoo, *gampang*," I said, bending to grip Achoo's collar. I kept my eyes down, not wanting to see Rats hood Goodwin like the nobles do their hawks. That's how I saw the movement of her hand as she gripped her belt. I'd forgotten the blade she kept there, disguised as part of the buckle.

I ground my teeth as they blindfolded me. In my trunk at Serenity's are my arm guards, which are reinforced on the outside with thin strips of metal. Those strips are in truth knives. I'd not worn my arm guards today, thinking we were out on easy errands. The problem with forgetting my training lessons is that one of these days the penalty will be fatal. As it was, all I had now were my back of neck and back of belt knives and my boot knives, all tricky to reach without drawing attention.

A rusher led me by one arm. I heard Achoo trotting at my other side. From the sounds, I could tell we'd entered a tunnel. Then we passed into a second tunnel, and into a huge, echoing chamber filled with the sound of rushing water. It stank like a sewer, though not as bad as some. This one must have gotten flushed out regular by the sea. I could smell salt water as well as scummer.

Then we climbed a set of stairs, crossed a small room, and climbed yet more stairs. At the top of that second stair, our blindfolds were stripped from us. As we blinked in the torchlight, the doxie put her hand on the door latch. "I'll announce you," she said. "Mind that hound. Her Majesty likes well-behaved creatures." She went into the next room.

"And I like Rats to leave me be," Goodwin said, pulling away from the cove and the mot who gripped her wrists.

The skinny cove, the shivery one, raised his hand. "Shut yer gob and mind yer manners, hedgecreeper," he told her.

In a flash she had her knife at his eyes. She had her other hand dug firm into his gems. His knees buckled. His face turned red in the dim light. I swung in behind her, my baton out. I thrust it into the gullet of the mot who was about to seize Goodwin. Pressing down on her windpipe, I backed the mot up to the wall and held her there.

"Achoo, *lindengi*," I said. My hound was already on Goodwin's other side, hackles up, lips skinned back. The other four rushers looked at us and held their hands up, palms out. It's amazing how scared folk are of a hound when she shows her teeth.

"I'll mind what manners I choose to mind, toad scummer, and you'll tell me 'please' and 'thank you' for them," Goodwin said to the bony cove. "What kind of Dogs do you kennel here, that you pieces of nose sweet think you can drag me and my partner all over the streets?"

"Rogue's orders, Guardswoman," the barrel-built rusher said, his voice very soft. "You know how life is. Bring 'em fast, she told us."

One of the others added, " 'A course, some of us allus got to add a bit o' sauce t' the job." He nodded to the skinny rusher who was still in Goodwin's grip.

The doxie opened the door again. She went still when she saw how things had changed since she'd left. At last she said, "Getting to know each other? It's lovely, but I'm sure Her Majesty don't mean to keep you here that long. If you'll come with me, she will see you."

Goodwin lingered, still looking at the bony cove. She sheathed her knife first, then released his gems. She wiped her fingers on her hip. "Come at me again, laddybuck, and I'll leave a hole big enough you can wear a bangle in them, understand me?"

I holstered my baton. "Achoo, good girl. *Tumit*." Following the doxie, Goodwin and I left the room. The rushers who were close to the door stood aside.

The room inside might have been part of a countinghouse or a warehouse once. It had been made nice, with benches, chairs, and tables. There was a bar against the far wall. Folk there waited in line for the tapster to fill their tankards. The place was lamp lit. I saw no windows. The door to what might be a kitchen was beside the bar. A second door, likely to lead to the privies, was in the same wall. Folk kept walking in through it adjusting their belts. A third door to my left was guarded by a couple of good-sized rushers. Next was the door we'd come through, and then a door was next to the hearth in that same wall. Two staircases led upward. There were plenty of holes these Rats could use to escape.

The folk that stood or sat closest to the hearth, about ten feet from Goodwin and me, were them that had the power here. There was a large open space around them, for one. For another, two guards with crossbows stood on either side of the hearth. Another stood at the back of the woman who sat in a rich, heavily cushioned chair placed beside the small fire.

I deliberately looked past her, because I knew the moment I saw her she was Pearl Skinner and she was going to be granite to the marrow. I'll say she is forty-five or forty-six, lean and fit. She would have to be, to still be alive and Rogue in Port Caynn. Her hair is like straw, yellow and brittle. I'd wager she killed whoever sold her the dye for it. Her eyes are large, dark, and quick, her nose long and straight. Her upper lip is near invisible, the lower lip full. She's got strong cheekbones. She dresses like a hillwoman, with a sleeveless overrobe covered with embroideries. Her dress was a rich blue silk, slit high up both sides. I could see black leggings through one slit, and black boots with dagger hilts all about the rims. Two hilts thrust from her sash, and I saw the prints of three dagger hilts along one of her sleeves. She wore dangling earrings but no necklaces, nothing an enemy could use to choke her. She did have a lot of rings for a knife fighter.

Beside her sat an older, white-skinned cove armed with a longsword. He wore his brown hair cropped two inches short. There were silver strands in his neat beard. On the mot's other side a younger Bazhir warrior sat. His long black hair was combed straight back and tied in a horsetail. At his waist he wore a slightly curved longsword.

The doxie walked up to the dais and stood next to Pearl, like a lady-in-waiting. "The two Dogs you wanted," she said, like we were a load of wheat she was delivering. The room went quiet.

Pearl tapped her fingers on the arm of her fancy chair. "Speak up," she said in a voice that brought Achoo's hackles up again. "Who by plague are you two? Ye're not Caynn Dogs. You come swaggerin' into *my* city, pokin' yer fambles in my banks, interferin' with *my* people a-doin' their jobs—"

Movement to my right caught my attention. Over by the bar the gixie pickpocket I'd caught earlier was ducking out of sight.

"Ye'll look at *me,* young mistress!" Pearl barked. I looked at her, keeping my temper gripped tight. Pearl leaned forward. "Yes, you interfered in *that* bit o' my interest, and ye'll tell me why! How do I even know ye're Dogs? Any cracknob can stitch up a uniform." She grinned at us, showing teeth. The fool trull had paid to have some of them mage-changed to pearls. Even though they'd doubtless break sooner or later, she had teeth in her head made of real pearls next to others that were gray and dying. I've never seen such a waste in all my days!

"They be true Dogs, Majesty, right enough," a man called from the back of the room. He got up and came toward us with the kind of solid gait that told a knowing eye he could walk all day at need. I remembered him—it was Steen, the cove who'd known so much about riot fountains and freezing spells. He looked just as I remembered him, dark-haired and dark-eyed, built like a badger with a wide head, wide shoulders, and thick arms. He's got a very thin beard that forms a circle around his mouth and chin, and he wears his hair close-cropped like the mot who'd helped to bring us here. His nose was broad and slumped, as if someone had hit it. "From the Lower City in Corus. Guardswoman Cooper, might you be rememberin' me—ah, I see that you do. Corporal Guardswoman Goodwin, good day. Steen Bolter. We met in th' riot."

Goodwin pointed to his beard. "I thought that thing was a mustache."

He chuckled and smoothed his thumb and forefinger over his beard. "Eh, some days it is, some it's longer. Hanse says I can't decide whether t' grow it nor give it a decent funeral." He looked at Pearl again. "They was hip deep in the Bread Riot I told yez about, Majesty. Hanse says it's a pleasure t' see these mots work."

"Hanse knows them?" Pearl asked. She used drinking from a tankard to hide the expression on her face.

"Helped 'em get their partner out first off. He'd broke both legs, poor cove. I'll ask after him at supper," Steen told Goodwin. "Hanse said we'll meet up. If Her Majesty's done wiv ye, a' course." He nodded at Pearl.

"What makes ye think I'll be *done* with these two?" she snapped, slamming her tankard down on a small table at her side. "*That* one"—she pointed at me—"snagged one o' my gixies at her work this mornin'! I know what you two bitches are doin', sniffin' about my turf."

Both me and Goodwin stiffened at that. Every Dog has insults thrown at her head, but none of us mots like to be called a bitch. Rogue or no, Pearl was trusting her luck to a bridge made of straws.

"You don't care for that, do ye, *bitches*?" Pearl asked. "But ye'll take it from me. Think I don't know how cuddlesome ye are with Rosto the Piper? Ye're here diggin' for Corus's own Rogue, *Rebakah Cooper,* lookin' for breaks in my shields!"

Goodwin looked at her nails and sighed. "We are here on assignment to the Deputy Lord Provost," she said patiently. "Our Rogue doesn't give us orders, any more than you do. We're not looking for a fight with you, though if one is requested, we might ask our hosts what the Port rules are about such things."

A scared-looking maid bustled over with a fresh tankard. She handed it to Pearl, who took a big swallow, then wiped her mouth on the back of her wrist. When she spoke, she *sounded* calmer. "Ye don't spook easy, do ye? I've had grown men wet themselves when I screeched like that."

"I'm not surprised," Goodwin replied.

Pearl gave her a thin smile. "I see ye're not, nor the quiet one, there. Does she talk?"

"When it matters," Goodwin said.

Pearl set her tankard aside and leaned forward, her hands on her knees. "It matters now, and don't ye mistake me," she warned Goodwin. "Cooper here got in the way of my business this mornin', and I'll know why."

Goodwin looked at me, wanting me to speak up.

I said, "The gixie was breaking the law. She stole a purse, and I caught her. I returned it to her coney, but she had a rusher guarding her back. She escaped me." I wasn't going to say I'd noticed the purse I returned was full of coles, nor that it was not the one that got stolen. It seemed like a very bad time to bring those things up.

"We do our work, Mistress Pearl, just as you do yours," Goodwin said.

Pearl rubbed a pearl tooth with one finger. "Clear off, Steen."

Steen tipped his hand to Goodwin and me. "See you over supper, I hope." He ambled off to where he'd sat before.

Then Pearl said, quiet-like, "How much would it cost me to make you two forget your orders, where it comes to interferin' with my business?" She was a brass-bottomed trollop, thinking she could buy us where the Rogue before Rosto and Rosto himself had failed!

Achoo caught my mood and growled. I leaned forward, about to spit on the floor, when Goodwin placed her hand on my arm.

"Cooper, manners," she said quietly, and gave my arm a little squeeze. She looked at Pearl. "These young folk are hotheaded. Of course we have to say no." Goodwin sighed. "We just got here, after all. How much trouble can two lone . . ." Her mouth twisted. Then she went on, "How much trouble can two lone bitches, off their hunting grounds, give? Doubtless this morning was only a fluke. You'll hardly know we were here." She let go of my arm and patted it. "Of course, if we did turn out to be trouble, you might want to offer higher than you were about to."

Pearl stared Goodwin in the eye for a long moment.

I hate playing the part of a loose Dog.

"Was I you, I'd stay blind to any Rogue doin's you might trip over, both of ye," Pearl said, her voice low. "Ask Nestor Haryse what I do to them that cross me. Ask 'im—" Suddenly she stopped. The Bazhir and the longsword man got to their feet, drawing their blades. "What's that racket?" Pearl demanded.

The guards moved up to stand at Pearl's back, their own

weapons ready. Everyone in the room with a weapon had it out as the door opposite the bar flew open. We could hear shouting as Nestor and five other Dogs poured into the room.

"We don't want trouble, Pearl," Nestor said, his voice booming above the noise. "But we'll trouble *you* to hand our friends back to us." He looked at Goodwin and me, then at the knot of guards that circled the Rogue. "Naughty, to go helping yourself to my people."

Pearl got to her feet and shoved her guards aside. "Cooper interfered in my business, and *my* folk had no way of knowin' who she was," she snapped. "I wasn't told two strange bitches would be crawlin' over my city, pokin' their noses where they pleased."

"No need to be harsh, Majesty," Nestor said, a touch of disappointment in his voice. "Is this how we want visitors to the city to see us, all crude and nasty-like? Doubtless you know by now that Corporal Guardswoman Goodwin and Guards-woman Cooper are here to study our methods. They'll be going freely about the city, with Sir Lionel's permission. And now that you know they're here, and I'm watching over them, there's no need to pop them off the street like this." His face went hard and dangerous in a way I'd never seen before. "In fact, if you think you've a Dog problem, in future? You'd do well to call Dogs to handle it."

Pearl's jaw clenched. "You get above yourself, *Sergeant.*"

"I remember how things are done," he replied. "It's *you* who seems to have forgot."

I held my breath. Achoo was pressed against my leg, her muscles tight. I don't think anyone in that room dared to breathe until Pearl waved at Goodwin and me and snapped, "Take them out of here."

We walked to the open door and into a long hall, three of

Nestor's folk in front of us, two more and Nestor behind. We passed through a second, smaller room where more Rats sat or stood, watching us. I whistled under my breath. Nestor had a sack, to walk in here with less than a full company of Dogs.

We passed through a final pair of open doors into the street. I was startled to find the sun had just reached the noon mark. Goodwin looked around, getting her bearings, same as I did.

"Eagle Street," one of the other Dogs said, guessing what she was about. "Three blocks into Lowdown below Money-changers' Street. Pearl don't hold court here all the time, though. Some days she's up in Gauntlet, some days Riverdocks, some days here."

"Not very trustin', Pearlie," a mot with Senior Dog insignia said with a laugh.

"No more should she be," one of the coves muttered. "Were she a cat, she'd have but two lives left. Folk've been tryin' t' kill Pearl Skinner since she was born."

Looking around, I saw a lad in a brown tunic and leather sandals standing at the corner. The boy was eleven or twelve, with brown hair and dark eyes. His face was naught to remember if you only caught a glimpse of it. Seeing our tracker full on like this, I recognized Nestor's serving lad Haden easily. I nudged Goodwin.

She looked where I did. "Did you put your boy on our trail?" she asked Nestor.

Nestor waved Haden over. He trotted up to us. "Did you think I'd let you amble off with no way to call for help?" Nestor asked, raising his eyebrows. "How did you know you were tracked? No one ever spots Haden."

The boy shrugged. "They did. They knew I was about afore they got t' th' docks," he said. "It hurt me pride, but they didn't fuss, so I stayed wif 'em. Figgered you'd beat me if I didn't, sir." He actually winked at me, the scamp.

Nestor looked at the Dogs who had come with him. "I think we're good. See you at muster out."

"Nice meetin' you two," one of them said. "Watch your backs." The other Dogs murmured their goodbyes and walked down the street, scanning already for Rats.

I glanced at Nestor, and at Haden. I am beginning to wonder who runs Nestor's house, him, or Haden and his sister.

"I suggest that Haden keeps trailing you," Nestor told us. "I hope Pearl leaves you be, but hope is like spring snow around her. It melts fast. Better to have Haden watch your back."

"At the least we owe Haden a meal," Goodwin replied. "And I was going to show Cooper around Flowerbed before we went back to the lodging."

Nestor smiled. "A busy first day. Will you take supper with us again?"

"We have a supper engagement at the Merman's Cave," Goodwin told him. "We ran into an acquaintance from Corus who invited us there."

Nestor whistled. "Interesting acquaintance. See to your afternoon, then. Will you have reports for me?"

Goodwin nodded. "Send someone tricky to pick them up?" she asked. "About five of the clock?"

"Me sister Truda can do it," Haden told us cheerfully. "She's a mouse, that 'un. Ye'll never see her comin' nor goin'."

"It'll always be Haden or Truda making the daily pickup at that time," Nestor said. "They have friends I trust who watch their backs." He saw my questioning look and grinned. "I got the idea from you and Gershom. Who better to work for you in the streets than the lads and gixies who are born there?" With that settled, Nestor took out his baton and wandered off, swinging it in an elaborate pattern at his side. I watched with envy. I've mastered some of the easier twirling patterns, but not the ones like Nestor was doing now. That's old Dog work.

I noticed a swirl of wind and leaves at the corner opposite. "A moment," I told Goodwin. Achoo and I wove our way through carts and walkers to get to that corner, where a spinner rose five feet high, made strong by the wind coming off the harbor. I took off my pack and rummaged in the pocket where I kept my dust packets. Sure enough, I had a few. I took out one and closed the pack, then set that in front of Achoo. "*Jaga,* please?" I asked her.

Achoo gave her soft whuff and moved until she stood over the pack.

"Good girl," I told her as I cut the stitches that held the cloth on my dust packet. When it was open, I stepped into the spinner's heart and gave it my offering.

The spinner went wide, then tall and tight around me. It had never met anyone like me before. It—no, *he,* Hesserrr—had to run dusty finger strands over my hair, into the layers of my clothes, and over my face. When he learned what I could do for him, besides provide tasty gifts of new dust and gravel, he quickly gave up his burden of human talk. I caught five- and six-word pieces that sounded like talk over cargo or rigging, sea talk borne in on the stiff breeze from the harbor. There were other pieces, too, about burglings, foistings, hard work done on cityfolk for some reason, and this.

"—die o' fright, did Sir Lionel know she's got folk servin' him." The coarse, pleased voice belonged to a mot. She must have stood right next to Hesserrr for him to pick up so much.

"How'd she *manage* it?" Another mot, younger-sounding.

"All Dogs got a price, my pet. This 'un along with the rest. Let's go git us some peck and cass."

That was the end of it, and the last bit Hesserrr had for me. I thanked him silently, as I always did, and stepped out. Achoo whuffed at me, as if she asked, "Did it go well?"

I bent down for my pack. "I've got one good bit. There's luck for us, eh, Achoo?" I shouldered my pack and started to brush the dust from my hair.

I'd finished that and gone on to my tunic when Goodwin and Haden tired of waiting and came over to join us. Haden tugged my sleeve. "Some'un offered t' feed a hardworkin' lad?" he asked, all pitiful eyes and innocent face.

Goodwin grabbed his ear between thumb and finger and dragged him down the street. "Nestor's saddled us with a pitiful scamp, Cooper. Tell us where to find a decent meal without getting our pockets picked, boy, and I *may* feed you."

When Haden told Goodwin that he could take us to a place that served Yamani buckwheat noodles, she almost adopted him. I'd never heard of noodles, but Goodwin got a taste for the things when she'd lived in Port Caynn before. They turned out to be long strings made of buckwheat flour dough, boiled until they were the same texture as dumplings. They were served in a broth with a poached egg. There was a trick to the dish. They were eaten with a pair of thin wooden sticks. Goodwin and Haden swore the Yamanis eat their food with these two sticks, and that even the youngest Yamani children use the curst things. Goodwin fumbled hers at first, being out of practice. Haden shoveled the slippery, tricksy noodle things into his mouth as fast as his hand could move. He didn't even let any of the egg drip to the ground. Once Goodwin remembered how to use the sticks, she was almost as nimble.

Me, I shared most of the dish with Achoo, who ate what I spilled. Luckily my reflexes are good, or I'd have worn it all. What I actually got to taste of the stuff was good. Not as strong as ground buckwheat, but well flavored, and the broth had a tang to it. I got a bit more of that, because I could upend the bowl into my mouth.

Haden led us then to a stall where they boiled the seagoing insects called shrimp, or grilled them on a stick. The cove who cut their hard shells away did it so fast I couldn't follow the moves of his knife. I could only hope I'd never find him in an alley some night. I liked the grilled ones with a spicy sauce so much that I had three skewers. Then I had to buy a skewer for Achoo. I didn't feel so greedy when Goodwin bought herself and Haden each four skewers. Next came a vendor of boiled seaweed. I didn't like that at all. I didn't notice, until after I'd spat my mouthful out, that Haden hadn't bought any. He was laughing himself silly over the look on my face, whilst Goodwin wolfed her bowlful. By the time we found a sweet-roll vendor Haden liked, we were well into the Flowerbed gambling center, and anyone who had passed us for at least two blocks was certain that if we were on duty, we were the laziest Dogs they'd ever seen, interested only in filling our bellies and gawping at the sights.

After lunch we finished our tour of Flowerbed. Haden pointed out the best bordels and taverns, and which meeting-houses were favored by the gamesters who gambled high.

"They follow the good cooks and the entertainers they think are lucky," he explained as we headed back toward our lodgings. "Gods help you if they decide you're unlucky—no one will hire you! Plenty of folk gamble here. They get in from sea voyages, they get paid, and they have coin in hand. Or the land caravans come in, and it's the same thing."

I looked at him. "Do you gamble?"

Haden laughed. "Me? I'm not so bored with coin in me hand that I'll throw it after dice or a horse. My da'd haunt me to my grave, sure he would."

I looked at him. Now he made sense. "Nestor said you're a street lad?"

"Aye." Haden shrugged. "Truda, too. Then Nestor caught me stealin'. Truda came at him with a knife, and her no bigger than a scrap. He said he figgered he oughta keep hold of us afore we kilt some'un. It were a struggle."

Goodwin smiled. "So you'll train as a Dog when you're of age, like Cooper?"

"*Dog* trainin'!" Haden snorted. "No, I study the music and fightin'. Okha's teachin' me those. Truda's learnin' to do hair and face paint for the lady-coves, and the fightin', too, from Okha."

I couldn't help it. I started to laugh at the look on Goodwin's face. She was used to poor children coming into the Dogs. The idea of Haden preferring to work for entertainers was not what she expected.

"It seems like a waste of a good tracker, that's all," Goodwin said.

Haden shrugged. "Nestor's put me to use plenty, and he'll do it even more afore I'm good enough with pipes and drums t' please Okha. Now, see, here's a good street to know, Trinket Alley. You'd think with the name it's cheap stuff, but it's not." So he kept Goodwin from trying to convert him to Dog work, by showing her where the scales of the port did business on Trinket Alley and other streets near the docks.

The city clocks were chiming one as we reached Serenity's. I hoped for a nap, but Goodwin said that we must write our reports. Gods be thanked she wrote the one on our suspicions that the Goldsmith's Bank knows there is a problem with silver coles. She called on me only for my exact report of my talk with the clerk who changed my gold coin, writing it down as I remembered it. She had me write up the pickpockets' switch of good purses for red ones filled with coles. I wrote of my morning for my Lord Provost back in Corus, including a separate copy of our encounter with Pearl. Then Goodwin made copies of the bank report and the pickpockets' switch. Once everything was done, she sent me to my room to rest before supper, reminding me that only five days past, I'd had my head broken. Instead I began to write today's events in cipher in this journal.

Slapper came back from his ramblings with five lady pigeons. Two carried ghosts. I listened to them and took notes of their complaints, though I did not know the three names they mentioned. I will put them into the reports that went to Nestor. Mayhap he will recognize the names. Once that was done, I returned to writing in my journal. It was when I wrote of our meeting with Hanse and his introducing himself to us that his name snapped into place for me. Hanse Remy. Otho Urtiz, the Player with the crazed slave, had told me that name scarce a week ago. I banged on Goodwin's door.

She opened it, looking grumpy. "Cooper—"

"Hanse *Remy*. The Player Otho Urtiz told me he won a lot of coles from a cove who'd come down the river named *Hanse Remy*," I told her. "They bet on a horse race."

Goodwin rubbed her nose. "Pox. Pox, pox, and swive-all luck. No, we did know Hanse might be involved somehow, if only because he gambles. He could know something, he could know naught." She sighed. "I'll add it to the report. To my lord, not Sir Lionel."

I scratched my nose. I wasn't sure I trusted Sir Lionel to handle things right, not when he was the one who let Pearl snatch Dogs off the street.

"Oh, and that dust spinner?" I said. "It gave me sommat useful. Pearl's got Dogs she has bought in Sir Lionel's service, waiting on him personally."

Goodwin nodded. "That stands to reason, Cooper. Rosto's probably got his own folk in Lord Gershom's house."

I ground my teeth. This is a boil on my bum. I know who two of them are, but my lord won't hobble them. He says it's better to know who the spies are than to suspect all his household. I don't see Lionel of Trebond being so forgiving, if he even knows who Pearl has set to spy on him.

"I'm glad you're able to tap your Birdies here," Goodwin said. "We need sources that are dependent on no one else, even if they're limited. Now, get some rest. I've a feeling we have a late night ahead."

Ten of the morning.

I should have written about last night when I came in, but I could not stay awake. I was not drunk, for I drank little, compared to my companions. Not that I could have known that Goodwin was drinking, had I not seen her raise and lower tankard or cup to her lips. Where does she put it all, a magic pocket?

No mind. I've yet to get my sleeping hours straight. I just woke, and must set this journal to rights before embarking on the day.

Truda came for the reports yestereve when the clock struck five, as Nestor promised. I watched the gixie trot off through the backyard of the lodging house, worried. If she was watched, or we were, she could have a hard journey home. Then Haden emerged from the bushes with two lads and a lass dressed just as Truda was. They closed around her and took the bridge over the stream away from the house. I smiled and went back inside.

Then I had to dress. It was possible Dale might join us, which made me edgy-like. I had but two dresses for walking out, plus a third for every day, so I had no reason to dither all night over clothes. I chose the blue dress with ivory, yellow, and pink embroideries. The sleeves are wider than fashionable, but they have to be. I strap flat knives to the inside and outside of my forearms, and I need to be able to reach them in a hurry. There are slits in the skirt's seams so I may get at the flat daggers that hang from the sash around my underdress. The outer dress tied with a yellow cord that matched my embroideries. That had weights at each end so I could use it as a weapon at need. I hung my purse and my eating knife from that. My leg knives were belted firmly around my calves.

I wear no earrings, since an enemy can rip them from my flesh. I do own a couple of necklaces of beads. They too can be turned against me, but I must have sommat pretty, and they are so cheap a good tug will break them. One of them was made of yellow glass beads, the color of my sash. I put that on. My hair I wrapped in a braided coil around my head, fixing it in place with my mother's ivory combs. They'd been her only nice things. Finally I put on a wrapped blue cape, using a fold to veil my hair like a proper mot. I pinned it on one shoulder with a brooch in the shape of a flying heron. That I'd bought myself, because I like herons, with my first wages as a full-fledged Dog.

"What do you think, Achoo?" I asked her.

Achoo put her head on her paws and sighed.

"I'm sorry," I told her. "I cannot take you where I'm going. It wouldn't look right, and you'd be bored." I gathered the rope I used to tie her up in the yard at home. *"Tumit."* I opened the door, but Achoo had not gotten to her feet. "Achoo, I begged the cook for some nice chopped meat for you. You knew when you joined the Provost's Guard that duty isn't always easy. Now *tumit!*"

Achoo rose with a groan, as if she were a crone instead of a mot of only two years. Down the stairs behind me she went, grumbling in her throat. She looked so pitiful that the cook insisted on adding a gravy to the bowl of chopped meat, which brought a slow tail wag from my shameless hound. I tied her in the yard and made certain she had a nice, deep bowl of water as well.

"Sergeant Ahuda would be ashamed to see one of her Dogs acting like a mumper," I whispered.

Achoo only sniffed and poked the meat with her nose, as if

she might find the strength to taste it. I looked back at her as I entered the kitchen. She was devouring her meat and gravy, her tail happily a-wag. "Mumper," I called, and went inside.

Goodwin raised her eyebrows at me when I met her in the sitting room downstairs. She wore a dress much like mine in a kind of coppery wool, with a darker brown cape. It was pinned with a crescent moon at the shoulder. She wore a small round hat, brown with copper embroideries, instead of a veil, fixed in place with bright beaded pins.

"Not bad, Cooper. I always say you clean up well. Are the animals safe for the night?" she asked me.

"Achoo's out back, and Slapper is asleep on the roof," I told her.

"Poor creatures," Goodwin said. "They don't know what they miss."

I was trembling a bit. I've never gone to a place where I was expected to be friendly with folk I barely know. "I wouldn't mind missing it," I muttered.

"You're so much bolder in uniform, I forget what a mouse you can be," Goodwin said as we went outside. A sedan chair waited for us. Goodwin had asked a housemaid to summon one for this hour. We climbed in, me trying not to step on my hem. My sister Lorine would kill me if I ruined her sewing.

"Pay attention," Goodwin told me as the chair lurched up and forward. "At least one of those coves will be there to see *you,* and that one the best-looking of the lot—though Hanse might be fun as well." She voiced an evil chuckle that shocked me. "Enough, Cooper, I didn't stop living when I married. I can *look.* They took to you during that riot, and you're going to be friendly if I have to shove you all the way. Pretend to be the person who wears that dress. I know you've been with men before. Surely they knew you liked them *somehow.*"

"It's easier during the festivals," I replied. "And the first one I knew from my lord's house."

"Well, now you'll learn how other mots do it when they haven't grown up with the cove and there isn't a festival." Goodwin sighed. "Goddess, I wish Tom was here. They say this Merman's Cave has good mussels, and my Tom does love his seafood."

"Couldn't he have come?" I asked. "He would've been good cover, you and him visiting the port, seeing the sights, gambling a bit, buying things for your house."

"No," Goodwin replied. "He's his own work to do. Let's not talk about work, though." She drew back the curtain on her side and pointed forward and back, to the men who carried the chair. I winced. I'd forgotten we had ears on us, coves who might pass on anything we said.

"Sorry. I'm all rattled from the day, I expect," I explained. "I'm not used to getting picked up and dragged before strange Rogues."

"She's harsh, isn't she?" Goodwin's voice was admiring. "You'd best mind your manners around her. She's no Rosto you can flirt with."

"I don't flirt with Rosto!" I said, knowing I could be heard. I giggled, settling into the dress and the necklace and the cape. Suddenly I wished I had some scent to make me feel like even more of a mot out for a good night. All this fuss over clothes and such, it could serve me like my uniform, as a different face from plain old Beka Cooper.

Now that I remember it, I'll pick up scent when I have a chance. Mayhap a blackener for my brows and lashes, and a bit of red for my lips. Or not. It's a careful balance, how much is too much. Okha might advise me. He uses far more face paint than Goodwin.

The Merman's Cave turned out not to be in the Flowerbed, but just a few blocks past Gerjuoy and three blocks up from the docks. There was a deep porch all the way around the front of the place, and windows with only one of a pair of shutters ajar. During the warm summer months they must set tables out and open all the shutters to keep the place cool. The night was cold for September, though. The fog had swamped the street, shaping the torches into globes of fire.

Goodwin paid off the chair men. I followed her through the double doors carved in the shapes of long-vanished merfolk. Once inside we saw a small room set off to the left. Two good-sized rushers who stood on either side of the entrance looked us over, then turned their gaze to the cove who entered behind us.

"The sword and the dagger, sir," one of them said. "Leave 'em here, if ye'll be so good. And whatever's hidden that might make for an unpleasant night for others of our guests."

Goodwin and I raised our brows at each other. Seemingly we looked too respectable to be asked to give up our weapons. We moved on into the eating house proper.

The noise swamped us. The smoke that floated along the ceiling made our eyes sting. It came from the fire in the great hearth where kettles full of wines and ales heated. Sweating mots wearing thin dresses and aprons filled pitchers from the kettles and handed them over to serving folk, then refilled the kettles to heat a new batch of drinks. I could smell spices, ale, wine, roasting meat, and hints of puke and piss. The tables around the huge main room were crowded with mots and coves drinking, eating, talking, and laughing. A cove walked past me carrying an eel pie. It smelled so good my mouth began to water.

"There they are!" Only Hanse could roar like that. He

beckoned to us from across the room. As if they were a wave rolling back from the land, those in our way moved off. Goodwin and I walked through like proper mots, holding our skirts above the floor and watching where we stepped. Though I have to say, the rushes were fresh, and as yet there were no nasty messes to avoid.

Hanse had changed clothes for the night. He wore a dark blue tunic with red and gray embroideries, very handsome, with white embroidered bands down both sides of the front. He even wore a short gray cape clasped with a twisted gold ring brooch at the shoulder. This was a man who didn't care if folk grabbed for his jewelry in a fight. He wore gold earrings and a broad copper wristband. There was a short knife and an empty loop hanging from his gray sash. They had taken his sword.

Steen sat with him, in the same tunic he'd worn at the Court of the Rogue. He had added two silver earrings in his left ear, though, and a handsome gray pearl in the right.

"Aren't you lookin' fine," Hanse greeted us. The coves helped us to seats inside their booth. "We feared mayhap you'd be thinkin' the better of joinin' us, after runnin' afoul of Queen Pearl."

Goodwin laughed in a coarse, brassy way as Hanse slid onto the bench next to her. "We won't say we weren't a bit twitched, will we, Cooper?"

I shook my head, since she wanted me to. Steen took the place next to me.

"Truth to tell, Pearl needn't have bothered," Goodwin went on. Now she was playing the part of the loose Dog for all she was worth. She sounded like other mot Dogs her age, bawdy and loud, not the daughter of respectable tradesmen. "Oh, Cooper here forgot her orders this morning. She's supposed to be resting while we're in town. We'll not meddle in Rogue business, not away from Corus. Never intended to. I put a word in Cooper's ear. She'll mind me now."

I looked down at my hands as if I were Achoo and I'd been scolded for sneaking food off the table. I was pretty good at guessing Goodwin's cues.

"You be talkin' riddles," Steen told Goodwin. He waved to a barmaid and signaled for drinks. "Ale's all right with you?"

"I'm happy with it, but don't expect Cooper to drink much. She's got some little bit of bird magic that makes her sick if she overdoes."

"Some mages is like that," Hanse said with a nod. "Others you could pour a trough full of mead and they'd drink it, then turn the trough into a horse and ride it away."

"Two pitchers of ale, and what manner of twilseys and waters have you?" Steen asked the mot.

She looked at him as if he'd turned into a winged horse, but said, "Raspberry and apple cider twilsey, and coriander water, sir."

"I'll have the apple cider twilsey," I said quietly. I would thank Goodwin later for making sure I'd do little drinking.

Hanse turned back to Goodwin as the serving maid left us. "You said you won't interfere in Rogue's business here? But what else is a Dog to do?"

Goodwin scowled. "Do her interfering at home, where she may make a profit at it, by Mithros!" She smacked the table. "My lord wants Beka away from some nasty Rats, with me to watch her, so off we go to Port Caynn to see how your Dogs work. That means we're assigned to *no* watch, with no share of a Happy Bag or the normal coin we'd get for doing good service. That's two-thirds of our income gone, by all the gods! No, I'll not stick my neck out getting up your Rogue's nose for one-third pay. No more is Cooper. We'll keep our skins in one piece and enjoy our holiday."

"Then you've run into the right fellows for that, haven't they, lads?" Dale Rowan had come up while Goodwin was talking. I near jumped when he spoke, then smiled up at him. He looked even better than he had on the boat, decked out in a blue wool tunic that brightened his gray eyes. His blue cape was fixed at the shoulder with a gold owl. He wore a broad gold hoop in one ear only, and a sparkling blue gem in the other. He grinned at Goodwin and said, "Between the three of us we can give your holiday a good launch, Mistress Goodwin."

"Clary, if you will," she replied. "It's hard to tell how good it will be with the ale not even here."

Luckily, since all three coves turned to yell for the serving maid, she was right there with the tray of ale and twilsey. And somehow, in the bustle of the drink service and our ordering food, Steen moved to the outside of the table and Dale sat next to me.

"To new friends met in riots," Hanse toasted when Dale had a tankard. We all laughed and drank to that. When Hanse praised the ale as a proper way to start the night, Goodwin said he was used to watery seaside ale. She, Hanse, and Steen started to compare ales of different towns from up and down the river.

Dale turned to me. "I heard you made Pearl Skinner unhappy today."

I followed Goodwin's lead. "So has all the town, seemingly. It was a mistake," I said tiredly. "I forgot I'm not at home and I'm not supposed to nab folk while I'm here. Why is everyone making a fuss? The gixie escaped."

"*That* surprises me," said Dale. "I don't see many filches getting out of your grip, Beka Cooper." He was leaning closer so I could hear him speak quietly. His breath stirred the hair around my ear.

Suddenly the cloth over my peaches felt over-tight, and I was finding it a little hard to breathe. I dared to meet his eyes for a moment, even though they were closer than a cove's eyes have been to mine in a long time. I forced myself to make a face and look away.

"She *wouldn't* have gotten away, Dale Rowan, if some big rusher hadn't rammed me in the back and sent me facedown in the street," I told him. "Nice work your filches have, if they all have bodyguards."

He ran his finger down the curve of my ear. How is a mot supposed to think? "Mayhap *you* should have the bodyguard."

"Dale," Steen interrupted, "tell Clary what Pearl said when you won that ruby necklace off her!"

Dale grinned at Goodwin, as if he hadn't been halfway down the side of my neck. "Oh, I won't repeat language like that when I'm having a good time," he said. "I did think of having a metal barrel made to wear around myself, to protect anything . . . valuable, though."

There, I thought, sipping my twilsey. He was playing with me, that's all. He's a playful fellow. *Very* playful.

Under the tabletop, I felt his hand brush my free arm.

"What's this?" The newly arrived mot was about twenty-five, all curves in orange silk, with tumbles of black curls and bright black eyes to match. She had a cat's pointed chin and draped herself across Dale's left shoulder and Hanse's right with a cat's boneless grace. "You lads havin' a party without Fair Flory?" Her voice dripped honey for the men, but her eyes darted murder at Goodwin and me. Goodwin simply grinned. I met the doxie's eyes with mine, widening my gaze until she looked away. I had to play Goodwin's shy young partner, but that didn't mean I should take sauce from a double-dimpled port mot.

"Flory, you've no call to ownership, you know that," Hanse said, giving her a slap on the bum that made her squeal and smack him back. "This here is Clary Goodwin—Corporal Guardswoman Clary Goodwin, so you mind your manners— from Corus. And this is Guardswoman Beka Cooper, her partner and strong right arm. *They're* our guests tonight, so unless they say you're welcome, you can shake that pretty round rump of yours elsewhere." To me and Goodwin, Hanse said, "Flory here is mistress of the Port flower sellers and orange girls. Flory knows how to have a good time, don't ye, wench?"

Flory sniffed at him and put both arms around Steen's neck. "I like coves as aren't cruel to me," she said, with a little girl pout.

"I say welcome, Flory," Goodwin said cheerfully. "The more the merrier! I never knew a flower seller who couldn't tell a mot where the best sparkles are sold, and where a cove wouldn't cheat her out of a week's pay for a length of silk!"

Flory laughed as she settled on Steen's lap. "Oh, if it's shoppin' you want, I can help you there!" she said, waving for a serving girl. "These lads have done me favors enough, and I'll do the same for any friend of theirs. On the sly, though, bein's how you vexed my Rogue this day."

"You're afraid she'll frown on you, being with us?" Goodwin asked.

Fair Flory's smile was thin and cruel. "They's lots of flower sellers and orange girls in Port Caynn, Mistress Clary," she replied. "We don't defy Pearl outright, and she leaves us well alone. There's peace in the Court of the Rogue!"

"We'll all drink to that!" Dale said, hoisting his tankard. The maid passed one to Flory, and we drank.

While I did not lose track of new arrivals, I do not precisely recall the order in which they came or exactly what was said after that. It was all laced with loud talk and joking, Goodwin's flirtations with Hanse, and the arrival of all kinds of food.

The great stew of sea creatures unnerved me, I am sad to say. As the maidservant placed our trenchers before us, I tried to peer into the large soup bowl without anyone noticing.

"What's wrong, Beka?" Steen asked. "Have ye never seen a great net stew afore?"

"No, nor even most of what's in it," I said, prodding a strange orange something with the tip of my belt knife.

"Here," Dale said, grabbing the ladle. He dumped a large serving into my trencher and gave himself another before he passed the ladle to Hanse. Then he speared one of the orange things on the point of his eating knife and offered it to me. The orange stuff wobbled on its own. "Try a mussel. You won't be the same thereafter."

"It's safe enough, lass," Hanse jested as he served Goodwin and himself. "If it were oysters, now, you'd be in trouble!"

I ducked my head. Everyone knows the reputation oysters have for putting folk in the mood for canoodling.

"Just open that pretty mouth," Dale wheedled.

I did, to tell him not to cozen me, and he popped the mussel in. My lady always forbade us to talk with food in our gobs, so I chewed. My mouth filled with sommat that tasted the way the sea smelled. The mussel was tender, with just enough garlic to make me happy.

Dale had popped two mussels into his mouth whilst I managed the one. He'd also managed to slide even closer to me,

249

so our legs pressed tight against each other from hip bone to foot. "Now, see? That was good, wasn't it?" he asked when I swallowed.

I nodded. He had another tidbit on his knifepoint for me. "Ever try skate?" he asked as he brought it to my lips.

He fed me a number of things, including the skate. I did not care for the clams, which were harder to chew than mussels, the too-salty sardines, or the squid, but the different fishes were nice. We had the eel pie that had so tempted me, a roast onion salad, a mixed green tart, and stuffed eggs. Whenever I showed I'd not tried something, he insisted on putting it into my mouth with his eating knife or, in the case of the sweetmeats, with his fingers. I let him do it, enjoying his play.

I have never been courted this way, all flirting, jokes, and quick touches. Rosto half insults me as he tries to tumble me. In matters of wooing, men are confusing. I'm far more comfortable when coves treat me as an ally, or a friend, or a student.

There were thirteen of us by the time we had gotten to the sweetmeats. Dale had teased me into trying his wine, a pale golden sort that was crisp and tingly on my tongue. I sipped it carefully, sensing it was the sort of drink that might knock a mot on her rump were she not careful.

"What do you say, then, Clary, Beka, Flory?" Hanse asked us. "D'you feel like a visit to the Waterlily? There's Gambler's Chance, dicing, music, backgammon, chess." He grinned at Dale, who laughed. "How about it? You can bring us luck, play a game yourselves . . . ?"

Flory rose from Steen's lap, where she'd been sharing his cup. "You'll never have to ask *me* twice!" she said, keeping an arm around Steen's neck as he stood. Most of the others were getting to their feet as well.

Goodwin laughed that unfamiliar laugh and swung her

legs over the bench where she sat. "I never pass a chance to rattle the bones, do I, Cooper?" she asked me. "Cooper's not much for play, but she loves the music and the watching. And maybe some kind soul will teach me this new Gambler's Chance game."

"You don't gamble?" Dale asked me, getting up from his seat.

I looked at him. "I have younger sisters, and our parents are dead," I told him. "Their only dowries come from me." Building dowries for my sisters was hard to fault as an excuse, but it was a lie. Lady Teodorie had already provided for them.

"Then you must bring me luck, and keep me from being sad should my luck turn," Dale told me. With that he wrapped his arms around my waist and lifted me bodily from my seat. I yelped and wriggled, then stopped as he set me down, laughing.

I couldn't help it. I laughed, too, but I gave him a small shove. "I manage on my own, Master Rowan!" I said. Goddess, for a slender man he has muscles like steel!

"I've no doubt, but isn't it agreeable to let someone else do it, now and then?" he asked me, helping me to wrap my cape about my shoulders.

"It is not," I said, adjusting his shoulder cape for him.

"Pretty liar," he teased.

"Saucebox," I retorted.

"Will you two flirt all night, or will ye come oan?" roared Steen from the door. We followed the others to the little room where the coves traded brass tokens for their swords and long daggers. Once they had settled their weapons around their sashes and belts again, the coves and Flory led the way out into the street.

"Dale, what's this Hanse tells me?" Goodwin asked. "Here I've been nattering about learning Gambler's Chance in front of the cove that *invented* the game? I'd take it as a kind-ness if you'd teach me."

"But teaching means I lose the chance to make coin of my own," Dale complained.

Goodwin showed him a gold noble, making it walk through her fingers. "Will this change your mind?"

I'm not sure buying lessons in Gambler's Chance was what my lord meant when he gave us that fat purse, but who am I to question Goodwin? At least in this company word would get about fast that the older Corus Dog was flashing gold. They'd be certain she was crooked. I eased to the outside of the group while Hanse and Dale started talking about the new game, one that was played with numbered cards and portrait ones.

I was happy to look at the crowds. Folk were out for their night's pleasures, and those who lived by shearing them were out, too. When most of the city ends its workday, the part I un-derstand best begins its hours of labor. Twice I heard the cry of, "Thief!" in the distance. I saw a Dog pair breaking up a rob-bery in an alley and felt downright homesick.

Hanse told Goodwin, "There's the Waterlily." I looked up and noted the brightly painted sign just four doors down the street. Then I saw a familiar face in the crowd. It was the scared maidservant from the Court of the Rogue, the one who had served Pearl her drinks. She wound her way into a thick knot of folk watching a lad juggle flaming torches.

I wouldn't get lost, not with the Waterlily so near. I strolled over to the gawpers. The maid had worked her way to the front. She watched the juggler, mouth agape, as he added the fresh torches given to him by his helper. She gasped when he set them to twirling yet still managed to catch each one without burning himself. And when he finished, she picked through her scant handful of coins and set one in the hat that his helper passed around. The juggler smiled at her, and blew her a kiss, even though others had probably given him a bigger tip. The maid covered her blushes with her hands and fled, giggling, while the juggler turned to flirt with another girl.

That little bit of kindness between maid and juggler pulled at my heart. Sometimes I forget there's kindness in the world. I remained for a moment to savor it, like a bit of honey on my tongue.

Then I hurried to the Waterlily, in case anyone had noticed I was missing. I suspected not, given how eagerly they'd been talking about that card game.

Inside the Waterlily all was light and noise. I dropped my cape around my elbows and sought my companions. The rooms here were larger than at the Merman's Cave, with comfortable chairs set for the gamblers and stools for their companions. The folk were well dressed and there were lamps hung over each table for light. Servants wound through the crowd with practiced speed, balancing trays of food and drink. In one large room I saw folk sit down to a meal, unhampered by dice or backgammon or chess boards. Two Players with lutes were singing a song back and forth as a talk between mot and cove, each of them doing a verse.

Dale appeared from the crowd and hooked an arm around my waist. "Come on," he told me. "You have to bring me luck!"

"And if I don't, you'll leave off pawing me?" I asked, trying to tug free of his hold. I confess, I tried very little. His arm was strong and warm, his hand flat against my belly. I could feel *that* as if I had no dress nor shift between me and his palm.

Dale swung me around and drew me up against him until our faces were less than a hand span apart. In his boots he was three inches taller than me, and his heels were small ones. I guessed him to be five foot ten in his bare feet, a nice height for a man. Close like this, it was as if we'd made a space alone in the crowd. Part of me cried to be let go, that everyone was staring at us. Part of me was noticing I fit against him, and he smelled a little like cloves.

I had thought only Rosto could make my head spin like this.

"Tell me to stop, if you don't like it. Tell me I'm unwelcome, and I'll go." He said it in all seriousness, his gray eyes sharp on my face. "I've yet to push myself on a woman who doesn't like me. Tell me piss off, Beka."

"No," I snapped instead.

I felt him chuckle, more than I heard it. "Then we still have a game!" he said, releasing me. He took my hand and tugged me through the crowd, bound for one of the rooms in the back.

When we got there, Dale paused as he drew the lone empty chair out from the table where Hanse, Flory, Steen, Goodwin, four of our other fellow diners, and two strangers sat. "Is Pearl in the house?" he asked. "I told you I won't play if Pearl's up to her tricks again."

"Sit down," Hanse told him. He'd already placed thirty silver nobles in front of his place and was arranging them in five-coin towers. Each coin was scored deep across the center, showing silver all the way through. "One of the guards told me she hasn't been here in a week. No more has Jupp, Zolaika, or Jurji. Play with an easy heart, Dale."

"Your Rogue gambles?" asked Goodwin. "Must be wondrous to win against her."

"What was wondrous was that a month ago, she paid when she lost," Flory replied. She shuffled two fat stacks of what looked to be fortuneteller's cards with quick-fingered ease. "All sudden-like, she had silver a-plenty, although I'da sworn the takin's for the Court of the Rogue weren't so special, even for a summer. Her and Jupp, all of them that's tight to her armpits, they were rollin' in coin."

Steen grunted, his chin on his palm. "They'd play till they lost, then keep playin' till they was winnin', an' winnin' large. Most of the rest of us would be emptied out for a week after playin' wiv them. That's why Dale's so jumpy, like."

"Well, she stopped playin' like that after ten days of it," Hanse said gruffly. "Our pockets are plump enough, and so are Dale's. Let's have some ale in here! Flory, deal them cards!"

"Aye, she stopped, after she made enough off us t' buy them cursed pearl teeth," Flory grumbled. "I wonder how much she spent on supplies for the winter?"

"Sour talk sours the play," Dale murmured. He took his chair as a maidservant placed a smaller seat for me just at his elbow. "Now, Goodwin," Dale said, "lean close so I can whisper what you do in Gambler's Chance."

There were four different sets of cards for the game—Moon, Sun, Coins, and Swords. Each set had its nobles—King, Queen, Lady, and Knight. There was but one Trickster card for the entire deck, who could be any card his holder claimed he was. Then each set had cards numbered one to ten. I grew bored after that, so I lost track of the combinations that made for more points.

I turned to watch the people as cardplayers arrived and left. While many came that had been with us at the Merman's Cave, there were even more who just knew Dale's game and liked to play. As the evening wore on, and I mean *wore,* other tables in the room filled with folk who played Gambler's Chance. No one let Goodwin bet tonight, since she was just learning. Neither could she collect when she won. At our table silver was bet, lost, and won. At one other table I saw gold being laid down. At a third table the coin was mixed silver and copper. If folk checked the silver to see if they had coles, they did it carefully. Did they know of the danger, or did they think they could get any coles back into play and lose them to someone else?

I had no way to check. As Dale's "luck," I blew on the painted backs of his cards before he turned them to see what meaning they held. Other mots and coves did the same for other players, but they didn't seem to be bored. They sat in their players' laps, fixed food and drink for them, gave them kisses when they won—or lost—and joked along with the players. I was curst if I would fetch and carry like a maidservant.

At last I quietly rose as if I meant to go briefly to the privy. Once outside the room of cardplayers, I looked around. Doubtless I should gamble a *little* bit, mayhap at the dice tables. I headed toward a table where I saw space for a new player. I confess, I was grinding my teeth at the thought of risking, and like as not losing, good coin, even though it was not my own. Then I heard folk go quiet as a singer's voice glided along the heated air. It was a lovely voice, deep for a woman's and throaty, raised in a wailing Carthaki song.

The singer performed in a larger room than most, another of those where folk came to sit but not to play. On a small raised platform stood a singer and a flute player. The singer wore a lovely gold-brown tunic with a wrapped crimson sash. Her sleeves were wide, almost like wings. When she raised her hands, she revealed gold cuffs on her arms. Her hair was glossy black, pinned in a knot at the back of her head, with golden chains twined through it. Her eyes were shaded in gold and lined with kohl. Her lips were painted a vivid red. She wore gold sandals on her feet. It was those feet, and her hands, with their gold-painted nails, that gave her away. They were much too big. I gave her face a second look. It was Okha.

"I'n't she splendid?" a cove leaning against the pillar beside me asked. "She's called the Amber Orchid. I seen orchids, down on th' docks. They're flowers, y'know. Brung in from th' Copper Isles. She's more beautiful. You sittin' down, dearie?"

I shook my head. The cove pushed off his pillar, walked in past me, and found a seat.

Okha sang three more songs, all of them wonderful. Then he kissed his flute player on the cheek and stepped down from the platform, while the listeners clapped and pounded the floor and threw coins. The flute player collected them. Okha nodded to me, then wandered through the crowd, stopping at tables to say hello to folk he seemed to know.

He then came to me at last and tucked my hand under his arm. "Now they'll think I'm a honeylove," he murmured in a voice that sounded like a mot's, though a deep-voiced mot's. "Shall I get you a glass of wine, Beka?"

"Cider twilsey, if you please," I replied. "I'm over my limit for wine tonight."

"I suppose they'll have to go out to buy it, but of course, dear." Okha beckoned for a serving man to come over. "Sweetheart, my usual, and a chilled cider twilsey for my friend, in my dressing room? I'd be ever so grateful."

The cove blinked at me, but smiled at Okha. "For you, the stars, Amber," he said. He trotted off.

Okha steered me down a hall and up a narrow set of stairs. There, off a hallway, he had a room to dress in and to relax in when he didn't sing.

"Where's Goodwin?" he asked, draping himself on a couch with a sigh. I watched him, wishing I had such grace. He arranged himself naturally, as liquid as water. In a woman's clothes, he was different than he was as a man, yet even more comfortable in his skin. It was the strangest thing.

I remembered my manners and his question. "She's card-playing with Hanse Remy, Dale Rowan, and some others."

Okha raised his penciled brows. "Dale Rowan! Now, there's rich company for a girl on her first night in the port! However did she meet Dale?"

I smiled at him. "We met him in Corus. During a riot, actually. And then on the boat here."

Okha laughed. It was a warm, rippling chuckle, the kind that made coves trip over their feet. "Met during a riot! Well, that's *one* way, I suppose. And Hanse?"

"The same way," I replied. "And Hanse's man Steen. They invited us to supper tonight, and we've been with them ever since."

"I can see you won't require Nestor and me to show you the sights, not if you're with *that* crowd. Come in," Okha called to the knock on the door. It was the young servant with his drink and my twilsey. Okha gave the lad a coin and a bit more flirtation, then let him go. As he sat gracefully again, he told me, "They're big gamblers, and they know everyone who plays."

"Good people to know when you're Dogging money," I said, thinking of all the coin that had gone through Dale's fingers already this night. I sipped my twilsey. It was very good, the best I'd ever had. "I hear even Pearl Skinner gambles. Is that her only habit? Or are there others?"

Okha grimaced, as if his drink was sour. "If you're planning revenge for this morning, Beka, forget it now. People who try to hurt Pearl have been known to end their lives flayed, gutted, and hung on the gates at Guards House."

He had a sad, distant look to his eyes. The person who'd

met that fate was someone he'd known—now there was something I would bet on.

"So she takes that ridiculous street name serious," I commented, when the silence got uncomfortable.

Okha's eyebrows went up. His thoughts plainly returned to this room and this conversation. "Skinner, a street name? Oh, no. It's her family's name and her father's old trade. Not that he plies it anymore. He was a vicious old sot who mysteriously fell into the sewers and drowned ten years ago. As did the trull who called herself his wife, and Pearl's two older brothers. All at different times, all in the sewers. Shocking luck, wouldn't you say?"

"Pearl seems to have a mean streak," I admitted.

"And an affection for coming at you from behind, though she hardly bothers anymore," Okha told me. "Not when she has Torcall, Jurji, and Zolaika to do her vengeances for her."

I thought that over for a moment. "Jurji. Is that the Bazhir who sits beside her at the Eagle Street court, the one with the curved sword?" Okha nodded. I guessed again. "The older cove, Eastern Lands stock, that's Torcall."

"Torcall Jupp," Okha said, and took a sip of his drink. "He's no hothead, unlike Jurji. He and Jurji are Pearl's main bodyguards. She changes the other around, but those two are constant."

"You mentioned a Zolaika?" I asked.

"Did you see an older woman in attendance?" Okha asked. "Heavy makeup, dreadful wig?"

It was my turn to make a face. "She led the gang that grabbed me and Goodwin."

Okha nodded. "She is Pearl's killer."

I stared at him.

He smiled. "She is not as stiff as she acts, nor as slow. The makeup comes off—it is painted onto a light piece of muslin she can pull off her face. A quick scrub with a wet cloth and you would not recognize her. The red hair is a wig." Okha leaned forward and tapped my wrist with two fingers. "Remember her, Beka, and tell Goodwin. If Pearl wants folk dead in silence, never knowing who murdered them, she sends Zolaika."

I remembered that lofty, mannered doxie, and I just couldn't fit my mind around it. But surely Okha would know. "How can you tell? How can anyone tell, if she is unseen? Pearl could just take a coincidental death and say she set it up."

Okha sighed. "If the death is an important one, or a threat, Pearl leaves pearls by the victim, or on the victim. It's what she did to Sir Lionel's children, when she thought he grew too nosy. She had pearls laid on their pillows, three years ago. Everyone knows. It's why he sent his wife and children to their home fief, and only visits them. I'd worry for Nestor's safety if it weren't for Haden and Truda and their friends. They're splendid guards." He rose and sat before a table laden with pots of paints and powders. Taking up a small, silver hand mirror, he began to examine his face. "Forgive me. They'll be calling me back soon."

"But Haden and Truda are just children," I said.

"Street children, for all Nestor's had them in his house for two years," Okha told me, wetting a tiny brush in a dish of water. He set about renewing the black lines around his eyes. "They run with their gang when there's no work to be done, and their gang sleeps in the basement during the winter. The things they do with knives and ropes! They're fine pickpockets, too, though they're careful not to interfere in the Rogue's trade. Nestor uses them for spies, or loans them out to Dogs he trusts." Okha smiled at me. "They're not cheap, of course. But as you learned with Haden, they are *very* good."

I was surprised Haden and Truda's friends had not robbed Nestor into poverty. Mayhap he had his own ways to discourage that. "I saw Haden," I told Okha. "Goodwin did, too."

Okha smiled. "And much put out about it Haden is, too. He says the two of you must have little ghost eyes flying behind you, because not even Nestor sees him, and Nestor knows he is there."

For a moment I watched Okha fix his makeup and check his hair. It was a wig, I knew, but unlike Zolaika's, it was a *beautiful* wig. With every move, every adjustment, he became more a woman. Lady Teodorie, with all her manners and elegance, could not match him for beauty and grace.

"How do you do it?" I asked him. "Become all wonderful and lovely like you are out there?"

He turned and looked at me with shock, something dark and sad in his eyes. It slowly vanished.

"You are an odd one, aren't you?" he asked from somewhere between his mot's world and his cove's. "You say little, but you make me want to talk about things that I don't usually babble about, you know. Maybe it's those eyes of yours. You don't judge. . . ."

I looked down. "Most folk find my eyes frightening."

"My experiences with 'most folk' are not so good that I am inclined to follow their standard," Okha said. His voice was very bitter. He turned back to his mirror. "I had very good teachers, people who took me in when my family cast me out. I worked and I studied, everywhere I went. But that isn't what you're asking."

I shook my head. Since he wasn't looking at me now, I added, "Not really. Your beauty comes from the inside. You don't put that on with a brush and powder."

"Inside I *am* a beautiful woman," Okha said, fiddling with a perfect curl. "The Trickster tapped me in my mother's womb and placed me in this man's shell."

I'd heard of many tricks done by the gods, but surely this was nearabout the cruelest. "I'm sorry," I whispered.

"At least I understand what happened," Okha said, getting to his feet and smoothing his dress. "How many like me live our lives without ever knowing? How many of us never feel right in the world where we live, and never realize that a god turned our lives all on end? Some of us even claim the Trickster is one of us, and makes us so She/He has company."

"Have you asked the god?" I wanted to know.

Okha gave me a tiny, bitter smile. "The god touched me once, Beka. I'd as soon not get his attention again."

Someone pounded on the door. "Amber, Amber, sorry, but Dale Rowan's looking for his girl. He says he's lost two hands of cards, and she's his luck!"

"I'm not his girl!" I said.

"But you're sitting with him at his table?" Okha asked me. He was already running his hands over my hair, smoothing it, using touches of his comb to tease locks out of my coil and forward over my cheeks. "The one who sits with a gambler is his luck, or her luck. Dale's a true gambler, especially if he starts to lose." He called to the cove outside the door, who'd begun to knock again, "Just wait, silly!" Okha snatched up a clean brush and dipped it in a tiny pot of paint. Before I could dodge, he'd set it to my lips. Next he dotted scent just under my ears, and tucked the bottle in my purse. It was a beautiful perfume. "Lily of the valley," he told me. "More suited to you than rose or violet. Now, let's go see Master Dale!"

I breathed it in. I felt strange. More beautiful. More like a grand mot like Okha. But that felt so strange, too, because I am no beautiful mot. I looked at my palms, to assure myself that I was still Beka. There were my baton calluses. I might smell like a flower in a noble's garden, but in the morning I would still be a Dog. I sighed my relief.

Okha led me downstairs to the room where my companions were playing. Dale was on his feet, arms crossed as he glared at the table, the other players, and the cards. "I won't touch a hand again until I see Beka," he told them. "How's a cove to know if a mot's his luck if she's not even here?"

"Because she stands right behind him while he roars like a bull, precious," Okha—no, he was all Amber Orchid now, graceful and grand—said with a laugh. "Good evening, guests. Welcome. For those of you who are strangers, I am Amber Orchid, a singer who is sometimes welcomed to these rooms, though *not,* of course, when there is a *game.*" Just the way he made his voice dip and flow turned his speech into a gentle joke on the players. They laughed.

Dale turned to look at me and bent down to speak in my ear. Amber swept forward, still talking to the folk in the room. Dale whispered, "Where did you go? I missed you! And I lost two hands!"

I stared up at him. "A mot has places to go where she isn't likely to want company! And I was bored. Don't go thinking I'm your property, Master Rowan!"

Plenty of coves I knew would have bristled right up. Dale only scratched his head, then grabbed both my hands and kissed each one. "I'm a bad escort, and that's the truth," he told me, a smile of regret on his face. "I get caught up in the play and I forget all my manners. I'm sorry. Do you *really* not care for the game?"

I was trying to get my hands back, but not very hard. He'd laced his fingers through mine. "I don't gamble," I mumbled.

"I don't even know the rules, and I can't see, on a little chair right behind you. Let me go, folk are watching!"

"But your hands are warm," he said in my ear. "And what's this lovely new scent? I like it."

"Dale, are you playing or not?" growled a cove seated at the table. "Your bet's not laid down!"

"A few more hands of cards, and we'll find someplace to dance," Dale wheedled me. "You *do* like to dance?"

Of course I love it. It's one of the few sociable things I can do without talking.

Dale grinned. "Oh, you like that idea? I finally found something that pleases her!" He glanced at the ceiling. "Thank you, Goddess!" He looked at me once more. "As for seeing the game—"

He turned to sit, and in turning, he spun me until I sat on one of his knees. I made a noise, I know it, and then I said nothing else. I only hung my head so my face wouldn't be so visible to everyone else. I knew I was blushing fierce. I peeked once to see where the strangled noises came from. Goodwin, curse her, was trying not to laugh, and doing poorly at it. Since I'd gone for Dog training, no cove save Rosto the Piper had been this careless with his hands around me, and even Rosto had never had the gall to sit me on his knee! Mayhap he knew he'd have got an elbow in the eye for his trouble. And yet I thought of doing no such thing to Dale. I don't know if it was the warm clasp of his arm about my waist, or the teasing jiggle of his leg under my rump, or the way his beard tickled my neck as he leaned in to explain what his cards meant. I only know that my dress, decent enough before, now seemed scandalously low-cut. Moreover, from the way his arm drew its fabric and the fabric of my shift tight over my peaches, he knew I was *not* thinking of the cards.

"What did I say?" he murmured to me. "My luck is back. Three Ladies and two Queens—the Goddess favors a humble courier tonight!" He slid two silver nobles out into the middle of the table. "See, that's a hand I'm betting on, five cards." He spoke loud enough that the others could hear, as if he taught me.

Goodwin tossed her cards facedown on the table. "I have naught to work with," she complained.

"Cold fingers, Dale?" Hanse asked with a broad grin. He threw five silver nobles onto the table. "Match me or kill your cards, man!"

"Kill?" I asked Dale, speaking as loudly as he did, taking my cues from him.

"Put them down. Leave this hand of the game," he explained. He inspected his small heap of silver coins, sliding one or two around as if he considered matching Hanse's bet.

I wondered how many of them were coles. Only one or two of them were scored to show they were all silver, unlike Hanse's nobles. "What if you do that?" I asked. "Do you get your two coins back?"

Everyone at the table laughed. "Once money's in the middle, it stays in the middle, same as a dice game or any other bet," Steen told me. "The winner takes it all."

Dale sighed and shoved in three coins. "I'm demented, mayhap, but my luck has to return sometime."

Flory thrust in four silver nobles and ten copper ones. Steen also bet.

"See, Goodwin figures her cards are no good," Dale told me. "She kills them and she wagers nothing more. She does not lose, but she does not win."

I glanced at Goodwin's eyes. They were sharp as they rested on Dale. She knows, I thought. He has fooled Hanse, his friend, and Steen, who knows him, too, but he hasn't fooled Goodwin.

She caught me watching her. One of her eyelids twitched a hair in the smallest of winks.

There was a lot of groaning and shouting, all good-natured, when everyone showed their cards and Dale proved to have the best hand. The pack of cards went to Steen. Dale explained how they were shuffled, or mixed up, so folk wouldn't get the same cards again, then the manner in which the shuffler gave out five cards each to the players.

Three games later, though Dale was still winning, he stopped the play. "I promised my luck a change, and I don't want her to desert me because I didn't keep my word!" he told the others as I got off his knee. "We're going to find some dancing."

"Now that's somethin' like!" Flory said, jumping up. "I'll get the girls. They'll have found some coves by now!"

Dale was scooping his last heap of silver coins off the table and into a bowl brought by one of the serving maids. She nodded and took it away, which seemed to me to be very trusting of Dale. Did they check the coins to see if they were pure silver?

He had kept two silver nobles back. Now he offered them to me. I scowled at them and then at him.

"Mithros's spear. What is that for?" I demanded.

He looked startled. "It's the custom. When someone brings you luck, it offends the Trickster if you don't give that person something in thanks. It's as if you say you don't value the luck."

"I'm sure he knows you value him, and I'll not be tipped like a backstreet trull," I snapped. "You brung your own luck, knowin' the game and the way of playin' the cards." I put a hand over my mouth, hearing myself slide into Cesspool cant. I hardly ever do it. Here I'd been thinking he *liked* me, but I might as well have been a serving maid or a doxie he asked to perch on his leg!

"No, no—curse it, Beka, you're the prickliest woman I've ever met!" cried Dale.

"No, I am," Goodwin said. She stood nearby, smiling, our capes over one arm. "But she comes very close, I have to say."

"It's not just about the luck. Yes, I had a feeling you'd be lucky for me, but I like you!" Dale stuffed the coins in his purse. "There! The vile money's all gone!"

I had to fight not to smile. He looked comical, his brows arching into his hair, his eyes alight with outrage and dismay, his cheeks flushed. Goodwin handed my cape to him. Carefully, as if I might bite, he came at me, holding it out. I let him drape it about my shoulders, my eyes on him the whole time. I supposed, if he'd thought of me like any wench he'd pay to blow on his dice or cards, he'd not be so upset.

As I pinned the cape with my brooch, I heard him mutter, "I'll just have to buy you something pretty."

I glared at him.

"Peace!" he said. "Peace! Otherwise how will we dance together?" With temptation in his voice he added, "I know where they sell the best spiced fried dough in all Port Caynn— better than Corus, too. Black God strike me if I lie."

I put my hand on his mouth. "Don't talk lightly of the Black God," I told him. "He's always about." I should know.

Impudent mumper that he is, he kissed my palm.

"Sir, yer winnin's," said the maid who had taken his silver. Now I saw why. She had exchanged it for gold. He'd have fewer coins to weigh down his purse. He tucked them away and gave her a copper noble for her trouble. I shook my head and followed Goodwin outside, thinking that they treat coin like sweets in this place. Do they know about the problem with silver coles? Not if the way I'd seen silver change hands that night was any guide. Was the trouble something known largely by the guild banks, that were keeping silent? Surely an educated cove like Dale would have heard something. Hanse at least was checking all of his silver, from what I'd seen.

We didn't have far to go to find the dancing that Dale had promised. There were pipers, drummers, and tambourine players in Seafoam Square, performing for all manner of folk. I noted sailors, tradesmen and tradeswomen, craftsfolk, even a handful of nobles, and a pair of Dogs in uniform. I saw one purse-switching, an exchange of a coney's purse of coin for a red purse of coles. I kept my gob shut while I marked the filcher's face. I danced with Hanse, Steen, Dale, and two coves I didn't know before Pearl's longsword guard, the one Okha had named Torcall, caught me up.

"Let go," I warned him. "Now."

"Calm down," he said. "It's just a reel. Soon over."

"I didn't say I'd dance with you, Pearl's man." I was deciding which knife was the closest. I'd have to be fast. Odds were he'd give me but the one chance to go for a blade.

"Afraid, King's Dog? Afraid of a little dance?" he asked me.

All right. I'd dance with him and see what he wanted. My friends were close enough, and my knives were closer.

If he had a point, he never said what it was, pox and murrain on him! When the reel was done, he bowed and went off into the dark. Had I not been among strangers, I would have shouted for him to come back and fight like a Dog. Instead I stood there, clutching my fire opal and cursing to myself in silence.

Dale found me. He grumbled how everyone was dancing with me but him. Not seeming to notice my foul humor, he swung me into the dance square that was forming. After that he didn't give me up until my feet ached and my mood was much better. He is a *very* good dancer and lifts me as if I weigh no more than a kitten.

When I mentioned my tired feet, Dale took me to a vendor who sold fried dough spiced with cinnamon and nutmeg, then drizzled in honey. I held on to these while he bought cider, which he carried to me in a leather jack he keeps hooked to his belt. I fed him knots of the dough as he gave me drinks of the cider, when I wasn't laughing at the jokes he made about the dancers around the bench he'd found for us. There were plenty of the crisp, sweet dough knots as I dished out one knot for me, one for him. Each time I put one in Dale's mouth, the tricksy fellow tried to nip my finger. Twice I let him. Twice more I smeared honey on his nose for a lesson and grinned at him. I could not have been giddier if the cider had been mead.

Wanting to slow things down and not wanting him to think he'd bowled me over, I was glad to find something to talk about when we reached the end of the knots. The vendor had heaped them inside of a large, curved shell. Since we sat near a cluster of torches, I had a well-lit view of the shell's inside. It was a beautiful, pearly, purple blue.

"How can people give these away? Aren't they valuable?" I asked Dale.

He looked at the shell and raised an eyebrow. "Abalone shells? The beaches are heaped with them. The food sellers gather them when the seafood harvesters have collected the meat. They're good for platters, and if folk make off with them, there's always more. Poor folk use them for plates, buttons— keep it if you like, but I can find you better."

I shook my head. "No. I was just curious." He gave me the last drink of cider. "Where can we find Steen?" I asked him.

Dale frowned. "What do you need Steen for when you have me? I'm better-looking, and I'm more charming."

I laughed. "I need to ask him something about Pearl's court. About one of her guards, actually."

Dale grinned. "Well, I'm as good as Steen for that! I spend almost as much time around there as he does."

I looked at him, feeling a nasty pinch of suspicion in my tripes. "*You?* In the Court of the Rogue?" Why does a bank courier have any business in that place?

Dale shrugged. "My friends go, and I can find some of the best games there. Up until a month ago, if I was careful to lose to the Rogue now and then, I won a lot of money off of her and her folk. Sooner or later I'll have to go back and lose to her for a while, just to prove I'm not afraid." He laughed. "What, do you fear for my tender skin already, pretty Beka?"

I nearabout said that's exactly what I feared. Then I remembered him in the riot, kicking high to the side with enough strength to knock his foe over. That kind of fighting took skill and training. He'd studied it somewhere.

"You give yourself airs," I told him. "Well, then, Master Quickwit, who's her guard with the straight longsword? He's forty or so, hair a golden brown, shorter than yours, light blue eyes, your height, broader across the shoulders." Okha had given me Jupp's name, but I'd hoped Steen would know more.

Dale raised his brows at me. "I'm no sergeant or Senior Dog, you know. I don't need the whole description. Are you always so definite about people's ages?"

I turned my nose up at him. Kora does that to Ersken, and it's a very pretty move. "I was the best in my class at it. I'd say you're twenty to twenty-two. Will you keep me here forever? My hands are sticky."

"I'll lick the honey off," he suggested.

I tried not to shiver as goose bumps wriggled all over my flesh. "I've a hound will do that," I told him, trying to sound cross and not like my knees had gone to jelly.

"Oh, cruel," Dale said, hanging his head. He cupped my elbow in one hand and steered me along the edge of the vendors' booths. "Your longsword guard is Torcall Jupp. He's from Barzun originally—educated cove. I think his family comes from the trading class, though that's a guess. He doesn't talk about them. He was the first one Pearl hired when she killed the last Rogue, about four years ago. He's her chief advisor—well, he and Zolaika share the honors. Pearl's brave enough, and she understands Rats, but she's not clever the way educated folk are. She needs advisors." We came into open ground, where a fountain rained water into a wide marble basin. We washed our sticky hands, and Dale his nose, as Dale asked, "What interest do you have in an old cove like him? He's strictly for the spintries, so don't get your hopes up."

I flicked cold water in his face. "Jupp danced with me. I don't know what game he plays at."

Now, at last, I had Dale Rowan serious. With a frown he took a seat on a nearby bench. "He *danced* with you."

I plumped my bum down beside him. "You don't see *me* getting jealous over *you* being nowhere in sight awhile, do you? Like as not you were dripping honey in some other mot's ear."

"Actually, Hanse and I were talking about a game tomorrow night," he said, as if he weren't entirely paying attention. Then he looked at me. "You were dancing, and he just grabbed you up?"

I nodded. "Told me he was there to dance. I thought mayhap he had sommat to say, but he never said it. He just finished the dance and left."

Dale picked up my damp hand and stroked it. "I don't

understand, either. Tor isn't the sort to play games." He cupped my cheek in his free hand. "Beka, what are you really doing here in Port Caynn?"

I sighed. "I nabbed a Rat with more Rats in his family," I told him, looking straight into his eyes. "Two of his brothers gave me a beating on Monday. Now my patron has sent Goodwin and me off until the Dogs can be certain no other members of the Rat's family will come looking for me. We're supposed to observe how Port Caynn Dogs work, so I follow Goodwin around and do as she tells me."

"Who's your patron?" Dale wanted to know.

I remembered a trick of Tansy's and tried it, wrinkling my nose at him. "Never you mind," I said. "It's nothing to do with us."

"There you are!" I heard Goodwin cry. Hanse and Goodwin, laughing, arms around each other's waists, ran up to us. Both looked windblown and happy, the best of friends. "Come along! They've got Carthaki sword dancers at a place Hanse knows of!"

We followed them.

The Carthaki dancers were wild, colorful, splendid. They showed us the big curved swords were sharp by chopping bundles of reeds and chunks of wood with them, then danced to wailing pipes and fast drums. They whipped the blades over their heads and around themselves, then over and around each other. Their wrists and hands were so fast that the blades started to blur in the torchlight. The sword dancers were men. Then came mots, little more than gixies, who tossed knives back and forth until they were silver butterflies in the air. After such dangerous pleasures came the mots who wore tiny bits of silk, only enough to cover their breasts, wide silk breeches, girdles made of coins, and an assortment of veils that could have been little protection against the chill of the night. They danced slow and fast, wriggling separate parts of their bodies that I never thought could twitch like that on their own, arching backward until their heads touched the ground, playing little cymbals on their fingers all the while.

It was *beautiful.*

After, our group found a tavern that served up a late supper. There were eleven or so of us by then, Steen with a new mot, Flory with a new cove, two more of Hanse's coves, and another of Flory's mots. I had only a bit of pie and some wine, being close to worn out. Goodwin saw it and told the men we were for home.

Nothing would do for them but that they walk us there, Hanse, Steen and his mot, Flory, and Dale. They left only when Serenity opened the door to us. It seemed that Hanse and Goodwin had already made plans for supper again in the evening to come. Dale told me he would see me there.

He didn't kiss me good night.

We weren't alone, of course, but I didn't expect that to stop *Dale.*

What is wrong with me? Was I too saucy? Too coarse? Too—Dog-ish?

I wish Kora and Aniki were here. They know so much more about coves than I do. I can't ask *Goodwin* what I did wrong.

At five of the afternoon.

Slapper roused me at what I later found was sometime after nine of the clock this morning. He landed on my face, sticking his clubbed foot into one of my eyes while he smacked me with both wings.

At least this once he calculated wrong. Hit by something, I did what any street Dog might do. I twisted sideways, grabbing for the dagger under my pillow. The cracked bird went flying into the wall nearby.

Seeing what had truly happened, I yanked off my covers and went to pick him up. I need not have bothered. He fastened his beak in my hand, striking me again. As I lifted him, he launched into the air, trilling in outrage. At least the claybrained bird was unhurt.

"D' you want me to feed you or not?" At the last moment I remembered I was not in my normal lodgings and did not yell. At home I would not have woken anyone. Aniki, Rosto, Kora, and Ersken all sleep like the dead.

Slapper whirled toward the window and perched there on the sill. The open shutters let in the full morning sun.

I turned and glared at Achoo, who sat on my bed, tail a-wag. "Not a *word*," I told her.

I scattered corn on the sill. Four pigeons waited there with Slapper, while others stood on the eaves nearby. "Splendid," I said. "Mumpers at the feast." I leaned out. The sill continued along under the other windows, a solid wooden ledge of a foot in width around the corner of the house. Reaching out as far as I could on either side, I sprinkled corn so more birds could feed.

Then I set about washing my face and cleaning my teeth,

listening to the birds as I did. Their ghosts spoke clearer now that I'd had a day and most of a night listening to all manner of Port voices.

"—told 'im I'd 'ave 'is goods in a week!" A cove, with defeat in his voice.

"I tol' Pa the babby broke it." This one was a gixie.

"Di'n't they warn me, yez don' cross Pearl—" A young cove, his voice trembling in fear.

I went to the window to see which bird *that* was, even though I knew I'd need more than a common murder to trouble the Rogue. Shutters slammed open nearby. The pigeons took off in a flurry, even Slapper, as a woman cried, "What are these curst filthy birds doin' here? Hey! You, what are you at over there?"

I stuck my head out. One of Serenity's maidservants, a mot I didn't know, glared at me from the room next door, on the side opposite Goodwin's. "What?" I called.

"You, is what! Feedin' these nasty things on th' ledge! You'll stop that, right now—I'm havin' a word with Serenity!" she cried. "They leave scummer everywhere, their feathers get into the house, they bring all manner of sickness—"

I couldn't just hide when I heard that. She was wrong about these birds that carry so much human misery. I leaned further out and clenched my hands into fists to give myself courage. "See here, mistress, I've handled pigeons for years. I've yet to catch so much as a sniffle from them. And they carry more garbage off the streets than you have, any day."

"They're no more than rats with wings. Serenity won't have them here!" With that she slammed the shutters closed. A moment later I heard her thumping across my neighbor's room, into the hall, and down the stairs.

"That went well," I told Achoo. She was in no mind to listen. Instead she stood by the door, doing her I-must-go dance.

I dressed quickly and took Achoo out and then back through the kitchen. It gave me the chance to wheedle food for her from the cook. The cross-grained maid was nowhere to be seen.

"Porridge and tea?" asked the cook as I prepared to take Achoo and her meal upstairs again. "Downstairs or in your room?"

"I'll have it downstairs, mistress, if it's no trouble," I said. "Only let me feed my hound."

As I climbed the back stairs, I heard her tell the cook maid, "I don't know what Berna was on about. She doesn't seem cracked to me."

With Achoo settled, I went to the dining room. Serenity and Goodwin were the only ones there. The Dogs of yesterday's earlier breakfast were doubtless in bed or on watch. Serenity and Goodwin sat on either side of a corner of the table, deep in talk. I supposed them to be speaking of Goddess affairs, both of them being temple officials. When they looked up as I came in, I felt as if I interrupted something. I saw that my breakfast, along with an apple turnover, was placed at the table, but wondered if now wouldn't be a good time for diplomacy.

"I can take my meal up to my room," I told them.

"You may sit down," Serenity told me. "And you will stop feeding pigeons in this house, mistress. Mine is a clean dwelling, not a coop."

"Very well, Mistress Serenity," I said, taking my place. "I'll find another place to meet with them."

Serenity frowned at me. "I don't understand."

"They carry the spirits of those who were killed, or those who died, with business left undone in the world," Goodwin explained. "Cooper hears those spirits. Sometimes she learns enough to hobble their killers." Goodwin looked at me. "Serenity was telling me the house had watchers last night."

The former priestess shrugged. "As I said on your arrival, this house is safe. I have placed my protections about it. I know when strangers watch us with ill intent. Two of them were here last night." She drummed her fingers on the table, then told me, "I mean what I say about the pigeons, messengers or no. My neighbors would be up in arms if they began to flock here. We have enough trouble with pigs and stray dogs in this district as it is. These spies—I think they were meant to watch us in shifts, but no more came when I blinded the first two."

"Blinded?" asked Goodwin. "For how long?"

Serenity's face was hard. "Permanently." Goose bumps went up my back as Serenity went on, "Everyone knows I am not to be trifled with. The Rogue was a fool to send them."

"You are certain they came from Pearl Skinner?" Goodwin asked. "How could you know?"

"I have a scrying bowl," Serenity replied, as calm as her name. "I watched the second of them and his keeper report to her. They knew there was trouble when my spell blinded the first one. The keeper stood three houses back and waited to see if the second watcher called for help, as he did. He took that one to their mistress after he was blinded." She sighed. "The stupid woman was gambling again. You would think the idiots at the gambling houses would realize that the more she loses at gambling, the more her folk will steal to fill her purse again." She looked at me. "Are you a mage, Cooper?"

I remembered my breakfast was in front of me, getting cold as I listened to her musical voice. "No," I told her, pouring milk into my bowl. With honey the porridge wasn't bad, even though it was barely warm.

Serenity smoothed the front of her gown. "Well. What resources the temple can give you in your work here, only tell me, and I will secure them for you."

Goodwin leaned back in her chair. "I thought you were a *retired* priestess," she said, suspicion clear on her face.

Serenity shrugged. "A retired First Priestess of the Mother. I am too old to welcome strangers on the great holidays, and I grew weary of factions and struggles in the temple. My retirement does not mean I am without power."

"We aren't here for anything but learning," I said. It worries me that Goodwin trusts the Goddess-folk too easily because she is temple magistrate at home. "We're not up to anything special."

"Then why does Pearl set watchers on you?" Serenity asked. "She has never showed interest in any other Dogs under my roof. Good Dogs, with plenty of hobblings to their names. You've drawn her attention. She's not one to forget those who do that. You may well need the temple. I will get help to guard this place." She pursed her mouth. "Pearl is like a stupid stray. She only remembers you've hit her for a time. Then she forgets and comes slinking back to try to steal from your kitchen again."

"You talk careless of a Rogue who had the sack to leave pearls with Sir Lionel's children," I said. Goodwin looked at me and raised her brows.

"Pearl has power only so long as people give it to her," Serenity replied. "Had Sir Lionel any backbone, he would have sent his children to our temple or Mithros's for safety, then hunted her down and broken her back like the Rat she is. Men like Nestor and a few others fight, while others make deals and Sir Lionel hides in Guards House. Some of us are tired of it. We are tired of her."

Goodwin got to her feet with a sigh. "Speeches are all very well, but if we don't show ourselves out and about, Mother back in Corus will scold." She looked at Serenity. "Don't get your throat cut on our account, Priestess." She walked past me. "Cooper, bring that hound of yours."

I went upstairs for Achoo.

She was glad to run downstairs with me, beating me with her wagging tail all the way. Goodwin waited for us in the courtyard. Achoo had to say good morning to Goodwin, which required standing and licking until Goodwin said, "Enough!" She didn't even have to say it in Kyprish. Down on all fours Achoo went.

"The plan for today?" I asked Goodwin as we turned right on Ashlie Lane.

"I'd like to see what we overhear at the gem markets on western Moneychangers'," she replied. "See what's said of Pearl and the Dogs here. And Sir Lionel. Port Caynn has always been wild, but not like now. I'd almost swear Pearl rules here, not the Crown." Her lips thinned. "That won't do."

Hearing her say that, so quiet, made me feel as strong, as awake, wary, and *eager* as the Growl of a roomful of Dogs. So *this* was what a hunt felt like!

We walked for a couple of blocks in silence until I settled and I thought she had settled. "Should we do aught about watchers on our lodging?" I asked. "Or do you think Serenity has it in hand?" I'd already glimpsed movement behind a cart stopped in front of a shop. I could tell it was Haden.

"I've been wondering that myself," Goodwin said. "We can't go to Isanz Finer's house without being sure we're not followed. If Pearl is involved, she'd kill to stop anyone from finding out where she gets her silver. I think she believes we're here, or actually, *you're* here, to spy on her for Rosto."

I snorted.

"Yes, but she doesn't know you," Goodwin said. "I want her to go on believing you are Rosto's spy. If she thinks that, she'll stop trying to watch us after a few days, when she realizes you're no such thing. Then we can visit Isanz and see if he has the source of the colemongers' silver. That's one of the things that makes me doubt Pearl as a colemonger. How would a city Rat like her learn of an unknown silver mine?"

"She'd be mad to be the colemonger," I said, surprised that Goodwin even considered Pearl seriously. "Rosto won't, and he's as greedy as any Rat. He says dealing in coles is cutting your own throat. True coin means everything to them."

"Aye, but Rosto's a curst wise Rogue for all his youth, and he's got some kind of book-learning to go with it." Goodwin picked up an apple from a stall and flipped a coin to the vendor. "Pearl's clever in a street way, but in a commonsense way? I've had the chance to meet eight other Rogues apart from Kayfur, Rosto, and Pearl. None of them made a display of being too rich, like she's done with those stupid pearl teeth. Even if she's only been Rogue four years, she should have learned some things by now. Either her bodyguards are poxy devoted, or she's a better killer than even Rosto." She bit into the apple and chewed like she was vexed with it.

"Mayhap her counselors warned her off coles," I said. "Dale says Jupp and Zolaika advise her. They'd tell her the pitfalls. Maybe they don't care about her teeth, but they'd say she dumps scummer in her own well, passing coles in her city. That her people, too, will bring coles back instead of real coin."

"But we know she handles some cole passing already, Cooper," Goodwin reminded me. "That red purse game—they'd have to get her permission to use rushers to protect the filchers when they swap purses. But that still doesn't mean

Pearl's a colemonger, and the more I see her, the more I think she's too stupid to be one. Still, we don't count her out." She ate some more apple, thinking. "It's our good fortune that our new friends gamble with the Rats of this town, eh?" She drew a Goddess crescent on her forehead with her thumb. "We were blessed at the Bread Riot, whether we knew it or not, falling in with them! They'll get us closer to the Rogue's court than we ever could have done on our own. Now, tell me how you learned that the Rogue threatened Sir Lionel."

As we walked along, I relayed everything Okha had told me the night before. About a block from Moneychangers' Street, we found an empty lot where I could scatter the seed and corn I'd brought with me. Goodwin added her apple core. Just as I suspected, Slapper and his new friends had been following me. They flew down in a rush, settling on the food. They startled a thin gixie, no more than twelve, wearing a much washed and tattered red gown, out of the bushes at the edge of the lot. She took off into an alley.

"One of Pearl's watchers, I don't doubt," Goodwin muttered.

I stood, listening to the pigeons. I heard a handful of voices, but none of them gave me anything I could use. The feeding ended when Goodwin nudged me and pointed out Achoo. My hound lay flat, her head on her forepaws, yearning on her silly face. It was as clear as if she spoke that she wanted to chase the pigeons. I broke out laughing. Mayhap the pigeons thought I meant them and got offended. More likely they'd gone through all the food. They took off and did not return.

"Achoo, *tumit,*" I said. She, Goodwin, and I resumed our walk toward Moneychangers'. "Did you learn aught of interest last night?" I asked Goodwin.

"Mostly about Hanse's group of caravan guards," she told

me as we dodged around a mule loaded with packs. "Thirty mots and coves work for him. Ten are on the road to Blue Harbor now, guarding a caravan. Ten more are on the river, taking a cargo to Whitethorn. It seems pirates get a little rough once the ships are past Corus. Hanse and nine more are right here in Port Caynn. We met four of them last night, not counting Steen."

I remembered. "What's keeping them in town? There's plenty of ships coming in. Business is at its peak with the harvests finishing up."

"Hanse says they're working on the docks for now," Goodwin said, "hiring out in small groups at night to guard ships or warehouses." We hurried around a string of carts to step onto Moneychangers'. Looking to the side, I saw a pickpocket swap purses. This time the coney caught wise. He grabbed the pickpocket's hand just as this one, a lad, was letting go of the red leather purse. I nudged Goodwin.

We looked on as the pickpocket's guardian rusher smashed into the coney. The cityman released the lad with a grunt, falling to the pavement as the rusher strolled off. The lad turned to run and saw that Goodwin and I watched him without making a move in his direction. He stared at us, then fled as the cityman staggered over to lean on a store wall. Some yards away, the young filcher turned to stare again. Seemingly he didn't know we'd been warned to leave him be.

There was a demon in me for a moment, I guess. I winked at him. Then I touched my forefinger to my eye and pointed it at him in the sign meaning, "I see you." The lad ran then, as if the Black God gave chase.

"I don't know that tweaking Pearl Skinner's tail is a good idea," Goodwin remarked. "You're lucky the rusher didn't notice. Nor did the coney."

"I doubt the lad will tell her I made it plain we saw what he did," I replied, stuffing my hands in my breeches pockets.

"Has Pearl set her filchers to swapping every purse they lift, do you suppose?" Goodwin asked as we walked away.

"For the three I've seen do it, there's dozens more who don't," I replied. "I can't help but wonder if these coneys are picked deliberate, or if they're just picked because the filchers or their rushers don't like the coney's face."

"The skinny gixie in red is on our rumps again," Goodwin murmured. "And Haden is behind *her*. At this rate, Cooper, we shall have a parade."

"I could circle around, ask Haden to rid us of her." I hated to do it. The watcher, from the glimpse I had of her, was half starved and might not fare well with Pearl if she lost us.

Goodwin shook her head. "Not yet. Let's see if she follows us all of the time, or if they swap watchers. What is Pearl so *nervous* about?"

"She's all over us like maggots on garbage, just because I interfered with one pickpocket yesterday." I whispered it. "I think we should do something to draw her into the open!" Achoo whuffed. I think she liked to see me so excited.

Goodwin sighed. "Cooper . . . Look, there's too much here that does not make sense." Goodwin's voice was soft, and we had the street noise to cover it. "Who makes the coles? *Where* do they make them? If all the Rogue's in it, why isn't Port Caynn soaking in coles and why hasn't Nestor told us they've been arresting cole passers? No, the group that's switching bad coin for good, at the gambling places or at the banks before they found out, that group is a small one. The secret would have spread elsewise. And what's the reason for those red purse swaps? Sure, it puts more coles into the moneystream, but it doesn't make the Rogue a big enough profit. What's it *for*?"

Goodwin had me there. I couldn't think of a sensible reason for the purse swaps. The good coin that the filchers got wouldn't be enough to buy the Rogue so much as a single pearl tooth.

We walked on in silence down Moneychangers', both of us thinking. Achoo stretched her *tumit* orders as far as they would go, stepping back or to the side to sniff at sommat. Then she would pop into place by my left heel, looking as innocent as if she'd never left it. As we passed the Gold- and Silversmith's banks, I heard Goodwin mutter to her, "You're not fooling Cooper, you know."

The street began to rise. Queen's Heights loomed some way up ahead, its granite cliffs rising even higher than the city walls. We were in Flowerbed now. I recognized this part of town a little, since we had been here only a few hours ago.

We turned down a side street that led us to a winding avenue just a block back from Moneychangers'. Here the gem merchants have their scales, their goods, and their guards. Merchants come here directly from their ships, small pouches in their hands or carried by their own hard mots and coves. We watched as they upended those pouches in the vendors' scales. They'd brought pearls, emeralds, sapphires, opals, rubies, spinels, garnets, and topazes, rough or polished into cabochons with fires burning at their hearts. One vendor had four clerks inside his small shop. Each of them was carefully weighing gold dust.

As we walked up the street, we noticed that business was slack. Then, from inside one shop, we heard a woman with a Sirajit accent snap, "I told you, it's gold or nothing!"

Goodwin and I looked at each other and halted by the open door. *"Tunggu,"* I told my hound. Achoo took her post by the door and I stepped inside. This mot dealt in opals. I saw

Tortallan fire opals, the black opals of northern Galla, and something new, stones that were labeled *Sirajit opals: tawny and dark*. The tawny ones were the color of a Yamani's skin, with orange, green, and red fires inside. The dark opals were mahogany brown, with red, blue, green, yellow, orange, and purple fires that made my fingers itch to pick them up.

The source of the argument was not the opals. A Tortallan noble was the only other person in the shop apart from the vendor, the guard, and me. The noble was dressed in the height of Corus fashion, with gold braid on his silk tunic and gold embroideries on his round cap. He did not look like the sort who accepted any block to his plans.

The vendor was a dark-skinned Sirajit woman. Heavy gold rings that dripped with rubies hung in her ears, while a gold chain with ruby drops on it swung between her nose and one ear. She wore a loose Carthaki dress made of colorfully striped wool. Behind her stood a large and muscular guard armed with a curved sword.

The vendor was thrusting ten stacks of silver nobles at the Tortallan. "I am forced to change my policy, honored sir," she told him politely. "I have received instructions from those I represent to accept payment only in gold."

The Tortallan clapped his hand to his sword hilt. "Impudent slut! You *dare* imply that my money is no good!"

The vendor stood, sweeping up her opals with one hand. The guard drew his curved blade. I made myself small in the shop's corner and took out my baton. I saw Goodwin move to block the open doorway. We had the same thought, that we might have to act as working Dogs after all, to keep the two Sirajits from a nasty death far from home.

The Sirajit woman glanced aside and down. "Honored sir, I may not gainsay my masters' orders, forgive me. The stones are theirs, and I must sell as I am bid." She glared at me and snapped, her voice far sharper, "You, get out of my shop! Your kind is bought and paid for!"

The noble turned to stare at me. I shrugged, which just happened to cause me to raise my baton. "Sorry, yer honor," I said, trying to talk like one of the Port Caynn folk. "I guess we're not welcome, unless ye've gold for the mistress." He couldn't say I threatened him, after all, could he? The baton just happened to be in my hand.

"Trull!" the noble said to the Sirajit mot. The guard rumbled and stepped out from behind the counter.

Now Goodwin came in. "My lord, let's be on our way. These foreigners don't know a nobleman such as yourself, and they don't respect our ways." I got in behind him, a little too close. Like most nobles, he stepped away from me. That took him nearer to the door.

"I want you to report these people to your sergeant!" he told Goodwin. "I want them arrested and their goods seized!"

"My sarge will hear of it the moment I see her, m'lord, don't you worrit yerself none," Goodwin assured him, following him out. I went after her, closing the door behind me. I heard bolts clack into their slots before I'd taken a step away. The shutters slammed shut beside my ear. I waited there as Goodwin tried to smooth my lord's feathers down. Finally he strode off in a mighty pet.

Goodwin turned back to me. "Goddess be thanked that was fairly quiet."

I could hear the Sirajit woman speaking, her voice sharp. I motioned for Goodwin to wait and stepped around the corner into the small alley. There I could put my ear against the thin wood of the shop's wall.

"Pack up everything, Usan," I heard the mot say. "Everything, down to the last crystal. We're leaving for Siraj—or Barzun, or even Carthak—on the next boat. Anywhere but here."

"But you haven't made the profit you want." That had to be the guard.

"Nor will I with the silver gone bad. I'm going to send word to the others, advising them to get out, too." She sounded shaky. "*Half* of what I took in yesterday was false. We're leaving!"

I thought, So the tale of her masters' orders was only a tale. It sounds like *she's* the master.

I heard the bolts snap. She was coming out. Goodwin peeked around the corner and watched, then said, "She's gone. Achoo is still sitting where you left her."

"Oh, pox," I said. "Achoo, *kemari*!" She came trotting around the corner. "Good girl," I told her, giving her some dried meat and an ear rub. "You did just as I said!"

"I wonder how many gem dealers will leave on that woman's say-so," Goodwin murmured as the three of us walked on down the street. "I'm no expert on those things, but it seems to me that if enough foreign merchants pull out, a country's in trouble."

"It may just be her and her kinfolk," I suggested. "She only said 'the others.' "

"True," Goodwin replied. She clapped me on the shoulder. "I'll put it in my report. Let it be Lord Gershom's headache."

At last we turned eastward again, into the area where mots shopped for ribbons, beads, jewelry, and such-like. Goodwin was much amused when I asked her to halt at a shop that sold face paint. I dithered only a little, then bought a small pot of eyelash blackener, a tiny comb to apply it with, a pot of red for my lips, and a little brush to use with that. Next we halted at a perfumer's shop. Goodwin was a great help to me there. I came away with a pot of carnation scent fixed in a balm, which she said would last longer than an oil. I can switch it with the lily of the valley scent that Okha gave me, so I won't tire of always smelling the same.

We ate our lunch in Tradesmen's District, sampling the goods from several vendors' carts and sharing them with Achoo. Then we bought two loaves. We found a fountain square with its own bounty of pigeons and set about feeding them as we let our food settle. Goodwin watched the folk around us as I listened to ghosts.

"I said I'd teach 'im t'steal another cove's woman—" A cove's voice, rough and bullying.

"It was right after the stew. I didn't feel right." A mot, this.

"Mam, they's rats down there!" A terrified lad.

"But look, we send out too much, don't yez see? We bring in plenty o' good coin, but folk are noticin' the bad!" A man with a Corus accent. I sat up, paying attention.

"Eight children I've had. I'm that afeered o' this 'un's comin'. I feel all, weak-like. He keeps throwin' the charm away, whenever he finds it." A mot who sounded weary to the bone.

"I said I'd leave everything to him. Why would he kill me if he knew he was my heir?" A cove, old and bewildered.

"I begged them, stop the coins for a time." It was the cove from Corus, the one who said folk are noticing. I sat up, looking for the pigeon who carried him. Which one was it?

"The stew didn't taste right. I saw her put sommat in it, but she said 'twas on'y spice—"

"Help! Someone help me, please! Who's seen a child, so tall, gold curls, a red luck string about her wrist? Please, have you seen her?" That was the voice of a living mot, coming from somewhere nearby.

The pigeons took off all at once, an explosion of wings. When they cleared, there was a mot in a wet apron running about the square, grabbing at folk. "Please, have you seen her?"

A tradesman shook her off with no patience or kindness for her tear-blotched face. "Get a Dog, that's what they're for!"

She scrabbled at his arm. "I tried, good sir, but—"

The cove gave her a hard shove then, sending her tumbling into the dirt. Then he checked his purse. To his companion he said, "Greedy beggars get worse all the time!" They strode off.

The mot put her face in her hands and wept.

Goodwin rose and went over to her.

"I thought I had something," I told Achoo, gathering the remains of our lunch and stuffing them in my pack. "I should come back tomorrow. That one bird . . . I wonder, if I ask Slapper, would he bring the bird to me?" Achoo made a tiny sound in her throat. I took it to be a question and explained, "I never did so before. Back home, all the pigeons knew where to find me. Here they don't even know me."

Goodwin came over with the mot. "Cooper, on your feet," she said, her eyes glittering. "This is Vorna. She was doing her wash. Her little girl wandered off."

"Shouldn't she get the local Dogs?" I asked.

"They told her that if she didn't have a silver noble, she oughtn't to bother them, Cooper," Goodwin said almost cheerfully.

I thought, Well, there's two coves in this city who don't question the silver.

Goodwin was still talking to me. "Now, is that poxy hound of yours for show, or can she earn all the food she's been gulping down?"

I put on my pack and looked at Vorna. Gods all be thanked Phelan had taught me how to do this. Gods all be thanked I do my memory exercises. "You were doing your wash. Have you something of the child's? Something dirty, that she's worn?"

Vorna hiked up her dress and raced off across the square, her wooden shoes rattling on the stones. Goodwin, Achoo, and I followed. Achoo's tail slapped my legs hard. Seemingly she knew she was about to do the thing for which she was made.

Vorna led us three blocks away into another, less popular square. This was a fountain square sheltered among poorer houses. The women who washed their clothes here looked at Vorna and shook their heads.

"No one's seen her?" Vorna cried. "I went all the way to Persimmon Square for help! Surely by now—"

An assortment of lads and gixies, some of them sweating and panting, shook their heads, too. "We went to your place, and her auntie's, and your cousin's," a gixie told Vorna. "None of 'em seen her."

I got down on my knees with my hound. "Achoo!" She was wriggling, her tail a blur in the air. "Achoo, *mudah,* all right?"

Like magic, Achoo sat and went still, her eyes watching me. I stayed beside her, one arm around her. I knew, just as she did, we were about to be put to the test.

A large, blowsy mot shouldered through the group of women and children. She came to Vorna, who had seized a basket of soiled clothes and was searching through it, tossing the items that didn't satisfy her on the ground.

"No luck, lass, and no word." The big mot looked at Goodwin and me. "Who are you two? You're not with the Tradesmen's kennel. I know every Dog there, and you don't belong."

"Falda, please," Vorna pleaded. "Don't start trouble."

Goodwin squared off to Falda. Once again Goodwin wore that strange new face, the one she'd had on last night. "You can waste time arguing our wheres and whyfores, while the babe stays missing," she told Falda, looking up into the bigger mot's face to do it. "But what *I* heard was that two Tradesmen's Dogs wouldn't do it without a silver noble, while Goddess knows what happens to that child. All *you* need know, mistress, is that Cooper and I are truly Dogs, and Cooper here has a scent hound." And she clapped her hand on the grip of her baton.

Falda reconsidered as Vorna handed me a filthy child's nightgown. It had been pissed in and dried. It smelled to the rooftops. "Will this do?" she asked me.

I stood, nodding, and took the gown. Phelan had said things with piss or scummer on them were the best. I don't know how poor Achoo can stand it. Mayhap the smells that made me like to puke were perfume to her. Gods all know four legged dogs will put their noses in places a human will run screeching from.

I looked at Goodwin. I wasn't sure how this worked with my human partner. "Do we go together, or—?"

Goodwin shook her head. "I'll stay here, in case someone else brings in the little one. If that happens, I'll find you and the hound."

I frowned, confused and worried. "How will you find me? Whistle? I lost mine in the riot, I think, and if we're too far off, I'll never hear."

Goodwin patted me on the shoulder. "Cooper, here I was

thinking you were healed from that clout to your head. Where's your Dog tag?"

"I have it right here, like I was told to," I said, tugging it from my belt purse. The glowing dot that was Goodwin was at the center of the compass drawn on the obsidian. "Why would I—?" Then I realized how she would find me if she had to. I was so embarrassed that I began to blush. "I'll just talk to Achoo from here on."

Achoo pawed my knee and whuffed softly. She wanted to move out. I thrust my Dog tag into my pouch hurriedly and looked at Goodwin. "Would you move them back?" I whispered. "They might respect it a bit more at the moment, coming from you."

Goodwin gave Falda a second look, just in case, then faced the cityfolk around us, her hands on her hips. "All of you, move back. If the hound comes at you, move from her path! And do what Cooper tells you, else we'll both know why!"

She gave me the nod and that tiniest of winks.

I knelt beside Achoo and offered the stinking nightgown to her. "Achoo, *bau*," I told her.

"Use only her name and a command word when you work," Phelan had told me. "That's all she needs to hear from you."

Achoo's nostrils flared. Then she leaned her head closer and sniffed. She sniffed again, then began to snuffle the nightgown, up and down, inside its folds, on front and back. She even stuck her head inside. When she pulled her head out, she began to sneeze.

My attention was fixed on her now. I stuffed the nightgown into my belt and got to my feet. Already she was casting forward, her nose in the air. She found her way to Vorna's things, wet and dry alike, stirring them with her nose. She sneezed again, twice, then set forth. For a few moments all was frustration as she went around the fountain and back, over to the edge of the square and back, up to the nearest corner and back.

I could hear Vorna tell Goodwin, "She's so restless, my little Aldis. She goes to play with the other children, to see a knight ride by—"

To get *stolen,* I thought, but I had no more leisure for thinking. Achoo found a scent that took her off the square and down a narrow alley. I ran to keep her in sight as she went at a steady trot, not too slow and not too fast. She had to go at a regular pace, both to keep me with her and to keep a steady flow of the scent in her nose, so Phelan had told me. Behind us I heard Goodwin yell to the folk in the square, "Don't you *dare* follow! You'll only get in the way!"

Achoo's narrow alley took us down two blocks. We turned into another small alley, then ran through a maze built of small outbuildings and sheds. Gods all above, how had the child known this was here? Then I saw where Achoo was bound and yelped. I covered my mouth with my free hand before I could do it again and distract her. Achoo had found a tunnel between two tumbledown buildings. Somehow the litter of years, including trellises of some kind, had fallen over the pathway between them. They'd left but a crawl space, a hideaway of adventure for children and a hound, and of misery for a full-grown mot. I dropped to my hands and knees in the muck, silently cursing. For this, I could just as well have stayed in the Cesspool in Corus, and raised my own muck-crawling toddlers to chase.

We came into the light again, where the path met with a

small street. Achoo stood, casting. I waited until I was certain she was confused, then drew the nightgown out with two fingers and offered it to her again. She sniffed. I stuck it in my belt once more, trying to get as little muck from my hands on it as I could.

Achoo raised her head, sniffing the air. I waited, quietly, ignoring the few passersby who stared at us. Achoo had not started to look bewildered, as Phelan said she would if she'd lost a scent. She seemed purposeful, alert. I wondered if she was like me, at her best doing what she was meant to do, hunting rather than flirting and telling lies to strangers. Then she took up her hunting trot, still following Aldis's smell on the currents of air.

Three blocks and two alleys later Achoo halted at the back of a small cart tucked into a narrow passageway between houses. The cart was a wooden box with a lock at the door. She stood up at the door, nudged the lock, and glanced at me. She'd been trained not to bark if her handler was in view. Her silence could mean her life and mine if there were Rats about.

I listened first. I heard only traffic from the street in front of the houses. No one was in the alley where I stood. I ventured first a glance under the cart, to see if anyone stood near it. No sign of feet. I took my baton firmly in hand and gave Achoo the hand signal to guard. Then I went to check, carefully, if anyone sat on the driver's seat of the cart. No one. Back to the locked door I went, sliding my pack off my shoulders. From the side pocket I took the pouch of lock picks Rosto had given me this last summer.

Aniki had taught me their use, though I barely needed training to open this lock. Once it was open, I put the picks away and stowed the lock in my pack. Only when the pack was on my shoulders again did I grip my baton and fling the door open, standing away in case there was a guard inside.

There was no guard. Who would need one for a set of hobbled children?

There were *seven* of them. Some were still weeping. Others had stony faces. They knew their fate. Poorer children, from their clothes. Ma or Da, someone had warned them that one day the child sellers would get them and they'd be slavers' bait if they didn't behave. It would do no good to cry, so most of them didn't. All of them stared at me, expecting their captors with another prisoner.

"Aldis?" I asked. "Which of you is Aldis?"

The one closest to the door, a beautiful little gixie with hair so blond it was near white, big brown eyes, and dimpled cheeks, flung herself at me, or tried to. The rawhide hobbles on her ankles yanked her down. I knelt and cut the ties, then let her hug me.

"Don't cry," I whispered as her face crumpled. "Quiet, all of you. I'll get the Dogs to return you to your rightful homes." I slashed the hobbles on their feet, then jumped out of the cart. "You must wait here yet a bit. Achoo, *hamun il Jugu!*" I told her.

Achoo leaped into the cart with the little ones and turned to face the door, her eyes sharp. I tried to decide what I should do next. How far would I get if I just stole the children away? Mayhap I ought to deal with the Rats who had taken them first.

"Hey!" A cove had come around the cart. He made the mistake of staring at the open door first, when he should have looked at me. I rammed the end of my baton into the top of his soft belly, hard into the muscle that works the lungs. He turned white and went to his knees, fighting to breathe. With no air, he couldn't yell for his friends.

Too bad for me they were nearby. They came running. I moved out into the alley, drawing them away from the cart and the little ones. One was a redhead, bearded, his tunic clean and well embroidered. He'd be their money man, the one in charge of selling. He drew the short sword hanging at his side. The other was bigger, bald, with a scar on his left cheek.

I waited for one of them to move, to see what I had to deal with. I was feeling better than I had in days. Fights are such clean affairs. There's no guessing what folk mean or what they're after. I *know* what they're after.

The redheaded one came at me first, doubtless thinking the sword would scare me off. I let him reach a bit too far and slammed him on the wrist, breaking it. He screamed and let the sword drop. I stood on the weapon to keep the bald one from getting it. Why had he not jumped me? I risked a look around.

Slapper attacked the bald cove from above, gouging his scalp with his one good set of claws and his beak. When the bald cove looked up, Slapper struck him in the face with those strong wings. He kept moving, darting in and out with that pigeon nimbleness. The bald cove wouldn't be attacking me while I was busy with the redheaded man. He was protecting his eyes.

I looked back at the man I was fighting in time to see the redhead fumble a dagger from its sheath with his good hand. I shoved the sword away and darted over, slapping my baton down on the redhead's good wrist. It broke, too. Now both his hands hung limp and he was yelling curses.

"Here, you—Dog! What be ye doin' wiv these coves?" a man called at my back. I glanced at the end of the alley. Some folk were gathering there.

"King's business—keep back!" I cried.

Now that I wasn't busy, Slapper dumped scummer on the

bald cove's head and flew off. With his hands free, the cove yanked a cudgel from the back of his belt and swung it at me. As I dodged, he kicked out. I jumped back. Instantly the redhead hooked one of my legs with both of his and yanked, to send me sprawling in the dirt. I hit my head hard enough that I felt it ring, but I had no time to be ill. I smacked sideways at his knee with my baton, making him screech as it landed with a crack, and threw myself over him, dodging the bald cove again. He'd been swinging his cudgel overhead at my skull. Instead he struck the dirt a good hard blow that must have hurt him far more than it hurt the alley.

He stepped back and watched me. I picked up the sword in my left hand and got to my feet. My poor head throbbed. I hoped Master Sholto's last healing was still good.

"What've they done to warrant yer interference?" the same pox-rotted busybody was demanding from the crowd. "We've seen 'em about fer days, deliverin' goods—"

"Stealing your littles, you cracknob bumwipes!" I yelled, out of patience and short of breath.

They went quiet, or mayhap I listened no more. The bald cove was feeling frisky, from the look of him. He grinned at me, showing off teeth stained brown, and tossed his cudgel from his right hand to his left like he had a mind to juggle. I just tested the sword's weight, settling it in my grip. He still grinned, but he watched that blade.

I've no notion of swordplay, but this blade was a short one. It wasn't much longer than a baton, and the weight nearabout the same as my lead-weighted baton. I could use it as I might a second baton, as a shield.

And I did, lunging toward the bald cove with the sword up to guard my left side, my working baton out to my right. He nearly dropped the cudgel he was flipping back and forth, and backed up to give himself some room. I swung to his right side. I'd seen enough by now to know he was left-handed, weaker on his right. The looby kept his eyes on that flashy blade. He tried to batter it down and never noticed when I swung on his left side with my baton. He turned on me with a roar, raising the cudgel again, and I slammed his right side with the flat of the sword. He swung on me backhand. I reached up, baton and blade crossed, and captured his weapon. It stuck on the sword. I let sword and cudgel drop, ramming my knee into the cove's gems.

That was when the cove I thought I'd left breathless rammed me in the back. Lucky for me, my pack got the worst of the blow. Still, I plowed into the bald cove headfirst, caught between the two of them. I took a blow to the shoulder from the one on my back afore someone yanked him off of me. I used my baton's grip to hammer the bald cove's jaw two good strokes, until his eyes rolled up in his head. Then I turned over, reaching into my boot for my rawhide hobbles. A cove and a mot, both wearing aprons that told me they were butchers, held on to the third Rat.

"You said child stealers?" the cove asked me.

I jerked my thumb at the cart. "See for yourselves. Only look careful. I've a hound guarding the little ones, and she won't like it if you get too close." I stayed seated on the bald cove until I'd bound his ankles and wrists. Only then did I get up and serve the redheaded cove the same, ignoring his whines about his poor wrists.

The two butchers came back to me, still holding on to the third Rat. The little gixie Aldis followed them. I looked around for the other children. They had gotten out of the cart but were staying there, guarded by Achoo.

I bound the third Rat at wrists and ankles, as I'd hobbled the other two. When I was finished, Aldis ran to me and clung to my leg. I picked her up and asked the butchers, "Are you satisfied they're child stealers?"

"How did *you* know of this?" the cove asked me. "You ain't from our district."

"Two of your district Dogs told the mother it was a silver noble for them to seek out her child," I replied. Then I spat on the ground to show them what I thought of such Dogs.

"They're not supposed to ask bribes to hunt little ones," the woman muttered.

"Lock it," snapped the cove.

"The mother, Vorna, she came looking for help. She found my partner and me with our scent hound. Achoo, *kemari*," I called. Achoo trotted over to stand beside me. I settled Aldis more comfortably on my hip. "We weren't going to say no to a mother, were we?" I asked the butchers. "Lucky for us Vorna was doing the wash and had the child's nightgown."

Aldis whispered in my ear, "I peed on it. I'm sorry."

I smoothed the mite's curls away from her face. " 'Twas well enough, this time," I told her. "It made the smell good and strong so's Achoo could follow you. That was a help."

Aldis looked at me, her face but inches from mine. "Mostly I don't pee the bed. I'm a big girl."

I frowned at her as I had at my little sisters, long ago. "I thought big girls listen to their mas. They don't stray where the child stealers might catch them."

Aldis hung her head, her lower lip a-tremble. "I was bad." Tears rolled down her cheeks. "They tooked me."

My heart pinched with sadness. I wiped her tears away with my hand. "Next time, will you wander away from your ma?"

Aldis shook her head. I believed her. "Next time, my hound Achoo might not be here to sniff you out. It's her you should be thanking." I set her down so she could hug Achoo. When she did, my hound licked her face.

I looked at the two butchers and at the small crowd that had moved into the alley behind them. "You're right, I'm not from this district," I said. "And I want to take Aldis back to her mother without more delay. I'd be grateful to you good cityfolk if you'd call for your local Dogs and tell them *you* caught these Rats in the act."

"But the Rats will tell a different tale," someone from the crowd said.

"Of *course* they'll want to say they was took by a Dog, even a lone small one," I told them with as much scorn as I could muster. "Elsewise they'll have to say they was grabbed by cityfolk with no weapons at all, big fine Rats like them. Mayhap you should, like, *persuade* them to tell the truth. *Before* someone finds a pair of Dogs and brings them back here." I went to the cart, letting the crowd talk among themselves. The little ones stood there, seeming a bit less frightened.

I knelt before the children so we were all nearabout the same height. "Tell the Dogs and these folk who your families are. Say no word of me," I said. The young ones nodded.

Then I looked at the two butchers, who seemed to be leaders hereabouts. "Have we an arrangement?"

The two butchers looked at the others, then at me. "Aye, though we think your nob is plain cracked," the cove told me. "Run along with this little one. Our own Dogs will come quick enough now that the Butcher's Guild has sent for 'em."

Finally! I picked up Aldis. "We're off. Achoo, *tumit*." We went down the narrow passage, around that child stealer's cart.

Behind us I heard the butcher mot say, "Now, ye scummer, what tale will ye be tellin' our Dogs?" I heard a meaty thump and a yell of pain.

"They'll be sad by the time the local Dogs get there," I told Aldis as we came out onto the next street. "Funny how folk dislike child stealers."

I made a few lucky guesses to avoid the route I'd followed to find Aldis. Soon we'd returned to the small square where we'd left her mother and Goodwin. Vorna was trying to do her wash as she cried. Goodwin was actually giving her a hand, something I never thought I'd see. Achoo barked a greeting, which made Goodwin look around. So too did Vorna. She screamed, seeing her child on my hip.

All the other laundresses flocked to us as Vorna snatched Aldis from me, kissing and crying over her all at the same time. Then she began to spank Aldis, crying, "Don't you ever wander again!"

The women were looking at us. With her spanking done, Vorna came forward. Aldis was sobbing on her shoulder. "I don't . . . ," Vorna began.

Goddess and Mithros, I hate the thank-yous. I thrust Achoo forward. "Achoo did all the work," I said. "She's the one you should thank." While they fussed over my hound, I slipped off the square into the street that would take us back the way we came. Goodwin and Achoo caught up before I'd gone a block.

"Cooper, Trickster laugh at you, someday you will learn you have to let folk say how they're grateful for what you've done!" she said, catching her breath.

"Not as long as I have partners," I mumbled.

"You think so?" Goodwin asked, giving me a raised

eyebrow. Then she pointed. "Look, there's a cart that sells grilled shrimp on a stick. Let's buy some, and you can tell me what happened when you got the child. Don't lie to me. Your hair is a mess and you have a bruise on your cheekbone."

I told her the whole of it as we bought and ate the shrimp. She chuckled over the story the cityfolk were going to tell their Dogs, about how they had captured three child stealers. Then she turned more serious as we set out for home. "You know, Cooper, it may be we erred when I said you should take Achoo and find the child. The Dogs may be fooled by that story, but Pearl will get the truth."

"You know we had to do it," I reminded her. "If Pearl goes for us because we Dogged child stealers, she'd best watch her *own* people," I said, crossing my fingers that I was right. "Rats that serve the Rogue like to think they're too good for such trade, you told me so when I was a Pup." I remembered Pearl's spy. What had happened to her?

Goodwin saw me look around us. "She kept back for a while—stayed with me while you and Achoo were on your hunt. She's good, but there weren't too many places she could hide and still watch that square. When you came back, she disappeared."

We headed east on Moneychangers'. We were almost to the turning for Serenity's when Haden caught up to us. "If yez were lookin' for Pearl's spy, she took off when ye brung the little 'un to her ma. I've not seen her since. Strange, innit?" He flipped a peach into the air. I doubted the fruit was paid for, and peaches are expensive.

"Why didn't you follow her, upstart?" Goodwin asked.

Haden grinned and offered her the peach with a bow. "Supposed t' be watchin' *you*, ain't I?"

Goodwin took the peach and bit it. Haden winked at her

and fit himself in among those who were walking along, until we lost sight of him.

I giggled. "I think he likes you," I told Goodwin as we turned down Coates Lane.

"Cooper, you alarm me," she said, but she smiled. "I have furnishings that are older than Master Haden. Oh, while I think of it—buy yourself another whistle. It's folly to go about without one."

When we reached Serenity's, it needed but one look from the priestess, and two raised brows, to remind me that I must be filthy. I took a bath and combed the dirt out of Achoo's coat, then went shopping for a good supper for her. She had earned it today. Once I'd returned, I settled at my desk to write my reports. That is done. I have given my copies to Goodwin, and I have written up this day for my journal. Now I believe it is time for a nap. Tonight we go to supper again with Hanse, Steen, Flory, Dale, and any of the others who might care to come along. Poor Achoo. It's the yard again for her. At least I'm giving her an excellent supper and a meaty bone this time, for an apology.

Pox and murrain. I never got to ask Okha how to use the face paint.

Well, I'll just try the lash darkener and leave the rest for another time.

Those we met the night of September 15 and such information as I learned of them, then and in succeeding days:
Lowenna Boller, orange girl, friend of Fair Flory
Kevern Pye, works for Hanse in caravans
Austell Goff, works for Hanse in caravans
Erben Worts, works for Hanse in caravans
Alisoun Nails, courier at Goldsmith's Bank, knows Dale

Wat Eavesbrook, works for Hanse in caravans
Viel Sperling, friend of Fair Flory
Bermond Tapener, master clerk at Goldsmith's Bank, knows Dale
Jaco Quilty, journeyman smith, friend of Hanse
Amda Threadgill, works for Hanse in caravans

At six-thirty of the morning.

concerning the night of September 16, 247

Goddess bless me, his hands. They are limber and warm, lighting every part of me he touches. He hasn't even touched the soft and secret parts. Not that I could stop *thinking* of him touching me everywhere once I'd gone to bed last night. Achoo finally climbed to the floor in disgust because I tossed and turned so. She is yet sleeping there.

And his kisses!

They came for us here at six of the clock last night, Dale and Hanse and the rest. We walked, the eating house being six scant blocks along the side of the ridge from Serenity's. They'd brought three more of Hanse's caravan guards with their companions. Everyone was full of good cheer. Some noble was having a birthday, and there was to be a fireworks display in the Ridge Gardens. The eating house looked out over Ridge Gardens where the fireworks were to be held, and Hanse and Dale, having planned this party weeks ago, had snagged a corner of it. We would even have a balcony where we might watch everything in comfort.

So caught up in Dale's joking was I that I didn't notice we had moved to the outside of the group. Suddenly Dale hooked me around the waist.

I reacted without thinking, bringing my bent arm up under the arm around my waist and slamming my free hand into the base of his neck. At the last moment I knew what I did and pulled my blow, but Dale still ended against the side of a building in the small alley beside us. For a moment we stood there, breathing a little hard, staring at each other.

Then I hung my head. "I'm sorry," I muttered. "You shouldn't surprise a Dog."

"Beka, I'm going to hold your hand now," he said, only half joking. He reached out and drew me into the alley with him. "I'm sorry. I've never taken a Dog around before. It never occurred to me there might be . . . hazards. But surely you have been courted this way before?"

I shook my head. I still couldn't bring myself to look at him.

He slowly put one hand under my chin and raised my face until our eyes met.

"What?" I asked him, my heart thumping. "I'll tell you right now, I've had a hard day, I'm bruised all over, and I am *hungry*."

In the torchlight from the street I saw his frown. "Bruised?"

"I'm a Dog, remember? I fight with Rats and they fight back. I bruise."

Dale picked up my hand and kissed the tips of my fingers. "Bruised here?"

I tried to yank my hand away. "Stop that. You're a flirt."

He looked at me, his eyes twinkling most wickedly. He kissed the back of my hand. "Bruised here?"

I tugged my hand again. "And a tease."

He turned my hand over and kissed my palm softly, his beard tickling my skin, roughened by my long grip on my baton. "Here?"

The peaks on my peaches went so tight I thought they might pop clean off. I pushed at Dale's forehead. "I'm not one of your toys." I tried not to sound breathless.

"I just found that out." He rubbed the base of his throat. "Never sneak up on the Dog. Very important, I think." He reached out to stroke my arm and felt my sleeve daggers. "Ouch! Not just fists—I've found your teeth! I'll check one more place—are you bruised here, Beka?"

He kissed the inside of my wrist. My knees were going weak *before* he licked it, just one little flick of his tongue. I turned to jelly, no more a sharp-toothed Dog.

Cool metal slipped around my wrist and he let me go.

"What?" I said, trying to catch my breath. I stepped out into the street, where I could see better. He'd slipped a silver bracelet onto me, the torc style that doesn't clasp. I turned to him. "What is this?"

"You won't take a coin, so I got you a gift. You were my luck last night," he told me, his eyes steady. "If we don't show our appreciation, the Trickster gets angry." He tapped my nose. "Besides, you don't have many pretty things, I'll wager. You'd never buy them for yourself. That's why you need me."

I scowled at him. "Oh, I *need* you now, is it?"

We heard a bellow from near two blocks away. "I'm STARVING!"

"I think Hanse's father was a bull," Dale said. He cupped his hands around his mouth. "WE'LL BE *there!*" He grabbed my hand, twining his fingers with mine. "Yes, you need me," he said as we trotted down the street. "You need me to make you laugh. You need me to tickle your—" He chuckled evilly. My skin rippled with goose bumps. "Fancy," he said at last. "You need me to remind you that you're a woman and not just a Dog."

I yanked him to a halt and tugged his hand until he was looking at me. "You can't separate the two, Dale," I warned him. "A Dog's all I've ever wanted to be, and sometimes I can't help being one."

He put his free hand around the back of my neck, warming

it, and me, all over. "I don't *want* to separate them. I think the combination is exciting."

He picked me up by the waist and swung me around, landing me in a doorway with my back to the door.

And then he *did* kiss me.

Oh, I came all undone. He wrapped me about in his arms. I got one arm about his waist and one about his shoulders and hung on. He wasn't a hard kisser, or a quick, fast pecker, or one that thinks he must suck your face off, like the other coves that have kissed me. He fit his lips to mine and went very quiet and gentle, breathing my breath, settling his hold on me until we matched, twined about like vines.

No more. I go all loose just thinking about it.

We kissed twice more, I think, slow. Taking our sweet time. Finally he said, "Hanse'll kill us if we're any later."

"Goodwin will think we got robbed," I managed to reply.

I was glad to hear some roughness in his voice. I don't think he'd sound so if he was just playing with me to keep his flirting skills good.

So we left that doorway and walked down the street, hand in hand again. We'd gone a block when he asked, "How many blades *are* you wearing?"

I began to laugh. He'd have felt the ones at my back, for certain, and mayhap the leg ones, too. "I'm used to Dogging in the worst part of Corus," I said. "And I don't know Port Caynn at all. A girl should be prepared."

"Well, this walking out with a Dog is proving educational," Dale told me. "You'll protect me, won't you? You'll have to if you keep bringing me luck. I'll have heaps of gold coin, and you'll be forced to stay with me to protect my skinny gambling body."

I couldn't help it. I giggled. He was so lighthearted, and so funny. I'd never known anyone like him. "You're not skinny, and I've seen you fight," I said. He looked at me and grinned, the torchlight dancing in his eyes. "Where did you learn that kicking style?"

"Some Shang friends who were better fighters than they were dice players taught me," he said. "Listen, did I hurt those bruises? And how did you get them?"

I hadn't thought of the bruises since he'd kissed my hand. I shrugged and told him, "We went about, around the gem sellers' street. And there were three child stealers. We disputed, and I won."

Dale stopped and turned to face me in the street. "You . . . 'disputed' with three Rats."

I put a hand on my hip—right atop one of my bruises, sadly. "I wasn't about to offer them cakes and wish them a fine day."

"And how many children did my fine, brave Dog save from whatever those Rats had planned for them?" Dale asked me quietly.

I looked away, grateful for the dark that hid my blushes. He sounded so proud of me. It made my heart flip over. A handful and a half. It wasn't even half a day's work. I'd've given them over for return to their families and gone back on the street, were I at home. Do we go to supper or not?"

He kissed me again, ignoring all the folk walking around us, the coves with their whistles and words of advice, the mots with their laughter and calls of "Lucky girl!" I grabbed his wrists as he held my face, blushing like fire at all the folk looking at us. I tugged, but Dale wasn't inclined to stop. I told myself no one could see my face, but it was dreadful, all those strangers staring.

Other hands tugged at us. Hanse and Goodwin had come.

"The night is young and we are about to bay at the moon, so come and tell us what you want," Goodwin said, towing me along. I pulled my veil over my face.

Hanse looked over at me. "Beka with eyes like moonstones, I hear you were up to Dog work again today, you and Clary," he said, his own eyes dead serious. "Weren't you warned?"

"Don't tell me your Rogue winks at child stealers," Goodwin replied boldly. She poked Hanse in the ribs—not gently, either. "That's what Cooper and her scent hound were after, my buck. A fine job she did, too."

"She's not *my* Rogue," Hanse protested, rubbing his ribs as we entered the eating house. This was a more elegant place than the Merman's Cave, though in truth I noticed little of the furnishings. Dale had taken my free hand again and was tickling my palm with a finger. I snatched my hand away, looking to see if anyone had noticed. I had never let a cove be so bold with me in public. For all he was Rogue, even Rosto had learned that.

Burly house slave guards, so much alike they could have been bought as a pair, halted us. "Swords," they told the coves. "Give 'em to her." They pointed to a mot who stood before a room where the weapons lay on shelves. Then the guards looked Goodwin and me over with knowing eyes. "What manner of trouble will we get here, good mistresses?" the one on my left asked. "We know you've got bits and pieces tucked away under those nice dresses."

So the house guards were better than at the Merman's Cave or the Waterlily.

"They're Dogs, lads," Dale called as he checked his sword.

"I'll vouch for them," I heard a familiar voice say. Nestor came in behind us with Okha—well, Amber—on his arm.

Nestor was out of uniform, but these guards seemed to know him. They bowed their heads and let him and Amber-Okha sweep by. Nestor smiled at me and tucked a coin into one guard's hand.

"Nestor, Amber, join us," Hanse shouted after them. "We're upstairs in the east corner!"

Amber-Okha put a hand on Nestor's shoulder. He smiled and nodded. Okha waved his fingers at us as they took the stairs.

"Sarge Haryse's word is good enough fer us, Guards-women," the guard who'd noticed we carried blades said to Goodwin and me. "You can go on in."

"I didn't know you were friends with the sergeant," Goodwin said to Hanse as he came back to us.

Hanse shrugged. "Oh, everybody knows everybody when they dance between the Court of the Rogue and the gamblin' houses," he replied. "I met Nestor because I bring Amber makeup and perfume from our Barzun trips. He's a decent cove, for all he's the law. Not bought law, neither. Straight law. A cove knows where he stands with Nestor, and it isn't on the good side of a coin."

"My feelings are hurt," Dale said with a pout as he joined us. "The guards don't trust Hanse and me, and we're such trustworthy lads."

Goodwin gave him a gentle push. "I wouldn't trust you farther than I can throw you, and you a bony bit of a cove," she said. "Look at you, toying with my poor, earnest Beka. I've been hearing about *your* reputation, Master Rowan! One foot in and one foot out of the Court of the Rogue, you *and* Hanse!"

"Lies, all of it, lies," Dale said, lifting my hand to his lips and kissing it. "Well, *mostly* lies."

"Caravaners got to be on terms with the Rogues," Hanse said. "Elsewise we lose too much cargo to them on the road. Better to be friendly and pay a little tax monthly, like."

"Now, what's this?" Sharp-eyed Goodwin had spotted the bracelet. When she took my hand to examine it, I got a better look than I had on the street. The front was set with three small, clear oval stones. They'd been invisible outside, but here, in the lamp- and torchlight, they sparked in different colors. Two held darts and chips of blue and light purple fire. The middle one, the whitest, held dots and sparks of pink, orange, and yellow light deep inside it.

I turned to Dale and started to yank the bracelet off. "I can't take this. It's too expensive."

He stopped my hand with both of his and gave me his I'm-very-serious wide-eyed look. "It's bad luck to return a gift, Beka."

"It is," agreed Goodwin.

"He's right," added Hanse.

Goodwin slapped me on the shoulder. "Besides, Cooper, most of your jewelry is scummer," she said cheerfully. "It won't kill you to have some nice things." She touched her moonstone necklace, which *is* lovely. "What are the stones on the bracelet, anyway?"

"Sirajit opals," Dale said cheerfully. "Usually you see the brown stones and the peach-colored ones. Now and then I get lucky and find something with the clear gems."

"Very lovely," Goodwin said. "Maybe some nice lad will buy *me* a present like that." We looked at each other, thinking of the opal seller who was determined to leave Corus. Then Goodwin took Hanse's arm. They began to climb the stairs to the second floor of the eating house. The first floor was already packed with diners.

"You have to be careful with opals, though," Dale said, taking my arm. "They're the Trickster's gems. Some last for ages. Others crack and go to pieces in months. If you get them just out of the ground, you want to hang on to them for a year at least before you try cutting them." He smiled at me. "I'm a bit mad for opals. I suppose it's because I am a Trickster's follower at heart."

Something in his eyes, as if he hoped I'd share his love of the stones, made me do something I rarely do. "I've an opal of my own," I told him, and fetched mine out.

Dale halted in the middle of the stair, drawing me to the side, next to a hanging circle of candles. Carefully he turned my stone in his graceful fingers, his eyes finding the cherry sparks, the green flares, the yellow lights, the orange ones, and the way a pink bit set in the surrounding pink stone might suddenly turn emerald green. "A raw fire opal," he said. "Not enough solid gemstone to make it worth cutting—"

I snatched it back. "I don't want it cut," I said. "I love it like it is."

Goodwin came back and grabbed us. "Goddess save me, you two are like children. Must we tie you to a rope and tow you to keep you with the rest of us?" She stared at my hand. "She showed you her fire opal? She *must* like you. Now come along and talk while we *eat*!"

She and Hanse weren't joking about the others' mood. They roared curses as we approached. The maids had placed us at tables set in a U so they might more easily wait on us. Better, we were in a sort of open room set off one corner of the building, so we could hear each other.

As luck had it, I got to sit beside Nestor, with Dale on my right. Goodwin and Hanse were across from us, on the opposite side of the U, with Steen and Flory. Dale and I were saved more curses as maids arrived with trays of small pasties stuffed with all manner of things. Okha, on Nestor's other side, had asked them for cider twilsey for me, while Steen had remembered Dale's wine, so we were well set up.

Dale asked me for my fire opal again. I handed it over to him, easier now that I knew he loved opals, for all he might joke about cutting mine. When he stood to eye it beside a lamp near the entry, Nestor leaned closer to me.

"I heard an unnamed Dog and her scent hound went on a hunt today," he whispered in my ear. "Later I get word from Deep Harbor that some cityfolk managed to seize three child stealers at their work at the same time."

I tried to look innocent. "Why are you interested?"

"It's not *me* who should worry you, sweetheart. It's Pearl."

I watched Dale cross the room to answer a question of Flory's. "I am curst tired of Pearl," I said, keeping my voice low. "Surely even that daughter of a scummer trull won't wink at child stealers."

"You wager your life on that," Nestor said. "Now listen close. I've news for you and Goodwin." He put two of the little pasties into my trencher. "Sir Lionel won't go after the guild banks for hiding their knowledge of coles in the city. He says 'twill only start a panic."

I stared at him. When I spoke, I kept my own voice soft. "But they risk the safety of the realm!" I checked to be sure that Dale was not close enough to hear. Now he was joking with Hanse. "They *can't* hide that they know there's a big operation going on!"

"The banks and Sir Lionel alike are panicking," Nestor whispered. "We must get word to my lord Gershom as soon as may be. I was told this afternoon that I'm forbidden to use the Crown courier service to Corus anymore."

Okha leaned around Nestor's back. "The head of the Silversmith's Bank took ship for the Copper Isles this afternoon," he murmured, passing me a dish of small tarts. "His family and servants left with him."

Nestor looked at him. "When were you going to tell me this?" he asked.

Okha gave him a very pretty smile. "Right now."

Dale was coming my way. I pointed to the tarts with my knife. "Onion, or spinach and egg?" I asked.

"Both, please," Dale said, taking his seat. "You and Nestor look very serious, so I thought I'd delay my return." He set my fire opal beside my plate after I'd given him the tarts.

I handed the dish back to Nestor, who traded me for the dish of pasties. As I did so, the gems on my bracelet glittered at me. Now it was my turn to rise and go over to the stronger light. The dancing colors in the gems were as captivating as the ones in my fire opal. I have never gotten so wonderful a gift. Did he mean to try to buy me with it?

When I returned to him, he was talking with Nestor about his card game. "There are all manner of variations," Dale was saying. "In my favorite, the Trickster can be any card the player says it is. If the player has four Ladies and the Trickster, and his opponent has four Kings, the first player can just say he has five Ladies, and he wins." He looked up at me. "Do you like your present, sweet?"

"You know I do," I told him, sitting next to him. "It's still too costly."

Nestor picked up my wrist and inspected the bracelet. "Not as a thank-you for—several won games?" he asked Dale, who nodded. Nestor looked at me. "It's a fair gift."

Something tight in my chest loosened. I didn't have to feel obligated to Dale, then.

Okha pulled his seat back so he could see us better. "Dale's one of the cleverest coves you'll ever meet, Beka," he said. "He's worked out variations on chess, backgammon. . . . He reworked part of the banking laws while he worked for the Goldsmith's Guild as a clerk—"

'Dale chewed and swallowed a bite of onion tart. "Until I got cursed *bored,* among those dusty books and papers all day!" he said merrily. "Never going anywhere, never seeing anything, staggering into my rooms at midnight—and such rooms! My *mice* lived better than I did!" As Nestor grinned and Okha chuckled, Dale said earnestly, "In truth, they did! I looked into their hole one night, and they were supping on sausage, ale, and cheese, when I had bread and cider! I tried to invite myself in, but they said I had no right to charge them rent *and* food!" I was starting to grin by then.

Flory's voice rose. "Don't you tell me what I must and mustn't say, Hanse Remy! Seems to me if folk stopped tippy-toein' about the subject of coles and came right out and *said* the word, we'd all fare better!"

She had everyone's attention. Hanse threw up his hands. "*Now* look what you've done, you forward wench! Why not screech it louder, so the whole place can hear you! All this nat-terin', when the world knows coles slide through this town like scummer in the street!"

"One true coin in *three,* you beef-witted shave pate?" she demanded. "My girls takin' in one true silver in *three*? I've not seen that afore!"

"Mayhap folk are givin' 'em to you an' yer mots a-purpose," jested Amda Threadgill. She was one of Hanse's caravan guards. She also sat a good distance from Flory. "Fer bein' so vexin' with yer dead flowers an' rotten oranges, pretendin' to sell when ye're nobbut doxies. That's what ye get fer lookin' down yer noses at mots that earn wiv honest work and don't pretend t' be better'n what they are."

Flory rounded on Amda. "Leastways *my* mots ain't half guard, half robber," she said, her voice as silky as Pounce's. "At least *my* mots give fair value for business."

Hanse glared at Flory. "Them's *my* caravaners ye're talkin' about, woman."

Flory glared back. "I bring up a true worry to us here in the city and you let your fawnin' baggage foul-mouth *my* folk?"

Lucky for us the chickens in broth arrived, together with white herbs, and rice with lobster and shrimp. As the maidservants dished out the food, everyone calmed down. Like Goodwin, I'd gone sharp, listening, watching people's faces. A touch on my leg made me jerk. I was about to jump out of my chair when I realized that it was Dale's hand, warm above my knee.

He took it away. "I forgot," he whispered. "Forgive me. Are you always so jumpy?"

"I was a Puppy for a year. I've been a street Dog since April," I told him. "It sharpens you some."

"Your muscles were as hard as the table," he said, carving some chicken and placing it in my trencher. "Does your scent hound do that when she catches the scent? Does she go all tight and stiff?"

I smiled. "Actually, she sneezes."

Nestor and Dale both looked at me. "Sneezes?" Dale asked.

"It's why she's named Achoo," I said. "A *really* good scent, she sneezes more than once."

"But Beka's not here to pick up scents," Nestor told Dale. "That's what she promised Pearl."

"*Goodwin* promised," I said, stabbing a bit of chicken with my knife. "I just nodded, to be neighborly. I can't promise what Achoo might get up to."

"I hope she is ready to take the blame for you, then," I heard Okha say. Warned by his tone, I looked to the door. So did everyone else. Two guards entered in advance of Pearl. With her came Jurji the Bazhir on her right, close to Goodwin's seat. Torcall Jupp, stern and dangerous-looking even without his longsword, stood on her left, close to Dale and me. I put my hands on my lap and stuck my right hand into my sleeve, touching the hilt of my closest knife. Dale slid his hand over mine and clasped my fingers, but gently. He squeezed them. I drew my hand away from my blade.

Why did I trust him? Still, it would be better to wait. Four more of Pearl's guards took positions outside our room, barring the exit.

Dale got to his feet and bowed. "Evening, Majesty," he said. "Have you come to join us?"

"*Dale.*" The low growl came from Nestor. "You *know* we don't get on."

Pearl actually threw back her head and laughed. It was a Player's move. Instantly we all saw why she'd done it. She'd had several more teeth turned into pearls since only yesterday. Was she *made* of gold, that she could afford such folly? It makes me sick to think of the waste.

"Dale Rowan, had some of my lads your sack, I'd rule this entire city." She looked straight at Nestor as she said it.

Hanse, Steen, Flory, and most of the folk who had to do business with the Rogue got to their feet then, to show their respect, I suppose. Flory was the last to do it. That left Goodwin, Nestor, and me seated yet. Dale lifted my hand and kissed it, then looked at Pearl and raised his brows.

This time Pearl gave out with a true laugh. "Oh, aye, sack enough for twelve men, doesn't he, Hanse?"

Hanse grinned. "I wouldn't know. I just let him travel with me from time to time." He raised his cup. "Will you have a cup with us, then, Majesty?" he asked. "You can drink to his sack. Even I will say it's considerable."

Pearl shook her head. "No, I'll not drink with you, Hanse. You know my rule. I only drink in my own court, from my own glass, and my own kegs. No, I'm here to pick bones with these two bi—" She started to say it as she pointed to Goodwin and me, enough that both of us stiffened. Then she smiled big, showing off those new teeth of hers, and went on, "Guardswomen." She looked from Goodwin to me. "After my warning, you two went Doggin' today."

"We weren't Dogging," Goodwin said, looking relaxed. "We were searching for a lost child." Like me, her hands were in her lap, out of view. "The mother was half mad with fright. The district Dogs turned her off when she didn't have a silver noble for a bribe."

Pearl smirked. "A silver noble, was it? The price has gone high. Too high, mayhap."

"Too high for this poor mot," Goodwin said. Her face hadn't changed, but I knew she'd noted Pearl's taunt about silver nobles. "She was seeking any who would help, and she found Cooper and me. Cooper has a scent hound, you may remember. Mayhap you could have told that poor mother no, but me and Cooper, we're made of weaker stuff." She lifted a hand to drink from her tankard, then set the hand in her lap again. "Would you kill us for taking a child to her mother?"

"I run no child stealers," Pearl told us. "Them Rats was none of mine. Still, I'd've thought you'd be more cautious, after my warnin'."

"I lost my head," I said, not wanting Goodwin to draw all of Pearl's wrath, if any was to come. "I never had a hound afore. This was the first time I got to try her on a real scent."

Pearl looked at me. "Guards as don't think afore they act don't live long. Ain't that right, Nestor?" She looked over at him and had the gall to wink.

Nestor shifted on his seat. Okha slung an arm around his neck, weighing him down. I wrenched my hand from Dale's and grabbed one of Nestor's heavy wrists with both sets of fingers, digging into his flesh with my nails.

Pearl smiled. "You've got friends, Nestor. You want to keep them, don't you?" She ambled out of the room, her guards falling into step around her.

Okha let Nestor go. I waited a moment, to see what he might do. When he turned and buried his face in Okha's shoulder, I let him go.

"I wonder if the fireworks will be this exciting?" asked one of Hanse's people. The laugh that came was shaky, but it was a laugh. The servants arrived with a pitcher of spiced wine from the owners, with their compliments. Compliments for what, they never said, but I suspected it was for not starting any fights.

The meal continued with no more such excitement. More food was brought and carried away. At last the sweets course came. Servants began to shove parts of the wooden walls aside, revealing the balcony with its view of the park and ridge where the fireworks were to be held. We could walk straight outside to watch, or stay where we were.

I went to find the privies outside the eating house. They were hid from the view of customers by stands of flowering bushes and trees. And a place so grand as this didn't keep just one or two privies. The women alone had a stone building with seven stalls inside, each stall curtained off, with a place to wash up after.

Waiting in the line that wound through the trees, I thought I could as well have been among a flock of pigeons, so many scraps of gossip did I hear. I hadn't expected that, not ever being at a place like this, so crowded, in all my days. At festival season I keep well to the edges of the gathering so I might bolt for home when I get uncomfortable, as I often do. I never go to large eating houses. How was I to know that even women who are strangers chatter as they wait?

"—told her, prices are creeping higher, but does she listen?"

"—poor thing had twins—"

"—couldn't believe it! Silver coles! As false as the governor's smile. You take my word—"

"—can't be had for love nor money. The merchant told me the grape crop this year was the worst—"

"Did you see that hussy! Walkin' in here, bold as brass, wiv pearl teeth bought with honest folk's blood!"

I agreed with that, but I was trying to hear the mot who'd complained of coles.

"—can't deal only in coppers! I'd need a servant to carry my master's coin for the shopping!"

The mot in front of me said, "The problem's not that bad, surely?"

The woman who stood two places ahead in the line turned to face her. It must have been her who spoke of coles and of her master. "Are you deaf—or blind? How much of your silver have you cut?"

"You'll frighten folk, talking wild-like of such things," the mot in front of me replied. "I'm a businesswoman. I can't afford such talk, not with prices on the climb."

The mot who kept house for a rich man propped her hands on her hips. "Do you check your coins, mistress? *Do* you?"

A woman coming out of the privy tapped her on the shoulder. "Stop jawin' and go about yer business," she said. "The line gets longer whilst you whistle up a fuss."

"Aye," called another mot. A second yelled from farther back, "We'll miss the magic!"

They nearabout shoved the mot who'd talked her alarm into the privy. Things were just settling when three more mots came out. I could enter at last. Sitting in my own stall, I could hear my neighbors' whispers still.

"—bad for business!"

"And silver coles aren't?"

"There's *always* coles."

"Take 'em to the silver bank or the gold, pay your fee, and get true coin. You'll also get writ down in the book, so it's recorded you've turned in coles, not tried to pass 'em off."

I dared raise my voice, since none of them would know who spoke. "What about goin' to yer kennel, then?" I tried to speak halfway between the Lower City and Provost's House, like these tradesfolk would talk. "Lettin' yer Dogs know?"

There was a space of quiet. I wondered if I'd startled them into flight, like a flock of pigeons.

"Ye're new, is it?" someone asked.

"Or cracked in the nob," another mot said. "As if they listen to the likes of us, unless we come with gold in our hands."

I tried again. "All right, then. What about your Rogue?" I heard naught. Finally I added, "Come on! The Court o' the Rogue lives on coin like the rest of us. They're just as hurt by silver coles as anyone!"

Someone gave a laugh like broken glass. It echoed in the stone privy.

Another mot said, "No one wise will rouse the Rogue, whatever the cause. She'll skin you."

"Who's to say this Rogue don't have her hand in it?" a new mot asked. "And if she does—"

"Cork it!" someone whispered. "We don't know from the Rogue's business, and we mean to keep it that way!"

The air filled with the whispers of women saying, "So mote it be."

I finished my business quickly. At the back of the stall was a gap between stone wall and roof, more than big enough for a skinny mot to crawl through. Before any of them thought to look for the one with all the questions, I kilted my skirt in my belt, hoisted myself to the top of the wall, and dropped down the other side. There I perched on the edge of the privy's stone floor where it stuck out beyond the wall. Below were the openings to the privy pits, where the muck handlers could reach in and dump out the barrels. Breathing through my mouth because of the stink, I walked carefully down the floor's edge until I reached the bushes. There I untucked my skirt and shook it out. All proper again, I could sneak away, hid by the greenery.

I eyed those still waiting in line as I went. No one seemed to be watching the privy door or the mots who came out of it. With a prayer to Mithros that I'd been careful enough, I found a different entrance to the eating house from the one I had used to come outside, and walked in that way.

The door I chose was tucked behind a long, carved screen that also hid the covered passage to the kitchens. It was only dimly lit. The servers could then see if anyone stood in their way before they came out into the eating house with their trays. At the same time no one would be able to see anyone behind the screen. I stayed there and watched the small group tucked under the rise of the stair inside. Pearl stood sideways to me, arms crossed over her gold and scarlet silk dress. Jupp stood with her, and Jurji. Hanse and Steen finished their little group. What were they doing hiding out with her? They watched the kitchen entry and the screen, their eyes darting over everyone who passed as Hanse talked softly to Pearl.

"—tell you, you're costin' me money, aye, and a good client on this! They never hire twice if you drop a job once!"

Curse it, I *couldn't* hear Pearl.

Hanse listened to her, then scratched his head. "Right. I fergot," he said. "We'll go. But don't you think—"

He stopped himself as Pearl thrust a ringed finger in his face and shook it under his nose. I could nearabout hear she was telling him, "I do the thinkin'," but it isn't my job to make up what Rats say.

Hanse and Steen made their bows to Pearl and went around to take the stairs up to the second floor again. I stepped back, deeper into the shadows. Pearl and her guards turned, looking to see if anyone had come near enough to spy. Servers emerged from the kitchen passage in a clump, laden with platters of food. I went back outside and walked around to the rear entrance, just in case.

Where is Hanse going for Pearl? It's a long enough trip, or it requires enough guards, that he has to cancel a job for one of his regular employers. I can't just decide it's got to do with cole-mongering, either. I'm sure the Rogue has her finger in all manner of puddings, just as Rosto has back home.

I returned to Dale, who sat at our table, finishing a cup of wine. Everyone else had gone to the balcony. He looked at me and frowned. "I thought you'd run off."

I sat beside him. "Delicate errands take time. And I was ducking Pearl. She was all over the downstairs."

"Pearl can swive herself." Dale slipped an arm around me

and pulled me closer. I looked quickly around. No one was nearby to see us. Dale went on, "I need to give you reason to come straight back to me." He kissed so sweetly, his arms just strong enough as he drew me tight to his chest. His tongue slid gentle into my mouth as I wrapped my hands around the back of his head, feeling his silky hair against my fingers.

When we stopped to breathe, I managed to say, "As reasons go, that's well enough."

Dale chuckled and bent his head to kiss the side of my neck. I gasped and dug my nails into the back of his tunic.

Then the first firework exploded, making us both jump. Laughing, Dale pulled me to my feet. We straightened our clothes and went out onto the balcony to watch the fireworks, his arm about my shoulders. The fireworks were very nice, too, what I noticed. Someone mentioned a piece like a flock of winged horses flying over the harbor, all made of brilliant white fire. I believe we were inside for that one, in a corner with our mouths locked together.

I am sommat sorry I missed that part of the fireworks.

Once the mages' display was over, our company returned to the Waterlily to gamble. Tonight Dale started with dice. I blew on them each time he rolled, as a gambler's luck should, and he did win often. The dice were fair, too. The Waterlily keeps a mage at each table to check that the dice are not false. Dale changed tables now and then, too. "To keep my luck fresh," he told me.

He and Hanse always played together. They've been doing so for years, Steen told me as we watched. Again I had that nasty twinge of suspicion low in my belly, where so many other things had been twinging all along. Dale did work for the Goldsmith's Bank. He went nearly everywhere with a sealed pouch that Dogs wouldn't search because it was Goldsmith property.

I dare not let my feelings blind me, not when the cole-smithing problem grows worse at an alarming rate. I like him so much, and yet who better to be part of a ring of colemongers? A clever man, too clever for the work he does, a gambler who plays up and down the river. A trusted courier for the Gold-smith's Bank. Known in the Court of the Rogue, and his friends Hanse and Steen have business with the Rogue herself.

Still, Dale isn't the Rogue. There's that to be said for him, unlike the other cove who chases me.

I wonder if Ersken ever has such trouble. He's bedded Kora for over a year, knowing she's the left hand of Corus's Rogue. Still, is it the same? Kora won't talk Rosto's business with Ersken. Ersken won't talk Dog business with Kora. They read books. They go to fairs and musical entertainments, and they have plenty of friends in common, so they have much to talk on. And Rosto has never set in play any sort of ploy that would pull the country down around all of our ears.

I have no proof against Dale. I will keep my eyes and my mind open, that's all.

Dale said that I could relax whilst he switched to a game of backgammon with a deep-pocketed merchant, so I was at my leisure to wander about the Waterlily. I listened to Okha sing for a time and watched Goodwin, Hanse, and Flory play Gam-bler's Chance with some young nobles who had more gold than sense. Goodwin lost as much as she won, but seeing her small moves of the eye and mouth, tip-offs I knew so well, I realized she lost some of those hands of cards on purpose. She always amazes me. Here was a game she'd learned only yesterday, yet she could have won a nice sum at it tonight, had she chosen to.

I looked at players' coins as I roamed. Much of the silver was marked. Had the colemonger started this way, trading bad silver for good at the gambling tables? If so, was he—or she—

mad, to be dumping so many coles into the city now? More folk every day were learning the silver was no good here. How could the colemonger make a profit from trading bad for good now, when folk would test silver coin or just refuse it outright? Unless he'd already made his fortune, or he was stupid, or he was out-and-out mad. That didn't even count the chance that the colemonger was a foreigner, bent on weakening our money so that our folk would turn on each other during the winter, leaving the country open in the spring.

If I thought longer like this, I knew I would get the shakes. I went to hear Okha sing again. When he was done, I returned to Dale and tortured him by drawing my fingers down the backs of his ears and his neck.

I was yawning when he won his game with the merchant and collected his winnings. Turning in his chair, he lifted my hand and kissed the inside of my wrist. "You need to work less during the day," he said as he sneaked an arm about my waist. "You don't have enough wakefulness for the night." Together we went in search of our friends.

Hanse saw us. He put down his cards with a nod to Steen. When they stood up, Goodwin and Flory did the same, to the protests of the other cardplayers. "It's time to call the night down," Hanse said with a yawn of his own. "We're off to Arenaver in the mornin' on a short trip."

To Amda and two of the other caravaners who were coming to join us, this was plainly news.

"But, Boss, I thought we had that Legann trip day after tomorrow," Amda said.

"This Arenaver thing is more important," Hanse said. "I sent a note to Master Dendall earlier that he'll need to find someone else for the Legann job."

One of the coves whistled. "He'll not like that."

Steen waved off his words. "I'm tired of workin' fer that ol' pinchcoin anyway. He argues over every copper we spend keepin' 'im from bein' robbed blind. You want that job, Kevern?"

The man Kevern grimaced. "He's a cheap piece of moldy cheese, he is." We ambled toward the room where the men could reclaim their weapons, the caravan guards talking over their various quibbles with the merchant.

Dale and I traded kisses in the shadows all the way back to my lodgings. Once we reached Serenity's house, Goodwin went inside while Dale and I found a dark spot just on the side of the house.

"Dream of me," he said, and kissed me so long I nearabout forgot what he'd said.

But not quite. "You don't want to be in my dreams," I said when we halted. "The only ones I remember are the bad ones."

"Maybe you'll remember mine," he replied, lifting me up a little in his arms. He didn't lift my skirts—I'd never let him— but I hoped I'd remember dreams of him when he set me down, for they'd be the best dreams of my life.

He said farewell and waited until the maid let me into the house.

Goodwin had waited for me at the foot of the stairs. "We'll talk about the night's gatherings tomorrow," Goodwin said, her voice very dry. "Write up anything you fear you'll forget. I've had a bit much wine, and I think your head's elsewhere."

"I won't forget anything," I told her. I was hurt that she'd think I was too giddy to remember what I needed to for my work.

Goodwin smiled and ruffled my hair. "No. No, I don't suppose you would. But I'm worn out, and I wasn't chasing a scent hound today. We'll take it all apart for our reports in the morning."

That was better. I went outside through the silent kitchen, taking care to wait and listen until I was certain the yard was empty. Achoo also waited, bouncing to her feet only when my hand was on her collar and I was untying the rope. Once free, the silly creature frisked around me, then stood on her hind feet. I danced the hound along for a few steps before I let her go and took her inside. I collected the bowl I'd left for her in the cold pantry, and gave it to her once we were in my rooms. While she ate, I undressed. The glitter of my new bracelet caught my eye. It made an odd picture, sitting below the arm sheaths of my daggers, but it is so very pretty and so very elegant. I put it away carefully, then removed my weapons. At last, wearing my night-gown, I wrote up this night in cipher. Now it is time to sleep.

Will I bed Dale? Should I? Surely what is between us cannot last. The hunt will take Goodwin and me away from Port Caynn, or we will finish it, and I will have to return to Corus. It wouldn't be practical, not a bit.

I think I should stop at a healer's in the morning and purchase a new charm to prevent babies. It's been so long since I needed one, I don't even remember where the last one went.

Eleven-thirty of the morning.

I'd been sleeping but a couple of hours when Goodwin hammered on my door.

"Get dressed," she told me when I opened up to glare at her. "Cityfolk clothes and a veil. Nestor wants us."

I blinked at her. "What's the hour?"

"The harbor clocks were striking two when Truda came. Move," Goodwin ordered.

I left Achoo sleeping in my bed. As I dressed in citymot's garments, she rolled over into the warm spot I had made.

When I came downstairs, I found Goodwin and the half-asleep Truda at the dining table. Goodwin plucked the note from Truda's fingers and gave it to me to read. It didn't exactly bleat with knowledge. It just said: *Tradesmen's kennel has something of interest for us. Truda will take you there.*

Truda led us west, toward Tradesmen's District, using alleys and lesser streets. I was impressed with her knowledge of the town. We encountered no trouble at all.

The Tradesmen's kennel was at the corner of Moneychangers' and Findler. Nestor waited for us inside the courtyard gate. Like us, he wore cityfolk clothes.

"Good girl," he said to Truda with a smile. "Can you stay on?"

Truda nodded. " 'M fine, Nestor."

"Then get out of sight," he told her.

Three lads Truda's age appeared out of the shadows on the opposite side of the street. She walked over to them, and together they merged with the dark again. One of them waved to Nestor before he vanished.

Nestor waved back, then looked at us. "This way."

He walked along the side of the kennel, rather than lead us through the front door. "I got word an hour ago from someone who knows my interests," he explained as we caught up. He kept his voice very quiet. "They brought this cove, Durant Elkes, in on suspicion of colemongering. The cage Dogs have had him to question since midnight."

"They called you so late?" Goodwin asked softly. We stopped before a side door. Like our kennel at home, Tradesmen's has a separate wing for the cages. It is even smaller than ours, mayhap because Rats were only stored here briefly before they are taken to the Rattery Prison.

"My friend heard them talk of a red purse," Nestor replied. "I'd set that on the list of things to watch for."

Goodwin stopped him as he reached for the door latch. "I had the idea that Sir Lionel was so affrighted by our news that he wanted any real work we did on the colemongers put aside. Now you tell me you've set friends to looking for colemongers? What game are you about, Sergeant?"

Nestor sighed and leaned against the kennel wall. "He was a decent man once," he told us. "Then Pearl threatened his children."

"We know," Goodwin said. "He sent his family north. Pearls on their pillows, all that."

"You heard. She also sent Sir Lionel's lady a pearl collar, the kind the gemsmiths call a choker. Sir Lionel gave way, that's all. He's terrified to block anything Pearl does. She had the sack to tell him if he resigned his post, my lady dies. So he does nothing."

"The governor?" I asked, looking around. A familiar sound was distracting me.

"A drunkard," Nestor said. "Useless."

"So if those who are paid to ward the city are a waste of air . . . ?" Goodwin asked, prodding Nestor.

I stepped back into the middle of the street. The sound grew louder. I knew it now. It was the scrape of dust, grit, and leaves as they blew over the roadway, rising on a circling wind and falling again. There was a dust spinner nearby.

"I know some good Dogs," Nestor told Goodwin. "Tried-and-true Dogs, tested in fire. We see what's happening. We agree it must stop. So we build on what we know, in the hope that something will break." He looked at our faces. "It's different in Corus. You've got knights coming and going. You've got the King's Own, and a good chunk of the army. And you've got Lord Gershom. The family calls him Granite, did you know? He doesn't bend and he doesn't break. The Rogue never got to be a great power in Corus. Here, the army is stationed up on the Tellerun or in the sea forts. The navy won't meddle in landsmen's quarrels. It's up to the Dogs alone, and Pearl and the Rogue before her bought as many Dogs as they could. As long as trade wasn't hurt, the Crown didn't care, so the Chancellor wouldn't give Lord Gershom the funds he needs to strengthen the Dogs here. We're doing our best, but truth to tell, we need help."

"If things are as bad as they seem, you'll get it," Goodwin promised, her voice grim in the dark.

Inside we went, to a corridor full of cells fronted by gates with tiny barred windows set in each. Nestor led us to the very end. Here was another door across the hall. A small window covered with a sliding shutter was set in it.

The whole building stank. The Rats inside knew better than to talk to us, them that could see out the small windows. Even in cityfolk clothes Nestor and Goodwin look hard.

The stink got worse the closer we came to the big room at the end of the hall. Nestor rapped on the door twice, then twice more. A cage Dog answered it. He was stripped to his loincloth, covered with sweat, his head and chest shaved so no Rat's flailing hand might catch in his hair.

"Sergeant Nestor Haryse, Corporal Guardswoman Clara Goodwin, Guardswoman Rebakah Cooper, to speak with the prisoner," Nestor told him. "Unofficial, like."

"Always so lovely when ye street Dogs come callin' on us poor cage Dogs," the cove said. There's no denying it, cage Dogs and street Dogs despise each other, mainly because cage Dogs do work like this. Master Sauce opened the door, letting a full drift of the questioners' room stink hit us in the face.

The room was the biggest of the wing. It had to be, to fit the instruments, even though kennel questioning rooms are just basic. This one had a rack, thumbscrew, irons, pliers, a long table, and a hearth fire. The fancier stuff is done at the prisons, if it is needed. This was more than bad enough for me.

There were only two shaved Dogs present, a mot and the cove who'd let us in. The mot was stripped to her breast band and loincloth. Questioning was hot work. I remembered that from my classes in it. The Rat we'd come to see was tied to the long table. They had tilted it so his feet were higher than his head. Then they had released the latch under the headboard so that it swung loose, tilting his head all the way back. He was bruised, covered with welts, naked, and soaked from the hair on his gems to that on his head and chest. They always began with a beating. I saw a strap that matched the welts hanging from a hook on the wall. They'd been giving him the Drink, I could tell. That's why he was so wet. I swallowed to keep the food I'd eaten from coming up. His eyes and lips were swollen, the skin around his nose red. There was a barrel of water next to the table. I clutched the fire opal in my pocket so hard I found later it had dug little holes in my flesh.

I got a mild form of the Drink in training. For him, they had poured water into his mouth without halt, making him swallow by holding his nose. Often, since the Rat was trying to breathe, the water went into his lungs. It was a way to drown a person on dry land. Now and then I have nightmares of it. I nearabout quit because of it, until our trainers said we actually had to volunteer to be cage Dogs. They wouldn't force us to question folk.

The cove's eyes were closed now. Was he dead or had he lost his senses?

His clothes were piled on a smaller table in the corner. On top of them lay a red leather purse, like the ones I had seen filchers switch for their coneys' original purse. Stacked beside his things were silver nobles. I went over to look at them. Each had been scored across the front, cut to show a brass center.

"Don't know why ye're takin' an int'rest in a lousy cole-monger as ain't even in yer own district, Haryse," the cove who'd admitted us said.

"You could've stayed in bed," the mot added. "He's a hard nut, this Durant Elkes. Keeps sayin' he's innocent, when he was caught with coles in hand and a purse full of them. We've given him the Drink three times, and still he wails the same tune."

"I hate these 'innocent' coves," her partner said. He spat on the floor. "Ev'ry evidence agin 'em, and yet they waste our time."

"Was his house searched?" Nestor asked them.

Goodwin went through the heap of things that had been taken from Durant Elkes's pockets.

"They're at it now," the cove replied. "Since he was brung

in, matter o' fact. Some of our folk is that angered, bein's how they've got stuck with a few coles in trade of late." Someone banged on the door. The cove went to open the little shutter, grumbling under his breath. He talked softly with whoever stood outside.

"Y'll find naught in his gear, apart from the purse and the coin," the mot said. She looked at Nestor. "Would you be rememberin' me, Sarge? I'm Shales. I served with you in Gauntlet, ten years back."

Nestor gave her a nod. "I remember you, Shales. You were a street Dog then."

Shales sighed. "That was before I had little ones, two fine boys. It's safer bein' a cage Dog now that I'm a ma. I don't get my head cracked so often. My partner over there's Anglesea. He's been a cage Dog pretty much his whole time of service."

"How was this Rat picked up, did they tell you?" Goodwin asked Shales.

"He tried to buy a fancy pair of earrings with the coles. The jeweler was on the lookout," Shales replied. "Seemingly he's taken in too many coles of late."

Anglesea, the big cove, came back. "Search turned up nothin' in the house. They've brung in his mot and son. They're already screechin' they know naught of his cole passin'."

Goodwin called, "Cooper!" and tossed me the red leather purse. I caught it one-handed. Why was Goodwin throwing it to me? I turned it over. It was just a cheap, red-stained leather purse, and yet it stirred some thought in my brain. I tucked my fire opal back in my pocket. I focused on the purse, thrusting away my own sleepiness and my sickness at the torture. I knew this purse, or one like it.

The filcher I had stopped. The other filchers I had seen, switching a coney's purse for a red one just like this. And I had

335

wondered, Why *this* coney and not another? The filchers chose the coney out of all the others on the street. Someone had *chosen* Durant Elkes. Why?

"Stop," I told the cage Dogs, forgetting I was the youngest Dog there.

Anglesea gave me a look that nearabout fried my gizzard. "Listen to this milk-fed Pup!" he said. "Givin' *me* orders!"

"Stop," Nestor told him. "Cooper, what is it?"

I made myself walk over to that table, to that cove. They had been forcing water into his open mouth while I thought. He coughed and choked, spitting gouts of water out. Thank the gods they hadn't gotten too far. It didn't take him long to get rid of the water in his nose and throat. One good set of the heaves, and he could talk again.

I held the red purse up before his eyes. "Is this yours?" I asked him.

"No, never! I never—" Durant hacked. "I never saw it—" Again he coughed, trying to clear his throat. He couldn't speak as he was, his head below his chest and tilting back. The muscles of his neck were pulled tight to make it hard for him to breathe.

I reached under his head with both hands. Gripping the board that supported it, I yanked it up until Elkes's head was even with the table.

"Hey, stop that!" Shales cried, starting forward. I ignored her and felt under the headboard for the latch that would keep it from dropping again. Durant started to hack out water mixed with snot as his muscles relaxed. I pushed his head aside with one hand, saying, "Don't spit up on me."

The latch twisted into place. I let go of the headboard. It stayed level, letting Durant breathe easier. His coughs eased. Goodwin handed me a cloth. I wiped the man's face.

"I never saw the purse afore, I swear on my mother's name," he babbled. "I don't know how I came to have—" He tried to sit up, straining against his bonds, his eyes wide, his mouth open in a silent scream. I looked back. Anglesea had struck him on the kneecap with a short whip.

Nestor turned to Anglesea. The cage Dog was just six inches from him, yet Nestor gave him such a punch in the gut that Anglesea flew back three feet. It was a mule's kick of a punch, and I will learn it if it kills me.

"When you stop your questioning, you *stop,*" Nestor told Anglesea, his deep voice very soft. "When another Dog asks the questions, you do not interfere. Understand?"

Shales walked over until she stood across from Nestor, with Durant's body between them. "This isn't your kennel, Sarge," she told him.

"But I can still give the orders," Nestor said. "Right now, your fool partner can't seem to remember that." He went to the door and opened it. "Get out of here, both of you. I'll call you when I want you back. Go on, I say, or you'll find yourselves on duty in the Rattery, I swear it."

Shales stared at Nestor for a moment, her hands clenched into fists. Then Nestor's left hand flashed. He'd just shown her a gold noble, where Anglesea couldn't spot it. That rough cove was too busy puking into the straw.

Shales swung over close to Nestor, bumping him rudely. Even though I was watching, I didn't see the gold change hands. Then she dragged Anglesea to his feet and looped his cleaner arm over her shoulders. "You ain't the King yet, Sarge," she snapped as she half carried her partner out into the hall. "You just watch yourself."

Nestor closed the door behind them. "Keep your voices down and they won't be able to hear," he said quietly, coming back to the table. "I don't know them well enough to trust them if we're getting any solid information here."

I looked at Durant. "So you never saw this purse, but it was in your pocket when you went to buy some sparkles," I told him. "You got it somewhere." He opened his mouth, but I shook my head. "Listen to me. Was your pocket picked today, or yesterday?"

Durant started to say no, then stopped. His eyes went to Nestor, then Goodwin, and back to me. He was trying to think up a lie to cover the thing he was truly guilty of. Didn't the looby realize what trouble he was in? I slapped his cheek, but gently, to get his attention.

"Don't be an ass," I ordered. "Give up the truth, however mad it sounds. You thought your pocket was picked, didn't you?"

He tried to shrug and winced. "Aye," he mumbled. "Some'un brushed agains' me in th' street. I felt for m' purse, an' it was there. I took it up, an' it were this red 'un. It was *stuffed* wif silver. On'y when I'd set out this mornin', I had but three silvers an' some coppers." He looked at Nestor, Goodwin, and me. "It wasn' stealin' if they *give* it t' me, right? An' I'm no colemonger if *they're* th' ones as gimme false coin!" His eyes were frantic. "I swear in Great Mithros's name!"

I patted his shoulder. "I've seen it happen several times." I looked at Nestor. "Maybe if I hadn't forgot I was away from home, and then gotten knocked down, I never would have noticed the others. They're as slick at it as goose grease. Dogs working the same places day after day would miss it."

"Your Rogue had Cooper and me lifted off the street. She threatened our lives if we interfered with her people again," Goodwin told Nestor. "Cooper and me, we're two suspicious mots. Why bother two Dogs picking up filchers? Why bother sending rushers to guard filchers, for that matter?"

"Especially when a few coins to the cage Dogs, or payment of the fine in Magistrate's Court, sends the filchers back to the street," Nestor added. "I know how it's played, you two. Stop trying to make me feel better because too many Dogs have gone crooked or careless."

I picked up Durant's tunic and folded it over, making a bit of a pillow so he might see us better. I slid it under his head. "The filchers are up to sommat special," I said, still trying to spin my thought out. "Something the Rogue wants done. So why would a Rogue *want* folk to have a purse full of coles?"

"So the coles get into the city's money?" Goodwin asked. She started undoing Durant's straps on one side, while Nestor undid those on his other.

"Then why not dump them in some fountains, or leave bags at street corners, or bake them in buns?" Nestor wanted to know. "Folk would grab them and run. Nobody would know who had the coins or where they came from."

"Instead she sets filchers to give them to certain people." I looked at Durant. "Who are your enemies?"

Durant looked at me as if I'd spoken in some strange tongue. "I've no enemies." His eyes flicked to each of our faces. I'd bet he wondered if he dared say Dogs were his enemies just now. "None."

"You ran afoul of *someone* of late, Durant," I replied. The idea was showing itself to me at last. "In business, mayhap in your social affairs. You beat someone to a prize, you bought someone out, you set up a marriage for someone who was wanted by someone else. It would be anything like that. Who did you anger?"

Durant lay still for a moment, thinking. Finally he told us, "Steen Bolter. He works in caravans, so why he wanted brass . . ." He coughed, then went on. "He wanted t' buy up all my stores of brass. He offered half what I'd ask. I said no. He wouldn't leave be. Kep' hintin', threatenin', like." Durant coughed again, turned his head, and spat a bloody mess onto the floor. "Said I was vexin' some'un in power. Said she'd ruin me an' mine. I said, I said, if she's so grand, she can make a better offer. Wha's a mot need with a warehouse full o' vases an' plates an' such anyways? He said never mind what she wanted 'em for, just sell." He stopped to cough again, longer this time. He gasped for a moment after he stopped. "My friends said he works for the Rogue. What's she want with all that brass?"

She wants to melt it down for coles, I thought. Folk kept track of brass ingots, in case colemongers buy them up. But they don't keep track of brass that's worked. How many coles would she get from a warehouse full of brass? Enough to bring down a kingdom? Is she really that stupid?

She uses the red purses to get even with those who anger her. But that doesn't make her rich. How does she pay for those pearl teeth? There isn't a mage that draws breath that does the work before getting paid.

A month ago she gambled high and won greatly. "Does Pearl still gamble?" I asked Nestor.

"Every night, nearabout," he replied. "Custom's fallen off with local folk, but the foreigners and sailors still make up for it in the gambling houses. Not just her, either. She cuts Jurji, Zolaika, and Jupp loose to play, and keeps the second-rate guards around her. She knows she's safe enough at those places."

"Her three gossips play as heavy as she does?" Goodwin asked. Her dark eyes were sparkling. She had the scent, too, I could tell.

"Heavier, and Jupp and Zolaika win more." Nestor wiped Durant's face. The poor mumper had fainted or gone to sleep. "They don't get excited like Jurji, or angry like Pearl."

"And at the end of the night?" Goodwin asked. "What do they do with their winnings?"

Nestor was nodding. "They swap their silver and copper coin for gold. All of them play silver games."

"Do you think the gambling houses suspect?" I asked them. "Surely some of them must."

"Even if they do, they're trapped," Goodwin said. "They dare not offend Pearl." She looked at Durant. "What happens to this poor scut?"

Nestor went to the door into the kennel and opened it, beckoning to the two cage Dogs. They came inside, looking sullen.

"Here's how this plays," Nestor told them, no longer a soft-voiced hunter but a hard-edged sergeant. "You end this questioning now, by my order. Send this cove to Deep Harbor's cages, on my order to hold him there." Both cage Dogs began to argue. Nestor reached into his purse and drew out a gold noble. He broke it in half. Immediately the cage Dogs fell silent.

"No more questioning," Nestor said firmly. "That's an order." He gave one half of the gold coin to each of them.

"You can't turn him loose," Shales reminded him as she slid her half into her belt pouch. As quick as she did it, you'd never think she already had a whole one for getting Anglesea out of our way. "He's on the record. He gets tried same as any Rat, and the law has him dead to rights."

"Even if a mage with a truth spell can get it out of him that he didn't know?" I asked. "Mayhap he can afford it. His worst crime is that he thought maybe he'd gotten illegal coin and didn't report it. He was greedy, but he never thought to break the law."

"Don't matter if he thought to or no, you oughta know that," Anglesea said. "Don't they teach you right?"

"Cooper, drop it," Goodwin said.

"But Goodwin—" I began. She glared at me and I shut up. If Durant went before a magistrate, he'd be sentenced. For passing coles, he would lose a hand and have the stump cleansed with a dip in boiling oil.

"His family is blameless," Goodwin said. She produced another gold coin and held it up. "Why don't you Dogs let them go home?" She waited until Shales nodded before she let Anglesea snatch the coin. Anglesea broke that one in one hand with a sneer at Nestor, as if breaking soft gold one-handed made him a better cove.

Goodwin gave him her frostiest look. "See to it they *just* go home," she told him. "Otherwise I'll come back here, and I'll take that gold out of your hides."

Nestor ushered Goodwin and me out of the questioners' room and into the chilly autumn air. "It's the best we can do," he said as we left the kennel. "There's a mage who owes me a favor. I'll make sure she offers Master Elkes her services when he comes before the magistrate. He can still sell brass with one hand."

I didn't want to think about it. I serve the law, but sometimes the law can be too hard for my liking. There is no give to it, no tiny openings through which mice can escape while leaving Rats to pay the penalties they have earned.

I don't want to be nabbing mice like Durant Elkes, who took a windfall and tried to spend it. How many of them have been questioned and given the Drink until they either drown or go mad? I want to be grabbing up the Rat, Pearl Skinner. I want her colesmiths. I want the ones who supply her with silver. And if the method to hand out the coins isn't all hers, I want them that helped her.

All these things I thought on, as I think on them now, while we walked through the streets. I was about to protest when Nestor left us at a shortcut to his home, until I saw that Haden and some other shadows moved off with him. Truda had met us at the kennel gate. She stayed with us, along with her, and our, half-seen guards.

I was about to enter the house when Goodwin shook her head and beckoned to me. She led me around the back to the bridge over the brisk stream that ran there.

"In case there are listening spells in our rooms," she said, talking into my ear. "I don't want Serenity or even Nestor to know what we discuss right now. This stream has a sprite in it. They hate mortal magic. It would take a powerful mage to set any kind of spell here." She reached in her pocket and tossed a silver coin into the stream. "I've come out here to make friends with the sprite after you've gone to your room."

I stared at her. "A sprite? But them's just folk in tales!"

In the half-moon's dim light I saw a crooked smile on Goodwin's mouth. "Tell that to my eyes and my ears, Cooper."

Without thinking, I gave her the tiniest of pushes, like I would give Aniki or Kora. "You said my dealings with dust spinners and pigeons were strange, when I trained with you!"

"And so they are. I'm used to the water folk. Except for the tail, they look like people. Now listen, Cooper, because we're both drunk for need of sleep. I think it's now safe to say that Pearl is our main target, but she's not our *only* target."

"No arguments," I replied. "And we'll need an army just to get at Pearl."

"Which is what I'm going to fetch, come tomorrow." I

stared at Goodwin. This was fast work! And yet I felt it, too, that we had to move fast to keep things from getting away from us.

She clasped my shoulder. "I want to come back with reinforcements in numbers. For that I've got to talk to my lord Gershom. I'll need your written reports before then—sorry, Cooper. I know it's late."

I shook my head. "It's all right." Heat was running in my veins. It was the way I felt when I knew a fat Rat was almost in my grasp. I was waking up.

"Maybe both of us should go." Goodwin chewed her lower lip.

"No," I said once I'd thought it over. "If you go, I can say you got to missing your man. After all, I'm supposed to be the one in danger until all the Pells are caught. You're using your day off, and I am idling about here. I can keep gathering bits and pieces, like where the silver comes from. We haven't heard from Master Finer, remember?"

She sighed. "I know. It's only been two days. We do need to know where they get that silver."

My mind was moving, thinking of what had yet to be done. "I can see what I may learn of Pearl's courts and hideaways, who's in the colemongering with her—"

Goodwin raised a hand to cut me off. "That's *just* the kind of foolishness I fear!"

"*Goodwin,*" I said, making my voice as firm as I dared, "am I ever reckless when I'm just sniffing around?"

"Yes," she replied.

"Of late?" I asked.

She thought that over. "Well, no. Not since you've had to think for you *and* a looby of a partner."

"I'll only sniff out word. I won't poke my nose in locked

rooms, I swear. But you know it as well as me, if you come back with Dogs or soldiers at your back, Pearl will run. I'll wager she knows every hidey-hole in this city. Won't it be good to be there waiting if she bolts?" I crossed my arms over my chest and shut up. It's always tricky, arguing with Goodwin. There is a line between just far enough and too far.

Goodwin walked across the little bridge and back again, then up the stream bank a way. I stayed where I was. Tunstall stands like an ox when he thinks, his owl eyes staring straight through you. Goodwin is a pacer.

Finally she came back. "How will you sniff out this information?" she demanded.

"I'll start with Okha and Dale," I replied. "Okha knows far more than he wants to give away before Nestor. Dale knows the Rogue, and he says he's welcome in her court. I can be there whilst he gambles with her. If I can find more dust spinners near the places where she holds court, there's extra benefit. I haven't even started to tap the pigeons and the dust spinners here, Goodwin, you know I haven't."

Off she went again, downstream this time. When she returned, she said, "You go to Nestor with anything big. You try *nothing* on your own. You're clever and quick, but you're still a first-year Dog, which means your chances to end up facedown in a gutter are almost as good as a Puppy's." She leaned in, her face but two inches from mine. "*Do not swive with this, Cooper,* or I'll have your tongue for a belt purse, so help me, Mithros."

I swallowed hard. "Goodwin, am I a good Dog or not?"

She looked away from me. Then, sudden-like, she wrapped an arm around my head in a rough hold. "You're a good Dog. I want you to live to be a great one." She let me go so quickly I stumbled. She leaned over the rail to gaze at the

stream. I was rattled myself, Goodwin not being the affection-
ate sort.

At last she muttered, "We should have come with more
Dogs."

"And be seen from a mile off?" I asked, feeling timid.
Sometimes Goodwin can be dreadful gloomy.

"Bull pizzles. There's no way to line this up well," she
replied. "Come on, Cooper. Go get your reports writ up, and
slide them under my door before you go to bed. I'll be gone before you rise in the morning."

So I did as I was told, writing the rough copy in my journal first, then the formal one on paper for my lord Gershom. I
promised myself I would do the copy for Sir Lionel in the
morning. Then I slid the reports under Goodwin's door and
went to bed. The harbor clocks struck four as I fell asleep.

My fine plans for sleeping until noon today were folly. Achoo
woke me around seven, I think, for her necessary business. The
cook was much amused at my sorry, sleepy state and gave me a
bowl of sommat to feed her as we returned to our room. I only
know that I went straight back to bed. My rest was destroyed
for good sometime around ten of the clock.

The maid was rapping on my door. "A Master Isanz Finer
is here," she called. "He asked for Mistress Goodwin, and he
didn't like it that she's gone off. He says he'll talk to you. I
wouldn't take forever to come downstairs, though, a'cos he's
that vexed about her bein' gone. He might well leave afore you
get there. I've put him in the dining room."

I opened the door a crack. "Thanks," I told her. "He's a bit
of an old crotchet, I'm afraid." I'd picked up two coppers before I answered the door. I slipped them into her hand. "Would
you say I'll be right down?"

The maid looked at the coins, surprised. I'll wager she was startled that I knew to give her a tip. She actually bobbed a curtsy and trotted off down the hall. I shut the door and set about getting dressed.

I found Master Finer where the maid had said he'd be. She had even set him up with a tankard of ale and a plate of cakes. I reminded myself to give her two more coppers and another word of thanks. I must keep in mind that tipping actually does good. Master Finer was setting down his tankard as I came in. There was a bit of foam on his upper lip. From the glare that he gave me, it was the ale alone that had kept him waiting. He'd spread a large map of part of Tortall on the table, anchoring it with a pitcher, the plate of cakes, what must be my tankard, and a bowl of apples.

"Here I've been, mistress, going half blind working over those coles of Clary's. What happens when I finally have word for her? That fribbety wench as answers the door here tells me Clary's gone gallivanting off and I'm to be dealing with you if I'm to deal with anyone!"

Well. Seemingly it was left to me to smooth the old bird's feathers. He couldn't be worse than Granny Fern in one of her pets, or the colonel across my street who comes to complain of all the wickedness that the neighborhood gets up to. I leaned forward with my most serious face on. "Master Finer, I may not tell you why she is away. I may only tell you that it could not be avoided." I carefully refilled his tankard. "Your work is vital to our hunt. Trust me, Goodwin did not wish to go without hearing your results."

He mumbled under his breath and took a swallow of ale. I noticed then that his eyes were bloodshot and red-rimmed. I sat straight and frowned at him. "I thought you had family to help you. From the look of your eyes, you have pushed too hard."

He waved his hand at me. "They helped. I never said processes and comparisons for differing silvers are easy, young Cooper. Never you mind my eyes. You're as bad as my grand-daughter. Have one of these cakes."

I took one and broke off a piece. "Goodwin would tell you the same, Master Finer."

He scowled at me. "Do you want my findings or no, Mistress Fussnob?" He patted the map with one gnarled hand.

As he did so, I remembered some of the things he had said on the day we met. "Sir, has your family heard from the Silver-smith's Guild or from your Watch Commander concerning the coles you reported to them?"

He shook his head. "Not a word, and I sent messages to both the day I spoke with you and Clary. And my fellow smiths and I are worried. Silver has doubled in price this week." When I blinked at him, Master Finer shook his head. "Of course a Dog attends only to the gutters. Now, Cooper, if the price of pure silver rises at all, it's wonderful if it rises a noble in a *year.* Ah—*now* you nod! *Now* you understand. Here's something that's more frightening still. *Gold* rose this week by *six silver nobles.* Folk are scrambling to get their hands on gold. I've in-structed my family to lay up stocks of food and other stores in our country house. Wenna and some of the other women took the children out of the city yesterday."

I stared at the old cove. If the other tradesmen thought as he did, Port Caynn was on the brink of disaster. And disaster, like scummer, runs downhill, straight to Corus. Goodwin's mes-sage to my lord might already be too late.

"My neighbors only think we're taking a late-year holi-day," Master Finer said. "We had no wish to start everyone to running."

You didn't want everyone else buying up all the supplies, I thought.

"Some folk are thinking the same in the money guilds, but only some," Master Finer said. "The rest think 'tis only one of those follies that come now and then. They call us fools. They tell us folk are just worried about the harvest. They're buying stores and laying them up here in the city." He shook his head. "*They* don't see how much bad money is out there. Now, mind this map."

Now that I took a longer look, I could see that the map showed western Tortall, from the Olorun River to the Scanran border and from Corus to the ocean. Master Finer tapped each place he named with his knobbed finger. "We had silver in the Coast Hills once, but it ran out thirty year ago, thereabouts. It was fine stuff, Coast Hills silver. It had a pearly sheen, buffed up. The insignia in the Silversmith's Guild Hall in Corus is made from Coast Hills silver, did you know?"

I smiled at the old cove. Tunstall sounded the same, talking about his tiny plants, or Aniki and Lady Sabine when they spoke of swords. "I'm as ignorant of the Guild Hall as I am of most things that aren't Dog work, Master Finer."

He barked out a laugh. "None of your sauce now, Cooper! Once you return home, go and look at that great shield over the Guildmaster's dais. Now. The coles. I had to scrape the silver off the coles, then render it down. By the time I had enough melts of it, I knew I had coastal Tortallan silver, but that might have been southern coast, too. There are some mines in the south, but those show a different color—" He coughed into his fist. "Never you mind! I did my treatments, that's all *you* need to know. The silver on these coles has some from other places. I suppose they bought or stole silver wherever they could and added it to their melts. But the biggest part of it is Coast Hills silver. *New* Coast Hills silver, that's never been worked afore this."

"But you said it was all gone," I interrupted. I expected his glare, and I got it. "Beg pardon, Master Finer, but you did."

He nodded. "So I said, girl, and so any silversmith in the guild will tell you. But this would be Dog work of a kind. If I tell you, on my honor as a silversmith, that this is new Coast Hills silver, what would you, as a Dog, be telling me?"

I shrugged. "One of two things. Either someone held back fearful big amounts of it, before the old mines failed, or there's a new mine."

He gave me a thin smile. "So Clary's partner is a clever Dog herself. You're right, Cooper." He pointed to the map. "Now, see, my process, the way I find silver, it shows me where exactly it comes from. No two places are alike. Here's the River Tellerun, as lets out just north of the city. The best silver mines were to the east of the Tellerun Valley," he explained. "And the best of the Coast Hills silver came from the mines here, a ways south of Arenaver, on the barony of Olau. I'd bet my house's fortune they've opened a new mine in secret there, and they're using that silver for the coles." He tapped the mark for Barony Olau with a knotted finger and sat back in his chair, all grim and satisfied.

I stared at the map, remembering Hanse's mention at dropping a job, and angering an old customer, to his people right after his talk with the Rogue. Their destination was near Arenaver, a safer destination to name than Barony Olau.

How did Pearl learn about a new mine at Olau? I wondered. I suppose the cage Dogs will get that out of her, if we catch her alive. It will serve her right to get the same Drink that poor Master Elkes took, just because he wouldn't sell her his stores of brass.

If she is looking for more brass, and bringing in more silver, she plans to make more coles. We have to hobble her, and catch her silversmith, before she does it. Thank the gods that Goodwin has gone for my lord's help.

"I've got you thinking, I can tell." Master Finer got to his feet. "Tell Clary to see me when she returns."

I scrambled to my feet as well. "Master Finer, we've stayed away because we're being watched by the Rogue. Gods, you came here in the open." My temples throbbed as I realized it. Just because Serenity kept the area around this house clear of all watchers did not mean there weren't others out of her reach.

"As if I would run yelping from that street trash!" Master Finer said, glaring at me. "I came with guards, and the guards and spells at my house are more than enough for the Rogue. Let her come after me! We'll bash those fool pearl teeth in!"

There was no arguing with him. I watched him go with the four strong guards who had waited for him outside, a tiny old man circled by muscle. All I could do was pray he was right and that his family could protect him.

I got up and let Achoo out. While she romped in the yard, I wrote a note to Nestor and gave it to one of Serenity's message runners. I asked Nestor to warn anyone at Tradesmen's kennel who still did proper Dog work to keep an eye on Isanz Finer's house.

With that taken care of, I returned to my room and changed my clothes for my weapons and the lone pair of cityfolk breeches and tunic I'd brought. I loaded my pack with seed and corn, then stuffed its side pockets with more of the small bundles of dirt I had brought here from Corus. Goodwin had kept us on the move, learning the city her way. I was inclined to follow her lead, not reminding her that I had other ways to learn news. In truth, information got from dust spinners and pigeons isn't the most satisfying, made as it is of bits and pieces, and it was so much slower. Still, I'd been itching to try the birds again, and there was that spinner I'd heard last night. I hadn't forgotten the Eagle Street spinner, either.

With my pack ready, I sat down and wrote up the day so far in my journal. Back it will go into my secret pocket, where I can keep it with me. My veins are still filled with that shivering fire. I'd thought to take a nap, but I can no more go back to sleep right now than I can fly.

I hate to say it, but with Goodwin on her way back to Corus, I feel like a hound that's been let off its leash. Now I can seek as *I* wish to. Let Pearl be suspicious of a Dog who feeds birds and stands in swirls of dust and wind if she likes. They will help me gather enough threads to weave for her a noose.

At half past five of the clock.
With Achoo at my side, I headed straight for the empty lot where I had fed the birds yesterday. As before, no sooner had I scattered seed than down came Slapper with his new friends. I settled on my heels to listen. In the bushes at the lot's edge I could see dirty ankles. I was near certain that the gixie set to watch us was with me again today. I got an idea.

Serenity's cook had given me a couple of my favorite Viviano apples. In the markets they were going for twice the price this year that they did last autumn. Certainly they'd be a luxury for a street gixie.

I pulled one out and, before I could change my mind,

tossed it high in the air, toward the bushes. It fell into the leaves, but I never heard it strike the ground. Quickly I set down a small pile of corn for Slapper, who was pecking my boots. I looked up under my brows. Those dirty ankles were still there, so the gixie hadn't run when I tossed the apple her way. She'd caught it, for certain. I can hit a Rat at a hundred feet when I throw a rock. That apple would have struck her or the ground beside her if she hadn't caught it.

One apple would not buy me any favor with my spy. It would take several to make her think well of me, if food could do that trick. In the meantime, I could hear what the pigeons might have.

The ghosts were talking as I bent all of my attention on them. They spoke of poison, a dropped load on the docks, a knife in the dark, a pain in a left arm. One had fallen from a ladder without telling his son of the moneybag buried under the back doorstep. An old man had died on his wedding night with a beautiful young bride. He feared to present himself to his old wife in the Peaceful Realms, knowing she would scold him for a fool. He actually made me laugh, which I'd never done with a ghost. I told him not to be a looby. He must go and take his scolding like a grown man. His voice faded from the mortal realms even as he said I was right.

None of them spoke of aught that sounded like Pearl Skinner or coles. Here, so close to the docks, I heard more of harborside and warehouse accidents than deliberate murder. I gave the pigeons a last scattering of corn as a thank-you before I went on my way, back to Tradesmen's kennel.

As we got downwind of it, the autumn breeze blew full into our faces, carrying the cage stink with it. Achoo looked up at me and whined.

"Sorry, girl," I told her, quiet-like. A pair of Dogs was passing us. "With luck we'll not be long."

We passed by the main entrance. The courtyard was busy with folk come to report crimes or to learn the fate of one who was nabbed. Achoo and I walked on down the long side wall that Goodwin, Nestor, and I had followed not so many hours before. I stopped by the door into the cages and looked around, listening for the scrape of blown grit that I'd heard last night.

The spinner lived on the corner of the kennel, where an alley ran behind it. It rose and fell from six feet in height to four, which was odd behavior for a spinner. The winds might snatch away the things that made up its sides, or a dust storm might blow them in, but usually their growth and shortening took place over days, not moments.

"Achoo, *tunggu,*" I said, pointing to the wall. Achoo whined again, because I was walking away. I'd left her ten feet from the spinner. I didn't know why.

I took out a packet of dirt, leaves, and bits of twigs from the Common. I'd gathered them when my friends and me were having a picnic there. It was a bright, clear summer's day. My brothers had come with Tansy and Joy. Rosto was there, laughing like a lad. Aniki and Kora taught us tumbling tricks. Phelan brought his curs, who had a splendid time chasing Pounce. I gathered five packets of earth from our picnic ground and sewed them up in bright red cloth, keeping them for very special spinners.

I stepped into this one. Instead of widening itself, herself, the spinner closed in, trying to weave its breezes in with my clothing. She told me her name, Shhasow. And then she dumped onto me all the human voices she held at once.

They were screaming. Begging, howling, praying.

I planted my feet in the dirt of the alley and concentrated. Shhasow had thrown those broken voices at me together, but I had learned years ago not to *listen* all at once. At first they slipped through my mind's fingers, just part of a mass of shrieks. Then I heard a voice say, "Charged me five coppers," and I nearly wept. I was hearing the awful backwash from the cages.

I was there some time. At last I had things sorted out. Over and over I'd heard a mot's cold voice say, "This one's inconvenient. A silver noble to leave me alone with her," or him. Other times she'd order, "Very good. Clean up." I'd heard that voice, the day Pearl had bidden its owner to nab Goodwin and me. It belonged to the old doxie, the one that Okha said killed for Pearl. Zolaika.

There was another familiar voice. It belonged to the cage Dog Shales. "—hit my little lad today. Just . . . hit 'im, because he wouldn't stop whinin' for me to tell 'im a story."

Anglesea was in Shhasow, too. "I b'lieve I'll just put a word in Her Majesty's ear, that Haryse was sniffin' around that Elkoo ocut."

At last Shhasow was empty of voices and tired. She couldn't understand why I hadn't run away like the other two-leggers who stepped through her. Though they couldn't hear, they *felt* her, and they fled. She didn't know why I was still there or why she could tell what I thought.

"Don't mind that. Look, I bring a gift," I said, and I up-ended my package of dirt in her heart. She slowed her spin, then opened up. Her coils were lighter. With everyday happiness inside her, she might fare better. I hope so.

I left her and went to Achoo. I sat beside my hound for a while, letting her wash my face and hands with her tongue. Finally, with only my clothes unwashed, she curled up in my lap. I bent to rest my face in her fur.

There are some things about being a Dog, and knowing all the things that Dogs do, that I cannot bear.

When Achoo's sharp elbows got uncomfortable, I decided we really ought to work some more. Down to Eagle Street we walked, sharing sticks of cooked shrimp, then cooked sausage. Achoo was not interested in my bunch of grapes, which meant more for me. I made it up to her with a slice of raw, boneless fish. I glimpsed Haden behind me once, and hoped that he and Pearl's spy were able to get sommat to eat.

As we got closer to Lowdown, I set two of my hidden knives in my waistband, hilts sticking out of the slits in my tunic. I also moved my boot knives up so the hilts were visible. Lowdown reminded me of my birthing ground in the Cesspool. A mot who walked there had best let everyone know she was armed.

I took a wrong turn twice, more because I was eyeing them that was eyeing me than because I misremembered my map. I found myself at last on Eagle Street at a familiar corner, where Hesserrr the dust spinner lived. To my left was a familiar alley. It ended in a building that sported no signs, only a strong door. That would be the entrance to Pearl Skinner's Eagle Street court, where she had talked to Goodwin and me.

Hesserrr was still on his corner, whipped to head height by the strong breeze coming off the harbor. I opened one of my packets of dust. Achoo whined as she watched.

"No, this will be much better," I told her. I always forgot she did not understand as Pounce would. For all I know, she does, and does not tell me. "I know this spinner. He's not cracked."

This packet was made of green cloth, meaning I'd taken the contents from the Palace Way by the Daymarket, the busiest street in all Corus. Shhasow had proved my belief, that the dust carried the flavors of the places it had been, even the feelings of those who had been on it last. I was bringing Hesserrr a taste of someplace he would never go. I cut the stitches on the packet, waited until there was no one close by, and stepped into the spinner. Achoo watched.

With my eyes closed, I released the dust and dirt from Corus into the spinner's breezes. Hesserrr greeted me with pleasure, greedily snatching the dust away from my nose and letting me breathe the air that shaped him. He released the scents caught in his breezes. I breathed in the sea, ships—wood, tar, and brass polish—seaweed, and fish. And, as the dust and grit I'd brought built up his sides, Hesserrr began to release the human talk that was trapped there. This was so much better than my visit with Shhasow. Much of it was nonsense, since breezes don't always linger for a whole conversation and Hesserrr wasn't trapped in an alley behind the cages. I heard bits about cargoes, storms, family matters.

Then I heard a gixie's voice. "—makes no sense, stealin' a purse only t' put another in its place!"

And a cove's rough reply. "Ye do as yer told. 'Tisn't yer place t' question Her Majesty!"

But the girl was stubborn. "I never had no guard t' filch afore, Dad! An' why are we only reportin' t' Queen Pearl or Jurji?"

The sound of a slap ended that.

Only the oldest spinners are able to keep so much. Hesserrr must be dozens of years old, mayhap even a century or two, like my friend Hasfush back in Corus. I was even luckier than I'd hoped.

More shreds were caught as folk opened and closed the

doors of the Court of the Rogue. I heard gossip about rob-
beries, murders, Dogs, gambling, prices, lovers, and anything
else under Mithros's sun. I tried to memorize as much as I
could. I heard Pearl tell a rusher that if he couldn't guard an
underfed little filcher, she'd find a rusher who could.

From the hollow sounds in that bit of talk, I knew they
were alone. No other voices or noises mixed with theirs. It con-
firms what I think. The pickpockets who give Pearl's enemies
purses full of coles are known to Pearl only. She keeps it secret
from most of her people.

I nearly jumped out of Hesserrr when the next clear piece
met my ears.

"Amber, she's *waiting.*" A man's voice, one I knew—
the cove who'd knocked on Okha's door at the place where
he worked. "You don't keep the Rogue waiting when she's
summoned—"

The breeze whirled away from them and I nearly began to
curse. Instead I held myself still and breathed, thinking about
naught but the smells in the breezes, just as I have always done.
There is always a chance sommat more will come.

"—way. She wants you singing for her court regular, once
a week!" It was the cove again. "And she'll pay whatever you
like!"

"All the more reason for me to treat her as I will any other
paying customer." Okha's woman voice might sound calm to
his servant, but to me, hearing as Hesserrr heard, there was a
hum of tension under his smooth words. "You think none of
them are dangerous, Zander?" Okha asked. "I've done this
longer than you've been alive. Trust me."

"What if Nestor finds out?" From his voice, Master Zander didn't like that chance.

Okha's voice was grim when he answered. "He knows the realities of our world. We don't *have* a choice."

The rest vanished, but it did not matter. I listened to the rest of Hesserrr's burden and stepped out of his breezes, filled with awe. Never, in all my days, have I known a spinner who was able to keep so much of a conversation together. I fumbled in my pack and fetched out two other packets of dust from other parts of Corus, all of the new stuff that I had. I opened them with shaking fingers and poured them into Hesserrr's grip in thanks. How old could he be? Older than my Corus spinner, Hasfush, who has lived mayhap for three centuries? I bowed to Hesserrr, not caring if folk passing by saw me and pointed. If they had heard and felt what I did, they would bow, too.

When I went to Achoo, she wriggled and whined until I said, "*Mudah,* all right?" I knelt and scratched her back, telling her that she worried too much. "I've been doing it for years, never mind what happened back at the kennel. That was very unusual. This was unusual, too, but a *good* unusual. Don't fidget, please?"

I hadn't known that Okha sang regular for Pearl Skinner's court. Now that I *did* know, I wanted to see him. If Okha was brave enough to sing for the Rogue, mayhap he would tell me where to find Pearl when she is not here on Eagle Street.

I sought other dust spinners, thanking them with Corus dirt for their bits and pieces as the sun passed through the sky. Achoo fussed, but she eased off as she saw that I was right. I did know what I was doing, and there were no other twisted spinners liked Shhasow. I found little more that was useful to my present hunt and nothing that was as good as the knowledge that Okha visited the Rogue's courts. Not being placed near spots where the port's Rats talked in safety, those spinners mostly trapped words about everyday matters.

I did wonder how Haden and my poor spy managed and what they thought of it all. When I bought pasties for Achoo and me to keep up our strength, I set two on a window ledge where they could grab them as they went by, though I hoped that Haden might be kind and leave both for her.

We made our way up to the square where Vorna had found us only yesterday. There I fed the pigeons while Achoo flirted with a rakish-looking cur. I'd hoped to hear the ghost of the cove who worried that Pearl sent out too many coles, but for some reason he was missing from the flock. There was no way to tell why, either. He might simply have decided he was done with life, and made his way to the Peaceful Realms. I'd heard bits from countless pigeons that turned out just like that.

I went to a bathhouse for a wash after all those talks with dust spinners. Achoo took the order to wait for me in the cloak-room as if I'd sentenced her to death by sorrow. A slave beat the dust from my clothes as I scrubbed all over. While I cleaned up, I watched to see where the slaves came and went. Dressed, my wet hair in a braid again, I collected Achoo. We did *not* leave by the entrance we had used to enter the bathhouse. The Rogue's spy and Haden doubtless waited for us there. Instead we took the slaves' way out of the place. It opened onto a different street from the main entrance, on the far side of the building.

I paid a carter two coppers to hitch a wagon ride. He let us off just a block from Nestor's house. Through our bumpy ride I had not seen any watchers at all, save for an occasional glimpse of Slapper. I was as certain as anyone might be that no one had followed us.

Truda answered Nestor's door, shocked to find me there

without Haden. "I'm visiting Okha, if he's in," I told her. "The barbarian watering your flowers is Achoo."

Truda giggled and ran off to tell Okha that he had a visitor. Quickly she returned to let us in. I gave Achoo permission to visit the kitchen with Truda, while I sat and waited for Okha to leave his rooms. When he did, he looked interesting. He wore brown breeches and an ivory linen shirt, like any ordinary cove. The rest was not so ordinary. He had makeup on his eyes, lips, and nails, and gold drops in his ears. He wore gold rings set with amber on two fingers of one hand, an emerald ring and two plain gold rings on the other. He was the very picture of what he was, someone on the border of man and woman.

"What, no Goodwin?" he asked in his man voice.

"She had to take reports to my lord Gershom," I told him. "She'll be back in a couple of days."

Okha smiled. "Poor Hanse will be unhappy. Last night he looked as if he hoped for good things from her, married as she is. Goodwin's just his kind of woman."

"He won't know she's gone," I replied. "Hanse and his crew took a job to Arenaver."

Okha looked at me, then away. "That's right. I'd forgotten. For a man who swore he'd never return home again, he's gone there often, these last six months."

That caught my attention. He'd said nothing of going *home*. "Hanse is from Arenaver?" I asked, as if it interested me only a little.

"No, from a little town on Barony Olau." Okha stood to take a tray with cakes and tea from Truda. "Thank you, dear. What was I saying, Beka?"

I watched Okha place the tray on a small table between more comfortable chairs than the ones at the dining table, the kind they'd keep for company. "You were telling me Hanse came from Barony Olau. Do you know why he left home?" My hand shook a little with excitement. There was my link between Pearl and the silver, between Olau and the silver, if Hanse could be made to talk.

Okha blew on his tea. "He ran off to join the army. It's sad. He did well for years, but . . . he struck an officer. He was lucky they only flogged him and kicked him out. And he landed on his feet soon enough, building his guard business with Steen and some other friends who left when he did. Why so interested?"

I shrugged. I trust Okha, but it is safer for everyone if I keep what I know to myself. "I like him. He saved Tunstall in the riot, you know. It's too bad Hanse doesn't have a chance with Goodwin, but she and Master Tomlan are like this." I showed Okha my crossed fingers.

Okha smiled. "I know. She flirts well, but she's a one-man woman. Now—what brings you here, Beka? How did you manage to come without Haden at your back? Truda says you're alone but for your hound."

I felt bad about that. I don't want to hurt Haden's pride. "I didn't lose Haden so much as the watcher the Rogue put on me. Haden was just part of it."

Okha lifted his brows. "Why must the Rogue not know you've come to visit me?"

"Because I'd like to know how the Rogue's courts are laid out. Nestor might not know that, but you do," I told him. "You sing for her every week."

Okha put down his teacup, frowning at me. "How in the name of the Crone Goddess did you find that out? *Nestor* doesn't even know it—I've managed to keep *that* secret so far."

I was startled to hear that, but on the other hand, what good would it do Nestor to know? Plainly Okha wasn't given a choice. He *had* to sing for Pearl Skinner. And Nestor would hate it.

"The only way you could handle that news without a fight is not to tell him?" I asked.

"And swear my friends to silence. He would be furious. My hope is that one day I will hear something that he can use to bring this Rogue down," Okha replied, his voice quiet. "That day has not come."

"Will you draw me rough maps?" I asked.

Okha looked at me, his eyes steady. "Beka, what are you up to? You're making me worry."

I shrugged. "I'm keeping myself busy till Goodwin comes back."

Okha's eyes were sharp. "Are you? Beka, the Corus Rogue is a delightful, sane fellow who understands the world. Our Rogue is mad with greed and power and she's stupid. She thinks that no one lives who can stop her."

"It's not my job to stop her," I said firmly. "I collect information, only that. Yes, Pearl will meet her match, but it won't be a junior Dog like me. It'll be the law, resting in the hands of a whole squad of hard, senior Dogs. *Please*, Okha? Tell me what I need to know."

Okha leaned back in his chair and covered his eyes with his hand. I drank some tea. Finally he stood. "Wait here." He was only gone for a few minutes. He returned with some rolled-up papers. Once I moved the tea things, he flattened the papers on the table. These were not rough-sketched. They were well-done maps of buildings, each room and door labeled very neatly. The top map was titled *Gauntlet Court, Basilisk Alley and Darcy Walk*. Okha pulled half of the map away to show the label for the one below. That was *Riverside Court, Cavall Street and Cecily Way*.

I looked at Okha. "You thought Nestor could use these."

Okha shrugged. "It's even better if you and Goodwin do so, and keep Nestor's name out of it." He pulled that sheet back until I could see the third map was of the Eagle Street court.

I looked greedily at the Gauntlet court map, noting the streets that lay outside each exit. "How did you learn so much without Pearl catching you?" I asked.

"A woman needs the privy, and a private room to collect her thoughts before she can sing," Okha said in the voice he used as Amber Orchid. "She might want a room to meet with a friend, or a room in which to oversee a game of Gambler's Chance. I am considered to be the most expert in the game in the city, apart from Dale himself."

"How can you stand it?" I asked. "How can you bear to explore those places, knowing what happens to folk that Pearl doesn't like?"

Okha looked away from me. "I think of Nestor, and the things that happen to Pearl's enemies." He met my eyes again.

There was an ancient cold in his eyes. I wondered if a god's eyes were like that, miles distant while still being up close. I wondered if Okha's Trickster was in the room with me right now.

I clenched my hand into a fist. I don't want gods mucking about in my life.

Okha carefully folded the maps until they were of a size to fit in my pack. "Make good use of them, Beka. Be sensible."

"That's me," I replied as I tucked the maps away. "Rebakah Sensible Cooper." Thinking of being sensible reminded me of another important errand I had to run today. I asked Okha to recommend the manner of shop I needed, since I thought women's healers might very well be something Okha would know about. I was right. He knew a fine healer with a shop on Tradesmen's Street, not too far out of my way home.

It was nearly four of the clock when Achoo and I left Nestor's. Haden and the Rogue's spy had yet to catch up with me. We hurried to reach the healer's, where I ordered Achoo to sit inside by the door as I looked around. The place was clean and orderly, filled with the smell of drying herbs. The charms were kept pinned to cloth hung on a wall behind the long table where the shopkeeper saw to customers. A curtained door led to other rooms, for patients, I expected.

I found the sort of charms I wanted and looked them over, ignoring the sweat that rolled down my ribs. Aunt Mya had given me my old charm, so I'd never had to shop for one. And mayhap I was thinking too highly of myself, hoping I might have a need for it.

"Exciting night ahead?" the shopkeeper asked me in a voice too loud for my comfort. I believe I shrank a foot in height. "From the look of you, silver or gold is out of the question."

I shook my head and forced myself to lean closer to her. "No good playing with these things," I mumbled. "I'll have true silver, if you please."

The shopkeeper looked at me and smiled. "Fortunate, to be able to afford it, dearie. I just happen to have this for two copper nobles." Her voice was quieter. She lifted a silver wire charm from the cloth and placed it before me. "The closed womb, in the Mother's own silver. No woman's ever had a big belly because a charm of mine failed her."

I fetched out the coins. The money came from my own funds, not my lord Gershom's. I could hardly account to Sergeant Ahuda for a charm to keep me from getting myself a baby! When I gave the money to the shopkeeper, she wrapped the charm in a bit of cloth and gave it to me.

"Put it on a chain or a bit of ribbon and hang it about your neck, or stitch it to something you wear all the time," she told me. "And have fun!"

I smiled and ducked my head. "I hope to! Achoo, *tumit*!"

On the way home I bought cooked chopped beef and a bone for Achoo. She isn't gaining the weight she needs, and I blame our rambles over the city for that. I need to feed her even better. I begged the cook for some goat's milk. It worked for Kora's and Aniki's kittens, so I am in hopes it will fill Achoo out some, too. One of the housemaids found me in the kitchen. She carried a rose and a note from Dale.

He invites me to supper at eight of the clock. Unless he hears from me differently, he will call for me here.

I took a nap and washed my face, then tried the lip and eyelash paint. I have written up this day's findings and put Okha's maps in the same hidden pocket where I keep this journal. I have asked Serenity if I may leave my poor Achoo in the yard with her food, bone, and water once more. The cook has also said, with a *very* broad wink, that she will give Achoo a fine breakfast if I am not home by dawn.

Now I must get ready. I tremble everywhere. I never felt such a wanting even over Rosto, but mayhap that is because I never let myself imagine that I might lay down with him. I am free to do as I wish with Dale, and that freedom makes me giddy. I tell myself I can search his rooms for evidence that he is connected to the colemongering, but knowing him better, I doubt that he is. Dale is clever. He has a gentleman's delicacy of touch. The colemongers have the grace and light touch of pigs rooting in garbage. If Dale were in a scheme, we'd never see the signs of it. It is plain enough that he is good friends with Hanse and Steen, and plainer still that *they* are in this to their eyebrows.

Also, Dale likes money. He likes *good* money, to buy fine meals, jewelry, clothing. I will keep an open mind, but why would such a man work to ruin the value of the money he prizes? A few coles, when no one was looking for them, he might use, but he would never shower them all over the city like this. Such behavior might be the work of someone both greedy and stupid.

I will search Dale's rooms, as I should. That is how I shall think of tonight.

And if I were to say that to Goodwin, she would laugh until she popped something.

Tuesday, September 18, 247

Ladyshearth Lodgings

Noon.

Last night was the finest I have had in my life. Dale took me to a good supper, then a puppet show, and a walk along the breakwater to see the sea lions in torchlight. After that, we returned to his room.

Not that I will be writing the details of *that.* I've heard tell of folk who write little books that are nothing but what happens when folk canoodle. How can anyone bear to write such things where other folk might read them? What he did to me and I to him, things I have never taken part in afore, they were too good to set on paper in my clumsy words. It would take the magic right out of them.

I know now why Aniki and Kora are forever saying to me I'd never lain with anyone as knew, *really* knew, what they were about. I wish I were in that good cozy bed still. He made me *laugh,* during. I didn't even think you were supposed to laugh then.

I want us to be together as much as we can, as long as we can. Never mind what happens when the hunt is done. "Have it all now," Rosto is forever telling me, "in case you don't wake up tomorrow." He is right and I want that, but not with him.

We breakfasted late. Dale went out and came back with the food, and fed me just as he had at the Merman's Cave. Master Sure-of-Himself had even told the bank that he had family business to see to and would not be available for work today! At last I remembered that I was supposed to be doing *sommat* to earn my fine lodging and all the coin Goodwin and I have been spending, so I bid Dale a rather long farewell. We promised to meet again tonight.

It was drawing on noon as I walked to Serenity's in a light rain. I stopped but once, at a pasty seller's cart. I bought six, and left four on stone benches near the places where I glimpsed Haden and the Rogue's watcher. It seemed to me I should make amends for losing them yesterday.

Before I entered my lodgings, I went around back for Achoo. I had tied her next to an open shed in case of rain, and now she huddled inside. Her water and food dishes were full yet. When she saw me, she leaped forward, barking with joy and trying to climb up the front of my gown.

I caught her paws. "What's this?" I asked her. "Why didn't you eat your breakfast?" She tried to lick my face as I held her off. "Achoo, easy!"

Nothing would calm Achoo until I allowed her to sniff me all over and lick my face and hands. She trembled as she did so, whimpering piteously. I began to feel like the biggest Rat in all the realm. The biggest wet Rat as the rain fell harder.

"Very well," I told Achoo, hauling her into the house before she got as soaked as I was. "All *right,* Achoo! I won't leave you overnight again, I promise! I promise!" I knelt and cuddled the poor creature's head. Who knew hounds are so much different from cats?

She shoved her wet nose in my eye.

"That's it, girl. I'll work sommat out with Dale, but I'll not leave you alone so long again. Easy, easy." She calmed down at last, to sag against my side, panting.

Dale will understand. Achoo loves and trusts me, gods know why. I won't betray her trust like those other bad handlers of hers. And I think I know Dale well enough that I can say he will welcome my silly hound. He has too warm a heart to turn her away.

We walked into the front of the house. Serenity was at the

dining table, working on her accounts, as I came in. "Someone looks like the cat who spilled the cream," she announced with a raised eyebrow.

I frowned at her, or I tried to. "I've noticed that people who give first prayers to the Goddess are uncommon interested in personal things," I said.

Serenity looked at her accounts with a smile. "So, did you have fun?"

Blushing, I ran up to my room to dry off and change into my uniform. I needed to write down the things I learned at Dale's. He told me that he and Hanse met in the army, when Dale was a paymaster's clerk. He'd been there when Hanse was dismissed. Seemingly everyone hated the officer Hanse had struck. That was why Hanse got a light sentence and discharge, rather than branding and time in the quarries. It was also why nearly twenty soldiers left when he did, including Dale. They felt the officer should never have been allowed to whip and bully his men to the point where one man would end his career to give a little of it back.

I found no signs of colemongering in Dale's rooms—I searched them as he went for breakfast. The silver coins in his hidden money box were all cut to prove they were true silver.

I'd drifted off, thinking of other things I had learned in Dale's rooms, when I heard loud voices downstairs.

I must go.

Okha's dressing room, Waterlily gambling house
One hour past midnight.
I've had days that drank donkey drippings before, but yesterday beat them all, Black God strike me if it don't. And it started so fine, too, as fine as a day could start, with me and Dale all warm and rosy in his bed.

It started when Serenity interrupted my daydreaming yesterday. "Cooper, you'd best come quick," she called through my door. "There's a girl here from Isanz Finer's house. She's nigh hysterical."

I opened my door and ran downstairs after Serenity, Achoo following. The gixie who stood in the hall was fourteen or so, dressed in a fine but rain-sodden tunic. Her braided hair was unveiled and mussed. Mud was splashed all over her slippers and hem. Her eyes and nose were red with weeping.

"Cooper? You're Cooper?" she asked, staring at me. "How can *you* help?"

"Why don't you tell me the problem?" I asked, steering her into the dining room. "I can't say how I must help until I know what the trouble is." Serenity had vanished into the house.

The gixie wouldn't sit when I pulled a chair out for her. "But you're barely more than a girl! The way Grandfather talked—I thought you'd be a *real* Dog!"

I held her shoulders and made her sit. "I am a real Dog. A junior one, but real nonetheless. And if you want a Dog, why aren't you at your own kennel?"

"Because they're the ones who took him, you ass!" she

cried. She shook all over. "Grandfather, my uncles, my *aunts*—*all* of them! They're charged with colemongering!" She began to cry. Achoo looked at me with reproach. Seemingly she did not care for my rough treatment of my visitor. Whining her sympathy, Achoo began to lick the gixie's hand.

Serenity came with a cup. "Drink this," she said. "It will calm you. You need to be calm if you're to help your people." She put the cup to the gixie's lips and held it steady for her. I took my fire opal from my pocket and turned it over in my hand to keep myself steady. Finer's arrest was very, very bad news.

"You're certain they said colemongering?" I asked when the gixie had quieted.

"The legal charge is nailed to the door of every house and shop we own. They even cried it from the corners of our street!" Though she was steadier, the tears still rolled down the gixie's cheeks. "And they found coles when they searched our house. Of course they did! Grandfather ordered us to put any we came across in the money box in his study, for when the guild chose to *do* something about it. But the guards found the box and said it was proof!"

"What about the guild?" I asked her. "He reported the coles to them. He said other silversmiths talked to the guild when he did. Did Master Finer tell the Dogs the guild knows about the coles? The guild will say he didn't make them."

"Of course he told the Dogs! One great brute hit him and blacked his eye. He said no talking from prisoners!" The gixie blew her nose.

"Did *you* go to the guild, then?" I asked. "They can help better than a lone Dog."

"It was the first thing I did, you stupid trull!" she cried. "The clerk I spoke to said they knew nothing about it, and if I was wise, I'd surrender myself to the Crown's mercy!"

I let the insult pass me by. I must seem like a complete lump, asking such basic questions, but I had to know what ground had been covered and what answers the gixie had been given.

The Finers were Goodwin's friends. With her gone, she would want me to do all in my power to help them. This was more true because I feared they would not be in such a mess had we not asked Isanz Finer to learn of the origin of the silver in the coles.

I used my training tricks to remember everything I'd learned of the Finers. "I have more stupid questions for you, mistress," I told the gixie. "I'd prefer it if you'd wait until I am done to scold me." I turned to Serenity. "May we have a number of sheets of paper—ten at least. Ink and a pen, also?" When she had left us, I asked the girl, "What is your name?"

She glared at me. "You waste time!" Achoo pawed her lap, as if she asked the gixie to give me a chance. Absently the girl scratched Achoo's neck.

"No," I replied quietly. "It will not do you, your family, or me any good for me to rush about with but half a plan in mind. I cannot be forever calling you mistress if we are to work together. And I *did* ask that you wait to scold me until we are finished." I smiled at her then, as if she was one of my sisters. She was Lorine's age, when all was said and done.

She sat up a little straighter and wiped her eyes. "I see. I'm Meraud. Meraud Finer. My papa is Grandfather's grandson. I'm really Grandfather's great-granddaughter, but he gets impatient with the *greats*."

"Meraud," I said, putting my hand on her shoulder, "if you know the names of those who went to the guild with Master Finer, remember them whilst I run up to my room. That's Achoo, by the way. She particularly likes a scratch on the rump. Achoo, *tinggal. Kawan.*" I raced upstairs.

First I opened my shutters and hung my spare tunic over the windowsill so that Haden, watching from somewhere behind the house, would know that I needed him. I took the maps that Okha had given me from under the mattress and set them in the hidden pocket of my pack.

My nerves were prickling, telling me to gear up. I obey my nerves at such times. I undid my braid and rebraided it with the spiked strap woven in. I thrust my sap into my pocket. I slid my arm guards on, checking to make sure that each slender knife was in its sleeve on the forearm parts before I did up the laces. All of my hidden knives went into their sheaths. My round iron cap I would put in my pack. Last of all, I checked the chain on which I wore my insignia before I put it over my head. There was my badge, marking me as a true Dog, if but a junior one. I gave the leather a polish on my knee. Then I took the round glassy circle of my Dog tag from my pouch and strung it on the chain as well. I took my supplies of coin and the letters of credit that Goodwin had entrusted to me, tucking them into the pack.

When I returned to the dining room, Meraud stared at me. "You look different." Achoo leaned against her leg, panting. The paper and ink I had requested lay near Meraud's cup.

"I just put the rest of my uniform on," I said as I set my pack on the table. I took out my journal, wet the pen Serenity had brought in with the ink, then sat cat-corner from Meraud. "Did you remember who went to the guild with Master Finer?"

She pulled herself up. "I'm not a ninny," she began. "Ouch!" Achoo had pawed her bare wrist, leaving white scratches. Meraud gave me a shamefaced look. "She doesn't like strife, your hound. He wanted me to take his share of the business, one day, Grandfather did. I went everywhere with him, and wrote it up for him. His memory isn't as good as it was." A tear rolled down her cheek.

"Are you the great-granddaughter he mentioned that might help him learn where the false silver comes from?" I asked. I opened to a fresh page in my journal so I could write down my notes.

She nodded and dashed her tear away. "I don't normally cry so much," she said, and glared at me. "Now, it was Grandfather that went to the guild, and my uncle Uthno—"

"Was Uthno taken up this morning?" I interrupted.

Meraud nodded.

"He's no use, then," I told her. "We need them that aren't in the cages."

"Well, there's Jelbert Moorecoombe, Honna Bray, Oriel Barber, and Rauf Makepeace. They came with us," said Meraud.

I wrote the names down. "Who spoke to you at the guild?" I asked.

"Senior Guildsman Tobeis Hawkwood and Senior Guildswoman Donnet Newmarch," Meraud replied. She sat straighter in her chair.

"You must write notes to them all," I told her as I scribbled the names down. "I have a message runner who will be here soon. He and his friends will carry them for us. In each note you must say that Master Isanz Finer and his family have been taken to the Tradesmen's kennel for colemongering. Say this regards those coles they spoke about when they met with the Silversmith's Guild, only give the names and titles of them your folk spoke to. Say that their aid is needed now. They must speak to the Finers' innocence before the Tradesmen's District magistrate. Do you need me to repeat that?"

Meraud shook her head. The moment I began to speak, she had begun to write on one of Serenity's sheets of paper. I was interested to see that she used a cipher I hadn't seen before.

"It must go to the silversmiths *and* to Hawkwood and Newmarch, this same note. Have you a way to mark that copies have gone to others?" I asked.

Meraud nodded.

"Be certain to put that on it," I said.

Meraud looked at me.

"Folk are sometimes more eager to help if they think others are watching," I explained.

Meraud gave me the tiniest of smiles.

I thought of something. "*Don't* sign your name, or give this address," I told her. "Some of them will give you up. They'll fear the Dogs are coming for them next. Some may think to hand you over to them to buy favor."

Meraud set her pen down. Her hands were shaking.

"As soon as you're done here, go to the nearest temple of the Goddess and sit at the statue's feet," I said. "They will have to prove you guilty to the Goddess's court before they can take you from the temple." There are advantages to having a partner who's a magistrate in the Mother's temple. Thinking of magistrates, I remembered something useful from my own days spent seated in a courtroom. "Does your family ever work with an advocate?"

"Master Rollo Liddicoat," Meraud said.

"Write to him first. Tell him what's happened and send him to Tradesmen's kennel with a sackful of gold. He can buy your family comfort if anyone may." I hoped this Master Liddicoat knew enough of how cage Dogs worked that he would buy Master Finer out of early questioning. "Be sure you tell him to take gold, understand?" I chewed my lip, trying to think. How long would it be until all the city heard that a family of silversmiths had been taken up for colemongering?

Who in Mithros's name had written those bills of arrest? Didn't he, or she, know that this was the worst possible move? A panic would start if folk stopped trusting *any* silver or worse, started to take their good silver out of the banks. Were all the Dogs in charge of things loobies at best?

I couldn't waste my time on Watch Commanders, that was plain. I had to get to Sir Lionel. He was the only one with the authority to order the Watch Commanders to lock the city down, if need be. He was also the only one who could release the Finers before they were tortured. I only hoped that he would take my word. I was *not* about to tell him that Goodwin was off gathering troops. Somehow I didn't think he would like knowing that we had judged him too fearful of Pearl to do what had to be done.

I went to the kitchen to find Serenity. She was talking with the cook. When she saw me, she beckoned me into the pantry. "What trouble have you brought to my doorstep, Beka?" she asked.

"I don't see where blaming *me* for things that began months ago will be useful," I replied. I was in too much of a hurry to be polite. "Will you give that poor gixie in there up to the Dogs?"

Serenity drew back. "Of course not!"

"Then don't go scolding me," I said. "She's writing up some notes that my friend Haden will take away when they're done. I'm off to Guards House for a word. When Mistress Finer is done, she'll need to go to the temple for safety. Will you see to it that she gets there?"

Serenity gave me the strangest look then.

"Now what?" I asked. I admit, I was feeling testy.

She smoothed her skirts. "You are very different when you

have work to do," she said, as if she remarked upon the weather. "Of course I will get Mistress Finer to safety. What of Achoo?"

I shook my head. "We're a team, she and I. We'll stay together." I slung my pack onto my shoulders.

"What should I say to Nestor?" Serenity asked me.

"Doubtless I'll see him before you will," I replied. I looked to the back door, which stood open. Haden waited for me in the yard, near the chicken coop. "Excuse me," I said, bowing to Serenity. I went to Haden.

"I saw the signal," he said, his brown eyes all a-sparkle. "Have ye business for me?"

I gave him twenty coppers. "There's a gixie in the dining room writing up some notes," I explained. "I need you and your friends to deliver them, *fast*. The one to the advocate goes fastest of all, understand?"

Haden nodded.

I held my finger up to make sure I had all of his attention. "Here's another thing. Hand those messages over to servants, say the thing is urgent, and *get out of there*. Don't linger. Don't wait for a tip. Don't answer any questions at all, understand?"

Haden's eyes widened. "Dangerous, it be."

"Mayhap even a cage matter, Master Haden. Be sure your friends take it serious," I warned. "Nestor will never forgive me if I get you in trouble."

Haden grinned at me. He'd lost an eyetooth in some scrap or other. "It'll get done and we'll vanish," he promised me. "We're old hands, never you fear."

I pointed him to the hall that led to the dining room. "Mistress Meraud's in there. Where are your friends?"

"I'll whistle 'em up once I've the papers and I'm away," he

told me. "Better like that." He trotted down the hall. I relaxed a little.

I said farewell to Serenity and Meraud, settled my pack, then left with Achoo. Half a block away I stopped by a railing for horses and bent as if to check my boot. I looked to the side. There was the flick of a much-washed red skirt.

Achoo could have run her off easy, but there was no danger to the gixie following me to Guards House. She'd never get in, so she would have no way to know who I spoke with there. I took off my pack and found another of the Viviano apples I'd filched from the kitchen and tucked away. I left it on the rail atop two copper nobles, then slung the pack on my shoulders again. That gixie had to keep Pearl happy. That's enough trouble for anyone to have in her life. I won't add to it. Achoo and I continued on up the street.

My mind kept me busy as we trudged up the steep hillside streets to Guards House. If Pearl had set the Finers up to be hobbled, why? Did her watchers see Isanz when he called on me? Did someone remember the old man's skill at naming the sources of silver?

It didn't even have to be that. If any of her people worked in one of the family's houses, they could have heard something. Mayhap the old man misspoke and told his family that he'd found the source of the silver in the coles. Mayhap a spy found his notes, if he kept them.

Pox! Isanz said a daughter and a granddaughter worked on the silver with him nowadays. I should have asked Meraud who the daughter was, and the granddaughter, if it wasn't Meraud herself. Was the daughter taken by the Dogs along with the old man?

I couldn't think that way. Goodwin will return with

reinforcements. It might take a few days, but if I can keep the Finers alive that long, they'll be saved. I was sure Sir Lionel would intervene, once I'd explained everything. He knew why me and Goodwin were in Port Caynn, after all. Better still, I'd be offering him a way to get free of Pearl Skinner at last. He could restore the balance between proper authority and the Court of the Rogue.

Sergeant Axman was on duty when I entered Guards House. I waited until he'd dealt with the Dogs already at his tall desk, then stepped up.

"Sergeant, Guardswoman Rebakah Cooper, on detached duty from Corus," I told him. "I need to speak to my lord the Deputy Provost on an urgent matter." I slid the gold noble I'd held in my hand since I'd left my lodgings across the top of his desk.

Sergeant Axman looked at the coin, at me, and at the coin again. Then he shoved the coin at me. "I'll take your word for it," he said, his voice gruff. "Nestor told us that're friends about you. Put that thing away."

I did as I was told. The sergeant whistled for a runner and spoke to her in a soft voice. I don't know what orders he gave her, but she took off. Then the sergeant looked at me again. "You'll need to leave your pack here, as well as the hound," he said.

I hesitated, but there was naught else I could do. The set of the sergeant's face told me I wasn't going to see Sir Lionel with my pack. I set it next to his desk. I pointed to the floor beside it and told Achoo, *"Dukduk. Jaga."*

"The weapons belt, too," Sergeant Axman told me. He looked a bit shamefaced. "My lord's list of them that wear the belt in his presence is a short one."

I stared up at him, shocked. No Watch Commander in

Corus had ever made his or her Dogs leave a weapons belt behind. What sort of milk-gutted custard spine *was* Sir Lionel? I looked at the floor, getting a grip on my temper. If I feared Pearl Skinner, and if I knew my Dogs were flea-bitten with Pearl's spies, mayhap I'd be wary of who carried weapons near me, too. If Sir Lionel did know many of us wore hidden weapons, he didn't think to ask us to drop them with Sergeant Axman.

"Has he always made his own Dogs surrender their gear?" I asked, quiet-like.

The sergeant nodded. He looked around, but the waiting room was empty. "Ever since his family was threatened," he whispered. "Me he lets come around armed, and Nestor, and a handful of other old-time Dogs. You didn't have to drop your gear last time because you and Goodwin were in cityfolk clothes. My lord hardly trusts his household guard."

It seems to me that a cove who is that afraid ought not to be a Deputy Provost.

The runner came back. "This way, Guardswoman," she told me. I followed her to Sir Lionel's office. He was seated behind his great desk. I stood at attention, waiting for him to give me the nod, as the runner left, closing the door behind her. Sir Lionel took his own time about going through his papers, signing a few, making notes on others, until he'd reached the end of the pile. Then he set down his pen, leaned back in his chair, and looked at me.

"This had better be worth my time, Guardswoman Cooper," he said. "I'm a busy man. Where is Guardswoman Goodwin?"

"She is unavailable, Sir Knight. This matter would not wait." I spoke carefully, trying to be as correct in my manners and speech as I'd been taught. Everything depended on me making the right impression. "Sir Knight, one of our informants has been falsely arrested on charges of colemongering. I come to you asking for your help in the matter. Master Isanz Finer and many members of his family, all silversmiths, were taken up this morning and brought to the Tradesmen's District kennel. Coles were found in the house, but these are coles set aside by the family. They have kept them out of the money-stream until the Silversmith's Guild answered their report of coles in trade throughout the city. The Finers made their report over a week ago. They also made this complaint together with other silversmiths in the guild. Master Isanz Finer also informed Goodwin and me of this the day after our arrival here." My mouth had gone as dry as paper. I licked my lips, but I dared not stop. "Moreover, Sir Knight, Master Isanz Finer was known in the past for his ability to identify the origins of different kinds of silver. That is why Corporal Guardswoman Goodwin and I visited him. He undertook for us to learn the origins of the silver in the coles. We now know where it comes from, thanks to his hard work. We also have a likely suspect in our eye. It is someone with no connections whatsoever to the Finers. An innocent family is being caged right now, Sir Knight. You must trust our word that these people are not involved."

I bit my lip to shut myself up. I waited, eyeing the floor. I'd already noticed Sir Lionel would not look at me. I felt a sinking in my gut.

"Have you documents from the Silversmith's Guild testifying that these silversmiths told them of false coins?" he asked, pouring himself a drink from a pitcher at hand.

"Sir Knight, we are trying to get those now, but my hopes are not good. The guild told the smiths there was no problem of coles," I replied. "You, with your greater understanding of such persons, would know better than I why they would say such a thing. To a lowly Dog like me, it looks as if they are trying to cover up the problem."

"I don't want the opinions of a lowly Dog like you," Sir Lionel said, his voice icy.

I looked at the floor again. "Of course not, Sir Knight."

"Have you documents from the other silversmiths who reported to the guild?" he asked.

"We are trying to get some, Sir Knight," I replied.

"You say you have a suspect?" he asked very softly.

I looked him in the face. His mouth was unsteady. His hands were shaking. Where was Goodwin when I needed her? I didn't know how to talk to someone of his position. He was the chief law officer here, even if we thought him tainted by his fear of the Rogue. Surely if he knew he could bring Pearl down, he would do his duty.

I thought of something. "My lord, today or tomorrow a caravan guarded by Hanse Remy will be coming here with smuggled silver. Isanz Finer told us where the silver comes from. We know that Remy went there. You can set a trap at the north gates to the city. If your people find smuggled silver in Remy's keeping, you will know that Isanz has served the Crown. He will have proved his innocence."

"What if he simply gave up his cohorts in crime, knowing that you and Goodwin were closing in?" Sir Lionel asked.

"We went to Master Finer for help, Sir Knight," I replied. "He could have had us looking up our own bums for the smuggled silver. Instead he told us where it came from. All I ask is that you send a writ to Tradesmen's kennel to spare the Finers until you learn if his information is good."

Sir Lionel was blinking too much. I never trust anyone who blinks too much. "Who is your suspect, Cooper?" His voice was sharp.

"Sir, I should not tell." I said it flat out.

"Answer me, you guttersnipe." He gripped the edge of his desk with white-knuckled hands.

I was on the very edges of my nerves, my whole body aquiver, or I might never have spoken as I did then. Writing it now, in cold blood, I can't believe I was such a fool. "You know curst well who it is, Sir Knight. If you'd been using your head instead of shrinking at every shadow, you'd have seen it for yourself. And if you hadn't let her run fast and far beyond all control, it might never have come to this."

"You *dare.*" He whispered it. His skin had gone the color of ash.

"There's yet time," I said like he was a fellow Dog and I his equal. "Pick her up. Put her to mage spells and she will talk. Better yet, question Hanse Remy. He'll name her in trade for his own life. She's at the heart of a rot that's spreading all down the river. Without her it will stop. You'll have the credit for hobbling her—"

He raised a hand. Purple fire flew at me from his fingers. I didn't even have the chance to dodge before it coated me, freezing my arms to my sides and clamping my lips fast together.

He put a magic on me. Gods curse him and his ancestors, he put a magic on me without my consent. I will have my vengeance for that, nobleman or no. I've been touched with other magics before. They never felt like this, but then, they were magics I'd agreed to, like healing spells, or Kora darkening my lashes and brows for a night's fun.

I'll have revenge for Lionel of Trebond's stinking trick. I don't care who he is. I have rights under the law.

"You ignorant, feckless piece of common get," he whispered, leaning toward me. "You're like a child playing with death spells. Did you stop to think of the lives you will destroy if your mindless accusations come to light? Of course not. You want the glory of arresting a Rogue. Mithros save me, you would see this city at war with itself! Well, not on my watch, girl. *Not on my watch*. Is that other one, what was her name—Goodwin—is she in this with you? Does she know of your insane idea? You may nod or shake your head. I am tired of your mouthings."

I only stared at him. He is as mad as a privy snake, I understand that now. He must be, to think he can cover it all up. I was horrified to know the city's law was in the hands of an out-and-out cracknob, but I was also enraged. He had to fumble for Goodwin's name—Goodwin, with all her reputation and honors! What had this Gift-lazy noble sop ever done with his life, save bring the whole country near to disaster by doing *nothing*?

Sir Lionel glared at me. He gave another twitch of his fingers. That purple Gift came swimming my way again. This time it made me feel as if a thousand burning needles thrust deep into my skin. I'd never felt such all-over pain. My eyes teared up and ran over. I ground my teeth. Then the magic on my mouth came off. I spat on his desk. He ignored it.

"Goodwin. Does she know of your ideas about the source of the false coin?" he asked me again. "The next time will hurt more, wench."

I swallowed. He wouldn't believe an answer I gave him too easily. I'd have to let him hurt me a second time. Don't take me wrongly. I *hate* pain. But guaranteed Sir Lionel had magic ways to talk to folk in Corus. I had to make certain there would be no killers going after Goodwin there. He'd have to hit me afresh before he'd believe anything I'd tell him about Goodwin, I knew.

The purple Gift came at me again. I felt like my skin was on fire. If the other magic hadn't been holding me up, I would have dropped to the floor. I shuddered, terrified that he'd do it again.

When I could, after the pain stopped, I started to spit blood from my bitten lip onto his desk and caught his eye just for a moment. He was giving me what I'm sure he thought was a frightening glare. I blinked a couple of times and looked away without spitting on his desk a second time.

"Does Goodwin believe you?" he asked.

"Di'n't even tell her," I mumbled. That part was easy. My lip was swelling.

"Speak up, slut," he ordered. "Be quick about it."

I closed my eyes and counted to nine, three times three for the Goddess, before I cooled off enough to answer safely. "She doesn't know." I said it slow and louder. "I never told her who I thought it was. She always gets the glory for the hobbling. I wanted it for a change."

He flicked another bit of magic at me. My lips froze together. "I can't have you stirring folk up with your wild talk." He spoke to himself. He'd made it clear I meant nothing to him. "Great Mithros, all I need is for you to spread rumors, and for the Rogue to hold *me* accountable. No, you must be safely out of the way."

He yanked a bellpull beside his desk. I closed my eyes, pretending the pull was a snake that dropped to wrap around his throat. Imagining that kept me from panicking. Whatever he meant to do with me, I was helpless. If Nestor even thought to inquire for me here, what could Axman say?

The door opened. A Dog came in, not one I recognized. Had he been listening at the door? He'd come fast if the other end of that bellpull was in some room far off. He was one of those rawboned, redheaded northerners who looked as if he never smiled—much like Sir Lionel, actually.

"Ives, this wench has committed a crime against the realm. I want you and Dogs you *trust,* Dogs who will speak to no one, to bind and gag her, and escort her to Rattery Prison," Sir Lionel ordered. He could as well have been asking this Ives cove to carry out the trash. "I want her in a Coffin cell, understand me?"

Ives bowed. "It will be exactly as you say, Sir Knight." He looked me over. "Enno and I can manage this ourselves. No need to involve anyone else."

"Very good," Sir Lionel said. "You will find me grateful. She must be gagged and bound *at all times,* understand? Do it immediately. The spell will not hold once you take her more than one hundred feet from me."

Ives bowed. From his belt purse he fetched the rawhide thongs every Dog carried. He bound my ankles so I could make short strides only. My hands he tied behind me, with very good knots. I'd be hard put to get at my weapons. I was certain he was waiting only until I was out of Sir Lionel's presence before he searched me for them.

The gag was harder—he had none. He left the room. Sir Lionel poured himself a cup of wine and began to write something. He was trying to show he was calm and in control. He would have been much more believable if he didn't keep blotting the page.

Ives returned with a length of bandage and a muscled hillman who was near as wide as he was tall. I guessed this was Enno. Most of his girth at chest and arms was muscle. Mayhap I could fight my way past Ives, but not this tree trunk of a cove. He was the one that gagged me.

Ives gave me a shove. I only rocked on my feet, which stuck fast to the floor. "Sir Knight," said Ives.

Sir Lionel raised his hand and beckoned. I felt the magic drop away, and I stumbled. Enno grabbed me and hauled me up with one hand clamped hard around my arm.

They half walked, half dragged me from Sir Lionel's presence. I spent no time worrying about my destination. I'd soon have the leisure to appreciate my Coffin, a tiny, dark room with no light and a door only in the ceiling. Instead I tried to work at the knots around my wrists without Enno catching me at it.

They marched me down a different corridor from the one I'd used to reach the Deputy Provost's office. We'd gone but fifty feet when Enno clamped his hand around my wrists and squeezed until my bones ground together. "None o' that, Duchess," he told me. "Swive with the ties and I'll break one o' your elbows, Mithros strike me if I lie."

They shoved me into a small room. There were logbooks on the desk, a bottle and two cups on a small table, chairs and a handful of cards that showed me Sir Lionel had interrupted a game. A bell hung on a rope that dangled from a hole in the wall. That would be the way Sir Lionel summoned Ives. Trays were stacked in a corner, I supposed for serving Sir Lionel. Another door led to the outside.

Pounce! I thought, calling to him. It was useless. He was in Corus, or among the stars. Of all times for him to be away! I stopped calling and tipped my head back. I would *not* cry in front of these two tarses. I would *not*. Somehow, between here and the Rattery, I would find a way to escape.

Then I bethought myself of my eyes. Many folk did not like them, especially when I was angry, and I *stared*. I turned my eyes on Enno, letting all of my rage fill them. When I'd done the same to Rosto, and I was not nearly so angry, he said he'd seen friendlier headsmen waiting to start their day's work.

"I'd best see if she left any gear with Sarge Axman," Ives told Enno. "It'll look bad if anyone comes hunting her and sees her weapons. Don't search her till I get back."

"You can have her," Enno said, backing away. "I don't want to tangle with this one. She's puttin' a curse on me."

"Hill barbarian," Ives said, putting his hand on the door latch. "They're just eyes. Mages have to speak to curse." He pulled the door open and shut up. Someone outside had placed a dagger right under one of Ives's own eyes.

Sergeant Axman shoved Ives into the room and came in, still keeping his dagger on Ives's face. Five other Dogs entered behind Axman.

"Shut the door," the sergeant ordered. One of the other Dogs obeyed. "Ives, what's Sir Lionel got planned for Cooper, here?"

Ives shook his head. He wouldn't betray his master's plans. The sergeant gave him a cuff that knocked him against the wall. Another Dog hauled him to his feet. The woman among them came at me, her dagger in her hand. With quick, hard strokes she cut the gag and the ties off of me.

"They were to take me to the Rattery and dump me in a Coffin," I said, rubbing my wrists. "Sir Lionel wants me silenced. He thinks if he can do that, his problems will disappear."

"He's got more of 'em instead," Sergeant Axman told me as two of the other Dogs set about tying up Enno and Ives. "Bread went up two coppers this mornin', and there's a Crown ban on rye. Seemingly part of the crop's gone bad, and they want to see what part. It's not sittin' well in the marketplaces." The Dog who kept watch from the door handed my weapons belt and my pack to me. He stood aside as Achoo leaped in. I dropped to my knees to hug her.

"I thought I told you to stay," I said quietly. I was trying to act like a proper Dog, when I wanted to cry into Achoo's fur. I looked at the Dog who'd let her in. He wore a padded leather coat and gloves that showed fresh scratches. He must have taken my gear from Achoo.

He grinned at me. "Yon's a fine hound," he said. "Hadda hold her up inna air afore we could get your things."

"Cooper, you need to get out of here and go to ground," the sergeant told me. He turned me away from the others and bent down to whisper in my ear. "We can't hold Ives forever. He's Sir Lionel's man. There'd be all Chaos caperin' in the halls if we killed 'im. Best we can hope for is, he'll be too scared to tell Sir Lionel that you escaped 'im an' Enno."

I nodded. That made sense. "Won't you and your people be in trouble?" I asked.

Axman showed me a wolf's grin. "We'll make us a bargain. He'll keep 'is gob corked an' we'll let 'im keep 'is sack. Now, you get movin'. You know who's safe to contact and who's not."

Ives shouted under the gag they'd put on him. I could tell he'd cried, "Traitor!"

The mot who'd cut me free kicked him. "You need to learn a bit of what's goin' on, laddie," she said coldly. "What's goin' on ain't as simple as you."

Axman hauled me to my feet and towed me through the door. He pointed down the corridor. "First left, down the stairs, through the door, second right down that hall, and out the door," he said. "It puts you two blocks downhill of here. Go."

"Won't they come after you for mutiny, Sarge?" I asked him. "You and them in there?"

"I ain't mutinyin'!" he said, his eyes wide and innocent.

"I'm gettin' rid of a cracked gixie as has been makin' trouble in my waitin' room, screamin' mad lies about the Deputy Provost! Gave her the sole o' my boot, didn't I? Dunno how she got runnin' loose here in Guards House!"

I stood on tiptoe and kissed his cheek. "You're a wicked one. Gods all bless, Sarge. Help is coming," I said. Then Achoo and I took off.

Sergeant Axman's directions led me through a door in a small alleyway that opened onto a street lined with small houses. I was on the north side of the ridge, the ocean harbor side. Coming outside with Achoo, stopping to catch my breath, I felt very strange. Only a few moments ago I'd been bound for a cell that was rightly called a Coffin. Instead, thanks to Nestor's friends, I was free, but to what purpose? Once Sir Lionel discovered I had not reached the Rattery, he would go to Serenity's house first. Meraud would have to get help without me, at least for the moment.

I knelt before a small shrine to the Wavewalker and put a copper in the jar. Anyone who saw me would think I was offering prayers. Truly I was buying time and peace to think. Nestor's would be the next place Sir Lionel would look. I could try to make contact with Okha at the Waterlily, but that had to wait until tonight. Dale would be at the Goldsmith's Bank. Besides, I didn't know if I could trust him for this. It was one thing to believe he was no part of Pearl's game, quite another to ask him to hide me from the Crown's law master in the city.

The idea struck me then. It was completely mad-brained, but what did I have to lose? I took off my pack and slipped Okha's maps from the hidden pocket. Pearl's Gauntlet court was closest to me. I reminded the Trickster that I deserved a little good luck just now and memorized the map before I tucked it away once more.

"We're going to have an adventure," I told Achoo, putting her leash on her collar. "And it's a very good thing Pounce isn't here, because he might try to stop us. But you, you're game for nearabout anything, aren't you?" Achoo pranced, wagging her tail. She was excited. "Well, then," I said, "I'll be Goodwin, and you'll be Tunstall, only fuzzier. And mayhap we'll live to tell this tale."

My body was filled with a strange quivering as we set out, a slight tremble that did not stop. Was it nerves? Kora and Aniki swore I had none. I only knew I was doubly awake and aware, balanced on a razor's edge. I took note of almost everything, even the soft thump of Achoo's pads in the street dirt as we walked. Since she kept looking at me with such lively interest, I kept my voice quiet and continued to explain as if she were Pounce. "The Court of the Rogue is where fugitives may find a welcome, isn't it? Well, we are fugitives, and we are looking for a welcome. It's the last place Sir Lionel will seek us. Mayhap I'll learn sommat into the bargain."

Achoo whuffed. It sounded as if she agreed.

We were passing some shops when I had another good idea. Achoo and I entered a jeweler's place. One of my lord Gershom's gold nobles bought me a strand of light pink pearls. It would do us no harm to greet the Rogue with a proper guest gift.

On we went, leaving the respectable homes and shops for the poorer streets of the Gauntlet District. Walking along, I learned for myself sommat I'd heard of last year, when a corporal in Highfields District back home murdered his wife. He went about the city after, just ambling. As long as he acted normal, folk ignored him. He was just another Dog. When Goodwin and me got noticed here, it was because we did something that brought us to local folk's attention. If I just walked like I belonged, flipping my baton up and around my hand, Achoo at my side, I was an everyday Dog.

I stayed ordinary until I went down Darcy Walk. A pair of coves who were idling near the entrance to Pearl's court halted me. "You just stop right there," the shorter of them said. "What's the likes of you doin' here? You're not one of th' Gauntlet Dogs. We never seen you b'fore."

I looked them over like they were privy scrapings. "I never knew I needed permission from as miserable a pair of Rats as you two if I wanted a word with Her Majesty," I said. I held up two copper nobles. "Or is it that I forgot the fee?"

The bigger cove took my coins. The little one was still not impressed. "You're wearin' blades. And you've a cur wiv you."

"That's no cur. That's a scent hound. And Her Majesty knows us." I spun my baton until I caught it neatly in my hand. "Will you let me by? Or shall I ring the Sunset Hymn on your skull with this?"

The little cove drew breath, doubtless to tell me off. The big one poked him in the ribs. "Let 'er go," he said lazily. "If she offends, one of 'er Majesty's blades'll cut 'er to cat meat soon enough."

They let me pass. Achoo and I walked between them, feeling the little one's glare as we went.

From what I could see of the outside, this court was a Guild Hall once, a great single building. Now it was enclosed by other, smaller ones built as the neighborhood got poorer. The lesser houses were attached to the place by corridors or breaks in the walls that joined them. The Rogue would own those places and make sure her trusted folk lived in them, to keep the court safe.

If anyone watched me from behind the shutters on the outlying buildings, I did not see them. Instead Achoo and I walked through the small door that opened onto Darcy Walk into the main building. Once inside, we stood in a narrow corridor that led to the left. The right-hand side of the corridor was bricked up. What light there was came from lamps that burned in sconces on the walls. Since the windows, too, were bricked up, it wasn't exactly a welcoming place to stand. We walked quick down that hall. I did not like the thought of being caught there if the lamplight died.

The door at the hall's end opened onto the main Guild Hall. It was a full three stories high, with a fancy ceiling framed in arches, wide galleries on the second and third stories, and hearths at each long end of the room. As at the Eagle Street court, there were tables, stools, and benches everywhere for Pearl's court to sit. Her own place, like Rosto's in Corus, was marked by a wooden platform beside the hearth farthest from me. A chair stood there, furs draped over it to cushion the seat. Two stools, one to either side, marked her bodyguards' places. There were small tables as well, to hold her cup and anything else she cared to set down.

Pearl herself was not in the room. A gixie a year or two younger than me came over, wiping her hands on an apron. "What'll it be?" she asked. "I serve till we gets busy. Then if you want more, ye go through that door there and gets your own." She pointed to a door where another serving girl leaned at leisure. Seemingly it was yet early in the day for the Court of the Rogue. "We've salmon in pastry, cheese fritters, honey fritters, onion tart, stuffed eggs, and mutton pasties. Chickpea soup, too."

"Have you barley water?" I asked.

She actually took a step back from me. *"What?"*

"Twilsey?" I asked. "Regular apple cider, not hard?"

The maid shook her head. "A Dog as won't drink. What's the world comin' to? We've apple cider for mages and them that bring their young ones. Will you have food?" She looked at Achoo. "Your hound had best have indoor manners."

"She's better-trained than I am," I said. "I'll have an onion tart, a stuffed egg, and two cheese and two honey fritters." Achoo would like the fritters.

The gixie held out her hand. "Five coppers, then."

I frowned. The same lunch would cost three coppers back home. "Do I pay extra for the honor of dining at the Rogue's?"

The gixie made a face. "I forgot my purse of laughter when I dressed this mornin'," she told me. "Have you not bought anythin', the last few days? Prices have gone up. Pay or starve, it's all one to me."

I paid and found a seat. The day was half over, yet those folk I could see in the hall were scarce awake. A pair of gamesters played dice with dozy slowness. A mot seated by the empty hearth opposite the Rogue's throne sharpened a series of knives most carefully. Achoo lay down and took a nap.

Sitting for the first time in hours, I thought of Dale. Things were so good last night, but what would happen now? He might shrink from me once he learned I was on the run from Sir Lionel. Or would Dale think this was some new game he might play, a game of wits with the Deputy Provost? He could very well do that. And there was the matter of Hanse and Steen. They'd be nabbed as soon as Goodwin returned with help. Would Dale try to save them from the Rattery? Or would he shrug and say they had gambled and lost?

They weren't the only ones who'd gambled, to be sure. I'd no way of knowing where I stood with the Rogue's people. If they knew nothing of what had passed between me and Sir

Lionel, I was safe enough. If word got out, though, I'd taken the most foolish step of my life. Much depended on whether Sir Lionel put up a hunt for me with more Dogs than just the two he'd sent to bury me in the Rattery. By now I knew that Nestor and Sergeant Axman were respected well outside their home kennels. If other Dogs believed them instead of Sir Lionel, I'd do fine.

I'd rolled the dice. I'd play the numbers I got.

Meanwhile, I was still hunting colemongers and evidence. It would be good to *prove* my suspicions of Pearl. I needed to lay hands on some pieces of her clothes, in case Achoo and I had to track her. And I had to think. I needed to work out each bit of the tale I was going to tell Pearl. I would have to give it before her, her guards, and anyone who stood within earshot.

I put my head down. This is why I hate Court Days, and speaking in front of Sir Tullus and a roomful of people. But there was no time to moan. Pearl would come at any moment, and I had to be ready with my most fanciful tale ever.

The maidservant returned with my tray of food and my cider. As soon as she walked away, Achoo sat up and whuffed at me.

"Yes, I remembered you," I told her. I placed a honey fritter and a cheese one on a small plate, together with half of the stuffed egg. Those I placed on the floor. Achoo gobbled them down as if she'd had naught to eat in days. In the end, I had but half of the onion tart and the other half of the stuffed egg. Achoo wheedled all the rest from me.

I was setting the dishes aside when them that were relaxing in the hall stirred. Pearl came down a staircase that led to one of the upper stories, guards in front and behind. A few hard-looking mots and coves followed the guards, talking among themselves. Once Pearl settled on her dais, a serving girl opened a door at the middle of the room, admitting folk from outside.

I had entered the back way. From the map Okha had made, these newcomers had come through the house that served as the court's main entrance. This place and the Eagle Street court were all set up like mazes, so the Rats had plenty of bolt holes if the Dogs came in force. It showed either how lazy Pearl was about safety, or how well she knew Sir Lionel's fear of her, that I had gotten in without challenge.

I watched, turning my tale over in my head. I'd learned more than a year ago that wearing a Dog uniform turned me into someone else, a proper Dog who only remembered she was shy in a courtroom. I'd already had the thought that mayhap I could be someone else in different clothes, and so I was bolder with Dale when I wear dresses. Now, to stand before Pearl with no Goodwin to hide behind, I made myself into the Dog of the story Goodwin and I told. I was Gershom's pet and a pretty Dog, the kind that gets the men to do her work for her. I bit my lips to puff them up and pinched my cheeks to redden them. I practiced fluttering my lashes. I thought of my peaches as fuller, my hips as rounder.

I watched carefully as them that had requests to make of Pearl lined up before her. Everyone carried a little something to sweeten the Rogue. The better-off ones had coin. The poor ones carried baskets of food or goods. The old doxie Zolaika, the Bazhir Jurji, or Torcall the longsword fighter would accept the gift. Once they gave Pearl the nod, she would hear what the giver had to ask. It made me grind my teeth. Rosto did not take gifts from everyone who came before him. Folk could talk with him outright. Sure, he accepted bribes, but in private, for important matters. If folk wanted to thank him, he asked that they just thank him. *Some* Rogues know what it's like to be poor.

I ordered more fritters from the serving girl. Achoo gobbled her share and much of mine, but that was all right. I was too nervous to eat. There was still that tale to tell, before as many people as sat below.

Achoo was begging for the last fritter when I heard Pearl's raised voice. "Cooper, you may be Dale Rowan's newest bedmate, but that doesn't make you *my* friend."

I wiped my sticky fingers on the inside of my tunic and hoisted my pack on my shoulders. *"Kemari,"* I told Achoo. Together we walked to the dais, me remembering to let my hips swing.

I gave Pearl a bow, though it wrung my tripes to do it, and offered her the pink pearl string, warm from my pocket. I had a tale to tell, and bowing to that rank maggot pie went with it, just as the pearls did.

Jurji reached out to me with his sheathed sword and poked the pearls heaped in my hand. I hung the string over the weapon, hating him for showing me so much disrespect.

He let them slide down the length of the sword until they rolled onto his wrist, where he inspected them. Only when he'd run them through his fingers did he stick the sheathed blade in his sash and hand the string to Pearl. She passed them through *her* fingers, not as he did, feeling for sharp edges or seams, anything that might show there was a trick in them, but in a savoring way.

"Very nice," she said at last. "A little out of range of a Dog's wage."

I kept my eyes on the floor. Let her think it was respect. "We had funds for this trip," I said. "I borrowed some."

Pearl set the string in her lap instead of handing them off to someone else. "A'right, then, Cooper. You've earned some speech wiv me. The gift is well done. What've you got to say, then?"

Now I could meet her eyes like I was innocent and my story was true. I was another kind of Dog now, and these folk were all people who might help me. That was the tale I'd spun. "Forgive me, Majesty, but I'm in a fix. I couldn't think where else to go that I might be safe," I explained. "And I couldn't leave Achoo behind. It's taken this long to get Achoo to trust me after her last handler beat on her. I didn't want her in harm's way."

To my surprise, Pearl's face darkened. "It's the lowest kind of scummer that will beat a creature who can't speak of it," she muttered. "Will she say hello?" She offered her hand, palm up, leaning down in her chair.

I hesitated. It would look strange if I didn't permit Achoo to greet the Rogue. "Achoo, *pengantar.*"

Of course Achoo went to smell Pearl's fingers, wagging her tail. The silly hound loves everyone.

Pearl actually looked at me for permission to pet my hound. I nodded. Inside I was shocked. I never thought Pearl would ask anyone for anything.

It wasn't long until Achoo was on her back, paws in the air, tail thrashing, whilst Pearl gave her a good belly scratch. It was plain to everyone that the Rogue was glad to play with my hound. It was just as plain to me that she understood them.

I hate to know good things of an enemy. It makes my life harder.

"Aye, I can feel a scar here, and another here," she said, her hands gently touching spots on Achoo's belly and ribs. "If her last handler was in this room, I'd mark him as he did her, see how he liked it." She looked to the nearest servant. "How about some chopped meat for my friend, here? Good stuff, mind, not street scrapings."

I smiled. I had to. "Thank you, Majesty," I said.

Pearl sat up. Achoo sat up with her so Pearl could rub her ears as the Rogue spoke to me. "Start talking."

"It's a bit of a tale," I replied, sinking deep into the other self I'd made. "See, Goodwin has these silversmith friends here, the Finers. She was good friends with one of their men ten years back. The old cove who's head of the family likes her yet. We visited them, the first day we were here."

Pearl glanced at me, an odd expression in her eyes. Was she the one who put the Dogs on the Finers?

"I heard today the family got taken up for colesmithing," I went on. "The problem is, Goodwin went off to Corus yesterday morning to visit her man. I figured she'd be grateful to me if I tried to help the Finers. If you knew the grandfather, you'd see he'd never go near colesmithing. He's one of those stern, right-thinking sorts. We report to Nestor Haryse, I s'pose you know that, but the Sarge is no good for sommat like this. He's not high up enough. For charges as serious as coles, I had to talk with someone *powerful*. I have some luck with powerful men." Someone behind me snickered. I ignored it. "So I dipped into Goodwin's cash box and went up to Guards House."

Around me I could hear Pearl's Rats chuckle. I turned and glared at them. "I didn't think it was a fool idea." I showed them my pout. My mask had worked. I'd wanted them to see a spoiled pet Dog, pretty and free enough with her favors that other Dogs cover for them. We didn't have any in the Lower City—they don't tend to last. But some of these Rats had seen me hanging on Dale often enough. I only needed to fool them, and Pearl.

"Forget my folk and tell *me,*" Pearl said. "I'm the one as decides if you linger here or get your arse kicked into the street."

"Oh, aye," I replied hurried-like, facing her. "So I go to that lard gut Axman. I tell him I *need* to speak with someone higher up, preferring Sir Lionel, and I slip him a sweetener. He calls for Ives, that collects the entry fees, I suppose. Well, Ives takes me to Sir Lionel, once I've given Ives *his* sweetener. And I start telling Sir Lionel about Master Finer. Only Sir Lionel interrupts me and says where's Goodwin. I tell him, she's gone back to Corus. Then he asks me if she's got my report with her. I ask him, what report. And he tells me, Don't play me for a fool. I know why you're here. Everyone knows you're Gershom of Haryse's pet."

"See, that's interesting," Torcall Jupp said from his chair near Pearl's. "All I can find out is that your family was part of his household, and he sponsored you to the Dogs."

I gave him the sidelong smile that the trulls give a cove to bring them racing across a street. At least, I hope I got that right. " 'Tis a very large house," I said, as sly as Kora working a new spell. "All manner of hidden passages." Forgive me, my lord, I thought. "Then my lady gets wind and *she* decides I need a trade that'll get my face broke in, only I like being a Dog. So I told Sir Lionel that my lord and my lady sponsor us to a trade once we're grown. Only Sir Lionel says I'm not to treat him like a coney. He says he *knows* my lord sent me and Goodwin here to spy on him, and make up lies about him so my lord Gershom can replace him or something worse." I let my voice climb, so more Rats might listen and laugh. "I told him no! But old Lionel kept asking what I would tell my lord. He wouldn't drop it and he wouldn't talk about Master Finer. I even put gold nobles before him. He dashed them to the floor! He said it were proof

I was my lord's spy, when it were Goodwin's gambling money. I figured even a Deputy Provost wouldn't turn up his nose at gold! When he said he'd not touch Lord Gershom's money, I lost my head and told him he was stupid."

I stopped to catch my breath. I felt as I did on Court Days, when I talked fast to get my whole story out before I began to stammer. It wasn't easier than testifying, to fork over a huge lie. I still had to spit it out fast. But it was done. The whole Court of the Rogue was laughing their buttons off, Pearl included. I figured that any tale that made Sir Lionel out as a fool would amuse her.

"What next?" Torcall Jupp asked me as folk began to catch their breaths. "You still haven't said why you are here."

I let my shoulders droop. "Because Sir Lionel said I could bed down in the cages for my insolence. His man came for me, but I got a head start on him, running. They know my lodgings. Nestor, that we've been reporting to, will have word to grab me up, I'll wager. I hoped to hide out here till I think of sommat," I said, looking at the floor.

"And what if the Deputy Provost sends his people here to find you?" Torcall wanted to know. "If you bring trouble on us—"

I glared at him. "I've been here two hours, maybe, and no one's come. They'd not seek me *here*. All the city knows Her Majesty's cross with me for trying to grab one of your foists. I hardly made a fuss up there at Guards House, anyway. Maybe I hit a few Dogs on my way out. Could be I made some horses rear in the courtyard. So a couple of the horses was already hitched to wagons that weren't too sturdy. They've got worse things to handle than one junior Dog, to my way of thinking."

That set them all to laughing again, as I'd meant it to. I

stayed as I was, wearing a sullen pout. Achoo leaned against my knees. I knelt beside her and hid my face in her ruff. Let the others think I was embarrassed at the uproar. I was on pins and needles, waiting to hear Pearl's ruling.

"Quiet down, you mudskippers!" she cried. They obeyed, though some were yet snorting. "You've given us a good laugh, Cooper, and you know how to treat a Rogue proper." She fingered the pearls I'd given her. "I guess Rosto taught you somethin'. You can stay until you give me reason to throw you out. Mayhap Sir Lionel will look for you harder than most. More like he'll just whine to my Lord Provost about you. That's more like him. He's a whiner, not a doer. You and the hound may stay, for now." She waved us off.

Achoo and I walked through the Rats, who patted my back and joked about my tale. I pouted, or smiled, or handed out little light slaps, playing my part, and held my course for the privies. Here they were set outdoors, up on a platform so them that drove the scummer wagons could empty the barrels from the alley behind. There was a fence closing the courtyard off, so folk couldn't leave this way easy. Looking at the brown stains on the fences and wall around the privies, I shook my head and breathed through my mouth. Seemingly folk who were in too much of a hurry to wait for the three stalls to clear used those instead. I wouldn't like to try climbing those slippery lengths of wood, for certain.

I did my business and sat there a little while, waiting for my shakes to end. I'd pulled it off. I'd played the part and they had believed. Now I had time to think of something else.

Achoo and I went back inside, to the second-floor gallery, where tables and chairs were set. These were yet empty and gave me a good place to view the floor below. Achoo settled beside me as I watched folk come and go. I even dozed, mayhap for an hour, if I judged by the light that streamed through the few windows. When I woke, Achoo had climbed to the bench next to me. Her eyes were filled with starvation.

I looked at her. "You're a mumper, plain and simple. I'm surprised you don't roll instead of walking, the way you eat." Achoo leaned against me and sighed. I gave her a strip of dried meat as I looked down at Pearl's court. Rats sat, eating and talking. Pearl was having a meal of shellfish and rice, chewing with her mouth open. She could have done with Lady Teodorie's fan on the back of her head, I thought. I would back my lady against Pearl any day. A doxie was towing a grinning cove through a door that led, so my map told me, to a private room off the hall. And Dale Rowan stood in the middle of the floor, speaking with Jurji. The Bazhir pointed up to where I sat. Dale nodded, clapped him on the shoulder, and made for the stairs.

I fidgeted with my belt pouch. What was I to say after last night? Should I leave, avoid him entirely? I really didn't think he was part of the colemongering ring, but that could just be my heart talking. If he was innocent, I was bound for all manner of trouble. Shouldn't I keep him out of it?

Dale came up behind me then. I knew his step, though I had only known him for a few days. He cupped my chin in one hand. Tilting my head back, he gave me a kiss that set my whole body burning. Finally he freed my mouth, though not my chin. "What in the name of Mithros and the judges of the under-world are you *doing* here?" he asked me, his face upside down before my eyes. "Serenity said you left with no warning, never came back. Then the Deputy Provost's men came looking for you at her place *and* mine!" He kept his voice soft. "Now I find you here? What manner of cow flop have you stepped in?"

"You give me a headache, making me look at you this

way," I said, buying myself time to think. "How hard do they search for me?"

Dale kissed me again, then sat next to me, putting his arm about my shoulders. "Achoo, you're supposed to look after her! Instead here you are, giving her your countenance and comfort!" Achoo wagged her tail and did her happy dance for him. Dale raised his brows. "Now I understand. You're just as bad as Beka is." To me he said, "Sir Lionel's Dogs are searching the markets. I didn't stop by Nestor's kennel to see if he'd heard. How did you manage to get up the Deputy Provost's nose, sweet?"

I looked at my lap. "I said he was stupid," I began.

Dale burst into laughter. Folk below turned to look up at us, grinning. No doubt they knew I was giving him the tale I'd given Pearl.

He heard my story out with snickers at all the right places, but at the end he took me by the shoulders and gave me a gentle shake. "Beka, you know better!" he scolded. "You don't go calling the nobility stupid, however stupid they may be! They're too prideful and they have long memories! Was anyone else there to hear you?"

I shook my head. I hated lying to him. He seemed honest and true when he was like this, but I couldn't trust my feelings entirely. He was a gambler. He was good at hiding what he truly thought.

"Gods be thanked for that. Without witnesses, there's a chance he'll lose interest," Dale told me. "With them, nobles always feel they have to make an example of you."

Dale picked up my hand and kissed the inside of my wrist slowly, as he liked to do. I'd thought that perhaps, now that we'd had a tumble, his touch wouldn't unravel my tripes as it had before. I was wrong. Now my every muscle went loose, knowing just what he could do with that warm mouth and those gentle, long fingers.

"Stop it," I whispered, trying to tug my arm away. "I'm in trouble and you're—"

Dale looked at me, his gray eyes bright and teasing. "You need to hide, I understand that. We have private rooms all around us, cozy little rooms with locks on the doors. You hide in one, and I'll keep you company. Much cozier than sitting up here." He kissed my cheek, then the side of my neck. "Hide, and tell me why you talked to the Deputy Provost like a looby, when I know you're no such thing," he murmured into my ear.

I was going to push him away, but my hands lingered on his chest. "He's a fool," I murmured back. "I hate fools."

"All the more reason for me to believe you'd never act like one yourself," he whispered, wrapping his arms around my waist. "You're either stupid or you're clever, pretty, pretty Beka, and I know you're not stupid." He pulled me half onto his lap. "Look, I brought you a present." He slipped it from his own neck over my head. The fine gold chain was still warm from his skin. I looked at the pendant that lay against my uniform tunic, a jagged piece of glassy, dark brown stone framed in gold wire. In the brown depths of one side, when I angled it toward the torches, I saw sheets of deep crimson. Flipping it over, I stared at the other side. Scales of blue and green light seemed buried just under the surface. It was a Sirajit opal.

"Don't screech about the price and how you're not bought," Dale whispered, trailing his fingers down the side of my neck. "I've won a lot of games in the last two days. Your luck stays with me. That's the best kind. And the stone wasn't that expensive. It was a piece off of a greater stone, too delicate itself to be worked. I told the cove who sold it to me that it was meant for one who'd love it for its own sake. *After* I'd bought it, of course."

"Of course," I agreed, knowing it did no good to argue with him about his strange gambler's code. It is a *splendid* stone.

"A bit of pretty to cheer you up, seeing's that you're having a bad day," Dale whispered. He touched his lips to my ear and then to my neck.

We were kissing greedily when a loud voice in the room below made us stop. We slid over on the bench to see who was so angry.

"Bread just went up two coppers the loaf, I told you, are you *deaf*?" Fair Flory stood before Pearl, her hands on her hips. "That's two increases in less than a month!" Behind her waited some of her flower girls and orange sellers. None of these were the tiny, pretty ones, either, but the ones built on the solid side, mots who worked the rowdy drinking and gambling dens. "Only two ships brought harvest wheat from the south this week. The captains say it's a bad year down there. We've no rye at all! Plenty of farmers are hangin' on to what they have, for their own winter."

"One captain says it's a bad year and you're panickin', Flory?" Pearl asked, a sneer on her face. "Ye'll stir up the Roguery with rumors and little to back 'em?"

"Not on the say-so of just one captain, and it's not just rumors," Flory snapped back. "And I'm here to ask you, you've put by to cover your own, *right*?"

"What's my supplies to *you*, Flory?" Pearl snapped. "I don't go thrustin' my nose into your business!"

"Rogue's stores *is* my business," Flory replied. "I pays you my cut, my people hand over their cut, all like our law bids. But

my ear's sharp, Pearl Skinner, and I've not heard of you layin'
up stores. There's no word *anywhere* of you buyin' grain and oil
to keep our people alive through the winter. That's Rogue's
duty!"

Pearl stood. Her hands were hidden in the folds of her
clothes. "As if I'd share my business wiv a brass-backed trull
like you!" The weapon must have been tucked under a slit
in her skirt. Pearl drew it now. It was a long knife with a dark
ivory hilt and a blade that looked wicked sharp. "Are you chal-
lengin' me?"

"I'm lookin' to our own good," Flory snapped, but she
looked nervous. "You spend our coin like it's ale. How're we to
know you're ready to feed them as give you a cut of all they
make? Them as do the *work*? How do we know it ain't all gone
to them curst *teeth*?"

I heard the Rats below mutter at that. It was hard to tell if
they approved of what Flory said or if they were angry with her.

Pearl leveled her long knife at Flory. "Either challenge me
or shut yer flappin' gob," the Rogue snarled. "Come on, Flory!
You want my throne?"

Flory backed up a step. Pearl looked at the others who had
muttered. "What about you? And you? No? You, then?" She
pointed her blade at someone else each time she said "you."
Each time that person flinched. Pearl's face twisted with disgust. She almost had my respect, standing there with her knife
out, wearing a long dress of stained satin over cambric. Her hair
straggled out of its knot, hanging in tangled locks. "Gutless
milksops, all of you!" she cried. "Easy to gossip in the shadows,
innit? Not so easy t'take the Rogue on! You lot wouldn't last a
bird's breath in my place, not with winter comin'! Well, keep
your cods dry! There'll be bread in the Roguery, aye, *and* meat

for all of you whinin', pukin' brats! And the next one to mutter wakes with a cut throat, my word on that!" She sheathed the knife. "Get out o' my sight, Flory, you and your whores." As Flory and her mots turned to go, Pearl yelled, "Leastways I never made my livin' on my back!"

Flory whirled around, a knife in her hand this time. "It's an honest livin'!" she cried, taking a step forward. "We don't suck the coin away from them that work for it!" Two of the flower girls seized Flory by the arms and dragged her from the room.

Pearl laughed. She picked up her tankard and drained it. "Stinkin' trollop," she bellowed, but the flower sellers and orange girls were gone.

Dale and I watched as folk who had stayed swarmed around the dais.

"Oh, they want to make sure Pearl believes they're faithful," Dale muttered sourly as he emptied my pitcher down his throat. There was very little cider left in it. "Goddess tears, Beka, why can't you drink like a normal person!"

I looked at him. "My head spins if I have too much. I don't like it, so I don't drink, most of the time."

Dale shook his head at me. Leaning over the gallery rail, he snapped his fingers. One of the maids looked up and nodded. As Dale settled back on our bench, he told me quietly, "Flory doesn't know the half of it. I heard two higher-ups in the Grain-seller's Guild tell my masters that if wheat went up, barley and rice will, too. If they don't go double in price by the end of day, I'll eat my boots. Rye's clean gone from the market."

My stomach dropped. Meat follows grain, vegetables follow meat. . . . At those prices, my savings will vanish by spring.

"It might be all right if King Roger has done as he should, and put by grain and oil himself," Dale told me, seeing the look on my face. "He'll see to it the guards are fed, the same as the army. The guilds will tend to their people, and the Rogues to theirs. The decent nobles will look after their people, too."

I looked at the table, knife-gouged and old. What of the folk who had no guilds or army or kennels to belong to? How many decent nobles *were* there, anyway?

"Here's what worries me, Beka." Dale placed silver coins in front of me, face side down. Each of them was cut through the side with the Tortallan sword and crown. At the bottom of the cuts I saw the gleam of brass. No doubt these were the coins I'd seen in his home. "I'd been hearing the word *coles* of late, so I looked at my own coins. My copper and my gold pieces are good. But far too many silver coles have come my way. One or two, for a cove like me, who roams all over the kingdom, that I expect. A friend melts them down and gets the silver for me. But not this many coles. I'm not the only one who's getting bit this bad. So I'm wondering, here are Beka and Goodwin, fresh in town. Maybe they're looking for colemongers."

I laughed. "If my lord Gershom was sending Dogs out for colemongers, don't you think he'd get his finest bloodhounds? Goodwin's one of the best, but she'd be part of a team, not holding the leash on one of Lord Gershom's pets!"

The maidservant came with a bottle, a cup, and a pitcher. The bottle was wine, for Dale. The pitcher was cider. Dale gave her a copper half-noble for thanks, and a pat on the bum. I kicked him under the table.

"I was just being polite!" he protested.

"Mayhap she'd like to keep her bum to herself," I told him. "If you need to be patting someone, pat me."

He sighed. "I suppose you're right, about not being on the hunt. But don't you want to know who's doing this?"

He's being canny, if he's one of them, I thought as I took a gulp of cider. Mayhap he thinks I'm so dazed with love that I'd never suspect him. I wish I *was* so dizzy with it that I'd quit wondering about him. This way, wanting him, liking him, then wondering if he is in it, hurts.

"I leave that kind of Dog work to the wise ones," I told him. "I get myself in enough trouble without trying to outthink Rats as use their heads."

"I know something we can do that doesn't involve thinking," Dale whispered, snuggling closer. He began to kiss me.

It turned out one of those private rooms was very near. Achoo guarded the door outside. Inside, Dale worked hard to make him and me forget things like higher prices, false coins, and the Deputy Provost. He even dozed after, though I could not. All too soon my brain was bustling again. I wanted to imagine our future together. Since that was a bad idea, I tried to figure out how long I had to stay hid and what else I might find out before Goodwin returned with my lord Gershom.

Where is Goodwin right now? I wondered as I smoothed Dale's fine hair with my fingers. I try to write it down now as I thought it out then. Goodwin would have reported to my lord and explained the state of things here. Would he believe her when she said Sir Lionel had lost control of his city to his Rogue? He must. It's why he sent her and me to Port Caynn, after all.

Say Lord Gershom did believe Goodwin. He'd have to convince the Privy Council that it was needful to mount an operation in Port Caynn. Goddess, at least a couple of days to get anything from that bunch of noble slugs. Then assembling all they might need and the return to Port Caynn.

I'd be on my own for at least a week. I could not flee to Corus, difficult as things are. I'd told Goodwin I would gather information here. That information is important, more important than my running the moment things get a little chancy.

Sooner or later Pearl would learn of my lies. I'd have to leave the Court of the Rogue before then. Would Dale put me up? Could I trust him?

Mayhap I could, for a day or so. Certainly I'd learn what he's made of, were I to ask. Truly I don't think he is in the cole-mongers' ring. He likes a game where the chances are more than good he will win. Pearl's game is not one of those.

Sunset was gleaming in the windows when we dressed again and left the room. Achoo greeted us in wriggling quiet. She knows she and I are on duty, even if I tried to forget with Dale for a time. We went back to our same table. A maid was just setting more drinks before us when a big-bellied young mot came before Pearl's dais on the floor below, breathing hard. Her face was marked with tears. She collapsed before Pearl as the Rogue and Zolaika admired someone's gift of a gold statue.

"Majesty, you must help us! Gods witness it, you must!" the mot cried. She actually reached out to clutch at Pearl. Quick as thought, Torcall had his sword unsheathed. He set the blade in front of her hands. The young mot pulled them away. "Forgive me! I'm out of my head with grief, I forgot—"

"What is it now?" Pearl asked with a sigh. "Have you a gift for me?"

The mot looked startled and frightened. "Oh—no, no, but surely in this case—"

Pearl looked away.

" 'Tis your business, too, Steen said it was!" the mot cried.

Dale sat up straight at my side.

The mot went on. "When he changed his plans so sudden-like, Steen told me 'twas *your* biddin'! And now they've taken 'im to the cages, him and all the others!"

Pearl drank from her tankard. "Steen is supposed to be away," she said at last.

"He said he might be home this afternoon, or tomorrow mornin' at the latest," the mot said. She kept her hands on her belly, as if to calm the babe within. "I thought I'd meet them. He told me, see, what gate they'd come in. The caravan got here, sure enough. As soon as it was through the gate, Dogs pounced on 'em. They cut at the packs. Most was just filled with bales of cloth, but there was silver blocks in the middle two."

"So they was carryin' silver for the Smith's Guild," Pearl said lazily. "So what?"

The mot shook her head. "They didn't have the royal stamp, Majesty. I was standin' right close, even though Steen was signin' to me to get back. The silver wasn't marked at all. The Dog Sergeant ordered the Dogs to collect it. Then he said everyone in the caravan was arrested for transport of illegal silver! They took 'em all to Guards House, in the King's name!"

"How can it be stolen from the Crown?" Jurji the Bazhir asked, confused. "We haven't heard of a large robbery. We'd know."

Zolaika answered him. Pearl was staring at the cup in her hands. "All silver mined in Tortall is the Crown's property," she said slowly, as if she gave a small child his lesson. "It goes to the Treasury, where it is registered, spelled by royal mages, and marked. Everyone must buy silver with the Crown's stamp on it. If the silver is unstamped, it is illegal. As far as the law is concerned, it is as good as stolen."

"They took all the guards and the merchants!" cried the mot when Pearl still said naught. "Hanse and my Steen and Amda are friends of your'n, everyone knows that! Can ye do nothin'? They'll start to question them anytime now!"

Pearl looked at the mot. "Do you think my arm stretches into Guards House?"

"Does it not?" the mot asked.

Pearl's face went hard. Her eyes were cold. The mot realized she maybe went too far and covered her mouth with her hand.

"Did you know about this?" Dale asked me.

He was staring down at Pearl. That made it so much easier for me to say, "No." It even made it easy for me to ask boldly, "Did you?"

"Don't be a looby." He still watched Pearl. "Me, a cole-monger? Before the Crown got me, the guild would administer its own punishments."

"Not if you escaped beforehand." I kept my voice soft. Only Dale heard me. "You could switch false coin for good and hide the good everywhere you travel. Lose bad coin at play, even."

He didn't answer me. His eyes were still fixed on Pearl. Suddenly he muttered, "Trickster curse her, she's going to let them rot. Her friends, and she'll leave them for torture! I have to get to the bank before they finish for the day." He gave me a swift kiss and stood. "Come to my place once it's dark," he ordered me. "I'll tell the landlord to open my rooms for you." He strode off, headed down the stairs.

I don't believe he's part of it. I think he means to buy good treatment from the cage Dogs for Hanse, or to get an advocate for him. That's the act of a friend, not a conspirator.

Pearl looked at the pregnant mot. "It'll take me some thinkin', to decide what to do," the Rogue said at last. "You leave it to me. Now go." She turned and beckoned to Zolaika. They put their heads together, with Pearl shielding their mouths with her hand so any who could read lips wouldn't

414

know what was said. From the way the air around them rippled, I'm positive that part of the hall is shielded by magic, too. If Pearl can afford pearl teeth, she can afford magical protections.

No one spoke as the mot left the hall. Pearl finished her private talk and sent Zolaika away. Once the older woman was gone, Pearl made some manner of joke to Jurji, who laughed.

"What's going through these Rats' heads?" I whispered to Achoo. She was on her feet, whining a little. She needed to go outside. "If I was one of them, I'd ask myself how far Pearl would reach for me, if she turns cold for good friends like Hanse and Steen."

I slung my pack over my shoulders. "Achoo, *tumit*."

We went outside, using the way we'd come in. Three small clusters of Rats stood near the door. One was the guards, but the others wanted to talk. Flory was there with two of her mots. Everyone went silent as I led Achoo to the gutter she needed.

When Achoo finished, Flory asked, "Where's Goodwin?"

I shrugged. "Off on her own business. May I ask sommat? The mot with all the face paint, that fetched me and Goodwin for Pearl—Zolaika, right? What does she do here?"

Flory and her friends made the Sign. Flory drew me in close. "Zolaika is Pearl's own private killer," Flory whispered. "The knife you never see comin'. Don't ever ask about her again."

So Okha was right. I didn't like how Pearl had sent Zolaika off after the news had come on Hanse and Steen. Seeing the tremble in Flory's hands, I don't think she liked it, either.

Flory turned her back on me to talk with her friends. The others did the same. Achoo and I took the hint and went back up to our table in the gallery. The atmosphere at the court had changed. Sullen voices drifted on the air. Folk watched Pearl from the corners of their eyes. She was having supper placed before her on a little table. From ~~abve~~ above I watched ~~convresa~~ conversations turn to ~~arguemits~~ arguments. Pearl's rushers broke up a dice game when the players started to punch each other. And I could heer bits of talk ~~abut~~ about stores, coles, and pryces.

I think I ~~mst~~ halt for a time. I've ~~dun~~ <u>done</u> a fearful ~~abont~~ amount of writing. Even in syfer I've writ a lot of pages. Ill write more of ~~yesstrday~~ yesterday, night, after a nap.

Okha's dressing room, Waterlily gambling house
Ten of the clock.
Back I come to the tale, the better for rest. My fingers quiver on
my pen. Too much is stirring in the city, and I have work to do.

I am shocked at the mistakes in my writing from earlier
this night. Lady Teodorie would switch my hands for certain,
did she see my cross-outs and blotches. Lucky for me she goes
nowhere near my journal now! Not that she would venture into
the snug hiding spot Okha has given me, in this secret room in
the Waterlily. Seemingly the folk who work here have hidden
fugitives before now. This place is made comfortable, with
blankets, pillows, small tables, and even a chamber pot. There
is a door that takes me onto the flat roof over the kitchens, with
an easy jump to nearby roofs for escape, or down inside the
house walls and out a hidden door. That's not an easy climb
with Achoo on my back in a sling, but it can be done at need.

But I need to continue last night's story, before it begins to
fade in my memory. I will have to tell it again later, before a
magistrate.

After Dale left, time ticked by. In the line for the privy,
mots and coves alike talked of higher prices in soft, scared
voices. My Dog's uniform never made them blink. Once Day
Watch ended, more Dogs had arrived. By Mithros, things were
slack here, when Dogs came in numbers to the Court of the
Rogue!

From the talk I learned *Dale* feared more for Hanse and
Steen than these Rats. And Pearl didn't utter their names
once after the pregnant mot had gone. Moreover, Zolaika never
returned.

By the time the city clocks struck the seventh hour, I was talking Corus fashions with two mots who'd come upstairs for a quiet drink. I was thinking it was time—and near dark enough—to find Okha when we heard noise below.

Pearl began to shriek. "What? She told that pukin' Sir Lionel I was *what*?"

I looked downstairs. Ives stood on Pearl's dais, next to her chair. Torcall and Jurji watched him, relaxed, as if Ives stood there often. Enno waited on the floor in front of the dais. Ives was talking softly to Pearl, jabbing his finger at the floor.

My tripes clenched. Axman had said he didn't know how long he'd be able to keep those two hobbled. The only safety he could guarantee me was that Ives would never tell Sir Lionel that I'd escaped him. I guess Axman hadn't known that Ives and Enno were on speaking terms with Pearl.

Pearl shoved Ives into Enno. "You mewling, gut-griping canker blossom! While you've fumbled your day down the sewer, she's been *here,* eating my food and drinking my ale!" She pointed up at the gallery. At me.

I seized my pack. "Time to go," I told my new friends. I'd been wise enough to sit at the outside of the table. Now I sprang for the long hall behind the gallery, Achoo on my heels. My gossips hadn't even worked out that Pearl meant me before I was out of their reach.

I thrust aside a cove leaving a private room with his clothes all mussed. He was trying to keep his feet when Achoo struck his knees and down he went. The hound and I kept running, no one chasing yet. Down the hall we turned right. If Okha's map was true, this corridor would lead us to a way out. Pearl wouldn't expect me to know where I was going.

I'd almost reached the turn when a hole opened in the

ceiling. A ladder dropped down with a skinny gixie on one of the rungs. I didn't know her, but the faded, stained red dress had a familiar look to it.

"Not that way!" she said, beckoning. "She'll have some'un on the doors! This way, quick! Up yez go!"

I might have argued, but I could hear the yells of pursuers. That settled the issue for me. I ducked under Achoo and stood with her thirty-odd pounds draped over my shoulders. Up the ladder we went, as I prayed it would hold our weight. The gixie scrambled up and out of our way as I hoisted us onto the ceiling. Good old Achoo never made a sound. Someone else in the ceiling yanked the ladder up after me. Quick as lightning the two young ones, my tracker from the streets and her friend, closed the trapdoor to the hall below. I bent down flat until Achoo could scramble away from me.

By lantern light I could see both young Rats had their forefingers to their lips. I cuddled Achoo and whispered, *"Di-amlah,"* in her ear. She made not a sound. Then we waited, knee to knee in a crawl space just high enough for us to sit up in, and so narrow that no two of us could move through it side by side. A lantern set between the lad and gixie was our light.

At least three groups of searchers passed beneath us and two over us. They made so much noise that I was surprised they didn't shake loose every mouse in the building. I looked around, marveling at our hideout. Was it here when the Rats moved in, or was it added when the Rats made it a court? It would be useful to a Rogue, but seemingly this Rogue knew nothing about it.

At long last things got quiet.

"She done give up," the lad said with a grim smile. "Inside

the court, anyways. No more patience than my lil' sister. Ye'd think the Rogue could do better'n a gixie of two."

"Hesh yer gob." My tracker slapped him with the back of her hand. "Don't go temptin' the Trickster. Could be the one time Pearl maybe uses her nob an' tries a new search inside."

"Nah, not her," the lad said. "If any o' her enemies marked how she does things, she'd be bottom up in the harbor by now."

"Maybe you should challenge her," I said, if only to remind them I was still there. "You seem to know her weaknesses."

They both flinched and looked at me. They hadn't expected me to have any thoughts on the matter.

"You need to worrit about yer own doin's," the gixie told me. "Don't think ye'll have me around to save yer breeches every time, Doggie. I'm not bought for a couple wormy apples and a coin or two."

"I wasn't trying to buy you," I said. "I've been hungry. I don't like to see a person starve if I might give 'em sommat."

"Well—good," the gixie said. "If Pearl thought we done this, we'd be breathin' out neck holes."

"Save she won't think it," the lad replied, "a'cos she's too frighted that her silver-freightin' boys will talk when they're questioned."

"So you know about that," I said.

The boy raised his eyebrows at me. "Don't we know everythin' as goes around here?" he asked.

I looked at him, thinking. "That's braggart's talk," I told him. "All steam." I'd fallen into cant again, grateful that street cant in Corus was the same as in Port Caynn. They relaxed a little, probably without even thinking about it.

"Says you," the gixie told me. "We knows where the store-rooms are, them that's got all the extry clothes and shoes, and them that's supposed to be loaded with grain against the winter. On'y those're half full."

"Don't say that!" the lad scolded. "Look a' her, she's a Dog!"

"Ask me if I care about your poxy stores," I said. I dug in my pack and pulled out a Viviano apple. I held it up. Their eyes locked on it. "Come winter, I'll be snugged up warm whilst yez grub for scraps. You'd yet have a grain o' chance to buy up food if yez told others about them storerooms." I handed the apple to the gixie, then found the other in my pack and gave it to the lad.

"Nobody lissens t' the likes of us," the gixie said before she bit her apple.

"Mayhap yez didn't tug the arm of the right person," I answered. "Fair Flory, now—*she'd* hear anything you cared to tell her."

They looked at each other. At last the lad said, "We done lived this long doin' as we're told and keepin' our gobs ohut."

I nodded and found a meat pie I'd tucked away, wrapped in a cloth. It was only a day old, still fit to be eaten. "Sometimes that works, sure enough," I said. "Most times it'll bring you an' yer sister to Starvation Alley, with the gulls waitin' to eat yer eyes."

"What is it?" the boy whispered finally. "Ye're wantin' somethin'."

I set the pie in front of me, taking off the cloth wrap. They were devouring the apples, but their eyes were fixed on my meat pie. I tried to remember how many times a week I had meat, before I moved to Lord Gershom's house. It wasn't often, for certain. And the meat in this pie hadn't been stewing in a pile of garbage for days.

I reached into my purse and set five copper nobles on one side of the pie, and five on the other side of it.

"Somewhere Pearl's got silver. I don't mean a handful of coin," I told them. "Bars of it. Heaps of coins. Tools for working it, and mayhap even a smith's forge. I'll wager you two know where that is. There's more coin than this if you show me where that silver is. I don't know your names, so I can't give you up if I'm caught. And if I know where Pearl's silver is, I can help ruin her. There are better Rogues than her. Rogues that will feed their people in hard times. Rogues that won't set a body to trailing someone like me all day without so much as a decent meal for it."

We sat there for a long, long time in silence. Achoo took a nap. I was starting to think they would turn me down and I should just go find Okha when the gixie broke the meat pie in two. She gave the lad half and kept the rest for herself. "Pearl beat me her own self those times I lost you," she said. She half turned toward me and lowered the collar of her too-large dress so I could see the edges of the whip marks. "She beat Elzie a'cos you caught her filchin' that purse, even though Elzie got away *and* switched the purses. I'm *sick* o' her fartin' Majesty."

The lad turned his share of the pie over in his hands. " 'Stead o' grain and oil, she's been spendin' the court's money on them fool teeth o' her'n. She ain't keepin' her siller for our folk, that's certain. We'll show ye."

I slid the coppers over to each of them. "If you can, there's more than double this price in it," I told them.

"But how can ye do anythin'?" the lad asked me. "Ye're on yer ownsome."

I smiled at him. "I'm inventive," I said. "And I've got friends."

The lad flinched and made the Sign against evil on his chest. "Ghost eyes," he whispered.

I made a face. "Never you mind my eyes." Dale likes them, I thought. "Eat up, and let's get moving," I ordered. "Unless it's here?"

The gixie shook her head. "The stuff's at Eagle Street court, and well hid. We'll go underground. Ye don't belong to the Rogue, so they'll not look for ye in th' sewers."

Then I had a very good thought. "Does Pearl have a room here? Where she sleeps, mayhap leaves some clothes?"

"She don't live at her courts," the lad said. "Too open, like. Too many strangers in and out."

My spirits fell.

"But she has a room for other things," he added. Both of them smirked. "She's got clothes there."

"She knows none o' these folk have the sack t' take 'em," said the gixie.

"Could we get into it?" I asked. "Now?" I set four more copper nobles on the floor.

The gixie scooped them up and handed them to the lad. "Just a ways back here. Start crawlin'. I'll tell yez when t' stop."

"Achoo, *tunggu*," I ordered. I didn't like to leave her—I certainly couldn't trust these two as I could Goodwin or Nestor—but I needed some of Pearl's clothes, and I needed to move fast. I stripped off my boots. Even when I crawled, my leather-shod toes would make more of a noise than would my toes covered by my stockings. I tied them together with my bootlaces and left them with Achoo. Praying that I did the right thing, I crawled until the gixie, who was right behind me, told me to stop. I was beside a trapdoor.

"Listen close," she whispered. "If you hear nothin', open 'er up."

The ladder let me straight down into Pearl's dressing room. Quick I went to the door and peered into the room beyond. It was empty. I could see magical letters written all around the edges of the door and the lock. It seemed Pearl thought that was protection enough for this place.

Both rooms were pigsties. Aunt Mya would have set Pearl to scrubbing floors for the condition of them. I was grateful for Pearl's habits. All those clothes heaped together were a stew of Pearl's scent. In a pile of what must be laundry I found, and took, two well-used breast bands and a pair of equally used loincloths. With my prizes in hand, I did not linger. I stuffed them into my pack and scrambled back up the ladder. The gixie and I returned to Achoo and the lad.

"What was that for?" he asked.

"She stole Pearlie's underclothes," the gixie said with a grin.

"Ye're livin' a dangerous life," the lad told me. "Are ye workin' a magic with them, then? It's the headsman if ye get caught with that, y' know."

"You're teaching law to a *Dog*? Never you mind what I need those things for," I said. "I'm guessing this passage wasn't something Pearl added?" I hung my boots around my neck.

The gixie shook her head. "None o' them knows about these."

"Then how do you know about 'em?" I asked.

The look that both of them gave me said I would never find out from them.

The lad took the lantern and guided us, crawling with it in one hand, stopping often to listen for footsteps and voices. Carefully we moved in that gap between the second and third stories, passing through the main building and into the next. At last the boy opened a door and stepped outside. I smelled wet earth and muck. He motioned for us to hurry through. We stood on a narrow stairway that led down the outside of a house on a side street, past the ground floor and into a cellar passage. No one was nearby to see us as we hurried down the splintered stair with only the small lantern to show the way. At the bottom the lad passed the lantern to the gixie. Then he worked the lock on the cellar door with some picks and let us pass through.

"I'll meet yez on Eagle Street," he told us. "I need t' make sure it's clear when yez come through there." He closed the door. I heard the clack as he locked us inside.

The gixie held up the small lantern so we could see the doorway cat-corner from us in the cellar wall. A cold breeze came from it. "Through that an' down the stairs," she told me.

"You trust your friend?" I asked.

"More'n I trust you," she replied. "Let's go, afore some'un finds us here."

"Wait," I said, hurrying to put my boots on.

"If ye went barefoot, ye wouldn't spend so much time on yer feet," she said. She spat on the floor.

Achoo and I followed the gixie across the cellar and through a new doorway. Beyond this one lay a number of uneven stone steps that led down into the chilly breeze. As we descended, I felt the earth rise higher and higher over my head. I did not like it. I miss the free movement of the wind and the sounds of birds. I feel as if I lose some part of my hearing in these damp places.

The smell got into my nose—scummer, mold, rotting muck, the gods know what else. I heard squeals when at last we stepped onto the walkway in the tunnel's side below the streets. Achoo lurched ahead. She liked to chase four-legged rats as much as the two-legged kind. *"Tumit!"* I whispered. She dropped into place, tail between her legs.

"Don't she bark?" the gixie asked.

"Sometimes," I said. "Mostly we work quiet. Behave," I whispered to Achoo. "You're on duty, same as me."

The gixie's eyes flashed as she looked back at me. "Ain't you off duty?"

"Not till I've caught my prey," I told her.

"As bad as Sergeant Haryse and his lot," she said over her shoulder, stepping past a heap of something or other. Achoo and I jumped it together. I landed too near the edge of the walkway, my boot slipping in muck. Achoo clamped her teeth on my belt and dragged me onto the stones.

"You know Nestor Haryse?" I asked the gixie, trying to keep my voice steady. I'm no delicate mot like my sisters, but the thought of landing in the soup beside us made me want to puke up my tripes. I ruffled Achoo's neck fur and gave her a strip of dried beef in thanks.

"All the city knows 'im. One day Pearl will tire of toyin' with the sarge and she'll serve 'im up flayed. 'S a shame," the gixie added as we turned down another, bigger tunnel. "He's one o' the good 'uns. He gives you 'is word, he's told you true—hush!"

We ducked into a deep tunnel I hadn't even known was there. The gixie closed metal shields over the lantern's sides, leaving us in the dark. We shrank back and waited as I heard the same thing she had, voices in the big tunnel. Six Rats, carrying torches, passed the opening of our hideaway.

"She's losin' 'er grip, I tell yez," one of them said, his voice a growl. "She's not keepin' Rogue business inside the court. She's lettin' Dogs into it, an' cityfolk, an' who next? The guilds? The Council o' Mages? The sarden King?"

"Hesh yer gab," a mot whispered. "Ye're makin' Stormwings fer yerself."

They were out of my hearing. I dared not follow to listen, but I wanted to. Instead I waited until I could hear no sound of theirs before I whispered to my guide, "Are they like the rest? Worrying about the attention Pearl is drawing?"

"Course they're afraid," the gixie said. "We belong in the shadows. Cityfolk don't look there. But Pearlie keeps drawin' their attention, d'ye see? What good are shadows if cityfolk start lookin' in 'em?" She led us out into the bigger tunnel again.

We had to hide twice more as other folk used the sewers to get where they were going. You'd think I'd grow accustomed to the stink, but it only bothered me more as we plodded along. By the time the gixie took Achoo and me up a narrow stair, my eyes watered so much I could barely see. I had to breathe with my mouth open because my poor nose was beyond stuffed. When we reached cleaner air inside the Eagle Street court, I was so happy I nearabout cried.

We entered quiet, like mice, but there was no need. The place was deserted, with Pearl being elsewhere that night. The only person to enter as we hid beneath a table was the lad.

"Plenty of them that was searchin' have stopped in the drinkin' dens an' eatin' houses," he told us when we stood. "They've set watchers in case Her Majesty comes by, but they're not wastin' time huntin' a runaway Dog. On'y Pearl's closest folk are still huntin'. You must worry them."

"So I should," I muttered. "Now, where's this room you told me of? Or was that just fumes?"

The lad took us behind a pair of storerooms. No one would come here to find the smaller room behind the first two unless they knew it was there. Once he'd closed and locked the door, the boy lifted the gixie up on his shoulders. She tugged on a grip set into the ceiling, then jumped as she clung to it. Her weight pulled down not just a large trapdoor, but a set of stairs built in.

"No ladders for Her Majesty?" I asked as Achoo bounded upstairs ahead of us.

"Her?" the gixie asked, and snorted. "That'd be work, and she don't work no more."

Up the stairs we went.

"Now, this part is tucked away, like," the lad whispered to me. He showed me how to grip the rope that would draw the heavy trapdoor-and-stair back up after us. Before I so much as touched it, I got the gloves I kept in my pack and put them on. They were special made, leather over silk with signs of protection woven into it, a gift from Goodwin and Tunstall when I was made a true Dog. Nothing I touched would hold a trace of my essence, should Pearl have a mage go over this place later. Such gloves are illegal, but magistrates look the other way when it's a Dog that wears them.

Once the gloves were on my hands, I grabbed the rope and dragged at it. Hauling that curst trapdoor up was no light piece of work. "We checked the building all round," the lad told me. "Unless ye measure the halls on all sides, ye'd never know there's rooms tucked between 'em. Figure this is where they useta hide them that's on the run from the Dogs, or them that was kidnapped for ransom, or them that was held for . . . other things."

"There's spells in the rooms so's ye can't hear what goes on inside," the gixie explained to me.

Down the narrow corridor we went, past three other doors. I had to ask, "You're certain no one's here? No one will pop out and put a magic on us or come after us with swords?"

The lad pointed to a black stone like a gem set in the center of each door. "When some'un's within, this lights up all blue."

So I felt like twice the fool, guided by these two who knew so much more than me.

The fourth door had a dark gem at its center, like the others. It also had a lock. I took out my picks. Luckily for my pride, I opened the lock as fast as my guides might have done.

"Pretty," the gixie told me with a pat on the shoulder. "If Doggin' don't work out for you, our chief might give you work burglin'. He's easier t' live with than Her Majesty."

"Thanks," I muttered as Achoo and I followed her inside.

The lad barred the door once we were in. The gixie used her lantern to light others inside the room, so I could see clearly what was there.

Even a little bit of it would have sent Pearl and anyone who helped her with this straight to the Rattery, and to the oil pots from there. With so much evidence, even the most pinch-coin bookkeepers at Guards House will pay for good-quality mages to lay spells of search and naming on it all, to find who helped Pearl. There were crucibles and tongs for metalworking, and a furnace made for the heating of small amounts of metal. The furnace was set into the wall. I was certain it would share a chimney with either the main room or a kitchen. A kitchen, more like, so no one would suspect the smoke that poured from it yearlong.

On the worktable someone had placed trays of block-shaped molds. The metals would be poured into them to cool. Under draping cloths I found metal stamps with King Roger's profile on one side and the sword-in-crown on the other, the most perfect copies of the legal stamp as anyone could want.

Chests on the floor held rounds of brass like heaps of thin noble coins, thousands of them. Small blocks of metal, blackened with soot to make them pass as charcoal with inspectors, turned out to be silver under the dirt. I counted only ten of those. None bore the Crown Treasury's mark, without which they were as illegal as those metal stamps.

What will Pearl do now that she is down to ten blocks of silver? Her fresh silver shipment is in the Deputy Provost's hands. Mayhap she'll try to steal it back.

"But this is mad," I said. "If she turns all those brass rounds into coles, she'll make no one rich, not even herself. She'll need a barrelful to buy a loaf of bread, because a silver noble won't be worth spit. The more coles that's on the market, the less they're worth." I looked into the trunk. It was full of red leather purses, the ones her filchers swapped for purses of good coin. "She gives these false coins to her enemies, did you know that?" I asked the lad and the gixie. "*They* get hobbled and questioned for colemongering, when they was set up by her. Innocent folk are tortured and killed while she ruins the money."

They both shrugged.

"It's naught to us," the lad told me. "We've got neither coin nor friends. No one helps us."

"We helped you, but that's b'cause I owes you, and I hates t' owe," the gixie added.

I shook my head and closed the trunk. Around the room I went, seeing what else was there. Smiths' gloves and aprons, files, cloths for polishing, buckets of water and buckets of ash, account books. Account books! Pearl was so prideful she never thought anyone might come here and use any of this against her!

"Speakin' of what's owed," the gixie said.

I came to myself and picked up a chisel from a shelf. "She

has clothing stores, you said. She hasn't forgotten that much of what she owes her folk?" Rosto had clothes rooms all over the Lower City. The Rogues always kept stores of garments, so their people might get clothes for cheap, or even for free, if they were in a fix.

"Sure," the lad told me. "There's one downstairs. I was just thinkin' I need a coat, what with it gettin' cold, like."

The gixie grinned at him. "We can help ourselves and never pay Her Majesty a copper."

I pointed at the second door. "Is that another way out?"

The gixie nodded. "Goes right down by the clothes room, even."

I opened the door we used to enter Pearl's colesmithy carefully, making sure no one had come along. Then I used the butt of my chisel to smash the gem that glowed if folk were inside. Now any Dogs I sent here would know which room to break into.

Stepping back inside, I closed the door and bolted it. Then I stuffed the lock full of a special clay I carried in a small jar in my pack. It would dry fast and as hard as stone, making a lock useless. Anyone who wanted to enter would need a ram to break the door down. I would make sure my Dogs had that.

I broke the gem on the other door as my two Rats went out. I locked it with my picks, then stuffed that lock, too.

This time we took a real stairway. When the gixie undid the catch that opened the secret door at the bottom, the lad slid out. A moment later he beckoned to us.

We went out and closed the hidden door behind us. I marked an iron cresset set in the wall. The gixie thrust it back to close the door. When I tugged it, the door opened again. A push of mine shut it. The door fit snug in the wall, its sides scarce visible.

The lad used his lock picks on the clothes room just across the corridor and used the gixie's lantern to light some lamps inside. Achoo and I followed them. Achoo quickly fell in love with the place, sniffing everywhere, while I closed the door behind us and looked around. My hound also did a small, rude act in the corner. I pretended not to see.

The light showed off crates and crates of garments and footwear, some good, some worn. I even saw fighting gear in a row of its own—no weapons, but padded leather jerkins, arm and leg braces, and armored caps. The lad went straight to that. The gixie dove into a crate heaped in velvet. I found a crate of religious habits. These rooms didn't just supply a Rogue's folk with new clothes when their old rags fell apart. Sometimes, when a gang was putting together sommat special, they needed special garb. With the right payment to the Rogue, they could have it.

As I'd hoped, there was a priest's robe for the Black God's order that would fit over my own uniform. Better still, this was a high priest's robe, with a thin veil stitched inside the hood to hide the face. My pale eyes would be hid as well as my uniform. I'd hoped to find the Black God's clothes. Being's that I was already in his service, he wouldn't be vexed, or so I hoped. The other gods might well be cross if I wore the habits of their servants. Achoo might give me away, or she might not. There were plenty of curly-haired mongrels running the streets of town.

I picked up a basket and a scarf. Into the basket went my pack, after I took what I owed my two friends out of it. I tucked the scarf over and around the pack, so it looked as if I carried foodstuffs.

"Achoo, *kemari*!" I called softly. *"Jaga."* Achoo sat beside the basket, panting happily. She didn't seem to mind that I called her away from interesting smells. I've never had so cheerful a partner.

The gixie had pulled a rich red velvet dress over herself, tangling the sleeves. The lad was trying to free her as he laughed. They went still as I came close.

"I said I'd give you more coin," I told them. On the floor I set ten silver nobles, each scored down the front to show it was good. I set another ten silver nobles beside that, then added my last bit of food, a good-sized hunk of cheese.

They stared. Then both lunged for the coin, ignoring the cheese. They tested each coin again with their belt knives.

"They's *real*," the lad said, staring at me with awe.

I just hope Goodwin thinks that their saving my life is worth it. Of course, they showed me where Pearl is making her coles, too. It seems to me the price is a proper one.

"I said I'd pay right. Now, if you're wise, you'll go to a bathhouse," I told them. "You don't want Pearl having a mage look at you and him sniffing out you was near me. Lavender oil in your wash water should do. And fresh clothes."

"Then yez need t' go afore we picks some," the gixie said.

I nodded and collected my basket. "Achoo, *tumit*. Lavender oil, you two. Don't forget." Achoo followed me out the door. Once in the hall, I listened until I heard the door lock behind me. Then I called my memory of Okha's map of this place to my mind. Once I knew where we were, I lit one of the wall lamps using my flint and steel and took it down to light my way out. Achoo marked the trail in her own way.

"I doubt we're coming back," I whispered to her at yet another stop. Achoo whuffed softly and wagged her tail. "I suppose you're one of them as says it never hurts to be sure." Achoo wagged her tail again and danced, which I took as meaning I had the right of it.

I opened the exit door I'd found remembering Okha's map and looked around. Outside was a pitch-black alley with no guards in view. Had I been Pearl, I'd have some sharp things to say to guards who left their stations even when she did not hold court there. An assassin could break in and wait for her return. I was me, though, so I left the door open. Even though the place belonged to the Rogue, folk wouldn't refuse the chance to help themselves to what was there.

Achoo and I walked onto a larger side street, then onto Barbers' Walk. I tucked my gloves into my basket and lowered the veil over my face, then doused my lamp and left it there. I moved forward at a slower priest's walk, my basket over one arm. Carefully, turning briefly down side streets or alleys if we saw any who might recognize Achoo and guess that the veiled priest was me, we moved uphill until, at last, the Waterlily came in view.

The rushers who kept rowdies from entering the place frowned at the sight of me. Since it's bad luck to offend the Black God's priests, even though they aren't thought to be lucky for gamblers, they let me in. One of the menservants came at me, fluttering, trying to offer me a table, private and unseen. I stopped him with a copper noble and a whispered request to see the Amber Orchid on sacred business. I knew I'd have to wait. I could hear Okha singing, his voice clear and beautiful on the too-hot air.

The servant was so glad to be able to hide me away that he not only escorted me up to Okha's room, he fetched me a pitcher of warm cider and a basket of cakes. Once he closed the door behind him, Achoo and I sat on Okha's couch. I leaned back gratefully.

Of course I went to sleep. All that excitement, with the

running and crawling beside, tired me out. The room was warm, the hound curled up with me was reassuring. Anyone would have taken a nap.

I was roused by Achoo's quiet whuff. I sprang to my feet, forgetting I was in a habit, not a uniform. I tangled in its skirts and went sprawling on the rug. I rolled over, fumbling for my sleeve knives, hidden by the habit's folds. Only then did I see that the butterfly-bright creature in a bronze silk gown was Okha. He wore a wig of marvelously looped white hair, each loop secured with a jeweled butterfly clasp.

Swiftly he closed the door and helped me to my feet. "Friend, I beg forgiveness," he said quietly. The Black God's priests are always called Friend. "I was not expecting so auspicious a guest." His fingers and his voice were trembling. He thought I was a real priest bringing news of a death.

"Okha, it's me." I tugged at my hood and felt the veil drag at my face. I hooked my fingers under the fine cloth and dragged the whole thing back. "Beka Cooper."

Okha collapsed onto a chair. "Beka! Gods preserve me, I nearly fainted!"

Somehow I doubted that.

Okha went on in his mot's mellow and golden voice, "Do you *know* how many people are looking for you? Pearl Skinner herself is downstairs with her guards, playing cards with Dale and watching his every move. When he went to the privy, she had Jurji follow him. Her people came to Nestor's house, hunting you. So are Dogs from Guards House. They have a writ from Sir Lionel that says you are mad and must be taken up for your own safety."

I flinched. I hadn't thought the milk-blooded cull would be so nasty as to label me mad.

"No one *believes* him, Beka," Okha reassured me. "Not when he sends Ives, his very own bully boy, to track you down. But plenty want to know what you did to cross Sir Lionel."

"It's hardly safe for folk to know, if I've got the Deputy Provost on me, right?" I asked him. "But I do need Nestor as soon as may be, and unseen by anybody. It's important."

Okha hesitated. I grabbed his hand. "If you don't," I told him, as serious as I could, "if you try to keep him safe in all this, he'll never forgive you."

"Curse you," Okha whispered. "When did you get so knowing?" He turned to his desk and wrote something, then opened the door. I scrambled to pull the veil and hood over my face. Okha whispered to whoever came to the door whilst I sat, gazing at a tapestry. Then Okha turned back to me when the door was shut and locked. "How did one young Dog cause so much trouble?" he asked me.

"I do my work," I said. "I'm going to need a place to hide tomorrow. Do you know one?"

"Right here is good enough," he said, gesturing to take in the small room. "No one comes here during the day. I'll tell my servant to stay out after the last meal of the night. You can turn anything in that chest into a disguise. Use the red or black wigs if you like. I have to say, going as one of the Black God's servants is brilliant. Don't you fear his wrath?"

I gave him half a smile. "We have an arrangement."

"Oh." Okha covered his mouth. His bronze nails caught the lamplight. They were quivering. Suddenly I felt bad. He'd been naught but a friend to me. "Okha, I'll go. You're afraid with me here."

He shook his head. "You'll do no such thing. I would never forgive myself if anything happened to you. Now, I must go sing. You may wish to step into that cupboard. There's a door to a hidden room in the back. They will bring my supper up soon, and it will be best for everyone if there is no priest of the Black God in my dressing room." He showed me the catch at the back of the cupboard. I had to stoop, but the door went through into a small, proper room, just as Okha had said. Achoo and I went into it. Outside the second door there was a flat rooftop where we could sit out if we wished and Achoo could do her business.

I settled onto the pillows that lay on the hidden room's floor. It seemed like a good time to catch up on the day's events in my journal, which I have done. Now I think I will sleep a bit more, if Achoo will stop snoring.

Thursday, September 20, 247

Okha's dressing room

Four of the clock in the morning.

Nestor woke me around one of the morning by setting a plate full of supper beside me. He sat on his heels, watching, as I struggled to sit up among the pillows. Achoo placed her nose beside my plate.

"You're shameless," Nestor told her. "And I left a plate of chopped meat for you in the other room. Let me get it." He fetched it and put it before her, grinning as Achoo gobbled her food. He waited beside me as I polished off a nice fish stew. "Now. What have you to tell me that has my dearest Okha so unhappy?"

I met Nestor's eyes. "Okha senses I can give you a way to hurt Pearl, but Nestor, it's really dangerous."

Nestor inspected me, his pleasant blue-gray eyes gone hard. They were Dog eyes now, and pleased I was to see them. "Guards House has a writ out on you."

"Because I told Sir Lionel he'd let things run wild here and he knew curst well who the colemonger is." I must have been weary or addled, because I kept on talking. "His gems are the size of millet seed. Folk in this city are dead for that. They'll have a long winter and more will die hungry, because he could have put his hand on Pearl Skinner long ago, and he never did."

Nestor sighed. "Pox," he muttered. "We were fools, thinking all would be well if we just swept up after him. But it isn't. And now our mess has leaked over Tortall."

"All over the Olorun Valley, anyway," I replied.

We sat in silence for a bit. Finally Nestor said, "I'll do what must be done, Beka. So will the folk I trust. That's a Dog's bargain." He made a fist. I offered my own. He tapped my fist with his, and I returned the tap to seal the bargain.

"I'm asking that you keep most of what we do secret until you talk to Lord Gershom. Sir Lionel and most of Port Caynn's Dogs never get a *whiff* of what you're doing. Not the slightest tickle in the nose," I told him.

"Very well," Nestor said.

"I can take you to the colemongery," I said. "You and them what you can trust will have to take all you can gather, if we can get in at all. I don't know how long it'll be until the cole-mongers learn someone's found the place. I made it hard for anyone to enter the room, but that alone will tip them off."

"They'll know the fair has left town if we loot it," Nestor told me.

"Not if we make it look like it wasn't Dogs as carried off the spoil," I replied. I flapped the skirts of my habit at him. "In-side one of these, they'd be hard put to name the dams that birthed them. Or use burnooses like the Bazhir wear, if you fear to offend a god." I plucked at my habit. "I work for this one sometimes."

Nestor paled and made the Sign. "We'll use burnooses," he said. "And we can go tonight. I'll have it all in a couple of hours, crew and wagon alike. A safe hiding place for the goods, too." He got to his feet. "I'll let you know when we're ready."

"Nestor?" I asked before he could go. He waited. "Is there any way you could get word about a Master Isanz Finer and his family? They're silversmiths. They were taken up and charged with colemongering by Tradesmen's kennel."

Something changed in Nestor's face. "Friends of yours?"

"Goodwin's more, Master Finer, particularly, but yes, I know them, him." I was starting to fumble my words, not liking the look in his eyes. "You *do* know sommat."

"Tradesmen's sent them on to the Rattery, Beka, all but Isanz," Nestor said gently. "His heart failed him on the way to the kennel. The Black God has him now."

I said something to thank him, something to make him feel I would be all right while he was out. He left to make his arrangements. I sat with Achoo, my appetite gone. I couldn't sleep, either. I'd failed Master Finer. If I'd been more polite to Sir Lionel, or if I'd just gone to Tradesmen's with some gold, mayhap I could have saved him.

I might have worried like that all night, but my memory is sharp like a Dog's. Nestor had said, "On the way to the kennel." Isanz was dead afore I even knew he was taken. It was folly for me to belabor myself.

Still, I wish I'd had a proper chance to save him. I liked him.

I tried to keep busy, so as not to grieve to no purpose. In between Okha's visits, his rest times between performances, I exercised, completed this journal so far, and sharpened each blade I carry. I even combed Achoo's fur and went over all of her commands to refresh them. And I prayed to the Black God for Master Finer.

The night for this place ends at two of the clock. Okha was just making sure I had food and drink and a chamber pot when Nestor, in a properly arranged and tied burnoose, came for me. He fairly crackled with eagerness and kissed Okha as a lover kisses his sweetheart after a long separation. Okha murmured a brief prayer, but he said no word against Nestor's undertaking.

I left Achoo in the hidden room, though Achoo liked it not at all. I had to give her the *diamlah* order twice before she would stop barking. Then I followed Nestor into the night, my veil and hood over my face, my gloves on my hands. All this secrecy would do no good if Pearl's mages tracked us by the essence we left on what we touched.

"No names," warned Nestor as we met up with three other folk in burnooses. One of them carried a torch for light. There was little of it in the streets. Nestor spoke quietly to us all. "Remember what happened to those who have tried to trap this Rat before. Eyes everywhere." We nodded. I settled comfortably in my skin. This wasn't the kind and careful Nestor of his house, or even the sharp-edged Nestor who had gone to supper with Okha, Goodwin, and me. This was Sergeant Haryse. He'd command us well. He'd stay calm, even if the Rat we were Dogging was a Rat he'd been after for a long, long time.

The streets were near empty. Nestor saw me looking about. "The fishing folk must be up two hours before dawn," he murmured to me. "If you don't handle the nets or the rigging, your work doubtless depends on those who do. Even rascals like your special friend keep fisherman's hours."

"Let's see if he's my special friend after the law books on this are closed," I said.

Nestor snorted. "Him a colemonger? No, not him. He's too fond of his life and his fingers to wager on so foolish a bet."

So I wasn't alone in thinking Dale innocent. That was a comfort. "He's friends with two others I know for a fact are in it," I told Nestor, feeling contrary. I realized I was touching the opal pendant Dale had given me, hidden under my robe, and took my hand off of it.

"Pecking at a lover because of his friends is a fast way to an empty bed," Nestor told me. He strode ahead to meet four more people clothed in burnooses. Every one of the folk he'd summoned wore not only robes and veils, but gloves. By daylight, or even earlier in the evening, we would have been a strange-looking crew. At this hour, no one was out to mark us. One of the newcomers carried a torch, which gave us two to light our steps.

We gathered more Dogs in disguise. There were fifteen of us when we came to a side street beside the Eagle Street court. There another false Bazhir waited beside a cart. A mule stood between its shafts, giving us a sharp looking-over. I was glad I'd left Achoo behind. She hates mules.

Nestor spoke to the carter quietly. Then he turned to the rest of us. He made certain that his hands were visible in the torchlight as he signaled. Two of us went to the cart and threw back a canvas sheet in its bed. There lay pry bars, heavy mauls and chisels, and a number of sturdy baskets. I grabbed one of those.

Nestor took my basket away. "You're guide," he whispered in my ear. "Get to it." He pointed to the shadowy door that was one of the Eagle Street court's side entrances.

I brought to my mind's eye the court's map until I knew where this door was. One of Nestor's friends was already there, dripping some manner of liquid into the lock.

"It's bespelled on it," he told me. "To bar folk from breaking in. It would never stop anyone from coming out, as our leader says you did." He murmured something. The magic smoked dreadfully. When the smoke blew away, the mage Dog motioned for me to employ my picks. "*Now* it's safe to unlock."

Within a moment I had the lock open. The mage went first, then beckoned me inside. He lit the hall lamps with snaps of his fingers as the others doused their torches and entered.

Happily, we were on the same hall as the clothes room. My friends were gone. It seemed they had escaped with their new clothes. I asked the gods to bless them, then went on to open the secret door to the hidden rooms upstairs.

"We'd never have found that," Nestor murmured in my ear.

Up the stairs we went. I'd thought they'd ask the mage Dog to open the lock I'd jammed with my clay. Instead a big cove came forward with a three-foot-long ram. He swung it by its iron grip, smashing it into the door. Three smashes later, we were inside.

At first all Nestor and his Dogs managed to do was wander about, staring at this complete colesmithy. I heard murmurs like, "The sack o' them!" and, "Right under our noses!" Some of them felt as I did, saying, "Are they *mad?*"

Nestor was the first to come around. "Get to it!" he ordered. "We haven't got forever!"

Nestor's Dogs got to work indeed. When they finished, the only thing that could yet be used for colemongery was the forge, set into the chimney as it was. Everything movable was piled in the cart outside, hidden under the canvas sheet. We waited until we were a good four blocks away before we halted for a quiet celebration, only slapping one another on the back or shoulder. We all knew that Pearl had never been the victim of so thorough and deep-cutting a raid.

The driver of the cart, Nestor, and two other Dogs took our loot off to a safe hiding place. The rest of us were left to go home with a last wrist or hand clasp. It's wondrous, to know you've aided in making Dog history.

As I let myself into the Waterlily with the key Okha had lent me, I wondered about Pearl's reaction. No doubt she would explode when she found her colesmithy had been stripped. She would be terrified that her goods might have gotten into Sir Lionel's hands, giving him a proper weapon against her. Ives would tell her soon enough that Sir Lionel had no knowledge of the burglary, but that surely would make Pearl's fears all the worse.

I needed to calm down before I slept, so I took Achoo out onto the roof. Okha had said that we could do that even during the day, the buildings around us being all warehouses without windows. Once I was calmer and Achoo had finished her business, we went back inside. I made us a bed of drapes and pillows, where she settled. Alas, my thoughts are still awake and lively. Might Pearl suspect that the Lord Provost himself would be informed of her colemongering? She'll be remembering I told Sir Lionel she was the colemonger. She'll be wanting me more than ever. Will she turn on her enemies when she cannot find her coles and her coin stamps? Or on folk she suspects of trying to seize her throne? If she does, she will drive off those she needs to defend her. It would be her gift to us if she did.

At last I am sleepy and my journal is caught up. I hope the rest of today is less mad than its start!

Guards House

Some time past the midnight hour.

being a chronicle of the events of Thursday the 20th,

beginning around the hour of ten in the morning of that day

When I rose from a lovely dream of Dale, it was just before ten of the clock. The hour struck as I cleaned up as best as I could and dressed in a lad's tunic and leggings that I found in the outer room's closet. My poor uniform was wrinkled and covered with all manner of smutches from my clamberings in Pearl's courts and the city sewers. I shook it out and draped it on a chair I took outside so my things might air.

Then I gathered crumbs from the food Okha had brought me the night before and went out onto the flat roof with Achoo. It is true, there are only blank walls to the east and west, but there is a splendid view of the harbor from the south side. I sat where I might admire it and began to scatter crumbs in the hopes that I might call pigeons to me.

A weight struck the back of my head and almost knocked me forward. I jumped to my feet, about to curse Slapper, when a familiar voice met my ears.

"Curse her for a lyin', two-faced scut with the heart of a weasel!"

Slapper had a passenger. The pigeon landed on the roof with a stagger and pecked furiously at the crumbs. He lurched. His clubfoot made it hard for him to stand.

The ghost that rode him talked on. "Didn't I know she'd turn with no warnin'? Didn't I? But clever lad that I am, I thought I could cozen her, buy her filthy presents, whatever it took to keep that pearl-toothed viper *happy*!"

I knew that voice.

"Hanse," I said, keeping my voice steady, because the ghosts panic or not depending on how I sound. "Hanse, you're dead."

"Ye think I don't *know* that?" Hanse snarled as Slapper grabbed for a nice bit of pasty crust. I scooped Slapper up, trying not to get pecked, and steadied him in my lap. Then I took a handful of crumbs and bits and held them for him. I yanked my head away as he tried to hit me with one wing. Then he settled to eat.

"I *know* I'm dead. Who's this, anyway?"

"It's Cooper," I told him. "Goodwin's partner."

"What're you doin' talkin' to a dead cove, eh? Why am I stuck to this gleekin' bird? Where is Goodwin?" Hanse was as restless as Slapper is normally.

"She's not here. Even if she was, she couldn't hear you," I said. "I'm the only one who can. The bird is Slapper. He'll carry you to the Peaceful Realms, *if* you settle your business that's left over from your life. As I understand it, anyway."

"So who gave you this stinkin' job?" Hanse asked. I had a picture of him in my mind, sitting on a bench, his elbows on his knees, a wicked glint in his eye. Curse it, I'd gone and gotten attached to a Rat. Now he was dead.

"I was born to it. My father had it afore me, my gran tells me. Hanse, listen, how'd you die?" I asked. "The last I heard, you were only arrested for smuggling."

" 'Only,' the wench says!" Slapper flailed in my lap. I let him go. He lit on the roof before me and strutted to and fro as Hanse talked. "The cage Dogs had me in a cell in the Rattery, getting me ready for questionin'. Then Zolaika came with one of her helpers. They weren't there to say, 'Goddess bless.' The helper put a silencin' spell on me before I could get a yell out, and Zolaika cut my throat."

I gulped. He was part of it all, the colemongering, but I had liked him. I remember him carrying Tunstall to safety in the Bread Riot. He'd roared with laughter at Goodwin's jokes and paid for more than his share of our suppers.

"What of the others that got hobbled when you did?" I asked. "No, you wouldn't be knowing, I suppose."

"But I do," said the man I could not see. "They killed us all. Zolaika said I was the last. Pearl wanted every one of us dead."

"Hanse, mayhap you can tell me." I had to ask as many questions as I could. I didn't know how long I'd be able to talk with him before we were interrupted and Slapper took off. "Have you any idea why Pearl is doing the colemongering? What she hopes to gain from drowning the city in coles?"

"Oh, that was my idea. Pearl's got her gain already. She told me all she wanted was to be richer than the King, richer than the Emperor down in Carthak. Now she's just adding cream to the pot," Hanse told me as Slapper ate. "The first two batches of coles we done, Pearl and any she trusted went to the Silver- and Goldsmith's banks here and in Corus and in Blue Harbor, and traded it all for gold. Nobody was lookin' for sacks full of coles, so—greedy pig that she was—she got all of it changed. She gave the ones that changed it a fee, them that she didn't have killed after. And her and her special pets went gamblin'. Mostly they won big, those first two weeks. They all warned her, if she kept dumpin' coles on the market, folk'd wake up. Prices would go up. But I knew her since we was little. I knew once she had the smell of money in her snout, she'd tear up the city rootin' for more, even if she was full." He sounded *pleased*.

More pigeons came. They'd finally seen the scatter of crumbs.

447

"Still moanin'?" I heard Steen ask. "Still grumblin'?"

"Why are you still here?" Hanse wanted to know. "You could've answered the Black God's call, same as the others."

"I'm *tryin'* to get you to come wiv me," Steen told him. "We don't belong here no more, ye great ox."

"Go, then," Hanse said. "I've business to finish."

"Ye're dead!" Steen cried. "Ye've got no body, no hands, no feet! What do ye think to finish?"

I cleared my throat. "Mayhap I can be of use, being's how I'm still alive and all." Hanse had given me plenty to think about, and yet another question I wanted answered.

For a moment they were quiet. Then Steen said, "Cooper? She can't see us. Or—"

"I hear you just fine," I said.

"Huh!" Steen replied. "How did that happen?"

"Who cares?" roared Hanse. "She can help!"

"Help against Pearl," Steen said with a laugh. "Pull t' other leg, it's got bells on't. How about Pearl pulls Cooper's tongue out an' wraps it about her neck?"

"I've got friends coming," I told them. "Me'n Goodwin aren't here for the reasons we told you."

"Thought not," Hanse said with grim pleasure. Slapper dropped to the rooftop to feed with the flock.

I dropped a heap of crumbs before me so he wouldn't go far. He returned to me. "I need to know some things before I do aught for anyone. Hanse, think about all the coles out there now. You brought her the knowledge of the new mine with silver the Crown doesn't know about, didn't you?"

" 'Twasn't a *new* mine," he replied. "My brother found a fresh vein in an old, abandoned one. He thought mayhap I'd find a way to turn it to account."

"And you went to Pearl," I said. "She took over."

"No," Hanse said. "Partners. You think I'd trust her with the mine's location?"

I found it hard to believe that Pearl would accept anyone as an equal partner, but I left that be. "So you bring her fresh supplies of silver. Are the two of you mad? If she had the silver you were bringing in made up into coles, there's hundreds more, am I right?"

"Does Goodwin know what you know?" Hanse asked.

"What does it matter to you? You're dead," I reminded him.

"She has you on that," Steen said.

"Aye, Pearl was ready to make plenty more with the silver we brung," Hanse said. "I told her to do it."

"But you were making silver nobles well-nigh worthless," I reminded him. "Didn't she understand that? Prices are going up! When did you plan to stop?"

"Never," Hanse told me. The word floated cold against the beautiful sky, as if I could almost see it, a patch of gray blight. The day was too lovely to hear a dead man talk of ruin for the land. "See, Pearl didn't care about aught else. She's got a fortune in gold, that's all that matters to her. Now she's got her smiths makin' up Yamani and Copper Isle coin stamps. When the panic begins and the banks stop takin' silver entirely, she'll be long gone."

"Cold," Steen muttered. "She's a cold, rabid Rat, that one."

"But you can't be that stupid and be the Rogue, can you?" I asked.

"What's stupid?" Hanse asked. "She made her fortune before anyone ever started lookin' for coles. She's already picked out her escape door. And the rest of 'em can go boil."

"Rosto's clever," Steen told me. "He makes allies. Pearl's one of them Rogues that rules by fear. She don't care for no one but herself."

"But *you're* not stupid, Hanse," I said. "You couldn't be and have Dale as your friend all these years. And I can't believe Dale was crackbrained enough to agree to this."

"He wasn't," Steen replied. "There was a colemonger a couple year back—Dale reported 'im. So we never brung Dale in on it."

A knot in my chest came undone. My instincts about Dale were right. I didn't relax as I wanted, though. That had to wait. Hanse had yet to answer me. "Hanse, why do it, if you're not a fool?"

Slapper had finally stopped eating. He was preening himself now, stretching out his wings and tail to go over each feather. The silence got so long that I was wondering if Hanse had decided to go to the Peaceful Realms after all. Finally he said, "I gave years to the army. Years to the realm. I've got bones that were never healed by fancy mages. They ache when rain or snow comes on. I'd earned myself a pension and a pouch full of medals. Then I make one mistake, and I'm out on my arse. Tossed aside like so much scummer, when I gave my youth for king and country. I got this scar—right, you can't see it. I got scars from fightin' hillmen, and Bazhir, Scanrans, Gallans, Barzunni, Tyrans, Tusaine regular army. Nasty bastards, them. No thanks to Tortall that I found a way to make a livin'. I always swore I'd have my revenge."

"I never knew this," Steen said.

"I didn't want you to know," Hanse said. "Not you, not Pearl—no one. 'Twas *my* revenge. I knew she was greedy enough to help. How many coves can say they brung a realm crashin' down?"

"By throwin' folk out of work? Beggarin' families afore winter?" Steen asked.

Hanse's voice was cold as he said, "Winter comin' on is a bonus. I never thought t'would all go so fast."

Steen's voice was shaking. "I guess you'll learn if it's true, that the Black God forgives. I can't. My ma, my da, my gran—gods, what if they lose their home now I'm not there to help? Flory's got a daughter. Half of our folk have families. What happens to them, did ye even care?"

"No," Hanse said, his voice quiet.

For a long moment I heard only the trill of pigeons and the cry of seagulls. Then Steen said, "If I'd known, Hanse, I'd've killed you meself. I won't stay to see yer plan for ruin succeed."

The pigeon that had carried Steen to me leaped and flew off.

"Ah, well," Hanse whispered. "He was always the better cove."

"The ruin you hoped for won't happen," I said. "Goodwin's bringing the Lord Provost's folk to break it all up. You can help me to catch Pearl, though."

"That'll have to do," he replied. "Truth to tell, it's not so amusin', destroyin' the realm. Not when you look at it from this side of things."

I heard footsteps inside my room. I stood. "How do I find you?" I asked.

"Old Greedyguts here, the bird, *he* knows where you are all of the time," Hanse said. "Just speak my name and we'll be along." Slapper and the other pigeons took to the air with a rush.

I turned to look at the roof door as Nestor stepped through. "Cooper, put on your uniform and pack up your things," he said, his eyes alight. "The storm is about to break!"

I blinked at him. "What in Mithros's name?"

"Come along, Cooper!" Nestor ordered. "No time to explain—we're needed at Riverside!"

Achoo waited in the secret room for me, tail a-wag. *She* knew there was the smell of a hunt in the air. I changed clothes. Soon I was out the door, wearing my rumpled uniform under my priest's robe. I had my pack slung over my shoulder and the robe. Outside, Nestor unhitched a pair of evil-eyed horses. Both were saddled and ready for some poor Dog to clamber onto their backs.

I froze. "I don't like horses and they don't like me," I told Nestor. "Why can't we walk?"

"Because we're wanted soonest," he said. "Beka, we've no time for you to flap your eyelashes and grope for your handkerchief—"

"I *really* don't like horses," I argued. "I will *run* the distance—"

I am quick enough, if I do say so, but Nestor had me in the saddle and was fitting one of my feet into the stirrup before I knew he had hold of me. Achoo barked, but I could not know if she disapproved of Nestor or laughed at me.

"Nestor!" I yelped.

He calmly mounted his own beast. "Follow close."

I gathered the reins Nestor had twisted around my saddle horn as my horse trotted after Nestor's mount. Achoo ran alongside us, her tail raised in the air. *She* was having fun.

I could not ask Nestor what was going on. There were too many people around us as we rode toward the harbor. I was puzzled. If we were bound for Riverside, shouldn't we go over the ridge? It was only when we crossed the main harborside road and picked up an empty, well-paved track that followed the land's edge that I saw where we were bound. Nestor had taken us to the Couriers' Road. Once we were on it, headed into the trees that covered the grounds around the governor's palace, Nestor looked at me.

"Gallop!" he ordered.

I didn't wish to, but I wasn't given a choice. My horse was so much in tune with his that the moment Nestor began to gallop, so did I. All I could do was hang on and pray that Achoo could keep up.

I need not have worried. Scent hounds can run for long stretches, and only the ones that last are kept for the work. From the way Achoo behaved as we raced over the height behind the palace and down toward Riverside, this was a treat we had arranged just for her. On we rode, until we had reached the waterfront that served the river traffic. Nestor slowed. Cursing, I pulled the reins and finally got my horse to do the same. At last we walked. We passed through traffic again, dodging other horses, carts, cranes, and the usual hordes of people.

Goose bumps rippled down my skin when I saw armed guards around the piles of grain sacks. *That* was new and unpleasant. Just as unpleasant were small groups of idlers in the warehouse shadows. Some were Rats, but many were ragged, ordinary folk. Their eyes were fixed on the grain, and the guards.

Near the wharf where Goodwin and I had entered the city, Nestor took a turn and rode inland for three blocks. He came to a halt at a countinghouse. A lad who seemed to doze in the doorway came forward to take the reins of our horses.

"Watchers?" I heard Nestor ask him.

"Nary a one," the lad replied.

Nestor beckoned to me and I dismounted with care. I handed the reins to the boy with thanks. I do not wish to see that hard-charging bag of bones again, unless it is in my soup.

"Nestor, I need water for Achoo," I said, looking at her.

She was still cheerful, but she was panting hard from her run. "It's bad to keep her so dry."

Nestor sighed with impatience, but he said, "I have a flask, but nothing for her to drink out of."

"My hands will be good enough," I told him, kneeling in front of Achoo. He poured three handfuls for us as the lad watched Achoo slurp them down. When I stood, wiping my hands on the insides of my habit's sleeves, I said, "Thank you, Sergeant Haryse."

He grinned and patted my shoulder. "She's a good hound, and you're a good handler. I think I'm going to owe you more than a little water when all of this is done."

Then we followed Nestor into the countinghouse. The room inside was filled with Dogs in uniform. They lounged on the counters, talked in small groups, compared weapons. I blinked, not at all certain of what was going on. Then I recognized some of them: Ersken and his partner, Birch. Nyler Jewel and his partner, Yoav. Three other pairs from Corus Lower City Evening Watch, four pairs from Night Watch, and nearabout forty more Dogs I had seen throughout Corus in the last three years, all hard Dogs. Three had scent hounds on the leash. Apart from Nestor, I knew only Sergeant Axman of the Port Caynn Dogs by name. I did recognize the team of Dogs who'd helped Nestor to take Goodwin and me from the Eagle Street court on our first meeting with Pearl. A few of the others also looked familiar. Axman gave a nod to Nestor and winked at me. Of the Port Caynn Dogs, their numbers were equal to the Corus Dogs. Everyone was dressed and armed for a fight.

Then I understood. This was the beginning of a major raid.

Goddess be thanked, Goodwin had returned. She stood at the rear of the room near a door, together with five Crown mages who worked with Dogs at Lord Gershom's bidding. Seeing us, she began to make her way through the crowd, using her elbows at need.

"Why do you look like cheese, Beka?" Nestor asked me quietly. "We've got help."

I was too flummoxed to tell him I hadn't expected help to come so fast. Miracles aren't for the likes of me, didn't Nestor know that? Only the nobility gets them. I was dreaming the sight of all these Dogs and mages, not to mention my partner, that I didn't look to see for a week.

I sat on the step from the entry to the countinghouse floor. Goodwin slapped Nestor on the shoulder, then hunkered down before me. Before she could say anything, my hound went half mad, wagging her tail and licking Goodwin's face and hands. Since Goodwin was tricked out in fighting gear, Achoo also washed plenty of metal studs and stiffened leather.

"Our early reports put my lord Gershom on alert," Goodwin explained when Achoo finally calmed down. "He sent a ship of Dogs to wait off Lurker's Point, out of sight from the river bridges, just in case. When I got to Corus and told him what we had, he didn't want to delay anymore. We rode to meet the ship once we collected Sir Tullus, the Flash District magistrates, the knights, and the mages."

I gaped at her like a country-bred looby. "*Sir Tullus* is here?" I looked around the room, trying to see him. I had spent plenty of Court Days stammering before Sir Tullus.

She grinned. "Yes. Think, Cooper—we'll need magistrates to issue writs, just like we need mages and knights. But first we have to know all that's gone on since I left. What's this Nestor and the sergeant have been telling us, that you're on Sir Lionel's 'wanted' list?"

"I was a fool," I whispered, looking down. "Tradesmen's

kennel arrested Master Finer and his whole family. I told Sir Lionel they'd made a mistake and you'd vouch for them if he'd intercede. But Sir Lionel wasn't listening. I lost my temper and spoke as I shouldn't have done. He put a magic on me, Goodwin! After that he wanted his errand boys to toss me into a Rattery Coffin, only Sergeant Axman and his friends saved me. He wouldn't do anything for the Finers. And now . . . Goodwin, I'm sorry. Master Finer didn't live. His heart . . ."

Goodwin took hold of my knee and looked down. Her free hand was clenched in a fist. I held still, waiting for her to say something, to tell me she never should have left me here, where her friends might look to me for help.

Finally she looked at me. Her eyes were hard, but she'd let no tears fall. "This is where we blame those who are responsible, Cooper," she told me, her voice very soft. "The colemongers, and the bought Dogs at Tradesmen's kennel. We'll leave an offering for him with the Black God when all this is done, and we'll occupy ourselves with tearing these colemongers apart, all right? We put grief aside for now." She straightened and looked from Nestor to me. I'd forgotten Nestor was yet right beside me. "How did Cooper enter the Black God's priesthood, may I ask?"

"Oh, my disguise," I mumbled.

I tugged it off, over my head and shoulders, as Nestor said, "She's been running from the Rogue *and* Sir Lionel. Pearl's set a price of five gold nobles for Cooper and Achoo, alive and unharmed. She needed a disguise. But Cooper's running has been to some purpose."

"It had better be to some purpose," Goodwin said. She looked at me. "Why *are* you running from the Rogue?"

I grimaced. "Sir Lionel's chief assistant Ives went to Pearl as soon as he escaped Sergeant Axman. I think Ives told her what I'd said to Sir Lionel. It's the only thing that explains the way she bounced when he was done."

Goodwin gently took hold of my ear. I flinched. Sometimes, when I am very stupid, she likes to twist it well. "Cooper?" she asked softly. "What, *exactly,* did you say to set both the Deputy Provost and the Rogue of this city against you?"

I tried to look at the floor, but her grip on my ear kept my head up. "I said he curst well knew who the colemonger was, and he'd let her run beyond all control. And I told him there was yet time, which is when he put the magic on me. He's out of his nob worried that I'll spread wild talk and the Rogue will hold him to blame. I didn't let on anyone but me thought so. I made him think I was trying to get all the glory and keeping good information from you, Goodwin. I—*owwwww!*"

I'd wondered when she would twist. Seemingly I had shocked her so much with my tale that she had forgot she meant to do it, until I mentioned her name. *Then* she recalled that she still clutched my poor ear.

"Of all the crackbrained dozy Pups it's ever been my curse to serve with!" she cried. "You just *had* to go and pluck the biggest Rat in all the Eastern Lands, didn't you? You couldn't have held your poxy tongue?"

"I thought she held her tongue well for a first-year Dog," Nestor said kindly.

"It's when she uses it that you have to watch her!" Goodwin snapped. "She'll say any curst thing when she's got the bit between her teeth, and never mind the consequences! I'm surprised she's lived to tell this tale!" She glared at Nestor. "And *you* tell me she's done well, these days I've been away?"

Nestor pulled my ear from Goodwin's hand. "You'll want to hug her, she's done so well. But I fancy she'll only want to give the tale once, because it's a long one. Let's get my lord Gershom and the others to hear it, too."

Nestor tugged me through the crowd of Dogs to the door where the mages waited. Goodwin and Achoo followed. I could hear Goodwin as she muttered, "I thought it was only the hill barbarian I couldn't trust on his own. I thought, Cooper's got a good head on her shoulders. She'll stay out of trouble. I'm getting too old for this."

Nestor opened the door and ushered me into the room beyond. It was a meeting hall, with tables set in rows, and chairs in lines on one side of each table. Lord Gershom sat at the first table, along with Sir Tullus and two other magistrates I'd seen at Provost's House. Three mages had also chosen a table. They were several cuts above what I was used to, which is street mages, hedgewitches, and the sort of folk who worked for the guilds. The very air around these mages hummed.

Nestor left us there, closing the door behind him. Achoo moved in close to my right side and sat. Lord Gershom looked at me.

I went down on one knee, properly, and bowed my head. "My lord," I said.

"Guardswoman Cooper," he greeted me, as if I were any other Dog. "Sergeant Haryse says you have much to report. I understand you are being sought by the Deputy Provost?"

"And the Rogue, my lord," I said.

"I imagine odds are on the Rogue," Goodwin said, her voice sour.

"If there is a betting pool, I will place a gold noble on Cooper," Lord Gershom replied. I heard a snort. I couldn't be sure who did it, of course, but I suspected Sir Tullus. I have been amusing that cove for a year and a half, somehow. "Both of you women find a seat," my lord told us. "We have no need for formality, and you will want to relax as much as you can. We have a busy day ahead." My lord pointed to a chair that faced the room. I rose to my feet and tried begging him with my eyes not to put me before everyone, a target for strangers to stare at, but he shook his head.

Sir Tullus said, "Cooper, is that a Sirajit opal about your neck? May I see?"

The necklace that Dale had given me must have tumbled out during my unhappy gallop. The opal lay atop my tunic, glinting in any light it could find. I walked over to Sir Tullus, slipping the necklace off. I gave it to him, waiting as he held the stone and turned it in the light. I'd never stood so close to him before. He smelled very pleasantly of sandalwood. He still had only one eyebrow, but I felt better to see there were two scars across the right end of it. You only get those lengthwise ones from fighting.

"Very pretty, Cooper," he said, giving the necklace back. "Setting the stone this way is unusual, but I like it. You can see more of the fire." As I took it from his hand, he added, "It is more expensive than I expect a young Dog to wear."

"It was a gift, Sir Tullus," I mumbled. I blushed, thinking of Dale.

"Your friend is lucky, to be able to give such gifts," Sir Tullus said. I looked him in the face, startled. He held up a hand. "I meant only that plainly he has gotten you to smile."

"Tullus, you're terrifying Cooper," Lord Gershom said.

Sir Tullus grinned at him. I wondered if I was having fever visions. I had never seen that expression on the magistrate's face before. "I assure you, Gershom, Cooper has proved she is well able to withstand anything I might tell her." I ducked my head at that, but it was a nice thing for him to say!

Others came in while Sir Tullus spoke to me and to my

lord. Jewel and Yoav were among them. So was Sergeant Axman. The working Dogs stood against the wall as knights took seats at the other tables. A group of scribes entered laden with parchment, ink bottles, and reed pens. They set up at two of the tables so they would have plenty of room. One of them I knew as Lord Gershom's scribe for his most important Dog work, the writer of all the documents that went out under his seal as Lord Provost. Had I not known this was serious unto death, seeing her would have corrected my thinking.

I bowed to Sir Tullus and returned to my chair, but I did not sit. I clutched my opal pendant in one hand and waited, sweating. I was going to have to talk before all these strangers, and this time I did not even have the lie of the pretty, flirty Dog to hide behind.

"While Corporal Guardswoman Goodwin reported the state of affairs to me three days past," my lord said, his voice loud enough to be heard by all, "Guardswoman Cooper remained here. She has information that we require before we proceed. Cooper, report."

I gulped and thrust my free hand into my breeches pocket to wrap it around my fire opal. Then I spoke as if I was in Sir Tullus's courtroom, reporting all of a crime from beginning to end.

When I fumbled, my lord Gershom would lean forward, waiting for me to find my thread. My mouth got dry. With my first cough Goodwin was there with a tankard of cider twilsey. Achoo leaned against my right leg to steady me.

So I told it all, from Master Finer's visit on Monday the seventeenth to Nestor's capture of the cole-making materials last night. Then, because Lord Gershom knew of my dealings with the dead who rode on pigeon-back and would expect me to include that information in any report I made, I repeated what

Hanse had said. The mages looked offended. Some of the magistrates acted as if I played a very foolish joke. It was hard to guess what Sir Tullus thought.

The questions came after that. The magistrates, mages, and knights wanted to see Okha's maps of the Rogue's courts. I took them from my pack and handed them over. I felt like I had betrayed Okha's trust in handing his dangerous and hard-won work to strangers, but at least I did not tell them his name. I would not get him into trouble with Nestor if I could help it.

One knight demanded I give up the names of the lad and gixie who had been my guides to the colemonger's works. I had to swear on Mithros's shield that I'd gone all that time without learning them a-purpose before he would believe me.

The magistrates wanted me to give a full count of Pearl's court. Nestor finally told them it was nonsense, that Rats came and went at any Rogue's court. There was no keeping count.

Some of them were vexed that I accused a noble of cooperating with his city's Rogue. I nearly told one suspicious, pinch-faced mot that I was sorry to ruin her pretty daydreams of what a noble might and mightn't do. I was opening my mouth to say it when I saw Goodwin tug one of her ears. I shut my mouth quickly.

At last my lord held up his hand. "Enough," he said wearily. "You have seen that her report does not change. Sergeant Axman, you and your folk know Sir Lionel best. Do *you* believe what she says of him?"

Everyone looked at the sergeant, who leaned against the rear wall. "It's why we got Cooper out o' Guards House, milord," he said, coming to attention. "Sir Lionel was good enough for the work once, but losin' his oldest lad to the Sweatin' Sickness five year back broke somethin' in 'im. When Pearl threatened his family, Sir Lionel cracked like a sheet o' salt. Plenty of us try to fight the Rogue, but when your own Provost's against you . . ." He shook his head. "It's just too hard, milord. The common folk trust the Rogue more'n the Crown. Pearl Skinner is worse than most, but still folk believe she'll help 'em where the Crown won't. They'll fight us if we go after her."

"So we must let her roam freely, destroying the realm's coin?" demanded a magistrate. "The realm will be fit only for Chaos if the common folk believe that we fear one lowborn thief!"

"No, milord," Axman replied. "But we'd best make curst sure the common folk know she's at the root of their money troubles."

"Enough. We're losing the element of surprise," Lord Gershom said. "Mistress Scribe, are the writs complete?"

"They need but my lord's signature, a magistrate's signature, and then my lord's seal." My lord's chief scribe took two parchments to one of the Port Caynn folk, a magistrate, seemingly. She looked them over, then brought them to my lord, who signed both. When she melted wax onto each one, my lord stamped them with his seal ring. She added her seal after his. Now the scribe brought one more writ for signatures and seals.

"These writs are for Sir Lionel at Guards House, the Rogue's person, and to lock the harbor against all outgoing traffic save for those vessels with passes," my lord announced. "Those to the Harbormaster and Sir Lionel must be delivered by knights and mages in addition to the standard forces." With that he began to make his assignments. Sergeant Axman and his folk would escort the knights and mages chosen to go to Guards House to have, as my lord put it, "a word with Sir Lionel." As I understood it, they would nab and hold Sir Lionel until my lord chose to speak with him. If Sir Lionel imagined all manner of cruel fates while two mages held him as he had magicked me, my lord Gershom would not cry so much as a single tear. Nor would I.

Beyond that, I lost interest in Sir Lionel's fate. He'd doubtless get away with a slap on the nose. Trebond was a rich, powerful house. What had he done, other than turn a blind eye to the work of Port Caynn's Rogue?

I was glad not to have the harbor assignment, too. Who wanted a basket of screaming ship captains in her lap, demanding special passes? And it wasn't going to be the Harbormaster who would get the job of searching each vessel for runaway Rats, either. It would be Dogs assigned to that task.

My interest lay with that greedy scummer snake Pearl. I wanted to be in on *that* kill.

A small group of Dogs was going to track down the Finers and get them to safety. Another group was sent to hobble leaders in the Gold- and Silversmith's guilds and bring them here, to answer my lord's questions when he had time for them. I didn't feel bad for them, either. Withholding knowledge of colemongery was a crime of its own. The guildmasters would wish they had been slower to shield their bums and quicker to notify Lord Gershom.

"Doubtless they'll bribe some Crown official to say they knew of it all along. They were trying to look into it when we made a mess of their inquiries," I muttered to Goodwin.

"Money talks and walks, but it does not bark," she replied. It is a favorite saying of Dogs.

I was appointed to the largest force, along with Goodwin, Nestor, and my lord Gershom. We were destined for Pearl's Riverside court, where she was supposed to be today. As soon as we got the nod, I sought out a small room. I left my priest's robe there and put on my arm guards, iron cap, and weapons belt. I was sad not to have my chest and back armor and my gorget, all sitting in my trunk at Serenity's, but it did no good to pout over what was missing. My weapons belt was enough for most Dogs. My arm guards, with their eight thin blades, and my hideaway knives left me better prepared than many. With those knives, my sap, and my baton, I had lived this long. I remembered to remove my jewelry before slinging my pack over my shoulders and going in search of a privy. With that taken care of, I returned to Achoo, Goodwin, and the rest of the main group as it mustered.

While I had armed, Serenity and thirty hard-faced mots had come to the countinghouse. Those women looked as tough as any Dog. They all wore long cloaks to hide the moon-stamped breastplates, back plates, arm and leg armor, and short leather skirts of women soldiers who guarded the temples of the Great Mother Goddess.

"I saw your arrival in my scrying glass, my lord," Serenity was telling Lord Gershom as I returned. "I knew you would need help. I have trusted these women with my life, and continue to do so. They are expert in street fighting."

"Your help is most welcome, lady," my lord said. "And from Goodwin, I know the weapon that *you* bring is your magical Gift. I thank you."

"I also bring two messengers," Serenity told him. She waved forward a lad and a gixie. They wore undyed wool tunics and light sandals. "When you give the word, they will carry news to the temples. The sisterhood will tell the people that Pearl Skinner's false coins have driven up the cost of food."

"Surely that will cause unrest," said a mage.

"If they don't know the truth, the common folk will be against us," Nestor argued. "We need to tell them something, or we'll have to fight for every foot of ground."

Standing close to my lord, I whispered, "Would it help to tell the people that Pearl's got a fortune in gold?" He looked down at me, one brow raised. Still keeping my voice very soft, I explained, "It's why she did all this, my lord. She changed coles for gold weeks ago, afore anyone knew there was a colesmith in town."

"We'll keep that between us," my lord murmured. "I don't want treasure hunters tearing Pearl's haunts to pieces looking for it before our mages can claim it for the King." He turned to Serenity and nodded. "Send your messengers, Daughter Serenity. And you and your women shall come with me. I do not expect Pearl Skinner to submit easily."

Serenity gave her messengers the word, then spoke with the mages. Lord Gershom went to give orders to the scribes and the magistrates. Gnawing on my lip, I took Achoo and sought Goodwin. She was with Jewel, Yoav, Birch, and Ersken. They greeted me and shared out some pasties they had gotten, including one for Achoo. I had the dreadful fear that I might weep, so glad was I to be among them again.

Goodwin eyed me with scant approval. "Cooper, you look like you slept in that uniform."

"I wish I had but slept in it." I felt like a sloven in my wrinkled clothes. "Goodwin, what does he mean to do about the city? He plans to nab Pearl, but what about after?"

Jewel grunted in agreement. "Take away Port Caynn's Rogue without leaving another ready to take her place, and it'll be a Chaos pit."

Yoav winced. "Food riots, money panics—"

"And no Rogue to keep a grip on the Rats? Goddess's mercy we'll be safe back in Corus," Birch said. "We'll have our own headaches, come winter."

Ersken's eyes, like mine, went from face to face.

"Rats will fight it out," Goodwin said, but she frowned. "They always do."

"Not if we nab all the best candidates," I heard Nestor say. I turned. He had come up behind us.

Sergeant Axman stood beside him. "Curse it. Why can't a problem ever be simple?"

"Festering, pox-rotted—I always hated this town," Goodwin muttered. She went to my lord and spoke quietly to him. He frowned, then came to our group with Goodwin at his side.

"What's this Goodwin's telling me? You think we should let some of the Rogue's top rushers go?" he asked, his heavy brows knit together.

Jewel spoke first. "Dogs don't admit to it, mostly, but we're too thin on the ground, everyone knows it. Without a Rogue, we'd never keep order."

"Have you any suggestions?" my lord demanded. "Is there anyone who won't make this worse?"

Everyone else looked at their boot tips. They didn't want to risk offending their master. It would have to be me who said it. "My lord, there's a mot—a woman, Fair Flory. She leads the flower sellers and orange girls. If she becomes Rogue, she'll keep order, or she'll do her best."

Nestor rubbed his chin. "She knows how things work, sure enough. And if Flory knows we're to thank for her freedom, she'll remember she owes the Dogs a favor."

Lord Gershom crossed his arms over his chest. "Can one woman do what's needed just now? These Rats will require an iron hand to knock them into line if we bring down a sitting Rogue."

Nestor coughed into his fist. "My lord, Flory has her own gang. She may not be a muscle-bound rusher, but Pearl isn't, either, and she took the throne. Flory's got more wits in her head than Pearl ever did."

Lord Gershom sighed. "Spread the word," he told us. "Fair Flory and her cohorts are to be allowed to escape, unless they kill Dogs. I can't allow that," he said, looking each of us in the eye. "My people come first. Those who are choosing the parties to strike the Riverside court, be certain you choose Dogs who can identify this Fair Flory."

"Yes, my lord," they said, and we all bowed.

"My lord, how do you propose to get us in position unseen?" a mage called across the room. We all looked at him. "Even if I place a spell of invisibility over us, folk will know a large group of something shoves them aside."

"Sergeant Haryse knows a secret way," my lord replied.

My gut lurched when Nestor grinned at everyone. I knew what he would say afore he said it. "We don't go on the streets, Master Mage," he said cheerfully. "We go under them."

There was an entrance to the sewers in the cellar of the countinghouse. Quickly we were sorted out and given our positions. The company charged with the attack on Pearl descended the broad staircase that led down below the streets. Achoo, walking at my side, whuffed softly when she smelled the chilly breath of the sewer.

"You have to expect everyone on Riverside has a finger or two in smuggling," Nestor told Goodwin and me as we reached the sewer's stone ledges. "That's why they make it so easy to come down here. Even if they don't handle smuggled goods, they turn a blind eye to whatever passes through."

"What happens when the tide comes in?" Goodwin asked.

Ahead and behind us, folk cursed. Someone called for Goodwin to shut her gob. Nestor told them to quiet down, then answered Goodwin. "The Rats of Port Caynn know the tides from the cradle. Anyone as gets caught?" He shrugged, our torches making his shoulders seem even broader. "They had no business down here, then, did they?"

"Tides?" I asked.

"The sewers flood for blocks when the tide is high," a mot said.

"Seems curst risky to use the stinking things at all," I grumbled.

"You're not a waterfront mot," Nestor said with a quiet laugh. "The sewers are the city's veins. Ask Dale, he'll tell you."

"She best keep her mind on Dog work, not canoodling," another Port Caynn Dog muttered.

Nestor started to answer, but I shook my head at him. Truth be told, the thought of Dale warmed me all over in this curst cold place.

Soon we left the sewer to climb out into the cellar of a burned-out wooden building. To my surprise, a cart drawn by a sailor waited for us on the street level. As we climbed up beside it, Nestor pointed out four pairs of Dogs and sent them to the cart. They lifted the canvas that lay over the contents of its bed and picked up four sturdy wooden rams.

Ersken came to stand beside me. "Didn't Ahuda teach us to never take a Rogue on his own ground?" he asked softly as the Dogs set the rams on end. The devices were made of heavy wood, wrapped in iron with iron grips at the back and at midpoint. The iron rams' faces stared blankly at the sky as the Dogs who held them waited for orders.

"She also says there's a first time for everything," I reminded Ersken. "Jewel?" I called. The old cove looked at me. "Why do we need rams?" I asked. "Unless they've word we're coming, the doors won't be locked."

He grinned a Dog's grin that showed all of his teeth. "Nothin' spooks 'em worse than a ram comin' through their doors, Cooper," he explained. "They feel all safe and cuddlesome with they doors shut. The Rats panic when we make the big noise and smash up the doors."

I nodded and stepped back. That was when Slapper found me. He lit on my shoulder and nearly slid down the front of my tunic before I caught him with one hand. Achoo leaned against my legs.

"What's this nonsense?" I heard Hanse growl. "Why are you standin' here with a crew of strange Dogs? My murderess walks the city alive!"

"These Dogs are delivering the bill to your murderess," I snapped, keeping my voice low. "The accounting for Steen, and Amda, and all your folk."

Ersken looked at me sidelong. "Still talking to the dead, Beka?" he asked.

"It's not something that goes away when I leave Jane Street," I told him. "How's Kora?"

"Missing you. So's Aniki. Rosto's heard you made a good, um, friend here. He's as mad as a bear with a thorn in his . . . paw." Ersken changed the part of the bear he meant to name, seeing that the fighter closest to us was one of the Goddess warriors. "Not that he's *pining*. He's gone through mots like ducks through water. But he's not happy."

"There's naught between us, even if I hadn't made a . . . a friend here," I replied. Was that what Dale was to me? *Friend* seemed like such a wrong word.

Slapper pecked my ear. "Will you stop talking of sweethearts!" Hanse bellowed. "I want *revenge*!"

"He'll still be glad to see you alive," Ersken said.

It took me a moment to remember we'd been speaking about Rosto. "I'm glad of it myself, so far," I replied. As Jewel waved us out, I told Ersken, "Lately it's been like living on the knife's edge, never knowing which side I'll fall off on."

Ersken clapped me on the shoulder as we stepped into the street. "Cheer up, Beka. Maybe you were going to fall off that razor's edge before, but not today," he said, as good-humored as always. "Today we're going to jump."

Nestor and Jewel formed us into columns with two rams each, our numbers mixed from Port and Corus alike. I ended up with Jewel and Goodwin, Ersken with Nestor. Watching Goodwin as she walked down our line, setting the column in order, I felt a weight come off my chest. This was where I needed to be, at last. The world was solid under my feet, not sand running out with the waves.

Jewel raised his baton and led us at a Dog trot down a side street. Slapper and Hanse took off, Hanse cursing as they flew away. Achoo ran alongside me, tongue happily lolling, tail a-wag.

I eyed windows and rooftops as I ran, but this part of the city was given over to the countinghouses and warehouses that served both river traffic and sea shipping. All of the shutters were closed, the day bidding fair for rain. Our street was too narrow for carts or wagons. Few persons were here to see us on the move.

Jewel and Goodwin halted us at a corner. As we waited, they called up one of the Goddess warriors and two of Nestor's friends. Jewel signaled the rest of us to wait. Then the five of them walked into the next street, as casual as if they were going to market.

Some Dogs trotted up to the corner and peeked around. One of them looked back at the rest of us and said in a quiet, carrying voice, "Four rushers on guard, dicing, the claybrains." She looked around the corner again and winced.

We heard a small crash, some grunts, and the clank of metal striking stone. The mot who'd spoken to us waved us on. We rounded the corner to find Jewel, Goodwin, and the others hobbling and gagging four Rats. Ersken gathered the dice, put them in the cup they had used for play, and tucked it inside one bound Rat's shirt.

"Let that be a lesson to you not to gamble," he told the Rat soberly. "The Trickster asks you to pay for any luck you may have, one way or another."

"Bless the boy, he's a priest with it," one of the Goddess warriors said with a grin. "After this, laddie, what's say I take you home and rub some of that off yez?"

Ersken actually winked at her! "Forgive me, gracious warrior, but my woman would turn me into something unnatural if I took you up on your kind offer," he replied, as if he truly regretted it. "She's a mage, and I'd best stay devoted."

All this was said no louder than a whisper, of course, as the Rats were towed into a nearby doorway. Up came our fellow Dogs who carried the rams. We drew our batons and got ready, me with Achoo at my side. Achoo was quivering, she was so eager. Jewel silently counted off on his fingers, one, two, three.

Together the Dogs with the rams swung them hard at the doors. Jewel counted off again, and again they smacked the doors with those weights of wood and iron. A third time they struck. The wooden doors burst open, swinging wide. A mage I hadn't even noticed threw a huge puff of fog at the gap. Under its cover we entered the court and spread out.

I am weary now. I must rest.

Monday, September 24, 247

Guards House
A little past six of the clock.
being a chronicle of the events of Thursday the 20th,
beginning around noon of that day

This court was a large, single room, almost a barn. It didn't boast the upstairs galleries or the side halls of Pearl's other two courts. There were plenty of Rats, though. They attacked, some armed with clubs and swords, others seizing tankards, stools, or whatever they could grab. Achoo and I joined up with Goodwin, who had helped to lead the charge inside. A pair of Rats came at us, screeching curses.

I did not wait for them, but stepped out to get the one in front of me. He carried a length of firewood gripped in both hands. It would crush my shoulder if it struck, so I darted under his swing and, one-handed, smacked both of his kneecaps with my baton. When he stiffened, his grip on his weapon going loose, I jammed the end of my baton between his thighs and yanked it up. Now he dropped the log and bent double. I smashed him on the back of the neck with my sap. Down he went, fouling the legs of the one who fought Goodwin. She knocked her cove back over my fellow with a smash to the jaw.

I turned and walked right into a blow to the belly from a club. I forced myself not to collapse, though my mind was white with pain. As I hung on, I heard Achoo snarl. Through the lights that covered my vision, I saw her clamp her jaws on the wrist of the cove who'd hit me. She had him by the club hand and she would not let go. While she hung on, I jammed myself sidelong into his belly, blocking his free arm to shield her, and grabbed myself a big fistful of him. Not of his gems—he was wearing a leather cod. Instead I grabbed a chunk of the inside of his thigh near to his cod and pinched hard with all four fingers and my thumb. He struck my back with his free hand, yelping. A glance showed me there was blood around Achoo's mouth, she was biting his club wrist so deep. The second time the cove brought his fist down, he plunged his arm onto the knife I'd yanked free. He wailed and grabbed my braid with that same hand. He screeched yet again. This time he'd jammed his palm onto the band of spikes in my braid. I stomped one of his feet with my boot heel and felt bones break.

"Achoo, *biarlah*," I said. She released the Rat so he could hobble away from us. I looked her over quickly. She seemed to be fine.

Forward I went, keeping to Goodwin's side. Achoo was expert at ripping a striking arm or a kicking foot. She had a good eye for my own attacks and never got in my way. She saved me from more than one knife. I promised myself, if I lived, that I would get her the meatiest bone I could find, climbing prices or no.

I'd stopped for a breath when I saw Flory and her mots trapped in a corner, knives out. A few of our folk kept the women there, but I could see by the way they held their bodies that they knew who Flory was and that they were not to hobble her. I waited until Goodwin had put down her Rat of the moment and let her know.

"Get my lord," she yelled. She began to move toward Flory, smashing any Rats that got in her way.

Lord Gershom was busy. A rusher with a longsword had decided today was his lucky day, seemingly. He was young and strong, faced with an old man with long gray hair. My lord must have ordered his guards to stay back. Now he smoothed his heavy mustache, a sign he was ready to do as he must.

"My lord, when you're finished, might I have a word?"
I asked.

"Certainly, Cooper," he replied, his voice as casual as if
we'd met in the market.

"Don't yez pay attention t' her!" bellowed the rusher. "Pay
attention t' *me*!"

"If you insist," my lord replied. He came in with that hard,
fast overhand swing of his. He does it one-handed, keeping a
small, round buckler on his other forearm. The rusher barely
parried the strike and tried an ox-handed thrust of his own. My
lord knocked that aside with the buckler.

I glanced around. There was a dais, of course. Pearl's
bodyguards were up there, holding off Nestor, other Port
Caynn Dogs, and some of the Goddess warriors. I did not see
Pearl herself. Was she at the heart of the ring of guards, hidden
by them and their attackers? I took a step toward the dais, but
there was a scream behind me. I turned back to Lord Gershom's fight. The rusher was dead already. My lord set his buckler aside. His guards closed in, making a safe zone around us. A
mage gave him a cloth so he might wipe his sword. My lord
couldn't do that on his clothes or the dead cove's. Both were
well marked with blood.

"These clothes will have to be burned," he remarked. "My
lady will not approve if she sees them."

If my lord was lucky, Port Caynn was far enough away that
Lady Teodorie would never know he'd been fighting again.

"Cooper?" Lord Gershom asked.

I pointed to the far corner. "It's Fair Flory, my lord," I said.
"The one we spoke to you about."

My lord sheathed his sword. "Very well. I'll talk with her."
He and his guards crossed the room.

I looked at the overall fight. We had caught them by

474

surprise, that was plain. The area near the tap and kitchen doors was empty of Dogs and Rats. I suspect many had escaped that way. Doubtless my lord had planned it so, given that Okha's maps showed there were exits in that part of the court as well as those we had used. It would have been a fair mess to take every Rat here before a magistrate.

Achoo scratched her ear and yawned. "Come on," I said, picking up my lord's buckler. "I don't like that mess up on the dais." Once I'd settled the buckler on my arm, I holstered my baton, keeping my sap in my free hand.

I muscled my way between two Goddess warriors, crouching down, the buckler over my head to shield me from the blows of those fighting there. I didn't have much room to swing my sap, but a little swing is all I need. Then someone screeched. The Dog in front of her yanked her out of the wall of Rats defending that dais. I slammed my sap into the knee of the cove fighting next to her and rammed him sideways. He toppled into the Rat on his left. The Dogs yanked those two down to the floor.

We had an opening through the wall of Rats. I slid the edge of my buckler up under the raised arm of the Rat in front of me, then stood and shoved it into his armpit. He couldn't get that arm down to strike me. As he grabbed for me with the other arm, Achoo seized his wrist in her teeth and dragged him down to the floor to be trampled.

I bashed the next Rat in the face with the buckler. There was more room to maneuver now. Rat after Rat was yanked away by the three Dogs who swarmed the dais along with me. And what we saw at the center of the dais, among the overturned chairs and tables and braziers, made me numb with rage.

"What're you fighting for, you clanking stupid bumwipes!"

I yelled at the Rats. No one heard. Of course not, it was too loud and their backs were to us. Then someone—Birch, Ersken's partner—hoisted me up. I stood on his knee, his arms around my legs, and tried again. "You Rats! You blind and mammering loobies, what do you fight for?!" I yelled.

Something happened in the room. The air felt tight. It was mage work. Birch's arms were trembling. I looked down for a better height where I could stand. On the dais someone had righted a table. No wonder it hadn't gotten destroyed in the fight—it was made of stone.

"Birch, you do it, please?" I asked. "You've got the bigger voice." As he got up on the table, the great chamber slowly went quiet.

"She's gone!" he bellowed. Now they all heard. The air felt looser again. I didn't want to know the name of the mage that had done the magic to make them hear the first time. The spell wasn't aimed at me, it was supposed to help. It would be poor thanks for me to punch the mage that cast it, but I hate being magicked, even as part of a crowd. "Your Rogue is gone!" Birch looked down at me. "Anyone else with her, y'think?"

"Jurji, Torcall Jupp, mayhap Zolaika," I said. "Her closest guards."

Birch called out the names and added, "You'll give 'em up now if you're wise!" No one answered him, so he got down from the table. "All this up here, 'twas a fakement," he said with disgust. "They was trained long ago, belike, to circle round the dais and make it look like they was protectin' her, whilst she scampered off some other way." He spat on the floor.

I nodded, full of my own share of disgust.

My lord Gershom came across the room, bodyguards and mages around him. In the shadows behind him, I could see where Flory and her mots had been cornered. They were gone.

My lord took the dais as the Dogs around it hauled unconscious Rats away. "Scent hounds, to me," he ordered. To everyone he said, "I will give a purse of ten gold nobles to the one who tells me where Pearl Skinner is. For every day that passes, it will be one gold noble the less. I am not a patient man."

"Who're you, t' be raidin' our court wiv your tarse-sniffin' Dogs?" a cove demanded.

Yoav backfisted him so hard that the Rat flipped bum over nob. "He's the Lord Provost of this realm, you slubbering piece of sheep scummer," she told him. "You'll talk respectful or I'll pull your tongue out."

"Yer Provost best sleep wiv one eye open, when Pearl comes after 'im," someone remarked. We didn't see who that one was.

"You must think I'm some lily-livered scut," my lord said. "Who stands on this dais now with a blade in his hand, and who's on the run? It's your Pearl Skinner with the price on her head. She won't come back, not to these courts. Why do you protect her? Do you *know* why we've come for her?"

Not one of them spoke. They only glared. I fidgeted, looking to see how Pearl could have gotten out. Did her guards only form a ring on the dais to distract us, as it seemed at first? She might have escaped with those who went out the back. Folk would have noticed her then, or if she fled through the kitchen. I drew closer to the dais—I had stepped off of it when my lord had taken over—and nudged a board with the tip of my boot. It was solid.

"Your Rogue is a colemonger," my lord said. "It's she who's been turning out those false silver coins. We have evidence. *Real* evidence, not whatever can be tortured out of some poor looby."

"Lies!" someone yelled. Soon all of them were shouting

sommat of the sort. The Port Caynn Dogs walked among them, cuffing them to silence, but they started again as soon as the Dogs passed.

I inspected the dais, remembering the magicked doors and secret stairs in the Eagle Street court. I even stepped up on it, shifting around the overturned chairs and tables. There was a rug, too, a nice thick one, wadded up.

"Shut yer gobs!" a mot yelled from the back of the room, near the entrance I'd come through with Goodwin and our Dogs. I glanced up. Fair Flory had returned, a cutlass in one hand, a maul in the other. I blinked. I'd never seen her outfitted for war. Seemingly flower-selling asked for more strength than I thought. "If you weren't such a herd of dozy scuts, you'd know the old cod cutter's tellin' the truth!"

Rats and Dogs alike gave way before her. Only my lord's bodyguards refused to move from her path when she reached the dais. My lord looked at Goodwin, who signed that Flory was all right. Only then did he give the nod to his guards.

Flory stepped up on the dais. "You know Pearl Skinner," she told the Rats in the room. "The greediest, cheapest trull in the world. Do ye *doubt* she's movin' false coin about this city? About this realm? Do ye *doubt* she's spent the coin that should've bought yez food for the winter? There's not a drop of oil in our storage rooms, nor a seed of grain. She left us t' starve!"

"Flory," I said. She turned to look at me. "Hanse and his people were bringing silver to her from the north for a new minting. I let the Deputy Provost know they were coming—but Pearl sent Zolaika to murder them all before they could talk under torture. Hanse, Steen, Amda, everyone who went north with him was killed last night."

"How do you know that?" she demanded.

"Cooper talks to the dead," Goodwin called.

Flory—almost all of them watching—made the Sign on their chests.

Nestor pushed forward. "I've seen where Pearl had the coins made. Mages will confirm it's all her property and that of those in her service." He looked around. "She's the one who shoved up the prices of bread and meat with her false silver. It'll be proved in Magistrate's Court for all to see."

"I saw 'er run out through the kitchens!" someone called. "Jupp an' that Jurji was with her!"

"No, she went up th' hidden stair, in th' wall behind the throne," someone else yelled. "There's a panel in th' wall back there. She went when we heard th' crashin' at the doors!"

I shifted the rug with my baton. A twisted wire loop stuck out of a crack between the boards. "My lord, excuse me," I said.

He moved aside. I gripped the loop and pulled. The trapdoor set in the floor of the dais rose. It brought with it a wave of cold air and sewer stink.

"Looks like we have three ways she could have gone," my lord said. "Scent hounds!"

There were four of us handlers and hounds in all. I knew the three brought in from Corus by sight. They nodded to me, and I nodded back. I was supposed to have gotten more scent hound training with them, before all this had begun. Did they know that I'd had to learn as I went from Phelan and on my own, or did they think I believed I was too good to learn from them?

My lord frowned. "Sergeant Haryse, have we only Corus scent hounds?"

Nestor grimaced. "My lord, at present we have but four in the city, and the lords of the district requested them this week for hunting. It is the governor's policy to always grant such requests."

I heard my lord curse softly. "Pray four's enough. Have we got something for the hounds we *do* have to use for scent?"

"I do," I said. I unslung my pack and removed the underclothes that I'd stolen yesterday. "I got these while I was at the Eagle Street court."

Elmwood, the oldest of the Corus handlers, picked them up, looking them over. "A good thought, Cooper. Though doubtless some of the scent from your pack clings to them now."

"She has bedrooms at the Eagle Street and Darcy Walk courts," I said. "We can find more there."

"*We* can?" Elmwood asked. There was no meanness in his face or voice. "You haven't got the training for a hunt like this, Cooper. Not after tricky prey that's got all manner of ways to go."

"You'll need fighting teams to back each of you up," my lord said. "Port Caynn and Corus Dogs mixed, and a mage for each." They moved closer to talk it out, choosing who would go and who might stay. Other Dogs began to move the hobbled Rats together and bind them that were still unconscious. I backed toward the wall, feeling as useful as teats on an ox.

Achoo danced and whined at my feet. Of course she did. She'd seen me take the pieces of Pearl's clothes out for other hounds to sniff. She'd heard the words *scent, hunt,* and *hounds.* She could see the other handlers kneeling to talk to their hounds. Achoo would know what all of that meant. She was ready for action, but I was not allowed to give her any.

Worse, I knew Elmwood was right. Achoo and I had successfully tracked a child, but we were not an experienced pair. She is a fine scent hound. I am the inexperienced one. It's the same as putting a lone Senior Dog with a Puppy. In looking out for the Pup, the Senior Dog can't be expected to work as well as she normally does.

"Sorry, Achoo," I whispered. Achoo whined, looking at the other handlers, who were giving their hounds Pearl's clothes to sniff. One already towed her handler to the exit by the kitchen. One dragged his handler to the door hidden in the wall by the dais. Someone had opened it for us. Elmwood's low-slung hound was halfway down the steps in the center of the dais already. I could hear his deep-chested bark exploding from the stone walls below as Elmwood and the Dogs who would back them followed.

Then I heard a cove yell, "You sarden loobies! Wake up!"

That was Hanse's voice, which only I could hear. I looked toward it, to the side entrance. A black pigeon attacked two Dogs who were going outside, striking at their heads with his wings. When they flung up their arms to protect their faces, I saw that their tunics fit badly, as if they were twisted, or pulled on over other clothes. Then Jurji stepped into my view just for a moment, his sword raised. He cut the attacking bird in two, then moved out of sight.

Achoo and I began to run, dodging tables, chairs, and bodies. The two Dogs dashed outside. I fell once as a rusher on the floor grabbed my foot. I kicked him in the face, struggled to my knees, and caught up with Achoo. She had beaten me to the dead bird. She nosed it, whimpering.

Slapper lay over the court's threshold. The blade that had

cut him was dreadful sharp, slicing him crossways. Doubtless he never felt a thing, I told myself.

I pushed his pieces together with hands that shook, not thinking of his blood on me. Wouldn't the Black God mend such a good servant? He must be able to.

Mayhap the god wants to give him a rest, Slapper working so hard for him while he was alive.

And Hanse—he would be gone. I'd never known a spirit to return if sommat happened to his bird. I did look, both times it had happened before. My guess is that the Black God takes them, whether their business is finished or no.

Time was passing.

Achoo whined. Her head was up, her nostrils were wide. She had a scent. She wanted to follow it.

I wiped my hands on my breeches and took two of Slapper's feathers, being as he won't need them anymore. I slid them over my shoulder, into my pack. And I remembered that picture, the two people walking through the open doors in stolen uniform tunics, the bird on the attack, and Jurji.

"Achoo, *bau*," I told her, pointing to the ground beside the door where Jurji had stood. His footprints were clear in the soft dirt there. Achoo sniffed it and the frame of the door, where a bit of cloth was caught in the splintered frame. She sneezed once, then went back into the court, tracking Jurji and, most like, the two in the stolen uniforms, back to where they'd hid themselves in the crowd.

I gathered up Slapper's poor body and carried it over to a small patch of grass. It bore a spindly tree. I placed him there, so what was left of him might return to the Goddess's good earth. He deserved better, but I had no time. I wiped my hands as clean of the rest of his blood as I could on the grass.

Inside, Achoo had circled back to the door. She was about

to go outside, still on her scent, when I told her, *"Berhenti."* She looked at me, whining, and sneezed again. She didn't want to hear "stop" from me. I knew how she felt.

I looked around. My lord, Nestor, and Goodwin were nowhere in view. They must have gone off to look at something else in the court. I was scared that Achoo might lose the scent. Then I remembered that Goodwin still had her Dog tag for me.

I grabbed Ersken, who was standing guard over a clutch of hobbled, seated Rats. "I'm off with Achoo—we're tracking Jurji, one of Pearl's bodyguards," I said. "Tell Goodwin I need her to find me. She knows how. I don't dare let the trail get cold." I didn't mention the two in disguise, in case they were only minor Rats.

Ersken scratched his chin. "Beka, maybe you should wait," he said, worried.

"He killed Slapper," I said, swallowing a lump in my throat.

Ersken's kind face went hard. "I'll find Goodwin and tell her. But how will she find you? She's no mage!"

"But she has a magic thing. She'll explain, maybe," I said.

Ersken clapped me on the shoulder and went looking for Goodwin. I returned to Achoo.

"Mencari, Achoo," I said. I should have told my seniors myself, but the trail *was* getting cold. And I confess, my heart was filled with rage. I wanted Jurji and whoever ran with him.

Achoo took off down the street. I drew my baton and followed at a careful trot, keeping her in view.

Jurji's scent took us down to the Riverside docks. Once there, we tracked it north, along the line of the warehouses. Folk saw us and turned their backs. I did not want to risk losing Achoo by stopping to ask anyone if they had seen our prey. She kept the scent in her nose and did not halt. The dock area ended by the breakwater, near a swampy mass of inlets. It was ground that was too wet for buildings. Achoo did not act as if she'd lost the trail because our prey had taken one of the little boats here. She trotted into a small gully that took us out of view of the docks and those who worked them. She stopped at the gully's bottom. Two uniform tunics lay there in a pile. Achoo snuffled them eagerly, then sneezed several times. Now she had not only Jurji's scent, but that of his companions. I bundled the tunics up and strapped them to the top of my pack.

Footprints led from the tunics up the soft earth on the other side of the gully. Achoo scrambled to the top easily. I tried to follow, with less success. I began to slide back down again. Achoo grabbed me by the sleeve, digging in on the level ground as I clawed for purchase with my feet and hands. When I reached the top, I fished in the front of my pack for some dried meat strips. Achoo did not seem to object to the wet earth that clung to them from my hands. She gobbled them.

"When this is done, I am putting a feast before you," I promised her. Once I gave her a drink from my palm and had my own drink of water from my flask, we got moving again. I fumbled out a handkerchief and wiped my hands and knees as well as I could while trotting forward. It did little good. Sadly, it was the only handkerchief I had, and Achoo was headed straight into one of the giant sewer openings that emptied out down here.

I followed. Of course these Rats would take to the sewers.

I'd have thought the stench would kill Achoo, but she never faltered. She seemed to know I could not run as fast as she did. Some light came down through grates high above, but Achoo understood I could not see as well as she could. She always managed to stop just at the edge of my sight, or just as my legs were getting tired. I began to feel bad for her, kept so much of her life to the slow pace of human living. She was clearly happy going at a trot with her nose in the air, all of her senses alive. I also realized how stupid I was, to leave alone like this. With more of us, one could always keep pace with Achoo while the others halted to rest, then caught up. For now, to my sorrow, it was impossible to mend my folly, only to pray Goodwin found me soon. The scent was in the air, Achoo had it, and I was bound to stay with her.

I don't know how long we were down there. From time to time Achoo would turn and turn, sniffing. There were other scents to confuse her. Did she have Jurji and those who were with him now? I stood well back, letting the hound decide. What would I do if she lost the scent this time?

But Achoo always sneezed twice or thrice and started forward again, her body purposeful. Once she was certain, she didn't waiver. I had to make her stop for water or a bite to eat. She obeyed, but she was restless. As clear as if she spoke to me, she was saying, "Very well, I know you want to keep my strength up, but scent *fades,* you know!"

And I'd say, "I know, girl, but you're what I have, and I'm going to take care of you."

Four times we met other folk. All of them looked at my uniform, my baton, and the hound. Then I would stare at them until they scurried away.

Finally Achoo did not halt at an entry. She turned and raced up a very long stair, so long I had to stop twice to rest. I was breathless again when she halted at the top. There was a grate in the way. I came ahead and thrust it up. Slowly the iron thing moved. My shoulders groaned as I thrust it higher. Achoo passed under it into the open air. I managed to get myself out then, and let the grate down quietly.

It was late afternoon. The air was chill and clinging, filled with the sound of great, ringing bells. They were too slow to be fire alarms. Was it some religious festival? Neither of us cared.

We stood, panting, in a fountain courtyard. A maid-servant, looking out a window, closed her shutters promptly. A couple of servants passing by saw us and rushed into another house. The place was deserted then. Achoo drank from the fountain while I refilled my flask. She cast around for her scent, sneezed in a way that was starting to comfort me, and trotted into the street.

Following her, I glanced around, trying to see where we might be on the maps of Port Caynn I had studied. Below us on the foot of the hillside lay the river docks where we'd begun this hunt. "No wonder those stairs were so sarden long," I muttered to Achoo. We were halfway up the southern side of the ridge, ten blocks or so below High Street and five or six blocks south-west of Guards House. Seemingly Jurji and his two friends were avoiding it. I was grateful for that. I didn't want to get caught up in whatever mess was unfolding there.

Achoo stopped in front of a town house. The torch over the front door wasn't burning. We went around to the back of the house. It too was locked tight. I cursed myself for ten kinds of fool. Mayhap the place was stuffed with Rats. Looby Beka, bringing no one else to help, and her whistle somewhere on the ground of Nightmarket!

Achoo whined and scratched at the door. That was that. I could not let her lose a good scent.

I hammered at the rear door with the end of my baton. "Open, in the King's name!" I cried. "Open!" Goddess, please let Goodwin get here soon, mayhap even now, I thought.

"Go away!" someone cried.

"Open, in the King's name!" I shouted, getting angry. It was a burning offense to invoke the King's name if I wasn't a guard. Everyone knew that. I hammered and hammered as windows opened all around us and the householder's neighbors began to yell. I moved to the side of the door, where I would not be visible when it opened.

Suddenly a cove flung the rear door wide. He thrust out with a short sword that would have skewered me, had I still been in front of it. I seized the hand on the sword hilt, slamming my baton down on the forearm just above my grip. Bone crunched. I dragged the cove forward and slammed my knee into his belly, then sent him sprawling into the kitchen yard. The manservant behind him went the same way, though instead of breaking his wrist I cracked his skull. Achoo and I darted inside. I slammed the door shut, thrust the bolts to, and glared at the three servants—a man, a maid, a thin cook—who stood there staring at me.

"Who's next?" I asked them. Achoo seized the cook by the wrist, though her teeth barely dimpled the mot's skin.

"There's no one else," the cook whispered. Achoo growled fiercely around her mouthful. "Just us and Master and his man." She pointed to the door. It seemed I'd locked those two out.

"You had visitors not too long ago," I said. I smelled ham, and fresh-baked bread. They sat on a table. I cut slices from the ham and chopped them into strips for Achoo. "Achoo, *biarlah*." She released the cook and came to eat what I'd cut up for her. I went to cut more for myself, but the maid had already done so, and sliced bread for me. I winced—I never should have let one of them pick up a sharp knife—and put my back to the wall as I looked at them. "Visitors," I repeated, as they all blinked at me. "Three of them, one a Bazhir. Like as not they smelled much like I do."

"Master didn't want them here," the maid said. "He said he were done workin' for them."

The manservant tried to signal her to be quiet. I pointed my baton at him. "I'm after colemongers. Unless you want to end up on the list of them that's involved, you'll stay out of this," I warned him. The manservant shrank back.

"He said she'd ruin him. The Bazhir wanted to cut the master, but the mot said they didn't want to leave no blood trail," the maid told me. "She ordered the master to empty his coin box of gold and she'd go."

"She?" I asked. "They had a mot with them?"

The cook laughed. "Ye don't know who ye're chasin', wench? Then ye'd best draw off now, afore ye're gutted. Pearl Skinner don't like Dogs as try t'bite her."

Pearl was with Jurji? But she'd escaped the dais, through one of the hidden doors, or the back way, in all the confusion! I'd gone for Jurji and his friends to avenge Slapper.

Well, now I had more than I thought. I'd best snap to.

"Did she say where she was going?" I asked.

All three shook their heads. They looked nervously at the door. The master and his servant were hammering there, demanding to be let in. "But they didn't go out on the street," the cook said. "If you go out the side, there's a passage, like, between the houses, covered over so folk can visit the High Street markets in the rain. I'll show you."

First I bundled up the food they'd given me in a cloth. Then I let the cook take me to the side door. She played me no tricks. I hoped for their sake that their master wasn't part of the colemongering. They seemed like honest enough folk.

Achoo cast around at the doorstep of the side entrance,

running scents through her snuffling nose. I offered her the bundle of discarded tunics from the gully, but she ignored them. She ventured a few steps past the door and sneezed heartily, her tail a-wag. Then she was off into the passage. For some reason it was getting dark early. What light we had came through arches that looked into other houses on this part of the ridge. Some houses were lit up for company, while others at least had torches in the kitchen yards.

I could see the end of the passage on High Street and was thanking the gods, the climb from the house being a steep one, when I tripped and went tumbling. I'd fallen over a length of wood. I was getting up when a boot caught me in the ribs and knocked me onto my back. When it came down, heel first, to smash my chest in, I rolled to the side and scrambled upright.

Two rushers and Torcall Jupp stood there. Jupp held Achoo by her collar, forcing her back on her heels so she could not lunge. He twisted her collar so she could not bite. It was the blond rusher who had kicked me. "Hardly a challenge, this," he said, showing me a gape-toothed grin. "She's all winded and tired after a day of runnin' about."

He moved to my right, a cudgel in his hand. The other rusher slid to my left. He was armed with a long knife.

"She don't look worth our trouble or pay," that one said. "Certainly not worth Master Jupp's time."

I drew a boot knife with my left hand, my baton with my right, as I tried to decide which of them would lunge first. It was hard to guess in such bad light. The one I feared most was Jupp, standing in the shadows, my hound's life in his grip. *He* was the one with a longsword and dagger.

The one on my right swung his cudgel, going for my baton hand. The one on my left lunged in. I darted away from the cudgel and back from the knife, slamming my baton down on the knife cove's shoulder. Behind him Jupp had moved two steps to my left.

The knife man cried out suddenly, gaping at the ceiling. He shuddered, dropping his blade. He shouldn't have done that, him being left-handed and me striking his left shoulder. He began to fold at the knees, clutching the air as Jupp stepped away from him.

Achoo, suddenly free, darted at the blond cove, snarling. She ripped at his tunic and jumped away before he struck her. As the cove turned, forgetting me to watch Achoo, I leaped forward and smashed my baton on his skull. He staggered, but he was still on his feet. I smashed him backhanded, across the temple, and he went down. I turned to face Jupp. He was calmly wiping his sword blade on the knife cove's tunic.

"I would have killed that one for you, too, had you given me a moment," he said, not looking at me. "I was trying to spare you the added exertion."

"What?" I asked him, panting. I felt plain addled. "What?"

"I was entirely prepared to kill both of them for you," he repeated. "I have had enough of Pearl's disasters."

I leaned on my knees, still panting. "Very convenient your timing is, Master Jupp."

"I wished to live beyond my departure from Pearl's service," he told me. "Now that she has other things to keep her busy, I believe I may escape with my life. That wasn't possible before."

I straightened up. "What's say I hobble you and take you before my Lord Provost? Mayhap he'll give you your life, too, once you've coughed up all you know."

He smiled at me. He actually *smiled*. "My dear, do you

truly think you could hobble me all on your own? There are no other Dogs within earshot."

"Pox," I muttered.

He nodded. "Pox indeed. Besides, I have something you will want very much."

I snorted. "Not likely."

Jupp dipped two fingers in his purse and came up with sommat small between them. He moved into a patch of light so I could see better. It looked like a tooth, but it had more of a shimmer to it. Then I realized what it was that he held. I stared up at him, startled.

He smiled. "Just so. She will not give up sticky sweets, though the mage warns her and warns her. She lost this only two days ago, and though we searched for it, we could not find it." He turned it over in his fingers. "I am told that magicked things like this are best of all for scent hounds. It is as if the magic that went to fix it in place takes on the owner's scent, and keeps it."

I sighed. "How long have you been planning this?"

"Since you and your partner came." He smiled sidelong. "Perhaps others believed your tale. I could not help but wonder why two such clever girls had been sent here for such silly reasons. It was only a matter of time until the counterfeiting scheme was revealed. I thought that you might be the advance guard of the law. And I was right." Jupp dropped the tooth into my hand.

"Since you're being so helpful," I said, "where's Pearl got to?" I held the tooth down for Achoo to sniff, which started a storm of sneezes.

He shook his head. "My dear, do you think she told me? I believe she suspected that, unlike Jurji, my loyalties were not what they could be. That is why she left me with these two dolts

491

and orders to kill you. After that, she said, I am on my own. Were I Pearl, I would try to take ship away from Tortall, but were I the Lord Provost, I would have the ships watched."

I nodded. Achoo was squirming and wagging her tail, running up the passage. As plain as if she spoke Common, she was telling me it was time to move.

I looked at Jupp. "I see you again, I hobble you," I warned.

"That is fair," he replied, and bowed.

"Thanks for the help," I said awkwardly. "And the tooth."

He grinned. It made him look ten years younger. "The pleasure was mine. Pearl has backhanded me on a number of occasions. Lately she has paid me with purses full of coles. This is how I express gratitude. Good hunting, young bloodhound."

He stepped into the shadows and left. I checked the other two rushers, not wanting them to rise and come after me. They were dead.

I took a breath. "Goddess, but I'm weary," I muttered. Achoo said, "Wuff!" softly, as if she knew we must be careful of other enemies, but she *had* to make me move along.

I let Achoo sniff the tooth again, which gave her another sneezing fit. I was beginning to worry when she stopped. With a sigh of relief I tucked the thing in the pocket where I kept my fire opal. "Very well. Achoo, *maji,*" I said.

The skies were darker, the air colder as we went on. The bells were still ringing in a steady, one-two pace. They sounded as if they were down by the harbors, river and sea, filling the air with ill omens.

On this steep curve in the ridge, the passage was no longer smooth. Steps were built into it to help servants and their masters to reach High Street without sliding downhill in wintertime. And there, on High Street, the passage ended.

Achoo's trail did not. She turned left, away from Guards House, and wove through the carts and horses on the street. Traffic was thin for late afternoon. Checking the faces of the passersby, the way they looked at me and cleared out of the way, I understood. If Port Caynn was anything like Corus, the law-fearing folk were behind locked doors and shutters, awaiting the outcome of the day's strange events. Word traveled through the city with every mumper and peddler. No cityman or mot would be out tonight, not with Dogs in pursuit of the Rogue herself, and Rats and Dogs fighting in the alleys and squares. I glanced back at Guards House. There was a force of Dogs armed for trouble at the gate. If only I could leave word with them, I thought, but I knew it would be no simple matter. I would waste time convincing them of the importance of a junior Dog's message, and I did not have that time.

Achoo whuffed quietly from the mouth of a narrow alley to my right. "Coming, my lady," I muttered, but I had to smile as I trotted to keep up with her. She was a very polite hound. "You must have gotten those manners from Phelan," I told her as she led the way. "Never from that last brute that had you."

Now I saw the cause of the early nightfall as Achoo led me sideways and down from the top of the ridge, toward the deep harbor part of the city. Half of the land basin on that side and all of the sea were under fog. Soon all of Port Caynn would be covered in it.

I asked Achoo quietly, "How far ahead of us is she, do you think? She was mayhap a quarter of an hour ahead down in the gully. Jupp slowed us, what, another half hour? We lost time at that house, but so too did she. Mayhap she has half an hour's lead on us. Mayhap we can eat up some of that if I pick up my pace." I did, too, ignoring my weary legs. I could rest for days if I nabbed Pearl.

Achoo led the way over a small bridge. I caught up to her as she went to the water's edge for a quick drink. Then she moved along the stream, following it downhill. "Aren't Pearl and Jurji getting *tired*?" I asked her. She huffed in reply.

We were twelve blocks deep into the moneyed district behind Guards House when Achoo came to a halt at a gated courtyard. She whined, looked at me and wagged her tail, and whined again.

Pearl had come this way. Danger might stand behind the closed gate, yet . . . Achoo said this was the path to follow. I switched my baton to my left hand and slid my back-of-the-neck knife from its sheath. With it in my hand, I used two fingers to raise the latch and pushed the gate open with my foot. Achoo darted inside and whuffed that all was safe for me beyond. I followed, listening and trying to see in the gray light. Then I took a breath. There was plenty to smell for us both. It would have been worse for Achoo, but it was no treat for me, that copper stink of blood, scummer, and piss. The dead were here. I closed the gate behind me.

Inside a shelter where guards could stay out of the rain, Achoo stood at the edge of the pooled blood around two dead coves in livery. One had bought passage to the Peaceful Realms with a neck slash from a very sharp blade, the kind of slash that would hack a pigeon in two. I almost missed the death sign on the other cove, until I saw the blood that ran from his ear. I crouched to inspect the wound. At a guess, I'd say that someone very knowing in the ways of murder shoved a thin blade into the cove's ear all the way to his brain. He looked startled.

"Pox and murrain," I whispered. "Boiling oil's too fast for any of them." I holstered my baton, stuck my knife in my belt, and rubbed Achoo's ears. *"Mencari,"* I whispered.

She led me through the open front door and we walked past the first body inside the house, a manservant. Two mots in the kitchen had died, like the manservant, of slashes from Jurji's curst sharp sword. The mot upstairs in a bedroom had a broken neck.

We found the answer to why Pearl had come here, or enough to guess with, in a room that must have been the study upstairs. We also found a dead young mot and a dead little gixie as well as the master, slumped on his desk with his throat cut.

There was a great brass stamp on the desk, and sealing wax, and a slotted wooden case with written forms. Those in one slot were mussed, as if they'd been put back wrong. They were *Special Orders for Passage from the Harbor.* The brass stamp was the Harbormaster's Seal.

So Pearl had come for that, and Jurji and Zolaika made sure that no witnesses survived their visit.

I hovered over the desk. I couldn't make up my mind. My lord should know Pearl was bound for the harbor with a pass. But getting word to him would mean finding a messenger and losing time. Going to Guards House or searching out the nearest Dog would also cost me time. Shouting in the street might bring folk to deal with me that I didn't want, or them that would fetch no help at all. Pearl's scent would get cold. She might yet escape.

Finally I wrote a note, telling him all I knew that he could use. I sealed it, wrote his name large on it, and used one of my knives to stick it to the front gate, where folk would see it.

Achoo had picked up the trail in the garden. She'd found a tunnel that opened in the floor of some sort of open shrine. It led down into the ground, again. I made her wait, though she wriggled and whined with impatience, then set a gardening shed on fire with a lantern I found in the stable. That would bring folk. They would find my note, and get it to Lord Gershom. The shed was a small one, nowhere near the neighboring houses. I made sure of that. It was the only thing I could think of to get attention.

I was not thinking at my best, but there was no one I could ask. With the shed starting to burn, I returned to Achoo. Down into the tunnel we went.

I can barely see my page. I must sleep.

Tuesday, September 25, 247

Ladyshearth Lodgings
Eleven of the clock.
being a chronicle of the events of Thursday the 20th,
beginning around four of the afternoon of that day

As we followed the tunnels down into the slope of the ridge, I hung on to the lantern, even if it kept one of my hands occupied. I didn't like blundering about with no light of my own. What light I found came from stinking little oil lamps kept by the mumpers who slept here. They told us that Pearl, Jurji, and Zolaika had come by. They had the bodies of their friends who'd been too slow to get out of Pearl's way to show for it.

We stopped for food and water from my flask. Well, Achoo did. I made the mistake of looking up and seeing the hunger in the eyes of the mumpers around me. These weren't the privileged tale spinners of the Court of the Rogue, with their false sores and dislocated joints, popped into place at day's end with no harm. These were folk with faces like skulls from hunger. I gave them my food. Then I gave them what copper coin and good silver I had.

I know it's never enough. But it's something. And it lightened the weight of my pack.

We left them behind as we followed the scent. They didn't like to get too far from the escape hatches, they said. The trail led us downhill, I could feel it. I wished I could stick my head aboveground to see where we were, but Achoo kept moving on. Then, in a space bare of all humans, she halted at a stair that headed deeper under the ground.

"Not the sewers again," I said. I offered her the tooth so she might check the scent. She sniffed it, sneezed four times, then trotted down those pox-rotted stairs. I whimpered like a pup and followed. My leg muscles were cramping.

Down and down we went. How much magecraft and how many people digging and dying had it taken to build these tunnels so deep in the ground? Every time I think mages are a pain in my bum, I should remember that I'd be wading in scummer if it wasn't for works like these. Except, of course, that nobody ever bothered to put such tunnels in the Lower City, so I *do* wade in scummer there.

The stair opened onto a large and dry sewer pipe. This one hadn't been used in a long time. It barely smelled. Reaching it, Achoo raced down the ledge along one side. I ran after her, the lantern swinging in my hand.

The dry sewer seemed to go on forever, perhaps because I was so very tired. My legs trembled with it, my neck and back ached. My arm and leg guards weighed so much now, when they had weighed so little this morning. I fell into a walk-and-trot gait, but the walking got longer, the trotting shorter. Achoo kept falling back, whining, as if to ask what was wrong with me.

The tunnel got harder to travel, too. There were places where the ledges had fallen in. We had to climb down into the tunnel bed and climb back up again. In one spot the roof had collapsed. We were forced to squeeze through an opening not much bigger than me. When the tunnel opened onto a real sewer, Achoo halted at a short, broad stair that led to a closed door.

"Achoo, *tunggu*," I said. We sat on the ledge, sharing out the last of the water. I gave her what remained of the dried meat. I wanted to rest so badly. When I began to nod off, I yanked myself to my feet and wearily climbed the few steps to find the door was unlocked. I was not as careful as I should have been. Shifting the lantern to my free hand, I thrust the door wider still and walked through with my hound.

A rough, gauntleted hand seized me and dragged me against an armored chest. Someone else wrested the lantern away as I fought my captors. My exhaustion had doomed us.

"Curse you for a stubborn, idiot Pup!" Goodwin snarled as she pounded my back. "Pox and murrain on you for all the worry you have given me this last day!"

"Good girl, good girl," I heard another familiar voice say, but Nestor wasn't talking to me. He was ruffling Achoo's fur as Achoo licked his face. Ersken thumped me more gently while Birch waited with a cup of something in one hand and a dish in the other.

Birch put the dish on the floor. Achoo made the contents vanish in three gulps. "Goodwin," Birch said patiently, "let the mot drink this, will you? She's near dead on her feet."

Goodwin let me go and Ersken handed me Birch's cup. I sipped. The liquid in it tasted wonderful, like some kind of spice. I drank it down, and a fire roared from my belly clean to the top of my head. I felt more awake than I had since I'd begun Dog training.

"Gods defend us, what *is* that?!" I cried.

"Something the scent hound folk told us to give you," Birch said, refilling the cup from his flask. "They use it on a long trail, when the hounds can go farther than the handler."

"How fresh is the scent?" Goodwin wanted to know. "I ought to kick your bum for vanishing on us like that."

"I thought I was following Jurji and his friends, only it was Pearl and Jupp with him. They disguised themselves as Dogs—must've taken tunics off the ones on the floor. Didn't Ersken tell you?" I asked as Ersken gave me a turnover stuffed with lamb.

"I told her," Ersken said ruefully. "Then she boxed my ear and called me a curst stupid scut. I didn't even know she liked me."

I patted him on the shoulder and looked at Goodwin. "While you were all sorting the hound teams, I heard Hanse yell. Slapper was attacking two Dogs who were leaving." I looked down. Magic drink or no, I was too weary to weep. "Jurji killed Slapper. We gave chase because I wanted to get Jurji. I only found out a little while ago that one of the false Dogs was Pearl."

I looked at Achoo. She was slurping down a bowl of water while Nestor grinned at me. "That's a good hound you've got there," he said, "but I'm thinking it's her mistress that's the true bloodhound. And I'm curst glad Goodwin had that Dog tag, or we might never have found you."

Goodwin held hers up. "I told you they work," she said. "Nearabout drove us mad when the Dog tag showed we were right on top of you, until we worked it out that you must be underground."

I looked around. We stood in an empty warehouse—long empty, from the boot tracks in the dust on the floor. Someone had set torches in the wall cressets. Three sets of footprints led out from the doorway that I had used, doubtless those belonging to Pearl and Jurji. I don't know how Pearl met with a third person, but I'd wager it was the killer Zolaika. Four more sets of footprints entered the place—that would be Goodwin, Nestor, Birch, and Ersken. I looked to the door they had used as entrance and Pearl as exit.

Achoo barked. She needed to go. *We* needed to go.

"Sorry, sorry," I told her. I gobbled the turnover that Ersken had given me. Goodwin went behind me to straighten my pack.

Nestor checked the lantern and blew it out. "Low on oil," he said. "We'll stick with torches for now."

The others all waited, their eyes on me. Finally Nestor smiled. "Cooper, you've got the scent hound. We're your squad. You have to issue the orders."

Mithros's spear. Three Senior Dogs and one of my year mates, yet they waited for my order. I took that pearl tooth from my pocket and held it for Achoo. She sniffed it all over and sneezed heartily thrice. We'd moved away from the tunnel door so we wouldn't stir up the footprints cast by Pearl and her companions needlessly. Now Achoo cast briefly over them, barked softly, and trotted toward the door to the outer world.

"Yes, Your Majesty," I said, running up to open the door. "A pity you need me for this."

We set off down the street outside the door. The air was thick with fog, muffling our footsteps. Achoo led us toward the harbor, her legs picking up speed. We trotted with her.

The city was as quiet as I've ever seen it, save for the fog bells singing from the harbor. The fog wrapped all of us around, making us draw closer so we might see each other clear. Those folk who were on the street rushed by on their errands, shrinking away from so many Dogs in a clump. When the clocks struck the fifth hour, I started at the sudden loud noise.

We were three blocks from the waterfront when Achoo halted at the kitchen entrance of a drinking den. She looked at me, but she made no sound. Her quarry was inside.

I needed to make sure. Birch hand-signaled that he and Ersken would stay on the kitchen door. Goodwin, Nestor, and I went around to the front of the place to see if Achoo picked up the scent again. She circled in front of the door, snuffling, then ran back to the rear. Goodwin and Nestor stayed in front as I followed her.

When I got to the kitchen door, Birch and Ersken settled their weapons and gear as I did. Then they looked to me for the signal.

"Achoo, *tumit,*" I said. I opened the kitchen door and we walked in, my two fellow Dogs behind us.

The smells of supper met our noses, and my belly growled. A hard-worked cook turned from her hearth to glare at me. "Here, you, this ain't no walkway! Just you back on out—" Then she saw my companions and my hound, and the finger I'd put on my lips. The maids were shrinking from us, eyes wide. Their mistress was made of sterner stuff. She slapped Birch's hand when he reached for a pasty and pointed the way to the front room.

Birch bowed. He signaled that the maids and the cook were to stand with their faces to the rear wall. He and Ersken bound their hands and mouths with strips of the muslin they used to steam puddings, then tied all three of them together by binding each pair of hands to the other. They could escape, but it would be difficult. They'd know soon enough it was easier to wait for someone to come and untie them. It was safer for us and them. We didn't know if they were Pearl's allies, and this way Pearl's friends would know they had not helped us.

Then we entered the front room. It was a tidy place, with tables and benches for common drinkers, a tap just to my right, and curtained booths along the wall past the tap. The stairs to the upper story were on my left. Only two booths had the curtains drawn. Did they hide folk having private suppers, or a captain doing business with a runaway Rogue?

I saw all this in the blink of an eye as I darted at the barkeep and put my baton up close to his throat. He knew I would crush his windpipe if he made any sound. Two sailor coves and a doxie were eating and dicing at a table near the stairs. They started to rise, but Birch shook his head at them. Ersken tied their wrists with their sashes or belts as Birch opened the front door to Nestor and Goodwin.

We heard a slight creak of wood. Achoo barked. Jurji leaped down the stairs and hacked at Ersken. He might have cut him in two had Achoo's warning not caused Ersken to whirl around as Jurji hit the bottom of the stairs. That turn saved Ersken from the sweep of Jurji's sword, though it did not save the cove whose mouth Ersken had been gagging. Jurji's sword cut deep into his shoulder, slashing a great vein. He screamed through the gag.

Ersken grabbed Jurji's sword arm and hooked one of his legs from under him, throwing Jurji onto his back. That was all I could see. I was binding the barkeep's hands while Birch, Nestor, and Goodwin went for the curtained booths. I made the barkeep lie down behind his bar as I roughly bound his ankles with his own cleaning cloths. I heard fighting on the other side of the bar and I was terrified my friends were getting hurt. At last I stepped out of that small space and looked into the room.

Jurji was trying to get to his feet, but Ersken had his sword arm up behind his back and would not let go. Jurji's longsword was still in the man he'd killed. Ersken had yanked him away from that poor cove before Jurji could free it. Then Ersken knelt on Jurji's legs, making sure Jurji couldn't move.

The curtains in both of the closed booths had been dragged from their rings. In one booth, two sailors had their hands in the air. Birch was tying the mot's hands. In the other booth, a cove in better clothes also had his hands in the air. "I'm an honest man!" he cried. He had a thick Barzun accent. "I am here to accept a passenger with a pass that will get me out of the harbor!"

Nestor and Goodwin stood off of the booth on either side

of a tall, gray-haired woman of Goodwin's age, dressed in a man's dark tunic and leggings. It was Pearl's doxie, Zolaika, without the mask of makeup, the wigs, and the fancy clothes she always wore. She was armed with knives in both hands. Her eyes, dark brown, were locked on Nestor, who was moving in on her with his baton. She'd already cut the left side of Goodwin's face from cheekbone to chin. The blood ran, but Goodwin didn't look as if she had noticed. She swung her baton sidelong, straight at Zolaika's shoulder.

Zolaika ducked the blow, but Nestor was waiting for it. He clubbed her arm with his baton. Bone cracked.

I did not see Pearl. I turned and glared at the barkeep. "Where is she? Where's Pearl Skinner?" He glared at me. I leaned down, grabbed his tunic in my fist, and pulled him up. "She's the reason half your silver is bad, you scut. Tell me, or I'll name you as her conspirator in colemongering."

He stared at me, then said, "She went to the privy."

Of all the idiot things to happen! "Where!" I demanded. It certainly wasn't by the kitchen entrance.

"Go right between here and the booths. There's a little hall, then the door t' the courtyard. Please don't give me the curse eye no more!" he babbled.

My eyes. It's always my eyes with folk.

I dropped him.

"Achoo, *kemari!*" I cried over the noise. She came to me as I clambered out from behind the bar. I put the tooth under her nose. She sneezed only lightly this time. Then she took off down the little hall I hadn't even seen yet, being that it was tucked back near the last of the curtained booths and the wall of the bar. She pawed at the narrow door, whining. I settled my baton in my hand, said, *"Tumit,"* and kicked the door open. The fog lay outside.

The privy doors in the stinking courtyard outside were open. No sign of Pearl. The gate on the opposite side of the yard swung wide, too.

"Achoo, *mencari*!" I whispered. Achoo went for the open gate. I followed.

The drink was ebbing from my veins, but something else was helping me along. I was close. The gate had still been swinging when I passed through it. Where could she go? Her last two loyal people were doing battle with my fellow Dogs. No one would shelter her. And I had Achoo.

Achoo knew our quarry was close, too. She led me down the block. I followed her into a stable, dodging the bites of sleepy horses. There was a door in the rear of the stable. We passed through that into an old courtyard.

At its center a grate lay beside an opening in the ground. Achoo stopped at it and whined. Her prey was in that hole.

"Pox," I whispered as I peered inside. Iron rungs led down into the dark. I ran back to the stable and stole a lantern. I left a gold coin in its place. It was all I had left, and Pearl had probably stolen a lantern, too. I waited to light the lantern with my flint and steel until I was outside again. Beside the hole with Achoo, I cut the tunics I'd been carrying in my pack, tying them into a rough sling.

"First the light, and then the hound," I told myself. I climbed down. It wasn't far. I set the lantern on a ledge, then went back for Achoo. When I settled her in the sling, she gave me a look that told me she had decided she would do any mad thing I asked, even though it might be *truly* mad. I scratched her ears and carefully fitted us both through that hole in the ground.

The moment she set foot on the ledge, she found the scent. She trotted quickly, all business, following each turn that Pearl made off that branch of sewers. A four-legged rat came at Achoo and squealed. Achoo snapped at it and trotted on while it dodged. It ran around me while I stood against the wall. I'm not afraid of animal rats as some folk are, but I've been bitten twice in the last year. I won't pay a healer mage for cleansing again if I can help it. Two more such rats came, and then more. What was the matter with the curst beasts? Was it Pearl that frightened them so?

It was when I heard splashing that my tired mind remembered something important. Something Pearl forgot, something I forgot, but something these smaller rats knew very well.

The tide was coming in.

I looked at the sewer. The water had risen almost to the ledge where we walked. Pearl must be closer to the harbor ahead, to be splashing.

"Achoo, *cepat*!" I whispered. Achoo picked up speed. I too moved faster, fear being a wonderful spur. Somehow the rats who were left ran through Achoo's feet and around me. There were less of them now. Most had found safety already, I guessed. For a brief, mad moment I wondered if Dale would like me now, dirty, weary, and wading in scummer. I'd need a daylong soak in a bathhouse before I'd feel fit to bed him again. I shook my head and forced myself to think of my quarry.

Pearl was not stopping. Her splashes ahead were louder, as if she floundered in deeper water. The flow was now up to my shins. Wavelets pushed at Achoo. The water was up to *her* chest. When the tiny waves shoved her off her feet twice, I knew we had to do sommat. There was an entry to my right with a stair, not a ladder.

"Achoo, *kemari*!" I whispered. I ran up to the top. The door opened up into the floor of a small shed. I looked outside that into a courtyard.

Achoo slunk behind me, whining. The scent was down below. She didn't want to leave, the silly beast. I took her leash from my pack and fastened it first to her collar, then to the latch of the door to the sewer, on the outside. *"Tunggu,"* I told her as she complained. "Dear one, you'll *drown. Tunggu!"*

I was crying as I ran back down the steps, Achoo's barks growing dim behind me. She'd earned the right to be in at the last, and I had betrayed her.

At the foot of the stair, I was unnerved to see the water now lapped the first step. I was even more unnerved to see that Goodwin waited for me there. The slash on her face was still bleeding, and the top of the ear on that side of her face was cut off. Once again she had the Dog tag in her hand. I was so relieved I almost kissed her.

"Gods be thanked for those tags," I murmured instead, keeping my voice down. I didn't want Pearl to hear.

"*Now* what is your excuse for running off?" she demanded in a whisper, glaring at me. "Tell me a god took you, because that's the only thing I'll accept!"

"All of you were fighting," I told her quietly. "I thought Pearl had just run out to the privy and I could snag her! But she kept going—"

Goodwin put a hand on my shoulder. "So should we. Later we'll talk about you leaving partners, girl. Now, look at the wall, at shoulder height."

I looked where she pointed. Some thoughtful soul had fixed a series of metal handholds there. If the water got too deep, me and Goodwin could hold on to one and not be swept away. I can swim, but I don't know if I'm strong enough to fight the tide.

"Gods all bless whoever did that," I told her. She grinned and motioned for me to take the lead. I nodded and plowed back into the vile water, which now came as high as my knees. It felt stronger, with more power behind the wavelets. Soon we could hear Pearl splashing along.

We pushed ahead as hard and fast as we could manage. Even when the most dreadful kind of trash brushed past us we said naught, straining to hear Pearl ahead. The water was up to my ribs when I saw her at the edge of my lantern's light, clinging to a handhold. She had lost her own lantern. With her free hand she fought to push away a mess of kelp, pieces of wood, dead animals, and whatever else had flowed in.

Unlike me, Pearl didn't have that drink to keep her strength up. She looked half dead.

I tried to draw closer to her. The waves were stronger. Twice my feet went out from under me. Goodwin hung on to a grip and caught me with her free hand, while I thanked the maker of those handgrips a dozen times for my own near misses.

A swell of water yanked Pearl from a grip and pulled her under. She surfaced with a scream and scrabbled at the wall until she seized a handhold by pure accident.

"Pearl Skinner, we arrest you in the King's name!" I cried.

"Not so *very* ambitious," I heard Goodwin mutter at my back.

I saw a niche higher up in the wall. I bounced down low and let the water help me to leap high, so I might set the lantern there. I sank down into the water again, wincing as some manner of trash tangled around my feet.

"Give up, Pearl! You can't fight us *and* the sea!"

"Pox rot you and all gutter-bred *bitches*!" she screamed. "I should have *gutted* you!"

"Wait a moment," I heard Goodwin say. She wrapped her

arms around me from behind, then let go. I felt something tug at my waist and reached to feel as she fumbled at my back. Goodwin always carried a hank of thin, strong rope in her pack. She had tied a loop of it around me.

"Go," she said.

Pearl was but ten feet away. She had turned to face us. I pushed myself forward off the wall, diving across the water's surface for the length of several grips. I grabbed on to one. Then I launched myself forward a second time. I had my free hand, the one that didn't grip the wall, under the water, where Pearl couldn't see I held a knife.

"Hands up," I said, bobbing in that curst water. Here the waves were swells. Shadows lay everywhere around us with the lantern half hid in its niche. "You're going back to Corus to face your trial." I risked a glance back. Goodwin was coming forward more slowly, passing the end of the rope through two handgrips and tying it off.

Pearl shoved herself off the wall and came at me, darting across the water. She had knives in both hands. I learned that when I caught one knife on my dagger's hilt, and took the blade of her second knife along my right hip. It hurt like fire had chopped into my side. I jammed my free hand up under her chin and locked my legs around hers. Down we went into the deep water at the center of the tunnel, sinking. I twisted my knife hand around her arm, trapping it. Pearl shook and thrashed, trying to make me let go as the tide dragged on us. I could not see or hear what else was going on, but I could feel another force tugging Pearl back by her upper body, or mayhap her neck. Goodwin was in the fight, gods be thanked. Pearl was jerking her free arm, trying to stab Goodwin, I think. Their movement thrust me back until I hit the tunnel wall. I ground

Pearl's trapped hand against the stone until her fingers opened. She dropped that knife. The pull on her body stopped. Somehow she'd made Goodwin release her. I clung to her arm as I came up for air.

I'm a poor swimmer, or mayhap I could have stayed down longer. I unlocked my legs but still clung to Pearl as I kicked for the surface. A bad, ragged pain dug into the wrist I used to grip her arm. I beat on Pearl's head with my free hand as long as I could, but I'm no hero of old. A bite *hurts*. Mayhap someone like Callun the Dead Man or Lita Flyingstar could have held her, but they were not there with scummer bouncing off them and four-legged rats swimming by. I let Pearl go.

She came up a yard from Goodwin and me, gasping. In her open mouth I saw three pearl teeth were shattered. One other was missing, but that was the one I had in my pocket, I think. She had a newly swollen eye as well as a broken nose that Goodwin must have given her in the water.

"Bitches!" she cried. "All of you, even the coves! Slinking, bum-licking bitches for any noble with the coin!" The tide shoved her toward us. I lunged and seized her shirt, Goodwin her arm. Pearl slashed at us both, having drawn another blade. We let go as the tide thrust her deeper into the sewer.

She thrashed and tried to paddle now that she had knives with both hands. Her head went below the water. She came up again, choking. Now the water was rushing back toward the sea, pulling her into the center of the sewer pipe, out of reach.

"Better the sea than your poxy law!" she cried, and she went down again.

"None of that," I whispered. I dove out after her. She would face her trial.

Somehow in that muck I found her and her knives. She cut me several times, light slices. I got behind her and wrapped my arm around her neck, settling her chin in the crook of my elbow. Now she could not bite. I shoved us up to the surface, where I choked her until she dropped the blades. And Goodwin reeled us in with the rope she'd tied around my waist.

We didn't really take Pearl from the water. Goodwin swiftly bound her arms behind her, working underwater, a skill I should practice. Then she untied the rope from the handgrips, and looped it around the bindings on Pearl's arms so there would be two ends to hold. Goodwin took one end and I the other. Those we tied around our waists. We went back up the sewer that way, towing the cursing and gasping Pearl along as we went from handgrip to handgrip. Goodwin retrieved the lantern from its niche when we reached it. It kept the rats at bay.

It seemed to take forever to find the stairs where I'd left Achoo. I knew they were the right stairs because there sat Achoo, looking at me as if I'd just killed her pups. She was covered in mud and dragging part of her leash. The free end was well chewed.

I blinked at her stupidly. "You're a mess," I said as we halted there. "What have you been doing, wallowing in street muck?"

Pearl struggled to her feet. I looked at Goodwin to see what her orders were. Let Pearl stand, or shove her into the middle of the sewer, where she would float? She seemed harmless enough, swaying on her feet from exhaustion, but she *had* gotten rich from her work as a liar.

"Keep an eye on our friend here," Goodwin ordered me. I kept my knife to Pearl's throat as Goodwin hobbled Pearl's ankles. She could walk in small, shuffling steps, but that was all.

Goodwin looked at Achoo and the steps, then at me. "I think you'll find a hole dug under the door up above. That and her being soaked from coming down here explains Achoo's state. I don't know what explains *yours,* Cooper. What's this?" She reached down and poked my hip. That was when I screamed and fell to one knee on the ledge, in the water. My vision went all white. I dug my fingernails into my hands until it came back, slowly.

"*Idiot* Pup," Goodwin muttered. She got an arm under one of mine and helped me higher up the stairs to one that was dry. Then she went back and tied Pearl to a grip in the stone, after testing it to make certain that she could not break free. I wanted to study the knots she tied, but my head was spinning by then, and throbbing.

Goodwin climbed back to me and set the lantern down. Then she took off her tunic and folded it in a square. All she wore beneath it was her breast band and hidden knife sheaths. "There's no help for it. All we have is soaked in scummer. Put this on your hip and hold it there to stop the bleeding." She helped me do as she'd ordered. "Why did you say nothing about being wounded?"

I blinked at her. "I was busy. You're wounded, too." I pointed at her arm.

"I'm going for help. Do *not* die on me, Cooper. Do you understand? Do *not* die. Promise me."

She seemed very intent, so I promised. Then she left us there.

"Let me go, Cooper," Pearl said. "You ever seen some'un boiled in oil? You'll never forget the stink. I'll make you rich, you set me free."

I tried to find a comfortable position for my hip. I wanted to puke. Achoo came and sat beside me, so I was warmer, at least. "Would you?" I asked while my teeth chattered. I was so very cold. "Will you do the same for all them that got the Drink when your filchers gave them purses full of coles? The poor loobies got caught passing them, but you meant them to, so I think you owe them."

"Cork it," she snapped.

I kept talking. "There's naught you *can* do for Hanse and Steen and their caravan. They're all dead. No more can you make it up to any of the folk killed back in Corus at the Bread Riot."

"They'd have served me the same, given the chance," she told me. "So would you."

"You're a wicked, vicious mot, and I will be there when you die."

I think I said it.

Friday, September 21, 247

Guards House
written Sunday, September 23rd
Goodwin and Pearl and I slept while mages worked on us. A scummer bath will kill someone that's all cut up unless Lord Gershom pours coin into mages' hands, saying, "Don't you let them die."

So I was told, anyway.

Saturday, September 22, 247

I slept while mages worked still more on Goodwin and me.

Sunday, September 23, 247

Goodwin and I slept most of the day, though Goodwin says she was up by afternoon.

Sunday, September 23, 247

Guards House
Near midnight.
I wasn't awake for three-odd days. Mage healing, losing blood, all of that.

When I did wake, I was in a small bedchamber on a bed with curtains drawn on one side. I saw wax candles burning wastefully on the window ledge, a fire in the hearth, and more wasteful still, a brazier next to my bed, burning something that smelled lovely and expensive. I tried to sit up, but that required more strength than I seemed to have.

"Easy there, Mistress Bloodhound." The voice came from behind the curtain. Lord Gershom drew it back. Over his shoulder as he helped me to sit I saw that there was a writing desk near the other window. He too had wax candles to work by. Outside the windows—all glass!—the day was gray and rainy.

As he settled my pillows to keep me upright, I drew lines on my coverlet with my thumbnail. "My lord, it isn't fitting that you do these things for me."

"Well, I'm here. We can't hardly talk with you flopping on your back." There was a pitcher and a cup on a table beside the bed. He filled the cup, then helped me to hold it as I drank. It was barley water with something tangy, mayhap lemon, in it. Then he drew a chair to my bedside and sat there.

"First, you're in Guards House," he told me. "Goodwin's here, too. Not everyone in this cursed cesspool of a city believes that their Rogue was behind the colemongering. They believe you and Goodwin hung the evidence on her."

I took a breath, about to protest, but my lord held up his hand. "It keeps them from blaming Nestor, Axman, and the other local Dogs, so you'll forgive me if I don't rush to try and change their minds. I'm not certain that I could. You two will come home with me as soon as you're able, and we'll make certain you don't return to Port Caynn for a long time. Understand, Beka?"

I didn't like it, but I understood it. "Yes, my lord." Briefly I wondered what would become of Dale and me, but I had no time to worry the problem now. My lord had more to say.

He patted my arm. "Good. Third, we had to get mages in to heal both of you and Pearl. Your wounds were poisoned, from her weapons or the filth down below, we can't say. But that's why you're so weak. They had to do something much like burning you out, top to toe."

Clumsy, Pounce commented as he jumped onto the coverlet. *But it did save your life.*

My lord raised his eyebrows at Pounce. "Your friend here almost got mage-scorched. He commented freely as the mages worked. I still don't know why he didn't heal you himself."

Pounce sniffed and came to curl up on my belly. *It is not permitted,* he said at last. My hands shook as I petted him. I don't think it was all from being weak, but I was not about to get sloppy with him in front of my lord.

"Then don't quibble with those who *can* do it, that's my advice," my lord told him. "Next time I'll let them scorch you."

"Goodwin's ear?" I asked. "Someone cut the top off it."

"The mages cannot create flesh to replace what was lost," my lord explained. "She says she doesn't mind. Now. Where was I? Fourth. Pearl and her fellow conspirators are on their way to Corus for trial. I say no reason to keep her in a bed here when she could recover just as well in Outwalls Prison. Her trial will begin as soon as you and Goodwin can give evidence. Fifth. Goodwin says to tell you that the Finers are home, and very angry they are. I believe the King will permit them to appoint the new officials of the Silversmith's Guild."

I stared at Lord Gershom. He grinned like an old wolf over a fresh kill. "Oh, yes. There will be changes here, and trials. Quiet ones, but the Goldsmith's Guild and the Silversmith's Guild have much to answer for."

"Sir Lionel?" I asked.

"In Corus, meeting with the Lord High Magistrate." Lord Gershom rubbed his eyes with his thumb and forefinger. "You know how things are, Beka. He belongs to one of the most powerful families in the realm, and the King's brother is his father-in-law. He will never hold another Crown position, and he will never leave his family's holdings again. Knowing his father, I think there will be all manner of humiliations there, but they will be private ones."

Lord Gershom inspected some old knife scars on my hand. "It will be a hard winter, Beka, but it could have been far worse. There are King's Awards waiting for you, Goodwin, Nestor, and Sergeant Axman, and commendations for all the Dogs who took part in this."

King's Awards. I sank back in my pillows. It was a medal—a medal, and a purse. Only a handful of Dogs ever got them. And the only reason I was in a position to get one was because Tunstall got his legs broken.

"Achoo?" I asked, starting up from my bed.

"She is quite well and on a walk at the moment," my lord said. "Pounce has been able to keep her from worrying too much. All you need do is heal. Then we can go home." He took both of my hands in his firm grip. "Mithros bless us, I knew that Goodwin and you are good, but you went so far beyond what I expected, and so quickly!"

I shook my head. "I know, my lord, but much of it was the

gods' own luck. Surely Goodwin is saying the same. Look how some coves we met in a riot were gamblers and connected to Port Caynn's Rogue—no, Hanse was even at the heart of the ring, providing the silver and encouraging her to do her worst. Goodwin's tie to Master Finer goes back years. It was all luck, and her guiding us to stay with Hanse and his friends, and connect the right links to make the chain."

My lord grinned. "She says it in nearly those same words, though she gives you more credit. But I tell both of you this. It took two of the cleverest Dogs in Corus to connect those links. You did it before disaster came not only to us, but to the Yamani Islands."

I stared at him, and he smoothed his mustache. "We took the ship she planned to use for her escape, once we had Jurji and Zolaika to question. Pearl's colesmith and his people were aboard already, with stamps for Yamani coins."

I made the Sign on my chest.

"Undersell what you have done if you must, and I know you will," Lord Gershom told me. "But you and Goodwin did far better here than even I expected, and I will not be forgetting it."

I smiled sleepily at him. "I have the very best of teachers, my lord." I might not have spoken so boldly, had I not been getting tired all over again. "I started with you, didn't I?" I fear very much that I went to sleep before his eyes.

When I woke again, it was dark outside the windows. Fresh candles burned on the desk, but my lord had capped the inkstand and put the papers away. That always meant he had finished for the night.

On the table beside my bed was a bowl of soup, the pitcher of barley water and my cup, and two soft rolls. I was strong enough both to sit up and to eat for myself. I even used the chamber pot tucked behind a screen. Seemingly I hadn't needed one before. Mage healings always dry me out.

Pounce watched me from the foot of the bed, where he and a freshly bathed and combed Achoo lay. *You won't limp for long,* he said. *The wound on your hip was the worst. Once it is healed completely, you will walk normally. It will give you pain now and then, though. The cut was a deep one.*

"Achoo, *kemari,*" I said. She scrambled up the bed to flop down beside me. Right away she began to wash my face.

"We managed without you," I told Pounce. "Achoo better than me, but we managed."

Did you doubt it? Pounce asked. *I did not.*

"I wish you could have chosen a quieter time for the lesson," I grumbled. "One of those long winter freezes, say, when no one goes out and nothing happens."

Pounce walked up and rubbed his face against my hand. *I wish I could have chosen such a time, as well.*

"Has Dale Rowan left any messages for me?" I asked. I hoped that he had, though I looked less than lovely right now.

He has not, Pounce replied.

Mayhap he doesn't know where I am, I thought. Or the bank sent him off for work. Or he heard about my jolly, ugly walk through the sewer.

"It's nothing," I told Pounce.

Liar, he said.

I got up again, to help myself to my lord's pen and ink and to find my journal in my pack. I thought it would be a sorry thing, soaked through and unreadable, but while it is much wrinkled, every word is there.

"Pounce?" I asked.

How will your descendants know what you have undergone without me? he asked, curling up by my pillow. *I could do that much for you.*

I kissed him on the head, which I know he hates, and began to write about Thursday the twentieth.

Monday, September 24, 247

Guards House

Two of the clock in the afternoon.

Goodwin found me as I had fallen asleep, with my journal, pen, and inkwell all around me. At least I'd had the wisdom to stopper the inkwell.

I woke to Achoo's "Whuff!" and Goodwin standing beside my bed, hands on hips. "Why didn't you put this aside, looby?" she asked, pointing to the things on the bed.

"I thought I'd just rest my eyes. I didn't know I was going to sleep," I explained. I struggled out from under the covers. "Can I take Achoo out? She must be fit to burst."

It was still raining, but light was coming in.

"I took her for a walk when I woke and again at noon," Goodwin said.

"Noon?" I squeaked.

She was not attending. "Cooper, I ought to break your skull and cook what's in it like an egg. Do you know how many things you did wrong? You *have* to remember your backup from the *beginning*, not trust that it will catch up to you! You're getting too old to forget!" Her heart wasn't in it, though. I could tell because she was petting Pounce.

I bowed my head. "Do you want to box my ears?" I asked meekly.

She gave me a light buffet on the shoulder. "I'm too stiff to box your ears. If you feel well enough, we have a cart and guards. We can go to Serenity's and pack. My lord says if we do, we will leave for home tomorrow."

I scrambled out of bed and looked for my things. Goodwin pointed. While I slept, someone had draped a clean uniform and underthings on a chair.

"Your old uniform is ruined," Goodwin told me as she carried Pounce over to the window by the desk. She stood with her back to me, looking outside as I dressed. "I went through the pockets, but—Beka, I'm sorry. Your fire opal cracked to pieces when it dried. Seemingly they do that if you get them wet."

I froze. I love that stone. It came from my first hunt. But what could I do, or say?

These things happen as the gods will, Pounce remarked from his seat on the bed.

"I doubt the gods were watching our frolic in the sewer," I replied.

"Don't blaspheme, Cooper," Goodwin told me. "I found a little pouch and set the pieces in that. It's in your pocket." She leaned her forehead against the windowpane. "I have to say, I'm feeling like that stone. I didn't even get to see Tom when I got to Corus."

"I'm sorry, Goodwin. I know you were missing him," I told her. She was showing a softer side to me. I didn't understand why, but I felt as if I should do something. I walked over and put a hand on her shoulder.

She covered my hand with hers. "We've seen a thing or two, Cooper." Her voice was quiet. "Older Dogs call a time like this a hard season. I've had too many of them."

Goodwin patted my hand and let hers drop. I took that as a signal to take mine away. We stood there a moment yet, until the sight of a flock of pigeons wheeling across the sky made my eyes burn.

"Jurji killed Slapper," I said. Then I remembered that I'd told her before. "I brought him here to die."

"Slapper came here on his own," Goodwin told me. "He didn't want you going out of his sight. And speaking of going—"

She looked at the door. Achoo sat there, scratching at it lightly. "You take her this time, so finish dressing. I'll help you pack. I want to return home to my man."

I was tugging my boots on when Goodwin said abruptly, "You did good Dog work, those days I was gone. Nestor told me. I'm proud of you."

I could feel myself turning red. "I only did as I figured you would have done," I replied.

"That makes me prouder yet. Enough sentiment, now. Take your hound out."

"Achoo, *tumit*," I called. We trotted outside, Achoo leading me to the proper door to the open air. "Who's in charge, eh?" I asked her as we returned.

I will not fill in the little here-and-there details of Achoo doing the necessary in the gutter, or of our return to Serenity's. I packed half of my things. I took a halt to rest and used it to inspect the contents of the bag where Goodwin had placed what she'd found in my pockets. One of the pieces made me go all over goose bumps. Had Goodwin looked closely at them? Did she know among the shards of fire opal was Pearl's magicked tooth?

I stared at it for quite some time. Then I stowed pieces and tooth in the little bag. They all marked lessons in my life. I didn't want to forget them. After, because I wanted sommat beautiful, I got my small jewel box and took out the bracelet and necklace given to me by Dale.

As if handling them had summoned him, a maid announced that he was here. If I wanted to see him, Serenity would allow him to come to my room. The mot laughed as I hurried to make myself presentable. She helped me to brush out my hair. Then she went to send him up to me.

For a long moment he stood inside my open door, his hands clasped behind him, gazing at me as I sat on the bed. I didn't know what to say. I felt as if the shadows of sewer filth lay all over my skin.

At last he came over and kissed me. His mouth lingered only for a moment. The touch of his hand on my cheek was cool. He smiled, then took a chair as Achoo danced over to him. "You've made quite the mark on our poor little town," he said, his voice teasing. "I heard you arrested the Rogue single-handed!"

I waved that off. "You shouldn't believe all you hear. More than a hundred of us was in it."

"Still, even being part of it is quite the feat for a young Dog, isn't it, Achoo?" She leaned against him so he could scratch her ears. He looked up at me as he did so, his eyes bright and questioning. They are wonderful eyes. "Nestor says his Dogs have a nickname for you now. Bloodhound."

I shook my head. "That's just folly."

He noticed Pounce sitting on the bed next to me. "Who's this? You never mentioned a cat. Here, puss." He held out his fingers. Pounce looked at him, then away. It was a deliberate snub.

"Is she shy?" Dale asked me. "Whenever did you have time to get a cat?" He seemed like his usual friendly self, but it wasn't quite right. He was *chatting*. I don't like *chatting*.

"Pounce has been with me for years." I glanced at Pounce, who still would not look at Dale. "He just doesn't know you."

Dale saw my open trunk. "So you're returning to Corus?"

I nodded. "Me and Goodwin, we're done here."

"You learned all you were supposed to?" Dale asked, smiling at me. "The Pells have promised to leave you be?"

I laughed. I'd near forgotten the reasons we'd told

everyone why we were in Port Caynn. "The Pells are done, and we learned plenty," I said. "We're curst stuffed with learning." I looked at my hands. "So, what will you do now? I hear that there'll be some ruction with the masters of your guild."

"Oh, the Crown magistrates are all over them, going through the books and money boxes. That's naught to do with me." Dale shrugged. "They questioned us couriers under truth spell three days ago, to see if we knew anything. The ones who passed, we're still doing guild business."

That startled me. "But if the Crown is looking into the guild's affairs, how *can* they do business?"

"Honest gold and honest letters of credit still have to move, Beka," he said, as if I were a slow student at my lessons. "I'm off to Port Legann tomorrow with a full pouch."

"Oh." I don't know why I was disappointed. After all, I was going to Corus. The someday I had pushed from my thoughts before had come. Mayhap we could go to his rooms tonight—save I was tiring again, and it would be a long walk there and back. "Do you think, when your work brings you Corus way, you might visit?" I asked. "I'd like that."

Dale looked rueful and sweet at the same time. "Beka, we enjoyed ourselves, didn't we?"

"Yes, of course," I said. It was the sewer, then.

"Then let's leave it at that. Let's not stretch it out. I've tried to see a friend when she is one place and I am at another." He reached out and took my hand. "Sooner or later it goes bad. I'd prefer our memories to be all happiness, wouldn't you?"

I said naught. I couldn't. Mayhap it wasn't the sewer, after all.

Dale frowned and released my hand. "I made you no promises, did I? We never swore undying—"

I cut him off before our talk *did* turn sad or ugly. "No, it's all right. I'm still weary from my last days of, of learning, and I'm slow to follow."

"We are friends, then?" Dale asked me, his eyes worried.

I could even muster a smile. "We are friends, still."

Dale rose, came to me, and kissed my cheek. "Gods go with you, Beka, wherever you may be."

"And with you," I said, feeling his lips on my skin for the last time. He turned and left me. Tears fell down my cheeks. I knew, because Achoo jumped on the bed to lick them off.

You let him off easy, Pounce said.

"I have my pride," I snapped. "I won't beg."

It's just as well, Pounce remarked, curling up on my pillow. *You're going to be busy. No time for boy-men and their games.*

I wanted to say sommat bitter in return, to say it was so much easier when you're a god-cat. Instead I took Achoo down to the garden. We sat by the stream for a while. After much thought, I tossed Pearl's tooth to the sprite that Goodwin says lives in it. I don't need that kind of reminder with me.

I hate it when coves say, "We'll be friends," then go. Still, how *would* we have managed? Him in Port Caynn, when he is home, me in Corus. Him wanting someone to be his luck at games, me being on duty when he begins to play and weary and cross, like as not, after my watch. And he had yet to be in my bed the nights I woke, screaming or sweating, from some dark dream of Rats, blood, and death.

But I had liked him. He made me laugh. He made me feel grand.

I closed my door and finished packing. I was trying to force myself to go down to the dining room when someone thumped on the door. Ersken stood there with a tray of food. "Goodwin said you might not want to come to supper," he said with a smile. "She and Birch and Serenity are arguing about something the King did ten years ago. Take pity on me."

So Pounce, Achoo, and I took our meal with Ersken, and carried our leavings down to the kitchen, and went for a walk. Ersken caught me up on more news from Corus. The Dancing Dove was open for business. Rosto had moved there already. Tunstall continued to loathe being kept abed, to the point that he enjoyed the paperwork that Ahuda sent for him to do. Aniki had bought a new sword of which she was amazingly proud, and Kora was suggesting that she and Ersken buy a house.

After Ersken took his leave, I finished writing in my journal all the events that led up to Goodwin and me towing a hobbled Pearl through the sewers. I even caught up the details of the last two days. The record is there, for when I write my official report.

By the time I went to bed, the ache over Dale was less, truly. I was going home.

Tuesday, September 25, 247

Home

Nine of the clock at night.

The trip downriver with my lord was quicker than ours was to Port Caynn. My lord had a royal courier's ship, manned by rowing sailors of the navy. All of us Corus Dogs traveled with him. My lord felt that Port Caynn law should now be left to the thinned ranks of the Port Caynn Dogs and the army. They would also have the army for two years more, while the trainee Dogs of Corus and Blue Harbor alike would go there to help fill their ranks again. All that was needed yet was a new Deputy Provost. Sir Tullus and my lord argued about it through most of the trip. Sir Tullus did not want the post, while my lord insisted no one else would manage the work so well.

"Couldn't you show Sir Tullus your eyes and convince him the gods want him to do it?" I asked Pounce as we lazed in the sun. Achoo was curled up beside me, keeping my mended hip warm.

I will not, Pounce said. *I have interfered in enough other lives of late, Beka.*

"Those stars you were seeing to," I said.

Those very stars.

"But now you'll stay home?" I asked, trying not to sound as if I begged. "We'll go back to normal, all of us in our places?"

"Not exactly," Goodwin said, crouching down beside me. She spoke quietly. "I want you to know first of all, you and Tunstall. When I was home last, Ahuda said they want her for Evening Watch in Flash District. She won't do it unless she has a replacement. I'm going to take it."

I sat up, about to yelp, but she put her hand over my mouth.

"Cooper, *listen to me.* I'm getting tired. I've done street duty and hunts a long time. Wading through sewers after first-rank Rats doesn't get me excited like it did. I need to slow down. Desk Sergeant is perfect for me." Goodwin clapped me on the shoulder. "And you'll be a perfect partner for Tunstall. He'll look out for you, and you'll keep him out of trouble."

She left me with that—just went off and left me with the worst and best news of my life. The great Clary Goodwin was going to be a desk sergeant, and I was going to have a real partner. How am I supposed to feel about that? How am I supposed to feel about anything, anymore?

At the dock, my lord had carts waiting for Goodwin and me. They took us home. Ersken carried my things up to my room. I argued that I felt fine, but Ersken just ignored me. Pounce and Achoo immediately settled on the bed. I stretched out with them, only because my head ached a little, and woke to twilight and a knock on the door. Ersken was there, dressed in cityfolk clothes.

"I'm ordered to take you to the Dove for supper," he told me. "The easy way or the hard way, but you're to come with me." He grinned. "I love to say things like that. Don't I sound like a hard Dog?"

"You look as scary as a buttered muffin," I grumbled.

"Don't be that way. Have supper. You'll still be surly, but you'll be a more cheerful sort of surly," Ersken told me. "I'll take Achoo out, and you can change clothes."

I did as I was told. I was in my own room, with my own bed, where Pounce was curled. I sprinkled cracked corn on my window ledge, a funerary offering, mayhap, for Slapper. I put on a blue wool tunic and gray breeches, and my opal bracelet and necklace. It made me a little sad to look at them and think of Dale, but they were too beautiful to leave in my jewel box. By the time Ersken and Achoo returned, I'd even straightened my braid and had a sip of the medicine the healers had given me to drink twice a day for two weeks. It was to fight the lingering poisons in my body, they said. Goodwin had some just like it. I wonder if Pearl does?

Achoo and Pounce walked beside us as we crossed the street to the Dancing Dove. It was brightly lit within and without. The taproom was busy with folk who'd come with business for the Rogue or folk who simply wanted to please him. For a moment I halted on the threshold, seeing Pearl's courts.

"Beka?" Ersken asked, one hand under my elbow.

I shook my head. "Nothing. It's nothing." Pearl was going to be tried. I had won. I walked into the common room behind Ersken. As he led the way to the stair, I heard the crowd quiet a little. Pounce leaped onto my shoulder.

A cove spoke out. "That's the one I was tellin' yez about. The Bloodhound."

I turned and looked for the one that said it. He was a sailor, mayhap one of the oarsmen from my lord's ship. "Don't talk," I said, shaken. "Not until you know what you say." Achoo barked, as if she agreed.

Ersken and I trotted upstairs. The door to the dining room we had always used for breakfast was closed. I thought it was to keep out the noise from downstairs, and opened it wide.

"Welcome home!" them inside called. It was our breakfast company—Rosto, Aniki, Kora, Phelan, Tansy—but it was also Lady Sabine and Tunstall, Tunstall being on a reclining chair. It was my brothers and the sister who still spoke to me, Aunt Mya and her husband from Provost's House, and my Granny Fern. Goodwin and Tomlan were there, as were Jewel, Yoav, Birch,

Elmwood, and the rest of the Dogs who had been in Port Caynn.

I might have dove under the table, overwhelmed by the notice, until I saw that many were here for Goodwin as much as me. That made it easier to take. Achoo was glad for the attention, which came in the form of food.

I was halfway through my soup when Lady Sabine tapped my shoulder. "He's tired," she whispered. "He shouldn't have come, but try to keep him away. I think it did him good."

So Achoo, Pounce, and I went over to Tunstall. He had red patches high on his cheekbones. Pounce leaped onto his lap. "So, when are you on your feet again?" I asked. He looked wrung out.

"My lord sends a Crown mage to me tomorrow," he replied, stroking Pounce. "After that, they say another week. It seems Crown mages can heal a little better than the ones available to common Dogs."

Well, we *all* knew that.

Tunstall beckoned me to lean closer. "Goodwin gave you her news?" he asked.

I nodded.

"Are you fine with it? Maybe you want a partner who's not an old man who goes flat for stupid broken legs?" Tunstall asked. Achoo stood between him and me, wagging her tail so hard she beat us with it.

Stop that, Pounce ordered him. *It's undignified.* Lady Sabine hid a smile.

I agreed with Pounce. I glared at Tunstall. "Did you break your nob, too?" I asked.

"I've felt curst useless, knowing you two might be in trouble there," he explained.

"There's plenty more trouble to get into," I said, hiding my trembling hands in my pockets. Did he mean it? Did he really mean it? "I'm going to get into it without Goodwin. Don't make me get into it without you, too."

Tunstall sighed. "Oh, very well. But only because you disgraced yourself begging and pleading this way."

I looked him over. "You're lucky you're a feeble old man laid up in bed, or I'd kick your bum up between your ears."

You're both so adorable I feel a hair ball coming up, Pounce told us.

"Vexing cat. You're lucky I'm laid up yet, Cooper, after you went for a queen Rat without your partner," Tunstall replied. "Oh, yes, Mistress Know-It-All, I've heard about your latest fit of idiocy. I'll have none of that when *I'm* your partner. Agreed?"

"Agreed," I said. Achoo barked. She, too, agreed.

Tunstall tapped his fist on top of mine, then I tapped mine on top of his. We'd made a Dog's bargain of it.

The Provost's Guard

Founded: 127 H.E. by His Royal Majesty King Baird III of Tortall

First Lord Provost: Padraig of haMinch (127–143)

Use of the terms *Dog, Puppy, Growl, seek, kennel,* and related terms in the Guard became popular about fifty years after the founding of the Guard.

Four Watches
Day Watch: nine in the morning until five in the afternoon
Evening Watch: five in the afternoon until one in the morning
Night Watch: one in the morning until nine in the morning
Fourth Watch: covers each of the other three watches on their Court Days and off days

In most districts, the best of the guards are put on Day and Evening Watch, when there is the most activity on the streets. The slackers are given Night Watch, when the least amount of activity is going on. The only area that is different is the Lower City, where the Day Watch is less active as well. Evening Watch is busy there. So is Night Watch, but while no one will say so, the truth is that the criminals own the streets during Night Watch. The very worst guards have duty then. They are the ones who just don't care about the work, the ones who are regarded as expendable. Everyone knows it.

Districts

Corus's watch districts, interestingly, often (but not always) correspond to the way the Rogues divide the city for their own organization:

Highfields District
Prettybone District
Unicorn District
Palace District
Flash District
Upmarket District
Patten District
Temple District

The Lower City: Conditions are very different in the Lower City overall. Since it is the poorest area, the bribes are the lowest and so is the prestige. The casualty rate is the highest because it is the most violent part of the city. Most of the guards assigned there are regarded as not being bright or promising enough to make a good impression elsewhere. Even so, the elite guards of the Lower City are the most respected. They are also the toughest and the smartest.

Chain of Command

Lord Provost: governs the realm's districts
Deputy Provost: assists Lord Provost (one per region in Tortall)
Captain (District Commander)

Per District
Watch Commander
Watch Sergeant
Corporals (varies by district)

Senior Guards (varies by district)
Guards
Trainees

TRAINING

Formal training in 246: One year in school. There is no screening or testing to enter the training program. Trainees are simply required to pass the classes.

All guards are required to attend combat practice for their first four years of service.

WEAPONS AND LAW ENFORCEMENT

Primary weapon: Two-foot-long hardwood baton with lead core

Guards don't use swords: A sword is a killing weapon. The majority of reasons a guard uses a baton don't demand an intent to kill. Wielded properly, the baton can stop most swords. Also, swords require years of training for proper use, they are expensive and require extensive maintenance, and they can break just when they're most needed.

The law and bribery: Law enforcement is a loose affair, something that is still being created. A law-keeping force under the control of the national government is highly unusual. Most law-enforcement groups are formed and run by neighborhood associations, guilds, or individual cities, or they are part of the military. The members of the Provost's Guard, like such groups, have a great deal of discretion in whom they arrest, whether they take bribes, and whether they do the thing they have been bribed to do. Bribery is the standard way to ensure that the underpaid people who protect merchants remember individuals and, at times, overlook their behavior. (Too much of a history of taking bribes and not following through on them does get a guard killed. It is wise for a guard to do what he's bribed to do most of the time.)

Guards memorize the laws and rules they are taught in training. They learn the rest of their skills on the streets and from each other. Some guards are smarter than others. Some guards are more motivated than others. And they all make up police work as they go.

Cast of Characters

Rebakah Cooper (*Beka*) — first-year Provost's Guard (Dog), protégée of Lord Gershom of Haryse (the Lord Provost)

Pounce — normally a constellation called the Cat, Beka's advisor and friend for the last five years

Achoo Curlypaws — scent hound assigned to the Lower City Provost's Guard

AT PROVOST'S HOUSE

Gershom of Haryse — Lord Provost of Tortall, Beka's patron

Teodorie of Haryse — Gershom's lady, patroness of Beka's brothers and sisters

Diona, Lorine, Nilo, Willes — Beka's younger sisters and brothers, all training for work in noble houses

Mya Fane — Beka's foster aunt, cook at Provost's House

PROVOST'S DOGS AND ASSOCIATES IN CORUS

Sergeant Kebibi Ahuda — Desk Sergeant, Evening Watch, Jane Street kennel, the Lower City Guard District

Corporal Finian Karel — Desk Corporal, Evening Watch, Jane Street kennel, the Lower City Guard District

Sir Acton of Fenrigh — Watch Commander, Evening Watch, Jane Street kennel, the Lower City Guard District

Sir Vannic haMinch	District Commander, the Lower City Guard District
Sir Tullus of King's Reach	Magistrate, the Lower City Guard District
Master Sholto	Sir Tullus's personal healer and mage
Senior Corporal Nyler Jewel	most senior street Dog, the Lower City Evening Watch, Yoav's partner
Senior Guardswoman Osgyth Yoav	street Dog, Jewel's partner
Senior Guardsman Wulfric Birch	street Dog, Westover's partner
Ersken Westover	street Dog, first year, Beka's friend, Kora's lover
Corporal Guardswoman Clara Goodwin	Beka's partner and former training partner
Senior Guardsman Matthias Tunstall	Beka's partner and former training partner
Corporal Greengage	street Dog, Nightmarket duty, the Lower City
Guardsman Marks	street Dog, Nightmarket duty, the Lower City
Guardsman Tillyard	street Dog, Nightmarket duty, the Lower City
Senior Guardsman Elmwood	scent-hound handler, the Lower City
Guardsman Sillsbee	Beka's partner at start of *Bloodhound*, the Lower City
Guardsman Ercole Hempstead	scent-hound handler, the Lower City

The Court of the Rogue, Corus

Rosto, called the Piper	Rogue of Corus
Aniki Forfrysning	swordswoman, rusher, chieftain in the Court of the Rogue
Koramin Ingensra	mage, serves the Rogue, Ersken Westover's lover
Phelan Rapp	former Guardsman and scent-hound handler, now working for the Rogue

Residents of Corus

Tansy Lofts	Beka's oldest friend from their slum days, now a respectable wife, mother, and businesswoman
Herun Lofts	Tansy's husband
Joy Lofts	Tansy's daughter and Beka's godschild
Granny Fern Cooper	Beka's paternal grandmother
Philben Cooper	Beka's cousin on her father's side, a carter
Tomlan Goodwin	Clara Goodwin's easygoing husband, a master carpenter
Lady Sabine of Macayhill	Lady Knight, Tunstall's lover
Zia	Lady Sabine's serving girl
Raaashell	new dust spinner at Duke Gareth's fountain
Otho Urtiz	Player, famed minstrel
Ashmari	Otho Urtiz's slave
Garnett	quality baker in the Lower City
Geraint Pell	brother of Kevan, whom Beka arrested

| Madon Pell | brother of Kevan, whom Beka arrested |
| Marco | sailor on riverboat the *Green Mist* |

Provost's Personnel in Port Caynn

Sir Lionel of Trebond	knight, Deputy Provost, District of Port Caynn
Sergeant Terart Axman	desk sergeant at Guards House, hound breeder
Sergeant Nestor Haryse	cousin of Lord Gershom, Beka's first crush, a Day Watch Sergeant in Deep Harbor District, Okha Soyan's lover
Guardsman Enno	guard on duty at Guards House
Guardsman Ives	personal aide to Sir Lionel at Guards House
Anglesea	Guardsman on duty in the jail cells at Tradesmen's kennel, skilled at interrogation
Shales	Guardswoman on duty in the jail cells at Tradesmen's kennel, skilled at interrogation

Residents of Port Caynn

Dale Rowan	courier for the Goldsmith's Guild, met Beka in a riot
Hansevor (Hanse) Remy	owns a company of caravan security guards, former soldier in army, met Beka in a riot
Viel Sperling	friend of Fair Flory
Lowenna Boller	orange girl, friend of Fair Flory

Kevern Pye	caravan guard, works for Hanse
Amda Threadgill	caravan guard, works for Hanse
Austell Goff	caravan guard, works for Hanse
Erben Worts	caravan guard, works for Hanse
Wat Eavesbrook	caravan guard, works for Hanse
Amda Threadgill	caravan guard, works for Hanse
Alisoun Nails	courier at Goldsmith's Bank, knows Dale
Bermond Tapener	master clerk at Goldsmith's Bank, knows Dale
Jaco Quilty	journeyman smith, friend of Hanse
Hesserrr	dust spinner on Eagle Street
Isanz Finer	cranky master silversmith, old friend of Goodwin's
Wenna Finer	Isanz Finer's daughter
Meraud Finer	silversmith, Isanz Finer's great-granddaughter
Okha Soyan	popular male-dressed-as-female singer/entertainer, Nestor's lover
Truda	Nestor Haryse's house girl, Haden's sister, former street urchin
Haden	Nestor Haryse's house boy, Truda's brother, former street urchin
Usan	gem shop guard
Vorna	laundry maid, Aldis's mother
Aldis	missing toddler
Durant Elkes	brass merchant, caught passing coles
Serenity	supposedly retired priestess of the Goddess and proprietor of Ladyshearth Lodgings

Members of Port Caynn's Court of the Rogue

Pearl Skinner	Rogue in Port Caynn
Jurji	Bazhir swordsman, personal guard to the Rogue
Zolaika	Pearl Skinner's personal assassin
Torcall Jupp	an older sword fighter, one of Pearl Skinner's personal bodyguards
Flory, Fair	leader of city's orange sellers and flower girls, a powerful figure in the Court of the Rogue
Steen Bolter	one of Hanse's caravan guards, part of the Court of the Rogue, met Beka in a riot

GLOSSARY

afore: before
aught: anything
bardash: male homosexual
Birdie: informant
bordel: house of prostitution
buckler: round, plate-like shield
buffer: thief of cattle, sheep, goats, or horses
canoodling: sexual activity
cipher: shorthand method used by Dogs, with symbols for entire common words
Coffin: narrow cell with no windows or doors, only a long, well-like opening overhead; prisoners are often left in one and forgotten
cog: cheat
cole: false coin
colemonger: someone who makes or passes false coins
colesmith: counterfeiter
Common Eastern: language spoken in Tortall, Barzun, Tusaine, Maren, Tyra, Saraine, and Scanra
coney: victim of a theft or any crime; sucker
copper noble: coin equivalent to ten coppers
corbie: raven
countinghouse: room or building where a business does its accounting; chiefly used here for buildings where shipping firms do business and keep track of what is bought, sold, and traded
cove: man
cracknob: madman
craven: coward; cowardly
cresset: metal wall fixture containing wood or oil to be burned for light

cutter: braggart

Dog: member of the Provost's Guard

doxie: female prostitute

dozy: sluggish

elsewise: otherwise; or else

fambles: hands

fen-sucked: sucked out of a fen (swamp or marsh)

Ferrets: street nickname for Crown spies

filcher: small-time criminal

flower sellers: women of that trade who are also prostitutes and thieves

foist: master pickpocket

fribbety: silly, frivolous

gab: speech

get bit: be cheated

get in the way of: become; learn

gillyflowers: older name for carnations

gixie: girl

gob: mouth

gold bit: coin equivalent to one-quarter gold noble or two and a half silver nobles

gold noble: coin equivalent to ten silver nobles or four gold bits

Growl: sound made by a roomful of Dogs about to be released upon criminal prey

Happy Bag: weekly bribes for Provost's office

hedgecreeper: cheap prostitute

hedgewitch: small-time mage serving lower-class clients, usually deals in healing humans and animals, fertility charms/potions, small battle/annoyance spells

honeylove: lesbian

hunter: hound specially trained to hunt escaped prisoners and slaves

Hurdik: language of Tunstall's native hill tribes

jabbernob: chatterbox

kennel: Provost's watch house; police station

lift: theft of a purse

looby: fool

loose Dog: crooked Dog: one who exceeds the normal allowance of bribery

mammering: wavering; hesitating

Master: Mr.; mister

maul: heavy hammer with one wedge-shaped head

mayhap: perhaps

Mistress: Mrs.; ma'am

moneystream: flow of money as it passes through the hands of buyers, sellers, and bankers

moonsong: idiocy

mot: woman

mumper: beggar

murrain (MUHRenn): pestilence or plague, mainly affecting domestic animals

nab: arrest

nah: bread

Oinomi Wavewalker: goddess of the ocean; she is believed by some to come when named, like the Trickster and the Smith God

orange girls: walking fruit sellers who are also prostitutes and thieves

peck and cass: meat and cheese

piece: lowlife woman; dirty woman

pigsticker: big knife

pluck a rat: do something really stupid, such as try to pull feathers off a rat

Puppy: trainee in the Provost's Guard

puttock: low-level female prostitute

raka: native of the Copper Isles

Rat: captive, civilian, criminal, or prey (to Dogs)

rook: cheat

rusher: thug

sap: lead-filled six-inch leather cylinder with loop for wrist to be held in the hand; a knockout or bone-breaking weapon

sarden: blasted; damned; detestable

scale: fence (receiver of stolen goods)

scummer: animal dung

scut: idiot

seek: hunt down a criminal or missing person

sheeplings: Player slang: those who are born to be shorn of their money

Sign: the Sign against evil; an X intersected by a vertical line forming a star on the chest

silver/gold kiss: bribe

silver noble: coin equivalent to ten copper nobles

sing on: inform

slubbering: slobbering, licking, or lapping

spintry: male prostitute

swap _____ for _____: move up a grade as a Dog: for example, "swap leather [1-to-5-year insignia] for bronze [5-to-10-year insignia]"

swilled: drunk

swive: have sex

tarse: piece of meat

tosspot: drunkard

tread a measure: leave; take off

trencher: "plate" cut from a stale loaf of bread, used to hold food

trull: very low-class kind of woman; the dregs

twilsey: refreshing drink made from raspberry or cider vinegar and water

Achoo's Glossary

bangkit (bangKEET): up/rise

bau (bow, like *cow*): smell

berdiri (bareDEERee): stand straight

berhenti (buhrHEHNtee): stop

biarlah (beeAHRlah): let it go

cepat (SAYpaht): go fast

diamlah (deeAHMlah): quiet

dukduk (DOOKdook, like *bookbook*): sit

gampang (gamPANG): steady/easy

jaga (JAHgah): guard

kawan (kahWAHN): friend

kemari (kehMAHRee): come here

kulit (kooLEET): leash

lindengi (lIhnDEHNgee, with a hard *g*): protect

maji (MAHjee): go

makan (mahKAN): eat

memberi (mehmBAREee, like *bear*): give

mencari (mehnKAHRee): seek

mudah (MOOdah): easy

pelan (pehlAHN): slow

pengantar (pehnGANNtahr, *gann* like *can*): greet

tak (TAK, like *tack*): no

tinggal (tingGAHL): stay

tumit (tooMIHT): heel

tunggu (toonGOO): wait

turun (tooROON): down

Coming in 2011
from Random House,
the third title in the
Beka Cooper trilogy

Mastiff

For a sneak peek
of Beka's next adventure,
turn the page!

Now the Summer Palace appeared through the trees on my left, a long building with another open corridor on this side. There were balconies and turrets and it had originally been very pretty white stone. Now soot streaks marred nearly every window frame. Part of this wing had collapsed into the cellars. Some of the windows stood open to the air. Others sported a single shutter, or half-burned ones. Tatters of burned draperies and furniture had been thrust from the windows to lie haphazard below. A chill ran clean down my spine and up into my skull. This was fearful business.

Achoo whimpered and scrabbled against the ties that held her to the packhorse. Something was frightening her.

"Would you release her?" I called to the men of the King's Own. "She needs to get down." The younger one rode to Achoo's horse to do as I asked while I looked around.

Between the palace and our road were gardens. Mayhap they'd been pretty, too, but now that I eyed them, and smelled them, I did not think they could ever be pretty again. Bodies lay among the flowers. Here were the missing Palace Guards, men of the King's Own, and the Black God knew how many servants, all sword-hacked or stabbed.

Lord Gershom swore. "Tunstall?"

Tunstall rode up to the older of our companions. "How many people have ridden this track before us?" he asked.

Achoo jumped to the ground. She ran over to my horse, her tail between her legs. She was nearabout spooked out of her fur.

I'd begun to slip from my horse when the man's voice stopped me. "A large group rode over this place last night in the dark. All of us were in it. And it is not this for which you are called. Come."

"Not this?" Lord Gershom demanded, but he set his horse in motion. The mage and I followed. Tunstall fell in with me as we passed. We heard my lord mutter, "What in Mithros's name can be worse?"

That same question worried Tunstall and me, for certain. I could not read Master Farmer's face yet.

"Is this what you meant?" I asked Pounce in a whisper.

It's the beginning, he replied.

Master Farmer looked at me. "So your cat talks," he remarked, as easy as if he rode by dead folk every day. "Doesn't it unsettle you?"

Easy, Beka, Pounce said in my mind, when I would have given the mage a tart answer. *He's frightened, too, for all he doesn't act it.*

"He's talked to me for years," I replied. "I'm used to it."

"Oh, good," Farmer replied. "I wouldn't want you to put a good face on it for me."

We rode past the flower gardens, but the landscape of the dead continued. They had fought in the trees here. Tunstall pointed to the far side of our road. There were footprints on a wide path that led down toward the sea. I nodded. Had the enemy come from there, or had people tried to escape taking that path? If Tunstall, Achoo, and I were supposed to make sense of this raid, we were sadly overmatched. I'd put at least five pairs on sommat as big as this, and more than one mage.

Thinking of mages, wouldn't that seaward path be magicked to the hilt? Wouldn't that wall down below be magicked just the same? Royalty came here for the summer. Surely those in charge of keeping them safe wouldn't leave their protection to a couple of walls and some guards.

Now we reached the pretty open circle where their majesties' guests might leave their chairs, horses, or wagons.

This had been cleared of the dead. That there *had* been dead I was near certain from the splashes of blood on the ground. Men of the King's Own, all as grim as the others we had seen, took our horses. I called Achoo to heel—she was sniffing the bloody spots now that I was on the ground with her—and followed Tunstall, Master Farmer, and my lord inside.

Our guides did not come with us. Mayhap they did not want to face the soot-streaked, blood-splashed entry hall. We were turned over to a fleshy, white-haired cove who had mayhap been very well satisfied with his life a few days ago. Now I had to wonder if he would live out the month, for all that he wore a rich silk tunic and hose and a great gray pearl in one earlobe.

"Your people may wait in there, Gershom" was the first thing he said. He pointed to a side room well fitted with chairs and small tables. "You will come with me."

My lord gave us the nod and we did as we were told. The room had escaped both fire and murder. There were pretty mosaics bordering the walls at top and bottom, as well as inlaid at the window ledges. The shutters were well-carved cedar, open to the air outside. The chairs were beautifully carved, too, and made of cedarwood as well. I made note of it, because my friends would surely want to know what the inside of a palace, even a summer one, was like. There were silk cushions with silk tassels everywhere, even on the floor. Pounce went over to one and idly batted a tassel. Achoo showed no interest in the furnishings. She went to the open door and whined.

"*Kemari,* Achoo," I told her. "*Dukduk.*" She looked at me and hesitated. I pointed to a spot next to the chair I meant to take and repeated my commands.

"What language is that?" Master Farmer asked. "It sounds like Kyprish, but it's pretty mangled. Doesn't she respond to commands in Common?"

I'd placed his accent by the time he was done. He'd come from the roughest part of Whitethorn City, off east on the River Olorun.

Tunstall had listened to him with both eyebrows raised almost to his short hair. "Now, would you go about giving away all your mage secrets to some stranger who asked?" he wanted to know. "Cooper has secrets for the handling of a hound. It's the same thing."

I ducked my head to hide a grin and pretended to be tucking my breech leg more properly into my boot. Tunstall wanted to test the mage a little.

"What kind of mage are you?" he asked Master Farmer. "The scummer-don't-stink kind, or the pisses-wine kind?"

Master Farmer scratched his head. "The I-just-like-to-be-friendly kind, I think. Ma always told me I was the friendliest lad, just a help to everybody."

Tunstall advanced until he was but three inches from the mage. He was half a head taller than Master Farmer and heavier in the shoulders, chest, and legs. In his Dog uniform he was overpowering. "Don't expect that lovable lout game to play with us. We're Lower City Dogs from Corus. We've seen it all, we've heard it all, and we've hobbled it all. What kind of name is Farmer, anyway?"

Farmer grinned. He looked like a fool. "It's my mage name."

Tunstall was about to spit on the beautiful rug when I cleared my throat and glared. I don't care where he spits normally, but not in the palace. He coughed instead. "Mithros's spear, what kind of cracknob picks a mage name like Farmer?"

The mage shrugged. "All the others kept saying how I walked and talked like I had my feet in the furrows and my head in the hayloft. I thought maybe there was something powerful, them all thinking the same thing, so I took Farmer as a mage name." He looked at me. "I've been wondering lately, though, do you think mayhap they were making fun of me?"

I scratched Achoo's ears. I was thinking that he couldn't possibly be as crackbrained as he talked, or else why would Lord Gershom have summoned him?

Tunstall shrugged as if he were settling his tunic more comfortably on his shoulders and stepped back. "Don't ask us," he said. "We're city Dogs."

"I was a city lad, once," Farmer said cheerfully. "I never had pets. At home we ate them. In the City of the Gods we sacrificed them for our magic." He crouched next to Achoo and me. This close, he smelled a little of spices and fresh air. "Is that why you bring your pets along? So no one will eat them?"

Try to eat me and you will regret it for what remains of your short life, Pounce said. I couldn't tell if Farmer heard. I didn't think so, not when he didn't even blink.

Achoo was thumping her tail just a bit, telling me she wanted to make friends with the dozy jabbernob. Pounce sauntered over to him and looked up into his face. Master Farmer stared at him for a moment. Then he said, "Now there's a pretty set of eyes. You don't often see a purple-eyed cat wandering about loose." He held out a hand. Pounce sniffed it for a moment, then bit one of his fingers. "And that's a lesson to me," said the mage, grinning. "Have you a name, Ebon Cat of the Amethyst Eyes?"

"I don't know what that means, but his name is Pounce," I said, frowning at the cat. "And he's not normally so rude." To make up for Pounce's bad manners, I said, "Achoo is no pet. She's a scent hound, as much a member of the Provost's Guard as Tunstall or me. And she's got more years on the street than me, too. *Bau,* Achoo." Since Achoo kept wagging her tail as she smelled Master Farmer's fingers, I said reluctantly, *"Kawan."* He seemed harmless enough. Lord Gershom trusted him. That had to be enough for me.

Achoo had rolled over so Master Farmer could scratch her belly when the door opened. The most beautiful lady I'd ever seen came in. She had masses of brown curls that hung down to her waist. A few jeweled pins hung from them. Her maids were lax, letting her go about with her hair undone like that. She had large, golden brown eyes, a delicate nose, a soft mouth, and perfect skin. Her undertunic was white linen so fine it was almost sheer, her overtunic a light shade of amber with gold threads shot through it. Strips of gold embroidery were sewed to the front and the left side of the tunic, vines twining around signs for peace and fertility. Golden pearls hung from her ears, around her neck and wrists, and in a belt with a picture locket at the hanging end. Pearls were sewed to her gold slippers. Gold rings with emeralds and pearls were on her fingers, save for the heavy plain gold band on the ring finger of her left hand.

I write all this, remembering her beauty purely, though she was smutched with soot from top to toe. Even her face and hands were marked.

Tunstall had seen her before this at a closer distance than I, but we all knew her identity. We were kneeling before she had closed the door after her. "Your Majesty," the coves said. My throat would not work.

"Oh, please, please, get up," she said, her voice as soft as the rest of her. "I can't stand—not now. Please. Look, I'm sitting down." It was true, she'd settled in one of the chairs. A smile flitted on and off her mouth, which trembled whatever she did. In fact, she trembled from top to toe, the poor thing.

Pounce walked over and jumped into her lap without so

much as a by-your-leave. The queen flinched a little, then stroked him. I'd been about to call him back, but I waited, watching those soot-marked hands move on Pounce's fur. He turned around and coiled himself there, not letting her see his strange eyes. As she petted him her shoulders and back straightened. Her trembling eased. "I'd thought all the animals had fled, or been . . ." She looked down for a moment, then turned her gaze to Achoo. "A scent hound? Is he yours?"

I looked at the men, but they, great loobies that they were, stood there dumbstruck. Tunstall flapped his hand at me. He wanted *me* to talk to Her Majesty! But one of us had to, and Achoo was staring at me with pleading eyes, her tail wagging. *She* knew the pretty lady wanted to admire her.

"*Pengantar,* Achoo," I said. I turned to Her Majesty, without rising from my knees. From talking to folk who'd been broken by something terrible, I knew I would be more of a comfort to her if I sat below her eye level. Having Achoo come over made it reasonable for me to stay where I was. As the queen offered her hand for Achoo to smell, I explained quietly, "Achoo's a female, Your Majesty. We've been partners three years now."

The queen looked at me, and at the men. "Partners?"

I pointed to Tunstall, then at my uniform. "Achoo, Tunstall, and me, we belong to the Provost's Guards. Senior Guardsman Matthias Tunstall, I should say. I'm Guardswoman Rebakah Cooper. And this is Master—"

The mage bowed. "Farmer Cape."

The queen smiled at the men, but returned her attention to Achoo. She'd not stopped stroking Pounce, either. "How does a scent hound partner a Provost's Guard?" she asked.

I hoped she knew the answer when she was normal. Seemingly she wasn't just now. There was a shaken look in her eyes, as if she'd seen things too terrible to remember. Thinking of the bodies in the garden, I knew the chances were good that our pretty queen had never encountered anything of the like before. "When someone is missing, or something's been stolen, we give Achoo a scent of it," I explained. "Then she goes off and finds it. I go with her to keep her on the scent and to summon help, should she need it."

The queen leaned forward and gripped my arm hard. There was more strength, or desperation, in her fingers than I would have expected. "Is that why you are here? To find my son?"

Acknowledgments

Many of you will have noticed I have taken an uncommonly long time between the first and second book of this series. For that I beg forgiveness. I also want to thank the people who got me through this saga of moving from Manhattan to Syracuse, an auto accident, physical therapy, foot and eye surgeries, and my fear that counterfeiting just wasn't that exciting: Bruce Coville, my reading buddy and all-around pal, who gave me plenty of useful feedback before I let anyone else see it; Mallory Loehr, my wonderful editor, who gave me all the time I needed to recover from everything, and then kept me slap up to the mark so I would finally finish the durn thing; Lisa Findlay, who heroically edited the manuscript almost literally between contractions and cheered me through uncharacteristic "Is it really okays?"; my beloved agent, Craig Tenney, who never once freaked over how long this was taking and eased my way elsewhere; my husband, Tim, who stood fast while I swayed in the wind and nursed me through all those ailments, and the fans on tammypierce.livejournal.com, who remember the things I forgot!

TAMORA PIERCE captured the imagination of readers more than twenty-five years ago with *Alanna: The First Adventure* (Atheneum, 1983). As of September 2008, she has written over twenty-five books, including three completed quartets (The Song of the Lioness, The Immortals, and The Protector of the Small), the Trickster duet, and now the Beka Cooper books, set in the fantasy realm of Tortall. She has also written The Circle of Magic and The Circle Opens quartets, as well as two stand-alone titles, *The Will of the Empress* and *Melting Stones*. Her books have been translated into many languages, and some are available on audio from Listening Library and Full Cast Audio. She and her husband, Timothy Liebe, also co-wrote the six-episode comic *White Tiger: A Hero's Compulsion* for Marvel Comics.

Tamora Pierce's fast-paced, suspenseful writing and strong, believable heroines have won her much praise: *Emperor Mage* was a 1996 ALA Best Book for Young Adults, *The Realms of the Gods* was listed as an "outstanding fantasy novel" by *Voice of Youth Advocates* in 1996, *Squire* (Protector of the Small #3) was a 2002 ALA Best Book for Young Adults, and *Lady Knight* (Protector of the Small #4) debuted at number one on the *New York Times* bestseller list. *Trickster's Choice* spent a month on the *New York Times* bestseller list and was a 2003 ALA Best Book for Young Adults. *Trickster's Queen* was also a *New York Times* bestseller.

An avid reader herself, Ms. Pierce graduated from the University of Pennsylvania. She has worked at a variety of jobs and has written everything from novels to radio plays. Along with writer Meg Cabot (The Princess Diaries series), she co-founded SheroesCentral, a discussion board about female heroes; remarkable women in fact, fiction, and history; books;

current events; and teen issues. SheroesCentral and Sheroes-Fans are now independent of her, but she still drops by and welcomes the Sheroes she meets on tour.

Tamora Pierce lives in Syracuse, New York, with her husband, Tim, a writer, Web page designer, and Web administrator, and their eight indoor cats, porch cat, basement cat, two birds, and occasional rescued wildlife.

For more information, visit www.tamorapierce.com.